I, SQUARED (I^2)

To Poly
Enjoy
John Brown

J O L O V

Copyright

Disclaimer

Dedication

This book is dedicated to Kurtis Moore. Where, while sitting on his terrace in St Vincent, the idea of a bucket list and a journey to discover the meaning of what it means to be human was born.

Contents

$I\hat{\ }2$

Preface

Is it the condition of man to always seek the impossible: the desire for immortality? That unwillingness to acknowledge the uncomfortable certainty of one's own transience as it climbs ever higher in the hemisphere of conscious thought. Like trees at the end of a late summer's day, their leaves honoring the memories of fine days past in a colorful symphony of reds and golds, shimmering and rustling in the cool breezes that signal the approach of autumn. A clarion call for the wildlife to hurry up and finish its work, for soon all will be barren once more. So must we live by this cosmic clock; like all things, we too are subject to nature's demands.

Yet still, we strive like vain peacocks in search of a mate. The chasing of celestial bodies whose orbits move ever further from our grasp as if somehow they would return to us the years already squandered: a forlorn quest to recapture the vigor of youth through drugs and cosmetic adjustments. Destined to end in failure, as all things do when the veneer peels away. What is left is like the contents of Pandora's box, full of the ambiguities of existence, safely locked away until the day fate finds a key.

And then, like Pandora, even hope is denied you. The news you never want to hear is waiting for you on the desk in front of your doctor. Your future is recorded on a single sheet of paper that might as well be emboldened with black ribbon, for the effect is just as devastating. Then those words, the ones you hoped would be reserved for others, not you: 'I'm afraid your condition is incurable.'

A single sentence delivered without a crumb of hope. No glimmer of possibility that there might be some path out of the dark forest. That one word – the essence of life reduced to that single stark word: terminal. When did a word that was once used to conjure up visions of travel and excitement come to mean that's your lot mate, the end, death!

And so it was for David Sherman – how he so understood that now. Every night he ended up chastising himself for being so vain – subconscious flagellation, that's what it was. He had to come to terms with his mortality. The problem he was facing was all of his own making. What would he have done differently, though? It was almost as if this path he was on, like destiny, had been deliberately conjured up. He was the victim here – to one of circumstance, conspiracy, and deceit. How else could he explain what was happening to him? Like Pandora, devoid of hope, his nemesis was waiting for him in the next room. He had to try and get some sleep before he went completely insane.

I^2

Big Mistake!

It was the only conclusion – he'd made a big mistake, huge! Sleeping on the problem only made matters worse. It was still there waiting for him in the next room. Only now did he fully comprehend the magnitude of the error he'd made. One he'd been more than willing to receive money for just a few weeks ago. For Christ's sake, why had he signed the non-refundable contract? Now was not the time to regret it; the voice of reason in his head kept repeating. But he so did, for sure. What was it they used to say – something in haste, repent at leisure. Leisure, now there was a joke! The android was simply impossible to live with. It was supposed to be an exact copy, but it was more like the resurrection of the Dark Lord himself. Sure, he recognized certain similarities; they both shared the same memories and some of the mannerisms. Some he hadn't even noticed in himself. For one, he hadn't realized how quickly he could lose his temper until now. Something Derek had ably demonstrated in the short time he'd been activated. But where he inwardly seethed, Derek was quite happy to let rip. It was like having to deal with the tantrums of a two-year-old. Maybe that was all it was. Was he ever so rebellious?

There was also no comradery between them; that was a given in the short time they had coexisted together. This was nothing like having a flatmate to share interests with. If Derek was meant to be an accurate replica, how had he not recognized this personality trait in himself beforehand – he basically hated himself and was impossible to live with? No wonder he was still single, not that there had been that many opportunities.

Dave was sure the neighbors in the apartment opposite had heard them fighting; they did everything possible to avoid making eye contact when he passed them in the passageway.

The android even swore like him. Loudly! Enough for the whole building to hear. Derek was quite happy to let him know exactly how he felt about the situation. They were too similar, that must be it, yet also too different; an unresolvable dichotomy.

If he didn't do something soon, it would end badly. All he knew for sure was he had to try to correct the mistake, or the direct route from the twelfth floor of the apartment might become the chosen way out for one of them.

He had to make a decision, try and decide what to do next. Maybe it was all his fault. Perhaps he needed to be more understanding – treat Derek more like a *he* than an *it*. Be more brotherly rather than perceive 'it' as nothing more than a perfunctory medical appliance. Perhaps he should go and see Craddock again and tell him it wasn't working out. See if he'd be willing to cancel the contract. Or maybe the technicians at Forever-Life could give Derek the 'once over' to see if there were any abnormalities. After all, his nemesis had been powered up for two weeks now, so they must have received some telemetry of *it* to analyze.

Why the hell did he finish with Tami… for this! He could have been so happy with her. If only he'd known what he was letting himself in for back then. He should have been more circumspect and not jumped in, despite the shortness of time remaining. Sleeping on the problem had been a fruitless exercise. He was still no closer to resolving this dilemma, something that only ten months ago seemed impossible….

I^2

So, Doctor

Mars, Earth year 2095…10 months earlier.

"I see you have the results." David Sherman scrutinized the doctor's face as he looked down at the report in front of him.

"There is no easy way to say this, David. I'm afraid your condition is incurable." Rhines peered over the top of his rimless glasses at his patient.

Dave hadn't the strength to look him back in the eye, preferring to stare at his feet instead. He suddenly felt drained. This was not the prognosis he was hoping for. Merely a formality the doctor had said when he carried out the tests. Did Rhines really just say he was dying?

"So, Doctor, what are my options?" Dave blurted out, trying to remain focused and objective. While all the time, he could feel the swell of anger growing and blossoming inside him. Why him? He was too young, only forty. Somehow the report had to be in error. They'd messed up the tests. That was it. None of it was true. It was just stress, that's all. They had it all wrong – he wasn't dying! He couldn't be dying….

"Well, basically Dave, there aren't any." Rhines leaned forward across his desk and intertwined his fingers. "What you have is so very rare; no one has invested any time or research into it."

"That sounds pretty final and not what I really wanted to hear." Dave retorted bruskly. He didn't like visiting the doctor at the best of times. Now here he was again, sat in a tiny spherical office that was no bigger than his own quarters. With all the additional equipment and the rows of filing cabinets along one wall, it suddenly felt decidedly claustrophobic. Dave shuffled about on his seat, impetuous to be done with it all. He really didn't want to hang around to hear the rest of the grim prognosis.

"No, quite," Rhines continued, unfazed by Dave's obvious discomfort. "There have been one or two studies done, but basically, you are suffering from an environmental deformity of the brain. The condition is a little like Motor Neurone disease in that the degradation progresses very slowly at first. And then bang."

"Bang?"

"Yes, bang," repeated Rhines. "You won't notice much change, not to begin with anyway. Some weakness spreading throughout your body to start with, most likely in your limbs. This will gradually become more noticeable. Then one day, without much warning, your brain will experience a cataclysmic trauma event followed by brain death. The best way I can describe it is that it will be a lot like suffering a stroke. The neurons in your brain will suddenly begin depolarising and start dying. Much in the same way they would if starved of oxygen. The only positive spin I can put on it is that you won't feel a thing. No pain receptors in the brain, you see."

"Spin it! So basically, you are saying I will have a happy pain free death."

"I'm afraid so." It was a measured response delivered without feeling. Dave could hear it in the Doctor's voice. He was trying to sound sympathetic, but it came across as dismissive and unconcerned. But then, how could you make the prognosis sound more positive? "It's only Mars-born that get it," continued the Doctor. "Something to do with being born into a low gravity environment. Your synapses are a little more fragile and susceptible to DNA decay."

"If it's so pain-free, why do I feel like shit stirred with a spoon? At times it's unbearable."

"Yes, I can quite understand."

Could he though? Was that just a doctor's get-out clause?

I^2

"It's all in the mind, you see. Put simply, the nerve impulses from your pain receptors are being misinterpreted by your brain. We can control this with drugs."

"So, will it go away?"

"Not entirely. Unfortunately, episodes like this will come and go. And later, when you start to feel weakness, there are drugs to help with that too. With the right medication, you can continue to live a near-normal existence."

"So, what you are basically telling me is that I was born with this problem?" Why was he still trying to sound rational? There wasn't going to be any good news tagged on at the end – no false dawn of hope. He should be more distraught about it all, inconsolable even, but the prognosis had left him feeling kinda numb and detached from reality. This was someone else's diagnosis the voice in his head kept whispering, not his. Refuse to believe it, it kept saying, and it will go away!

"Look," continued Rhines, the hesitation in his voice quite noticeable. Was he trying to find words to lessen the blow? "It doesn't immediately show itself up as a problem, but as the nerve cells die, the symptoms start to manifest. I suppose it's a good job we have so many to start with; it makes the brain quite a resilient organ. Fortunately, your higher brain function will remain mostly intact. You won't become a vegetable."

"So that's good then? You think being fully conscious of your own imminent demise is preferable to being ignorant about it. What you are basically saying is, I'm going to end up being the Martian equivalent of Steven Hawkins."

"I wish I could even offer you that, but no, it will be a lot quicker than that. By the time you have need of a wheelchair, you'll only have a little time left to make use of it."

"So it's curtains then? That's what you're telling me. There's nothing anyone can do." Dave bit his lip nervously to try and stop it quivering.

"I wish I could offer you better news, but I can't. You asked for it straight up. When the time comes, we can move you into a care facility."

"How long?" The words struggled to form around the lump in Dave's throat. "How long before I become an inanimate embarrassment?"

"Two years maybe."

Dave considered the words carefully, Was Rhines tried to sound overly optimistic?

"Like I said, the disease will progress so slowly at first; you won't notice any changes, apart from some increasing clumsiness and maybe a little weakness. It won't be until the final few months you'll start to lose mobility. I suggest you do everything you intend to now while you still can."

Dave found his mind wandering. What could he possibly do 'more of' while living and working at the Anders mining station? It wasn't known for its nightlife and leisure amenities. In fact, it was dowdy and dull, a bit like himself really. Apart from his living quarters, a garage to house the vehicles that ferried them around, a refectory, a landing pad, ore processing labs, oxygen and waste recycling, and the Red Dawn, there was nothing else. His life here was uncomplicated: he worked in the lab, slept in his billet, and spent his free time in the refectory and the Dawn!

"Well, Doc, thanks for being straight. And I thought it was just a touch of Martian flu affecting my balance. Never believed for a minute there an underlying cause."

"I'm sorry it's not a better diagnosis, but the brain scan and blood tests were quite conclusive."

"Maybe it's time for me to think of taking some time off before I fall over and break something irreplaceable," Dave tried to sound upbeat, but the humor in the response was lost on Rhines. "Maybe that trip to Earth I've always promised myself. You know, I've always wanted to go, but the physical issues for Mars-born visiting there have always stopped me from taking it any further. Seems irrelevant now!"

Rhines studied him carefully – he just might be an ideal candidate. "If that's your intention, there might be something on Earth that can help. A form of treatment; a different way."

"You know of something then?"

"It's not a cure," Rhines replied firmly. He didn't want to give Dave any false hope. "But, there have been medical advances in the field of cybertronics that may help."

"Really, cybertronics, how?"

"It's not for me to say, and you might not consider it as being of any benefit. If you are interested, you will have to talk to the experts yourself. Only they will be able to advise you on what's best. You certainly have enough money to pay for the journey. What else would you spend it on here? And I'm sure your health insurance could be used towards treatment costs if needed."

"Okay, thanks, Doc. I'll think about it," Dave replied, trying to remain positive. It wasn't a cure, he understood that, but at least it was a hope of something better than watching the clock on the wall of his module tick-off what minutes of his life remained.

"So, have you ever visited Earth?"

"No, don't they say the gravity there is too much for a Mars-born. We don't have the bone density."

"To some extent, that is true, but your bone density is just fine. Do you not remember your childhood here? The compression suit and the anti-growth hormone drugs you had to take to stop you growing nine-foot-tall in the low Martian gravity."

I, SQUARED

"Yes, I remember the compression suit. It was uncomfortable at best, and also my father having to pump it up at bedtime. You couldn't move even if you wanted to."

"Well, it worked, didn't it? See, you are no taller than me." Rhines, comparing heights with the palm of his hand, traced an imaginary line between the foreheads of them both. "Now, muscle density, that is something else."

Getting up from his chair, Rhines walked around his desk and placed his hands over Dave's feeble biceps. "You will have to work on these if you intend to go Earth-side," he said, squeezing them. "You will get tired, of course, and you will feel as though you are carrying a large load around with you on your back. Eventually, when you lose your mobility and end up in a chair, you'll find sitting down less strenuous. Besides fresh air rather than the recycled crap we have to breathe, day-in, day-out, may help slow the progression of your disease."

"Do you really think it could help that much?"

"Can't hurt, can it." Rhines perched himself on the corner of his desk. Reaching around, he picked up Dave's notes. "I see you are a lead scientist here. In that case, you are well-off. Being paid to live in a bubble all of your life is one thing, but isn't it about time you spent some of it? I also see from your records that you have no family here. So, there's really nothing stopping you from leaving."

"That's true, I suppose. I only have a sister back on Earth, Jane; she was born there. It's a long story: basically, my family split while I was still a young child. My father stayed here with me while my mother returned to Earth after getting pregnant again. She just couldn't take the claustrophobia anymore. My mother and father are both dead now. Not exactly sure of my sister's whereabouts; it's somewhere in Texas. We call each other at Christmas but never really say anything. She is as much a stranger to me as

I^2

I to her."

"Well, if you are interested in the alternative therapy available on Earth. I will give you the name of a good friend of mine, another doctor, but of science, working in advanced cybertronics. He runs a company called Forever-Life, they deal with cases just like yours. Their treatment is radical. Like I said, it's not a cure; it's different. So, just let me know what you decide."

Taking the business card Rhines held out, Dave placed it into his standard-issue blue jumpsuit's top pocket. The doctor, quick to his feet, put his hand on Dave's shoulder and squeezed it gently. It was a shallow gesture; Dave knew it, but how else could the doctor pretend to be sympathetic. Rising unsteadily from the chair that had seemingly sucked what little life remained out of him, Dave extended his hand. The doctor shook it willingly as he ushered him towards the door.

"See you again soon. If you let me know what you decide, and I'll make the necessary arrangements." Rhines patted him on the back as he exited the small hemispherical surgery – a sympathetic 'keep your chin up.' It didn't make Dave feel any better.

Dave checked the clock on the wall of his habitat module; it was time. Gazing through the porthole that served as his only window to the outside, he looked up at the tiny vivid blue sphere glowing high above the desolate Martian landscape. Being so far away, it appeared not much bigger than the stars around it, but in the stillness of the moment, the beauty of it out-shone everything else in the sky. It was calling to him: 'Do it, what have you got to lose. Come to Earth, come and see your family.'

Although he wasn't Earth-born, he would not exist if it wasn't for that crucible of humankind: that distant blue dot. Without their endeavors, there would have been no exploration, no colonization of Mars, and no David Sherman. He was as much a product of their accomplishments as the walls constructed around him.

His grandparents were born on Earth at the dawn of the 21st century, and here he was ninety-five years later living on Mars. The technology push of intelligent devices on Earth at the start of the century had reached a nadir; everybody had everything they would ever want. People had grown weary of it all, even social media. The technology companies, tired of persuading people they needed products that did precisely the same as the thing it was replacing, only faster; lighter; more expensively; had started branching out in other directions: space travel, robotics, AI. These were the new gods of avarice and covertness. As far as buyers were concerned, smartphones only did the same things as before, but in more creative ways. Cars were still cars. 'Stuff' worked well enough. Being inherently more impoverished than previous generations, many had finally learned the wisdom that saving had its merits. Saddled with paying back their forebears' excesses, they had less disposable income to spend on such technological frivolities.

No, he might enjoy Earth; it would be like revisiting the world of his grandparents. To him, they were just names, strangers he had only ever spoken to on a video link when they were alive. All he could seem to recall of them was how they'd tell him of how proud they were of his father, one of the original pioneer settlers back in 2040. By the time he was born in 2055, Mars had become sustainable, and twenty years after that, independent – no longer the property of corporations. He remembered that day well and the full-blown crisis it triggered on Earth, almost a pre-cursor to another World War. A situation only prevented in the eleventh hour by common sense and the undertaking that Mars would remain politically neutral. So,

I^2

by de facto, Mars ended up with its own government, not beholden to Russia, China, or the US.

Now it was his turn to be a pioneer and see for himself the birthplace of man. Or, should that be the birthplace of Mars and the scientists who made it all possible: the dreamers; the explorers; those who'd dared say this is doable. Why spend what little remained of his life staring up at a minuscule blue dot in the dark of night when he could see it for real?

It was decided. Tomorrow, he will go and book passage on the next transport. In a week's time, he'll be heading for Earth on the biggest journey of his lifetime. This was his only chance; the next flight wouldn't be for another eight months. Far too late with what little time he might have left. Buying a ticket would be the easy part – telling his friends and leaving everything he had only ever known, well, that would be much harder.

The following morning, from his small domed window, Dave watched two micro twisters dancing outside. Twirling around each other against the rich ochre earth, they intertwined and raced over the surface, reaching forty meters up into the milky tea-colored sky. 'That's what I'd like to do,' he thought quietly to himself, 'a chance to dance.' He reflected on his life as they swirled on by. It took seconds. His was a dull, boring existence, one he didn't wish to micro-examine. Even his name was boring. His parents decided that picking something 'retro' would be popular, just like his friend's parents had. They all enjoyed the same mundane existence and were equally blessed with boring names: names devoid of charisma or a hint of the exotic in any way. In fact just four uninteresting guys in a pub. But they were his friends, and departing for Earth would leave a big hole, more than he would ever reveal to them.

I, SQUARED

Red Dawn

Dave laid a clean jumpsuit out on his bed. Did he feel like it? After the day he had experienced, was a trip to the Red Dawn such a good idea? His friends would be there for sure, expecting him to show up as usual. Besides, they already knew he'd been to see Rhines again today. The doctor seemed pleased to hear he'd decided to return to Earth. But, so far, all his friends knew was that he'd been off work for a week with the flu. A strain of the influenza virus that originally came from Earth. Initially traveling out with a cosmonaut, it managed to find its niche in the recycled-air systems. Everyone came down with it eventually. However, his friends would easily see through this deception. What should he tell them of his intentions?

In the space of a few hours, the doctor had made all the necessary appointments for him back on Earth. All he had to do now was get there. He was also starting to feel a little better. The new meds were beginning to take effect. He still felt rough, and his joints still ached, but some of his strength had returned; he could at least now stand without feeling he'd collapse straight back down again. Maybe give it another hour. By then, the pills should have worked their magic, enough to stop him from feeling dizzy and grasping for the nearest object for support.

Dave watched the second hand of the wall clock tick mercilessly around the dial, taunting him about wasting what precious time he had left. Why shouldn't he go to the pub? Fuck the illness. If he was going to feel worse as the days wore on, maybe he should get it over with as soon as possible? Was telling his mates such a big deal anyway? Perhaps, but he didn't want sympathy; that feigned concern when no one knows quite what to say for fear of offense. No, tonight was a night for getting drunk in the company

I^2

of his mates. To laugh and enjoy himself as much as he could on a red dustbowl of a planet he had called home for 40 years.

Unlike him, even his friends had ventured outside occasionally. In all the years he'd been here, well, all of his life, if he was being honest, never once had he stepped outside onto the surface just because it was there. Sure he'd visited other colonies, but only by transporter. Nowhere on this red dust of the planet was his footprint. No mark to say this is me; this is my home.

He had always fancied trying Martian Golf – exactly the same as Earth golf, except here you could hit the ball 700 yds from a small piece of astroturf you carried around with you. To reach the green, you traveled to it on a Segway. A green in name only, a simple boundary scratched in the dirt, rolled hard-flat with a hole placed in the middle. Yes, maybe he would have liked to have tried that, but now he knew he'd never get a chance; he had made his decision. He was going to leave for Earth and die there, and everything was booked.

"Ah, you made it then," exclaimed Topaz, eyeing up a slightly disheveled Dave approaching the bar. "What will you have?"

"Do you have anything drinkable tonight, Toz, or is it just the usual Witches' Brew?"

Topaz took the humor as offered. Dave was one of her oldest regulars. "Your friends are already here in the Glass-House. Apparently, there's a cargo shuttle due in, and they wanted to watch it arrive. You get such a good view of the landing zone from there. I guess they must be readying the big ship in orbit for return to Earth."

"Yes, that's about all we do these days; talk about traveling rather than actually experiencing it."

"You feeling okay, Dave? You sound a bit down."

"I'll be okay after I've had a few glasses of your magic

potion."

Extracting a transact card from his top pocket, Dave tossed it onto the bar. "I'll just take a Red-Dawn Special, please, Toz. You know, that exclusive beer that is only sold in one outlet and made out the back in a bucket."

"Coming right up. And, it's a rusty bucket if you don't mind; I have standards to maintain." After reaching up to relieve the shelf of a drinking vessel, Toz turned smartly in a single practiced movement, placed it under the dispenser, and opened up the faucet.

Dave picked up his beer as soon as it stopped foaming over the rim. After carefully wiping the base on a beer mat, he turned and headed off to seek out his friends.

Dave entered the Glass-House through a set of emergency decompression doors. Or as he liked to keep reminding himself – the Polycarbonate-House. It's funny how some things just stick. Whenever someone said glass, a little voice inside his head would say – it's polycarbonate, not glass!

Glancing around the multi-facetted domed structure of triangular-shaped transparent panels set into an aluminum frame that some called the diamond, he soon located his three drinking buddies sat at their usual table over by the far wall. Judging by the number of polycarbonates cluttering the table, they were already halfway down their third round of inebriating beverages. Biting his lip, he approached them tentatively. How should he tell them?

"Hiya, Dave, still breathing then," piped up Terry, Tezza to his mates. Terrance, when they wanted to rib him.

"Yes, Tezza, just about. For a little while longer anyway."

"Good on yer," interjected Frank in his fake Australian accent. Dave knew, like him, he'd also never visited Earth. Frank's only claim to being Antipodean, as he

I^2

would often refer to himself, was his Australian parentage and was unswerving when challenged about it. In his opinion, this gave him the unequivocally right to practice crude approximations of the stereotype.

"Look, guys, it wasn't all good news," he tried to cough back the lump forming in his throat. Even now, he could feel his confidence ebbing away. If courage was water, then someone had just pulled out the plug. "I might have to go away for treatment." It was a half-truth, he knew it, but it was all he could get out at that moment.

"Really, where? There is nowhere in this one bar town," exclaimed Robbie. Where they sending you, Enterprise?"

"Er, well…, no actually, Earth. I'm going to Earth." Dave stuttered; he was finding the words hard to come by. "They say I have a brain abnormality, and Earth is the only place they can treat it."

It was a lie and a cop-out, but it was enough not to force his mates into offering him faux sympathy. He didn't need any of that. All he wanted now was to enjoy a beer with friends and not think about it anymore. Be one of the lads talking about girls. One who could laugh with the rest of them about Terry's latest knockback from the canteen girl who had only arrived on the transporter from the capital, Enterprise on Acidalia Planitia, the week previous. Not that there were many girls to talk about at the Anders mining station, just a few working in the mineral processing lab. Deep down, he hated the idea of breaking up the gang. He would miss evenings like this and the friends he had here, a tableful of them leastways. The alcohol was starting to make him feel nostalgic.

Dave looked into his half-finished beer and reminisced on his life. He hadn't lived! He had spent all his life at Anders, except for the time he spent in Enterprise. The only place on Mars where there was a senior school.

He had boarded there and stayed on afterward to enter the university. The John F. Kennedy Academy of Science was probably the smallest university on two worlds, but then, for a while, it was the only place to be. He'd studied geology there and met Erika, his first, and in all truthfulness, his only love. They were quite an item back in the day. He wanted them to settle down and get married, but she being an Earth-sider, left to go back there after obtaining her degree. She'd told him she couldn't contemplate living in a bubble for the rest of her life, and he found the idea of leaving Mars too daunting a prospect. But then, when did he not feel insecure about everything. Maybe he'd look Erika up when he finally got Earth-side, or would that be too embarrassing for them both? Besides, he didn't have her address, and they hadn't exactly kept in touch all these past years. He must also call his sister and arrange to visit – this might be the only chance he'd get to connect with his family again.

A new life on Earth, as short as it might be, would be an adventure. His life, so far, had had so little excitement in it. He would welcome the challenge. He realized that now it was almost too late. There had been nothing in his life to say wow to. It would be a shame to die so ignorant of the gift he had almost chucked in the bin for want of experiencing. Surely there was time for at least one adventure in an otherwise mundane existence.

"Look, guys, thanks for a wonderful evening." Dave tottered to his feet, almost falling backward. Grabbing hold of Robbie's chair, he managed to steady himself. "I'm not going to stay and watch the shuttle come in if you don't mind. I don't think the beer and the tablets are agreeing with me too well."

"You mean you can actually be clumsier than you already are," piped up Terry, trying to lighten the mood on what so far had been something of a somber evening. Dave

I^2

could tell the thought of one of the 'gang' leaving had left them all feeling slightly deflated.

"Yes, and they say it will get worse. Gee, I don't mean to keep falling over things."

"It's okay," Robbie replied, trying to defuse the situation by being sympathetic. There was a time and place for badinage, and this wasn't one of them. "Terrance didn't mean it. You know what the great oaf is like yourself. The only one I know who can get stuck in an airlock for over an hour."

"It was defective, I tell ya," decried Terry, feigning hurt at the suggestion he had forgotten his access code.

"Yes, I'm sure it was," scoffed Frank, imitating the pushing of buttons on an imaginary pad in front of him.

Everyone laughed. Here, Dave mused, in this one corner of a repurposed habitat module was the only thing he'd miss: four friends sitting around a table in a makeshift bar that had over the years become a permanent fixture. And soon, all he would have left would be the memories. Just like Erika, a faint recollection of something that once used to be important. In hindsight, would he come to regret the decision he'd made to leave? Suddenly he was once again filled with doubt, but he mustn't let it show. He was too proud for that.

Purposely, he steadied himself against the effects of the alcohol. As surely as an acrobat balancing on a tightrope, he crossed the room, waving to Topaz as he passed by the bar on his way towards the exit. She waved back and smiled, as she always did – he would miss her face too.

After hitting the button on the decompression doors that led into the connecting corridor, he waited for them to open. They slid back with a slight 'psst' as the air pressures equalized. On the other side, the cooler air of the passageway made the hairs on the nape of his neck stand to attention. Unwelcoming and sterile, the route that would take him back to his billet, Alpha 26, awaited his footfall.

Every corridor at Anders was equally nondescript, five of them in total, evenly spaced around the circumference of a main central hub. They were uniformly light grey and hemispherical. Made from a composite of two aluminum sheets with a filler of dense insulation sandwiched between them. Along the inside surfaces on both sides ran the trunking conveying the cables for all things electrical. Above, another carried the air supply lines. At the end of each corridor, the habitation ring ran all around the circumference.

From space, the five corridors made the station look a little like a ship's wheel. Each of them, being designated by the first five letters of the Greek alphabet, Alpha to Epsilon – even the corridors had a more inspiring name than his. As Dave made his way along Alpha corridor towards his billet, he thought about changing his name. Why shouldn't he? Maybe something explorer-like. Livingston. Livingston Sherman had a nice ring to it. Why couldn't his parents have chosen something more inspiring than Dave? Dave the mundane, Dave the uninteresting, or more typically: Dave the bore.

I^2

Farewell

One soft-sided holdall didn't seem much for a lifetime, but there it was. All packed and sitting in the corner of the habitat. Dave opened up his itinerary again and stared at it. Overland Rover to Enterprise in Acidalia Planitia, and then eight months aboard the Deep-Space Ranger: Endeavor, journeying to Earth. Eight months of boredom sealed in a tin-can traversing the eternal blackness. He would be swapping one habitat for another but still as much a prisoner. Just thinking about it made him shudder, being kept alive by engineering and good fortune. And, eight months would eat a long way into the time he had left.

The doctor had given him a prescription for the meds he would need to take on the journey. Dave decided he'd pick them up in the morning on the way to the Rover Terminus. But tonight was his last night on Mars, and he would spend it in the Red Dawn with his friends and wish them well.

Dave pondered a while; should he tell them he was dying? Maybe he'd just let the alcohol talk for him. Did he really want to reveal to them that his condition was terminal and he wouldn't be returning? At least he could spare them that. What would he do if they pressed him for details? So far, he'd been pretty elusive over the whole matter. But now everything had been finalized, they might ask, after all, this would be the last night they could enjoy the pleasure of his company – forever.

Still deep in thought, subconsciously, he trod the route he'd walked a thousand times. Almost by surprise, he found himself back in the Dawn. The House Special beckoned if only to quell the turmoil running wild inside his cranium, the whispering voices of doubt that had become his constant companions ever since he'd booked passage.

I, SQUARED

They would soon be anesthetized, for a little while at least. One final evening to unwind with friends before the big adventure. Maybe tonight, against his better judgment, *he* would let down his guard and lay bare his soul. He knew they deserved better. How could he call them his friends if he deliberately kept the extent of his illness from them?

"First here then, cobber," Frank shouted out across the bar as he strolled over with a pitcher of beer. "Here top-up's," he said, banging the jug down on the table, enough to make the beer froth-up over the lip in the reduced gravity. "We'll down a few tonight. I mean, eight months with no alcohol. Gee, you could have knocked me down with a feather when you said you were going to Earth the other day. Shit, I couldn't do it!"

"Thanks," Dave replied, carefully lifting the wet pitcher and topping up his glass.

"Tezza and Robbie are on their way. It should be a good evening; they're showing the World Cup final between the USA and Argentina tonight. Live, well, you know, as live as being three light minutes away will allow."

"Yes, It will be good. Never thought the day would come when team USA would be favorites to win a game of soccer."

Quickly downing another glass of Red Dawn Special, Dave turned his attention to the broadcast. What he had to say could wait.

"Here they come," Frank shouted out, unnecessarily pointing to the two remaining chairs around *their* table. "Over here, guys."

"Okay, everyone, sorry to be last," Robbie offered by way of an apology. "Guess we'll need another of those," he said, pointing to the half-empty pitcher sitting in a puddle of condensate and spillage.

Signaling the bar to catch Topaz's attention, he gesticulated the number two on his fingers and pointed to

I^2

the pitcher. Toz acknowledged with a nod.

Presently, Topaz made away over to the table where they were sitting. Dave watched all her years of experience on display as the beer lapped gently up the sides of the pitchers without ever dribbling over.

"Okay, who's paying for all this?" Toz demanded, placing them down carefully on a table that was in danger of running out of space.

"I am," Dave replied. "It's my farewell party. Tomorrow I'm leaving for Earth."

"For good?"

"Yes, Toz, forever." There he had said it. What he couldn't say to his mates, he had glibly divulged to the barmaid.

"Forever, did you say forever," Frank exclaimed, without any sign of an Australian twang.

"I was going to tell you tonight. My condition...my illness, there's no cure, it's a one-way trip. I'm going to Earth to try some radical new treatment, and that'll be it. For as long as I have left, I'll be spending it closer to the Sun!"

A stunned silence seemed to suddenly permeate the bar – a perfect moment of nothingness. The status quo of familiarity had been ruptured. Within that single tick of time, the very fabric of space had folded in on itself around their little table, and with it the dawning realization that from now on, all their lives would be different.

"Gee, that's a bummer. We'd better get another round in, quick, Dave's paying," piped up Frank. It was just what he wanted to hear. He didn't want sympathy. He wanted a great night with friends. Tonight he was in the chair – let them not say after his passing that Dave was a tight-fisted bastard when it came to buying a round or two.

After three more pitchers of beer and the satisfying taste of victory watching the USA beat Argentina, Dave was starting to feel a lot better than he had of late. Thanks to the drugs, the headache he'd had all week had abated, and now the alcohol was kicking in. He was starting to feel mildly euphoric. In the warm glow of the evening, the four of them mused over their lives together; most of it sat around the very table they were occupying now. Four drunken friends trying to recall some of the more memorable anecdotes the beer would allow them to access.

"Dave, do you remember the time Frank also got trapped in an airlock when the mechanism failed. You see, I'm not the only one," offered Terry, deliberately trying to unsettle his friend about the perils of venturing outside. And also in part to get his own back for the other night. It still rankled, being so absentminded as to forget his personal access code.

No, but I can recall the time you got caught with your pants down, giving the nurse one," countered Frank.

"I keep telling you it was the other way around. She was giving me a cortisone shot in the backside."

"It's not what you said at the time, and you saw her socially as well," butted in Robbie. "We started putting a symbolic beer mat down where you sit while you chatted her up on that little table for two over there," he continued, pointing towards the darkest corner of the room. "We were going to start a sweepstake to see how long it would be before she blew you out the airlock!"

"Didn't get anywhere though, did I. She was only standing in as relief. She went back to Enterprise before I had a chance to woo her into my bed."

"She certainly didn't give you any relief if I recall," mocked Frank. "And I seem to remember you saying she wouldn't shut up. In fact, we all had the pleasure of listening to you moaning about it for a month afterward. That, and the fact the rash came back!"

They all laughed, Terry included. To Dave, his was it, a microcosm of life, all of them sat around one table. It was

I^2

all he knew, and soon not even that. "So, who are you going to elevate to my seat when I've left?" He was going to say 'gone' but thought better of it. It would dampen the mood, and this evening if anything, he only wanted to remember the laughter.

"Who said we are? We might just press the beer mat into service again," Frank picked one up and symbolically slid it across the table to where Dave sat. He liked the idea of being irreplaceable, more than one of being as so inconsequential and disposable as a beer mat.

It was late when they all finally staggered to their feet. Each of them trying to remember the moves necessary to perambulate without falling over, while Toz collected five pitchers from the table.

Dave, relieved to have managed to get to the counter without visiting the floor with his head on the way, sought support from it. After fumbling around in the pocket of his trousers, he managed to extract the transact card that had somehow become entangled in the lining.

"So it was a good night then?" Topaz enquired, forcing a smile. "I'll miss you, Dave. A lot."

"I'll miss you too, this place, and your welcoming smile. And don't you just have a great name," slurred Dave; he was drunk but at that moment didn't have a care. "Don't you ever get lonely? Working here, I mean, it's not like the Ritz or anything."

"No, not really, It's all mine, my own little kingdom. And, I get to see real life here and meet great guys like you. We could have been an item, you know – if only you'd asked."

Dave blushed. Was it a come-on or just bar banter? If he was worldly-wise, he would have known. "Thanks, Topaz. Your words, they mean a lot, as does all my time spent here."

"Have a good life, Dave, don't waste what's left. That's

your bar person's advice. I hope you find someone who can make you happy."

After hitting the button on the decompression doors, Dave waited for them to open. They seemed reluctant to slide back, almost as if they were trying to hold him captive. Refusing to let him leave for new horizons. For one final time, the passageway would be his escort back to his billet. The beer and the kind words of friends had eased his anxieties about going. He patted the corridor wall and ran his hand along it as he staggered back to his quarters. Tomorrow would be the start of the biggest adventure of his life, and now he was ready for it.

I^2

Departure

A shrill synthesized bell interrupted his fitful dreaming. A prelude to the monotonous replay of the itinerary that greeted him every morning. And every morning, it was usually the same, but not today.

"Good morning, Dave," chirped Bellinda, a name he had bestowed on his longstanding, sleep-destroying, invasive electronic assistant. "It is now time to arise. Your schedule for today is as follows: Seven a.m. MST; vacate the room and return the room key to security. Eight a.m. MST; board Rover bound for Enterprise. Arrival at Acidalia Planitia; six p.m. MST. Seven p.m. MST; board transit shuttle for Earth transport ship: Endeavor. Have a nice life. Would you like me to play some music?"

His eyes, as if stuck together, refused to open and acknowledge the new morning. Today he was starting out on a trip into the unknown. He couldn't help but think; wasn't that also a metaphor for life? Isn't every day a journey into the unforeseeable? Slowly he eased himself out of bed and sat on the end of it. Bellinda reminded him that he hadn't acknowledged her yet. "The time is now six-fifteen a.m. Martian Standard Time. Please respond."

"Thank you, Bellinda," acknowledged Dave, "and no music."

Begrudgingly, he made his way over to the closet and removed the luminescent green Low Atmospheric Pressure Suit from its hanger along with its corresponding helmet sitting on the shelf above it.

Lightweight! The LAPS, as it was more commonly known, was supposed to be lightweight, yet it felt as heavy as a crate of rock samples. Maybe it was his illness; were his muscles so wasted already? How would he survive the journey – he was panicking before he'd even got dressed.

I, SQUARED

Breathe deeply; he had to calm himself. He hated wearing the thing at the best of times, something he'd only regularly done when emergency drills were called for. Even then, he hadn't had to leave the muster area. Else, wear it as a precaution when he seldomly traveled by Rover to another site. But not once in the last 20 years had he used it to venture out onto the surface of the planet, just because it was there. No, he was a stay-at-home type of guy, and now he had to put the fear and anxieties of moving on behind him.

Laying it out on the unmade bed, he cringed at the sight of it. Turning hastily, he headed for the bathroom so it was no longer in his field of view. He was hyperventilating. He needed water, if only to stop him gulping in vast quantities of recycled air.

Only when he could no longer feel his heart bouncing against his rib cage, he dared raise his head from the sink. It was a very bleary-eyed face staring back at him in the mirror. Fuck it, why shave? Why did he even get out of bed? He could die here just as certainly, and very soon, judging by how he was feeling. Last night had been very enjoyable with the beer flowing like it was about to run out, but now he felt the worst for it.

He tried not to wretch as he cleaned his teeth, more as a way to remove the fur from his mouth than to actually polish his molars. After knocking back an extra painkiller, he rinsed his mouth for the second time. He was prevaricating; it was time to leave – for Mars and Rover wait for no man. He tried to recall who he was paraphrasing, but no name was forthcoming. Stooping like some lethargic octogenarian, he retrieved his bag from the corner of the room and placed it alongside his spacesuit.

After re-reading the instructions on how to use the suit, he reached back into the closet to retrieve the other pieces of clothing he needed. He had subconsciously forgotten about undergarments. The heated under-suit: a

I^2

vest and a pair of long-johns woven with fine electrical wires, designed to provide a small resistive load for the circulating electrical current. Essential if he didn't want to morph into a block of organic ice as the temperatures plummeted to a bone-shattering low of -70 Celsius at night.

Everyone affectionately called the undergarments toasters. Dave could understand why they were so necessary, though totally impractical and a pain to put on. But before he'd even get to climb into those, he first had to put on the dreaded sanitary underwear – specifically designed for those long journeys between bathroom breaks.

Absorption pants, or APs for short, were just a fancy way of saying diapers. Everyone called them Ass Poohs, but hell, when you couldn't just pop to the bathroom, they were essential. The last thing you'd want is to be electrocuted and broiled in your own bodily juices. Was death by toaster even a possibility? Surely the current would be too small?

After straining on the toilet for what seemed an age, Dave hoped he wouldn't need to use them but doubted his bowels would be so cooperative after the previous evening. He certainly wasn't looking forward to sitting in his own excrement on the Rover for ten hours. But then, one day soon, that would become the highlight of his day – when the wiping and cleaning of his backside became the responsibility of a carer. At least today, he could skip breakfast and drink little, even though he was feeling dehydrated.

After struggling into the suit and connecting up all the internal wires, he was as ready as he would ever be. Half kneeling, he fed the strap of his holdall over his shoulder and pulled himself back upright, instantly wishing he'd left a few items behind. After repositioning the buckle, so it was at least comfortable, he turned towards the door. This was it: the last time he would ever occupy these quarters; four unpretentious grey walls and a small circular window.

Reaching for the light switch, Dave reminisced: he'd

resided in these same quarters ever since he'd graduated. Actively choosing to come back to Anders to work, just as his father had done. Most other graduates in his year had all departed for Earth and lucrative careers on a world that wasn't trying to kill them at every opportunity. When it came to benchmarks, he was at the top of the class for Nerdy! With a sigh, he switched off the fluorine lighting.

Despite his pledge to skip breakfast, he found himself waylaid by two sobering drunks as he approached the central hub.

"We couldn't let you off that easy! Could we, Frank!" Robbie said, steering their friend towards the refectory. "Tezza's already in the queue, ordering the pre-flight special."

"You know, all those foodstuffs with extra fiber," quipped Frank.

"Gee, thoughtful of you all, thank you."

"I see you got your spacesuit on okay then, Diaper-Boy," ribbed Terry as they approached the table in the refectory. "I just got you a single piece of toast, okay? I know what it's like having to go in those. Did I ever tell you about the time I was working out on a remote bore-hole and filled my boots…"

"No, I don't want to hear," complained Dave. "It's going to be bad enough holding it all together after last night, without listening to your embarrassing BMs."

Sitting down, he knew he'd miss them more than they would ever know; they were his only family on Mars. He wasn't hungry, but he picked at his toast anyway, hoping it would quell his churning stomach. He listened to their banter for the last time, realizing he'd lived all his life through their eyes; it was all he knew. He had no one else who'd care, not like they'd care when the time came. Why was he doing this again? There was no cure. Was it solely to track down a sister he'd never met? Partially, but it was

I^2

more than that – he hadn't lived at all. He hadn't experienced life, and life hadn't experienced David Sherman. Who was he to deny the universe the opportunity to feel his presence, however fleeting?

"Look, I have to go soon; we'll keep in touch though, won't we? I'll sign up for a Video Over Laser Transmission account on Earth so we can still raise a beer and have a chat, even if I'm sitting fifty-four million kilometers away."

"Sure thing, Tezza's got a VOLT account here," Frank responded.

"Yes, he still uses it to show everyone his rash," Robbie quipped.

Everyone laughed, for a moment leastways, as if trying to delay the inevitable – the encroachment of a final farewell.

"This is your ten-minute call," crackled the voice of the announcer over the public address system. The words bouncing off the refectory walls made them sound reverberant and less coherent, but their meaning all too obvious. "Will everyone leaving for Enterprise," the anonymous voice instructed. "Please make your way to the embarkation area."

"So, then, this is farewell." Dave pushed back his chair and attempted to stand in the cumbersome spacesuit that seemed to want to resist any form of movement. With some difficulty, he eventually found himself upright. One by one, his mates clustered around and hugged him, patting him on the back and wishing him well. The emotion of the moment was overwhelming, making it difficult to focus on what each of them was saying.

Turning to pick up his helmet from the table next to the one they'd been sitting at, he was determined not to look back as he left the refectory. He didn't want them to see the tears that had started to dribble down his cheek.

Quietly and as unassumingly as possible, he picked up

his holdall from the collection point and shuffled off towards the airlock, his feet strangely reticent to stride out with any confidence towards their ultimate destination.

I^2

Shuttle

The EA or embarkation area was less crowded than Dave was expecting. In essence, a fancy name for a departure lounge connected via two airlocks to a cargo bay and a third to isolate it from the rest of the mining station. Apart from himself, three others were waiting to leave. He'd seen them in the Dawn the previous evening. They'd been visiting Anders to extract terbium from the nearby mountain range. A rare-earth metal used in fuel cells to power the emergency generators back at Enterprise. An essential system, should a dust storm hit and last for weeks like the one last year.

Dave watched the miners maneuver a transit case containing the precious metal into an airtight trailer. Soon, this would be hitched to the back of the Rover along with all his worldly possessions, not that there was anything worth keeping. It was like watching parents wrapping up a newborn in a pram for the first time. Not that he'd had any experience of being a parent, other than what he'd gleaned from the entertainment channels.

As soon as the miners were happy their cargo was secure, Dave stepped forward and handed his holdall to the operative charged with loading the Rover. Someone Dave had only spoken to a few times and just knew him as Whyte. Carefully Whyte placed Dave's luggage into the container, next to the miners' personal belongings.

Dave looked around, more for nostalgic reasons than concern. Was it only the four of them traveling? Just then, he noticed Tamara, Tami to her friends, one of the mission director's assistants heading towards him. She'd often been his point of contact when there was a science briefing to present. "Hello, Miss Gleeson. Are you traveling with us today?"

I, SQUARED

"Oh hello, Dave, don't be so formal, you know only too well it's Tami when we're not on duty. And yes, I'm going back to Earth. I've got a new job at NASA."

"Me too, well not NASA, but Earth anyway."

"Good, then we will have plenty of time to catch up on the journey. See you later."

Dave scrutinized her as she handed her luggage over to the loading technician. Even in a spacesuit, she oozed sex appeal; he could feel his heart racing. Following her with his eyes, he studied her, oblivious to the fact he was staring. Was it her hazel eyes he found so alluring, or the dark chestnut-colored hair perfectly framing her flawless features? What could he, Dave the drudge, possibly talk to her about on an eight-month journey? She was everything he ever desired in a woman but too afraid to ask. He'd probably spend most of the trip in his quarters anyway, shying away from human contact. Much as he'd done all his life, really, especially when it came so attractively packaged as Tami. Following behind her, he made his way through to the transfer area, but not so close as to make either of them feel uncomfortable.

After re-checking the passenger list, Whyte sealed the decompression doors that separated the EA from the rest of Anders. A warning panel above the door turned red as soon as Whyte engaged the interlocks. The EA was now isolated. Dave shuddered; this was it. He had reached the point of no return.

Whyte, turning to a console in front of him, started decompressing the cargo bay. A loud 'clang-clang,' followed by an automated warning message on the PA, told him when the pressures had equalized. Placing his hands over two safety interlock levers, he turned them simultaneously to the open position. Through the observation window in the transfer area, Dave admired the graceful elegance of the cargo bay doors as they split down the center and swung effortlessly outwards like theatre drapes to reveal the

I^2

Martian landscape beyond and their transport.

Using his feet for leverage, Whyte glided along on his chair to the panel that controlled the first airlock, the one the luggage container had been sealed into, and started to decompress it. As soon as the panel light on the console turned green, he flicked a second switch to open the external door into the cargo bay. Still on his chair, Whyte sidled across to a third panel and powered up the remote camera on the luggage trailer. Moving his hand over to the joystick standing proud next to it, he expertly steered the trailer out of the airlock, across the cargo bay, and straight onto the back of the waiting Rover.

Dave, trying to clear his mind of the upcoming journey, waited patiently at the back of the small queue in the transfer area for the Embarkation Manager to catch up to him. Picking an Oxygen Environment Pack up off the deck, the EM thrust it into Dave's chest hard enough to make him cough. Flinching from the impact, he just about managed to grasp hold of it and prevent it from falling back to the floor. It was definitely as cumbersome as it looked. He put the ease by which the EM seemed to be able to hurl heavy bits of kit around like balloons, down to the fact he was Earth-born – his muscular physique in the low gravity environment endowing him with superhero strength. The EM huffed and walked off, unimpressed by Dave's inability to securely hold onto the life support unit.

As soon as he reached a lectern, the EM turned to face his charges. "Okay, this is how you use the OEP," he started, picking up a demonstration unit off the floor. Dave tried to follow the perfunctory instructions being relayed to him. If he'd been a wall, his absorption of the facts would have been just as effective; his mind too wrapped up with his own insecurities to pay much attention.

Without checking to see if his students had adequately understood the mechanics of the OEP, and more importantly, how you attached it to the onboard oxygen plant when they boarded the Rover, the EM moved on to show them the correct way to wear it on their backs. Gratified that they'd all managed not to strangle themselves in wires and pipes, and everyone had correctly connected the heater circuits, he moved on to the helmet and how to securely attach the OEP's oxygen supply.

Dave was convinced he hadn't understood any of it. How did you attach the oxygen pipe to the outlet thingy and the inlet bit again? And when was it you should turn on the air supply? Tentatively he raised the helmet over his head and guided it down onto the metallic receiving ring. Relieved to engage the sealing flange on the suit with the one on the base of the helmet by touch, he felt for the lever that would lock them together. It's now or never, he told himself as he twisted it into the closed position, half expecting to suffocate.

The EM walking down the line, checked each passenger in turn. He was satisfied; they were all compliant and not gasping for air like some gigantic goldfish in a bowl without water. Returning to the console, he signaled the driver on the Rover over the intercom.

The second airlock was bigger than the first, enough to hold them all comfortably. After being ushered in by the EM, they waited for him to seal the inner door. "Okay, I am about to depressurize," he said over the intercom after securing it. "You will feel your suits balloon outwards slightly. This is quite normal. The trapped internal air in your suit will expand as the external pressure drops away. When the outer door opens, make your way across the cargo bay and over to the Rover. Once inside the shuttle, wait for the driver to repressurize it before removing your helmet. When he takes his helmet off, you can too."

A little gasp of air from the last remnants escaping through the outer door's broken seal welcomed them to the

I^2

real Mars. As he clanked his way along the metal deck-way towards the Rover, a voice kept tormenting him: 'Go on, do it, before its too late.' Unable to resist its call, Dave jumped off the deck-way and planted both feet in the red dust – finally, he had left a mark on the surface. Did the sky suddenly seem a little less orange than usual? But then, maybe looking through dirty windows for the last 20 years would make everything appear brighter.

Dave waited at the back of the queue to board. As expected, Tami was first on, then came the miners, and he followed up behind. Clambering up the small ramp extending down from the back of the Rover, Dave squeezed past the solar panel inverters and charge accumulator to get to the seat at the rear of the passenger compartment. To say the space on board was cramped would have been generous. After contorting around in the confined space, made all the more awkward by the inflexibility of the spacesuit, Dave finally took to his seat. Locating the cable coiled up in the armrest, he extended it outwards and plugged it into the receiving socket on his forearm control panel. The unit beeped in his helmet to indicate his intercom was now live.

It was deliberate as much as hoped for that he'd find himself at the back of the Rover. The seat next to the Oxygen recycler unit, where the OEPs would sit in cradles once the Rover had been secured for departure, suited him perfectly. Here he could pretend not to exist, just like he always would in unfamiliar company.

Immediately in front of him, the brusque broad-shouldered miners occupied three seats across the width of the Rover. Dave liked the way they almost obliterated him from sight. He could see Tami had buckled herself in at the front, in the row behind the driver and his second.

The mechanical whirring sound of motors and a slight vibration told Dave they were getting ready to depart; the gangway was retracting back into the body of the Rover and the hatchway closing up. As soon as it ceased, the driver introduced himself over the suit intercom. "Hi, Tim here," he said by way of an introduction. "My second-in-command is Ronni. Anything you want to know, ask her."

Ronni turned round to acknowledge everyone. "Trip time will be just under nine hours, No problems with dust-storms, so it should be a comfortable ride," she said over the intercom. "So, sit back, everyone, and enjoy the Martian landscape."

"The back of the Rover is now sealed," informed Tim, "and I have a green light for pressurization, so you can remove your helmets. If you'll take off your OEPs and pass them to Dave back there, he'll fit them into the cradles. You'll find somewhere under the seats to stow your helmets."

After struggling to recall the EM's instructions, Dave eventually successfully connected seven Oxygen Environment Packs into their cradles before settling back into his seat. The miners grunted when they gave him theirs as expected, but Tami had definitely winked at him. That knowing wink, almost as if she was handing him a piece of clothing after removing it as a prelude to more. Dave was unsure what the 'more' might be, having only watched certain movies where beautiful women handed clothing to strangers. Tim and Ronni had shaken his hand, which was nice. Tim was as close to the dashing space pilot stereotype as Dave could imagine, a real Dan Dare. Ronni, however, was petite, with stunning auburn hair and high cheekbones to help support her broad smile. He hoped he wasn't staring. Was he staring? Never mind, she was probably used to it. Clicking his belt buckle back into its retainer, he couldn't help but wonder if she had a boyfriend. As long as it wasn't Dan Dare, the pilot. No, she would definitely go for someone less shallow than that.

Dave settled into the seat, trying to make it feel a little

I^2

more comfortable, but knew he'd fail. There was a lump where there shouldn't be a lump. And no lump where there should be one in the lumbar region. As he fidgeted around, he felt the Rover lurch. They were moving. Not wanting to, but unable to stop himself, he looked through the window and watched the whole of his past life disappear from view. It made him shudder. Not the type you get from the cold, but the one where your nerve-endings jangle and cause involuntary spasms in the muscles. This was going to be more challenging than he imagined. He was alone, and now the Rover had left Anders; he didn't mind admitting it to himself – he was scared.

The double dose of medication he'd taken was starting to take effect. He felt drowsy, and the gentle rocking of the Rover didn't help. Trying to keep his eyes open was turning into a losing battle, one which he welcomed. It would render the need to make conversation unnecessary....

Stirring from his drug-induced slumbers, Dave tried to stretch. Everything was stiff or numb, and his head felt woolly, which was hardly unexpected. It was the type of blurriness that comes from drinking too much the night before. In an attempt to snap his mind back into focus, he looked out of his small porthole window. As the Rover rounded a small ridge, he could just make out the capital in the distance. Set against paprika-colored hills, small silver spires glinted in the sunlight of a fine summer's day. Dave glanced up at the environment panel above the driver. The external temperature was 14C, positively a heatwave for Mars.

I, SQUARED

Endeavor

"Okay, everyone, docking in five minutes," Tim called out, much to Dave's relief. Nine hours without a toilet break had had him consciously clenching his pelvic muscles since waking. Soon he would be disembarking at the transfer point and able to use the bathroom. It couldn't come fast enough.

"And don't forget to take your helmets from under the seat," instructed Ronni. "There's no need to get helmeted up as the Rover will be docking straight onto the airlock via the side door. So leave the OEPs on the cradles and just carry your helmets, as you will need to hand those in with your suits."

Dave felt relieved; thank goodness he didn't have to hand the oxygen packs back out – moving and stretching over the seats might have exhorted more pressure on his bowels than he could control.

With some sense of urgency, Dave collected the key for shower-room six from the disembarkation officer. Tensing his abdominals, he shuffled away as quickly as he dared towards the transfer facilities.

Once inside, Dave frantically locked the door and sighed. He'd made it; all he had to do now was free himself from the LAPS. Was it him, or had the unwieldy spacesuit chosen this moment to inconsiderately keep him incarcerated? Flailing his arms rearward, he made another attempt at grasping the lanyard that would spring open the neck. This time, his fingers caught hold of the elusive chord. With one downward tug, he was, at last, free of the damned thing. Hurriedly, he headed for the toilet cubicle before suffering any further indignity.

He'd made it, his AP's, unsoiled but still

I^2

embarrassingly damp. He quickly disposed of them in the specially provided AP disposal unit. Feeling relieved, he showered and freshened up using the purposely provided toiletries. After drying off, he felt the chill of apprehension prickle at his skin, enough to make his body hairs stand proud. This was something more than the waft of dry recirculated air over his naked body. This was a palpable feeling of fear. Fear of the unknown and his next obstacle – getting ready for space.

His luggage, such as it was, had gone straight on ahead; it wouldn't be required while he was in transit. Opening up the shower room's locker, he checked the IVA hanging there, took it out, and carefully laid it across the wooden bench seat. A label emblazoned with his name had been fastened by Velcro to the top pocket, and the suit was the correct size. At least they'd got that right; hopefully, the flight suits everyone had to wear on the spacecraft would also fit.

He was also relieved to find that this time he was only required to wear regulation boxers and a vest underneath the Intra-Vehicular Activity suit. In one hour, he would be on the shuttle and then hopefully another ninety minutes after that, aboard the Endeavor – the first of the Deep-Space Rangers, one of only two DSR spaceships that could make the Mars run.

After replacing the LAPS on the hanger he'd taken the IVA off, he placed it in the locker, ready to be taken away for cleaning. The IVA was just as challenging to get into as the LAPS had been to get out of. And if anything, even more rigid. Eventually, after breaking into a sweat that all but nullified the shower, he had it on. The satisfying sound of him pulling up the zip that made the suit airtight; a relief. He wouldn't have to call for help and look like a complete idiot. Sitting back down on the simple brown-slatted bench provided, he re-read the checklist he'd been given when he collected the bathroom key. According to the instructions, he was passenger number eighteen out of twenty-two and had to report for embarkation thirty minutes before boarding. Was that a lot, he wondered; twenty-two? Just how big was the ship he was about to spend eight months on?

The Embarkation Officer, another large burly man with a definite military disposition, checked his suit thoroughly without much more than a grunt. Satisfied that everything was fastened correctly, he waved him through. Stepping into the holding area beyond, a glorified waiting room of grey linked chairs set against equally grey walls, Dave walked over to the shelving area where twenty-two metal boxes waited for owners. Picking out the one with his name on, he opened it and removed a helmet. The Endeavor's third-in-command called him over as soon as he had returned the box to its slot.

"Name?" the TIC asked, glancing down the passenger list without looking up.

"Sherman, David." Wondering why the officer didn't just check the name tag.

"Been in space before?"

"No, sorry."

"Okay, watch. This is how you fasten your helmet when you get in the shuttle."

Dave watched the officer demonstrate how to attach the spherical head-wear to the suit using a dummy head-and-shoulders model on a table next to him.

"Okay, is that clear?"

"Yes," Dave replied, relieved to find it was exactly the same fastening mechanism as on the LAPS. Satisfied, the TIC reached over to pick up a dummy umbilical cord.

"Now, when you get aboard, you have to fit your earpiece before you seal your helmet. Then, connect this umbilical," he said, wafting the end in front of Dave's face.

I^2

"This will supply you with the air you need for the journey, and it also powers up the communications. It all connects here." Dave watched the officer insert the umbilical into the connection plate on the side of his suit. "Insert it like this, and rotate ninety like that until it clicks. You got that?"

"Seems straightforward enough."

"Good, to release it; press this button here on your suit to free the catch and rotate it back," demonstrated the officer. "Are you comfortable with what I've shown you so far?"

"Yes, perfectly."

"Good, then if you'd step this way, please," indicated the TIC, pointing Dave in the direction of the open airlock doors and on into the shuttle.

Once inside, Dave couldn't help himself but count the seats: sixty for passengers and ten reserved for crew. His question had been answered – the ship would barely be a third full. An image of the Flying Dutchman crossed his mind. But, at least he knew one of them to lessen the voyage of the damned.

After fifteen minutes, he had the final count: thirty-two. No one had chickened out at the last minute. Not like he'd thought of doing, right up until the moment he had buckled himself into the seat. As hoped, the berth next to his remained unoccupied, not that there'd be any opportunities for conversation – they all had to stay 'suited-up' in their helmets for the short journey up to the orbiting Endeavour.

"Welcome aboard, everyone. This is your Commander speaking," came a disassociated voice over the intercom. "Please fasten your harnesses and put your helmets on as you've been shown. The airlock is being sealed, and soon we will begin depressurization. Everyone, press the green button on the seat-back panel in front of you as soon as you've successfully switched over to the onboard air supply."

Dave attached his helmet as proficiently as any astronaut before locating the umbilical. Like a baby in the womb, he plugged the lifeline into his suit. Instantly he was rewarded with a 'psst' and a slight inward rush of cold air, making his now unreachable nostrils itch.

The Commander's voice squawked loudly in Dave's earpiece, "All green. Next stop: Endeavor. First, we have to make some preliminary flight checks, and then we will be off. Once we reach the ship, you will remain in the shuttle until the internal environment on the Endeavor has been checked and the shuttle repressurized. Once the Endeavor is underway, it will remain in weightless operating mode until we have completed all course corrections. Artificially induced rotational gravity will be a new experience for some of you. So please take some time to get used to it. I know many of you know this, but we have two Mars-born first-timers on board, so please try and help them. If you see them struggling, try to lend a hand."

Dave wondered who the other first-timer might be. Both of them would have to adapt to being three times heavier than now! A lot of gym time would be needed to build his muscles up sufficiently, two hours a day, rising to four as they approached Earth. At least it would be something to do.

"Okay, prepare for departure. Lift-off in ten, nine, eight, seven," counted down the voice of the Commander over the PA. Dave, gripped by a sudden panic, never heard 'six' He had closed his eyes as tight as he could for fear that his eyeballs might pop and….

Did he blackout for a moment during lift-off? Unquestionably, the weight he felt on his chest as the craft accelerated away from the surface had him struggling to breathe for a while. But now, all he felt was sort of floppy. His legs seemed to want to float off from the floor, and the

I^2

slightest movement of his arms resulted in wild flailings. Weightlessness was going to take a little getting used to. When he had read the pre-flight manual before leaving Anders, it had warned him about overcompensation. There was nothing for his muscles to work against. He had to try and remember to move in small precise increments.

Turning his head slowly, for fear of wrenching it off, he looked out of the window. He could just make out the crescent of the surface. In the distance, he could see Phobos, the largest of the two moons of Mars. At only 6000Km above the surface, you could watch it traverse the Martian sky three times a day. The Endeavor's orbit was twice as far out as that and halfway between Mars and its other moon: Deimos. Well beyond the possibility of colliding with either of them.

"Commander here, we have reached our terminal velocity and are now flying on an intercept course to rendezvous with the Endeavor in one hour. The onboard systems have been activated by remote telemetry to rewarm the ship and to start pressurization. I'm sure you will appreciate that after being in orbit for 60 days, it will take a little while to run through all the preliminary flight checks and make it habitable."

Dave couldn't help but wonder what the crew did on Mars between journeys and how they managed to cope being away from family for so many months at a time. Dave guessed that besides maintenance runs and refueling the ship from the frozen carbon dioxide they took up to pass through the ship's UV reactor, the crew's time would be very much their own. At least staying in the capital gave them more options on how to spend their free time than at Anders.

An hour to pass, maybe time for another nap, anything would be preferable to watching his home shrink away below him. He didn't want to dwell on the thought of having made a big mistake – not now there was no possibility of going back.

Every time he tried to close his eyes, images of his friends and the Red Dawn would swirl about in front of him as if being projected onto the back of his eyelids. Giving up, he switched on the terminal in the seat-back to activate the forward camera. The outline of the Endeavor appeared in the distance, shimmering in the sunlight against the pitch blackness. The sizeable circular habitation ring, located just behind the bridge at the front, reminded Dave of a wheel attached to an axle. At the rear end, the plasma drive engine cluster provided balance. In between along the rest of the body, substantial directional solar panels gave Dave the impression of wings. It was almost as though he was looking at some giant space-bird that could fly through the spacial void. Like a mother feeding fledglings, they were soon to be the worms, ingested for later regurgitation in eight months' time. They were closing on it quickly. The shuttle would soon be turning to come alongside the giant spacecraft hanging there motionless, yet traveling around the surface of Mars at thousands of miles an hour.

As Dave watched the shuttle close on the Endeavor, he wondered what adventures awaited. His fears had abated somewhat, replaced by the inquisitiveness to explore. Whatever the following days brought, it would undoubtedly be different.

"Commander to crew, get ready to dock," squawked Dave's earpiece again, still too loud to be comfortable.

The slight clunk on the side of the shuttle was hardly noticeable. But everyone on board recognized the significance – they had docked.

"Okay, everyone, we are running system checks now," continued the Commander. "So far, everything looks good. In a few minutes, I will be pressurizing the shuttle. This will only commence after I have established the

I^2

habitability of the Endeavor. So hang tight."

How long had they been waiting? Dave checked the clock on the panel in front of him. It seemed longer. He was just starting to think that there might be a problem and one last chance for him to change his mind, but the sudden sound of air rushing into the shuttle was undeniable. The Commander was soon back on the intercom. "Okay, I can confirm the cabin pressure has now been normalized. Mitch, my TIC, will help you disembark. You can now safely remove your helmets, but don't forget to take them with you. They will be needed again."

Dave removed his helmet with little difficulty. It was all becoming second nature to him as he watched Mitch float weightlessly down the shuttle. It looked effortless. All that was required was a little push off and then, using the grab rails protruding out along the craft's sides and roof, he could work his way methodically towards the airlock.

Gingerly, when it came to his turn, Dave unbuckled his harness and started to feel himself wobble about on the chair. No longer restrained, he rose slowly and gripped the closest grab rail with one hand while gathering up his helmet with the other. As soon as he felt confident enough, he aimed himself in the direction of the exit and pushed off. Thankfully Mitch was there to hold out his hand and slow down his approach into the airlock.

"Mind your head, and then you're through into the main craft," he said. "Make for the Transit Lounge, so that's through the airlock and then left. There you'll find your seat. Strap yourself in, and wait for further instructions."

Dave floated down the Transit Lounge, or TA, until he found the seat-back with his name on it. It didn't come as much of a surprise to see Tami buckled up in the one next to it.

"Not long now, Dave," she said.

I, SQUARED

"No, I suppose not," Dave responded, at a loss for anything else to say. Smalltalk was not a gift he possessed unless it involved football or alcohol.

When everyone is waiting for something to happen, time passes indescribably slowly. Dave decided it was one of those irksome quirks of quantum mechanics. He didn't need to look at his watch, hidden under his spacesuit, to tell him it was way past being late. They must have been waiting for over an hour for something to happen? He looked up at Tami, who had somehow managed to carry her e-book reader on board with her. Why had he not thought of doing the same? It would have been infinitely preferable to staring at the sterile walls of the Transit Lounge for two lifetimes. Dave found himself considering the possibility they'd all been abandoned, or else the entire crew had suffered some sort of catastrophic accident. It was one of unfettered relief for him to again hear the voice of the Commander crackle over the intercom.

"Okay, we are a go for the initial burn. Everyone get ready to say goodbye to Mars. Don't forget, stay buckled up as we will be remaining weightless until we reach our terminal velocity. Only after then will we start up the gravitation motors. During this phase of the flight, everyone is to wear their helmet as a precaution. You will find the air supply umbilical connection in the left arm of your seat. I will speak to you again once we are underway."

Tami leaned across. "Why is it Commander and not Captain?" she asked, leaning forward to locate her air supply port.

"I presume it comes from the early space flights to the Moon," Dave responded, unsure he was relaying fact or conjecture. "The lead astronaut was always a Commander, and this is not a military vessel. It's not like a warship, is it?"

"No, I guess not. Mind you, with the uniforms they give us, it feels very military."

I^2

"Yes, I suppose it does," Dave nodded in agreement as he plugged in his air supply. "Still, I guess they have to run it like it is one, too dangerous to let the inmates just please themselves."

Placing the helmet over his head, he soon found the locking ring and engaged it. Pressing the oxygen supply button on his suit resulted in instant gratification – a slight breeze of chilled air rising up from the aspirator around the helmet's base. After pressing the green button on the seat as before to signal he was ready, he sat back and thought about the adventure in front of him, unsure whether it was excitement or nervousness he was feeling. But at least it was invigorating.

The earpiece intercom in his helmet buzzed back into life, and with it the voice of Commander Andersen. "Commander to all crew and passengers, we are all green. Starting the engines now."

As the ship accelerated away, Dave turned his head to catch one final glimpse of his home for the last forty years through the single rear-facing observation window set high up in the wall behind him. Tami saw it too. Together they watched the red ball slowly but perceivably start to recede in the window. Fifteen minutes later, Mars had shrunk to a quarter of its size.

"Commander again," buzzed Dave's earpiece. "We have now reached our terminal velocity. You may now remove your helmets. In a short while, after we have completed our checks and made our final course corrections for Earth, we will start up the motors on the habitation ring to simulate gravity. This will be done very slowly to check they are working properly. It will take two hours to reach Mars Standard Gravity. As soon as the panel light on the wall indicates the gravity motors have been successfully activated, you may unbuckle. Until you get used to it, some of you may also feel a little nauseous. This is temporary and will pass, I can assure you."

Dave couldn't help but wonder what would happen if the motors didn't work – would he remain buckled to a chair for eight months.

After successfully unlocking his helmet, Dave was in time to catch the Commander's continued instructions over the ship's PA intercom. "Please understand there will be very little simulated gravity to start with. You will still need to use weightless protocols to maneuver about until we get up to speed. My TIC will be acting Purser for the journey. He is on his way to the Transit Lounge now to assign you your quarters. So it just remains for me to say, see you all at dinner."

Dave looked across at Tami, "dinner?" His stomach started churning at the very thought of it – he hadn't eaten since morning. "But it's now well past two a.m.!"

"Yes, dinner!" Tami replied. "The ship is always on Earth Standard Time. So now it's six p.m., assuming the clock on the wall is always right. See you at dinner; twenty-hundred hours? It will be lovely having someone I know to talk to."

"Yes, it will be," Dave concurred. "Tell me, do you know any others traveling on this flight?"

"Just a couple, Tegan, she is from the Mars Directorate department like me, and her husband Johan, they are returning to Earth to start a family. They didn't want to give birth to a Mars-born – too many potential health issues. You're Mars-born, aren't you, Dave?"

"Yes, never been anywhere else. This will be my first visit to Earth." Maybe he'd tell her later about his health issues. Now was not the time.

I^2

Flight

Dinner-time and he was nearly ready, but in truth, he really wasn't. Was his condition making it difficult to stand with any confidence or the effect of artificial gravity? And he was still overcompensating and knocking things over. This was the third time he'd retrieved the electric toothbrush off the floor.

What would he talk about? In his sad life, what had he done worth boring everybody with? And then there was Tami, she was lovely and someone he'd like to get to know better. But would she like him? Should he tell her about his life-limiting condition? All questions he had no way of answering, yet here he was, worrying about them all the same.

After knocking the toothbrush onto the floor again, Dave decided it would be safer to place it back into its holder. Taking a deep breath, he took a moment to regain his composure. These questions could wait. Why worry about it? Getting used to moving about his billet without bashing into things was his immediate priority, rather than distressing about hypothetical situations that might or might not transpire.

To say his accommodation was bijou would be generous. As grey as the rest of the ship, the living area consisted of a bed, a desk with a built-in swing-out chair, and not much else unless you counted the in-wall stowage and the small galley where he could make drinks from a shiny metallic automated dispenser.

Above the desk, a computer terminal, come entertainment console, dominated the remaining wall space. Opposite, on the far wall, a small circular window looked out forward, not unlike the one he had back on Mars. As he peered out through the thin perspex pane at the infinite blackness of space, he suddenly felt homesick. What he wouldn't give now to be looking at the reddish-brown landscape that had been his view for so many years. As unchanging as he – just how he liked it.

Turning back around to face the shower cubicle and toilet, Dave checked his appearance in the small mirror above the gravity sink. Just above the sink, a panel light glowed red, next to a warning sign. 'Facilities only to be used when the green light is illuminated.' Dave wondered how much longer he would have to wait. Until the habitation ring was rotating sufficiently fast enough to suck the water down the waste pipe, using it was prohibited. Would he even be able to pick his feet up by the time they had accelerated the ring to match Earth Standard Gravity? But that was still a few months away, and they said the sink would be okay to use by the morning – once the waste processing systems had become fully operational. The thought of having to continue to use waste bags was something he didn't want to dwell on.

Walking over to the storage units, he slid back the frosted Perspex and selected one of the three grey flight suits that had been provided. It was the same system of rotation they used on Mars: Wear one, wash one, save one. Picking out the first one, he returned to the bed and laid it out next to his discarded IVA. After removing his undergarments, he walked back across the room naked to extract fresh ones from the drawer below the storage unit. Finally, he picked up his IVA and hung it in the storage locker reserved expressly for it. The next time he'd need it would be when they reached Earth orbit. If the room felt small now, how much smaller would it seem after eight months?

Tami was already sat down in the refectory, next to Tegan and Johan. More awkwardness thought Dave, almost

I^2

of a mind to sit at a vacant seat he'd noticed in the corner. But no, that would be discourteous. And maybe eight months in solitary confinement of his own making would not be living up to the rationale behind making the journey in the first place.

"Hello, Tami, made it," he said, maintaining a firm grip on the nearest grab rail for fear of floating off or falling over.

"Hi, Dave, meet Tegan and Johanus Hofstalt."

"Hi, David Sherman," Dave responded, raising his free hand by way of an introduction. "But, just call me Dave. No point being formal while we're all held hostage on a spaceship hurtling through space, that may or may not get us to our destination!"

"Nice to meet you, Dave, and for us too, it's just Johan and Tegan," Hofstalt acknowledged, pointing to the vacant seat with his outstretched palm. "Please join us. And I advise you to use the lap belt still."

"Okay, I'll just go see what Chef has prepared."

"Don't expect much; it's just protein bars tonight. Galley won't be up and functioning until tomorrow," interjected Tami.

"It seems that most things around here will be working mañana," Johan replied. His jocular nature coming to the fore.

"I noticed, but then this is my first trip," Dave eased his grip on the rail, ready to risk life and limb to get to the servery.

"Ah, Mars-born then?" Johan surmised.

"Yes. I would have to be, wouldn't I!" Dave replied confidently. If Johan could make light of the situation, then so could he.

After selecting a protein bar and drinks pack, Dave returned to his seat. Having three friends would help him settle in, not so unlike his old life back on Mars. But tonight was not the night to bore everyone with his life story, that could wait, and he was tired. The day had been arduous, more than he cared to admit. After finishing up his meal, he would make his excuses and leave. "I hope you don't mind if I cut-and-run after I've chewed my way through this leather strap! I'm starting to feel very tired. Maybe see you all tomorrow for breakfast?"

Yes, sure thing, Dave," Johan replied. "Don't think we are going anywhere for the next eight months."

He was unsure how long he'd slept for. All he knew for certain was that it was way past breakfast time. The communications and entertainment console said 11 a.m. However, he was relieved to see the green light glowing away over the gravity sink. After a spruce up, he would check his itinerary on the terminal. As a Mars-born, he had twice the gym time allocated to him. A necessity to prepare his slender frame for the rigors of life under 9.8 Newtons of gravity.

Dragging himself out of bed, he switched on the terminal and plonked himself down on the chair in front of it. He didn't bounce – it felt like he was on Mars again. The rotation of the habitat ring must be up to speed. Checking the calendar, he noted his first session had been scheduled for between sixteen-hundred and seventeen-hundred hours. Then he had a meeting with the Commander at six. Everyone on board would be given a job to do, and he was no exception. Even the sick had to work. He guessed he and his fellow passengers wouldn't be asked to fly the ship or maintain essential systems; that was the crew's work. But every passenger was given something to do to stop boredom turning into psychosis. Space sickness they called it, and he had seen it first-hand. Why was he suddenly thinking about the guy at Anders who just lost it one day and stepped out onto the surface of Mars in nothing except his pajamas? He was a goner in ten seconds. Was it the idea of not being in control anymore that was giving him the jitters? Imprisoned in a flying bullet for the duration!

'Ping,' the console messaging system flashed a message on the screen just as he was about to step away from it.

'Tami here, going to lunch in the refectory at one. Can you make it?'

'See you there,' he typed back, noting that they were not yet friends enough for her to engage video mode.

Lunch was pleasant. The reconstituted freeze-dried stew was edible if not helped by Johan reminding everyone that all water on the ship was recycled. Eventually, they'd all be drinking water that had passed through every other crew member.

"So, Dave, what exactly did you do on Mars," inquired Tegan. "Tami told us it was something to do with geology."

"Sort of, more like sample testing in a lab, rather than doing any real science." Dave fidgeted in his seat. It suddenly felt like he was being interrogated. "Working on a mining station is all about making sure the minerals and elements we extract are of the required quality. For shipment, I make sure they are all sealed in their containers and labeled correctly before being sent up here or put on a direct unmanned shuttle to Earth. Did you know that between arriving and leaving, the orbit of this ship has to be adjusted five times to compensate for the additional weight being stowed." Well, that was his life story very much told. It certainly didn't sound anywhere close to exciting now he'd said it.

"Johan's a teacher, did you know. And Tegan's a doctor," Tami offered by way of an introduction.

"Really, at the University?" Dave asked, reluctantly peeling his gaze away from Tami, desperately trying not to visualize how she'd look 'au naturel' and failing. Beneath its fabric veneer, the flight suit Tami was wearing promised much. Something he doubted he'd ever get to see beyond fantasy. But at least he was grateful his moment in the spotlight had reached closure.

"Yes, I *lecture* there, not teach," Johan replied, deliberately emphasizing 'lecture.' It was as if being called teacher was somehow inferior. "Modern History and Politics. When I say modern, I mean anytime in the last thousand years, but mainly focusing on events post-second World War, all-in-all a fascinating period. There is nothing so dangerous as man than when he is being his most creative. Was not space exploration a big political game of one-upmanship? Were not advances in technology driven by mankind's desire to kill one another? We are benign now by comparison. Lulled by the need to cooperate and bring back to Earth the profits from our extra-terrestrial activities."

"Sounds very interesting," remarked Dave. Guessing that Johan liked to hear the sound of his own voice and opinions. He would definitely be interesting to listen to in the coming days. If only to take the pressure off him and stop his mind from wandering into forbidden territory – one that involved Tami and being in some sort of relationship. It was an impossible daydream, and he knew it. Were they not already work colleagues? If anything were going to happen between them, it would have done so already. Had Tami not been stationed on Anders for two years now. In all that time, his dealings with her had only ever been professional. There had been no signs of there being any 'spark' between them. Tegan, however, might be useful. When Tami had said she worked at the Mars Directorate, he'd falsely assumed she was another secretary. Not a member of the medical faculty within the directorate. And now he knew she was a doctor too. It was good to know, just in case.

I^2

After changing into his gym-wear – basic shorts and a t-shirt, he couldn't help but wonder how they reclaimed and recycled sweat? But he was prevaricating – the fear of stepping through the hatchway from his cabin and out into the connecting corridor of the habitation ring beyond hadn't lessened any. He must try to overcome it. Try not to think that a few centimeters away below his feet was the vacuum of space. But, also, at least here, there was some familiarity with home. He must stop calling it that! As he walked around the gentle curvature of the ring that made the floor in the distance become obscured by the curve of the roofline, he compared the similarity of the layout. On the forward-facing side, there were doorways to the cabins. On the rear side, stowage and common areas, including the gymnasium, much like Anders.

Above him, every ninety degrees around the habitation ring, he came to a shaft with a warning plate fixed next to it. Low gravity area, it said. Like wheel spokes, all the accessway tubes led to the center – the spacecraft hub. Apparently, while the gravity was as low as MSG, Johan said that if you could jump high enough to reach the tube, you would carry on towards the center by your own propulsion. Well, Earthers could; his muscles were nowhere near strong enough yet. He had tried and been rewarded with a bruise for his efforts, hitting his head on the bottom rung of the ladder protruding out from the shaft's edge. If he ever felt like visiting the center of the craft, he would just do the sensible thing: pull down the ladder and use it as intended.

Eventually, he reached the ninety-degree segment of the wheel that housed the refectory and the medical center. Being almost diametrically opposite his quarters made his chosen direction of travel irrelevant. Next to the medical center, the door he was dreading, the one marked fitness center. He shuddered as he looked at it. An electronic panel glowed in the half-light outside the entrance, displaying his personal session time and schedule. Disappointingly, it hadn't changed any. Exercise was something he had tried to avoid all his life, but now it seemed there was no getting away from it.

Opening the bulkhead door, Dave was greeted by the sound of light tubes clacking into life. Thankfully apart from the exercise equipment, the room was deserted. At least, there'd be no one to see him making an absolute fool of himself on the apparatus. After inspecting the equipment, Dave decided the mechanical contraptions had been expressly designed for torture and nothing else.

Making his way over to the diagnostic station, he pressed the only button flashing on the panel. It had already recognized him. The console in front of him immediately displaying the readout it was receiving off the remote sensor attached to his wrist – something everyone on board had to wear for the duration. The figures shown for BP, Heart rate, and $O_2\%$ meant little to him. All he knew for sure was that his performance would be relayed to the terminal in his berth after every exercise cycle. There he would be expected to meet or exceed the target curve plotted out in his personal flight journal. This would show him how much progress he was making. And there was no possibility of 'winging' it – the medical officer got the results at the same time, leaving him with no alternative. He'd much rather be in his berth gazing out at the stars; that would be more than satisfying enough and far less sweaty.

Below Dave's bio readout, glowing back at him, his first exercise: cardio and muscle build. Walking over to the treadmill, he flashed his wrist sensor over the receiver. The treadmill display acknowledged him by name, the day's exercise program, and a request to fasten the rigid restraining tether around his waist to stop him from

I^2

bouncing off it. Essential if the workout was to be successful in a low gravity environment. How else would his legs obtain the necessary downforce to work against the resistance of the moving belt?

As soon as the system detected the tether had been fastened correctly, it turned the start button green. Dave pressed it and nervously waited for the belt to start moving. Walking pace at first, slowly building momentum up to a steady jog. He was running! The words bouncing around his cranium in disbelief. Dave, the docile, had suddenly become Dave the dynamic.

But the euphoria of the moment was short-lived. His breathing had shallowed and become labored, short sharp gasps that seemed to achieve little. And the pain in his leg muscles could best be described as continuous cramp, only without the contractions. He already wished he could just push the big red emergency stop button and make everything go away. He stared at it. It was calling to him – 'Go on, do it, push me.' It seemed to be the only thing in the room; everything else had disappeared. 'Blink, Blink – go on, you know you want to.' He would resist, his breathing had at least now settled down, and he felt he was no longer trying to suck air out of a vacuum. And was feeling as though your heart had relocated itself to somewhere under your chin normal? And he could hear it beating inside his ears. It must be; he was still alive! Something he'd have to get used to. Looking at the stop button was too much of a temptation; he would concentrate on the distance display. 1km done, 2 to go; he might make it. All he had to do was focus on the prize.

"Hello Dave," came a voice from behind him he'd come to recognize.

Hindered by the restraining tether, he turned as best he could to see Johan walking towards the second treadmill.

"Hi," he managed back between gulps of air.

"So, how's it going."

"To be completely honest ......, I'm finding it......, quite strenuous."

"Ah, good, then it's doing what it's supposed to. You will sleep well tonight, my friend."

"Yes, I believe I will."

How could they give him two sessions of this a day? This was day one, level one, the easiest! He was already fretting about his body's ability to quickly adapt to the punishment regime; otherwise, one day, Johan would find his lifeless body slumped over a machine. But then who was to say that wouldn't be the case anyway? His condition may have been correctly diagnosed, but how could they know for sure how much time he had left?

Dave noted the Commander's Office wasn't much bigger than his as he stepped through the hatchway. Apart from an enlarged area for office administration, it was practically identical.

The Commander, a man, tall-ish, fifty-ish, with greying hair that conveyed the impression of intelligence and authority, beckoned him to sit on the additionally provided chair.

Dave complied.

"I see from your notes you have a medical condition," he said, without looking up from the digital tablet he was holding out far enough in front of him to give Dave the impression the Commander usually wore glasses.

"Yes, Sir."

"You don't have to call me Sir; you're a civilian. Tom or Commander will do just fine. I would prefer Tom, however."

"Yes, Tom."

"Any issues, see the medical officer or come talk to me. Now, your onboard assignment: I actually have the

I^2

perfect job for you. Seeing as most of the rock on this ship has come from Anders, you can have the task of monitoring it and ensuring everything remains as it should in the cargo holds. So, stowing, maintenance of seals, condition of cargo, etc., all yours. Just inspect it twice a day and fill in a report. Easy for you, but important, right? Does that sound okay?"

"Yes, Tom, it does. In fact, it sounds just like a home from home."

"Good, nice to meet you, Dave. Send in the next person if he's arrived yet, and, no doubt, we'll get to talk some more during the voyage."

"Nice meeting you too, Tom," Dave replied, rising from his seat. He suddenly had the feeling that his best-kept secret probably wasn't as secret as he'd hoped for. He'd soon have no option but tell his new friends of his condition before it became common knowledge. It wouldn't be long before everyone knew everything about everybody with such a small contingent of travelers. Maybe he'd tell them tonight at dinner – Tegan would understand. But, he didn't want pity, not eight months of people watching him, seeing if he would keel over anytime soon, or tiptoeing around him for fear of being insensitive.

Dave pensively approached the dinner table; he was last as usual. His mind wholly preoccupied, playing out various scenarios as to how he'd tell them. Trying to imagine his response to any question they might ask. It was like playing mind-chess. He had to get it off his chest now before sitting down and losing his nerve. "Look, I need to say this before we start dinner," he started while reaching to pull out a chair. Did he have the courage to continue? He must, if only... Well, if only, at that moment, seemed like a pretty good reason. "I don't want it to become common knowledge, and you hear it from someone else first."

I, SQUARED

They were watching him intently now. Staring at him, waiting on the delivery of his next syllable. He could feel his resolve weakening – get it out now, quickly. "I'm dying!" he stuttered. It wasn't how he'd planned it, but then these things seldom do, no matter how much you practice it beforehand. He needed to qualify it quickly before they called the medical staff, mistakingly thinking he was having some sort of seizure. "Not straight away, so don't call the medics." Better, almost humorous, he congratulated himself and plonked his backside down on the chair.

"I owe you all an explanation," he had their attention now. He was no longer Dave the uninteresting. "Look, I might get ill before we reach Earth. I'll probably be okay, but I have something called Low Gravity Motor-Neurone Disorder. Or LG-MND, to give it its abbreviated form. I suppose that makes it seem less severe. At most, I probably have two years, a little longer, a little less; no one knows for sure. But it won't really start to affect me until a few months... well, a few months before the end. So, I'm going to Earth because there is some sort of treatment available there. Everyone is a little vague on exactly what it is. All I know for sure is that it's not a cure."

Dave was suddenly conscious that Tami had placed her hand on his and was squeezing it lightly.

"I don't want you to treat me any different, okay. I'm just Dave, and we'll say no more about it, okay?"

"Whatever you wish, Dave," offered Tegan, "but do come and see me at any time if you want to talk."

"Okay, I will. Promise," Dave replied, relieved that no one seemed to be making a big deal out of his news. "But let's enjoy this evening. I hear they're going to show the Alien movies over the next few nights. Shall we all go and watch them? I love the cinema."

The evening had been a great success. The film was as

I^2

good as Dave ever remembered it being, having already seen it a handful of times. Maybe it was the company that had made it special, that, or the popcorn that had been thoughtfully provided. Tami seemed more than friendly, perhaps it was just his imaginings, but he secretly hoped it was more than that. It might make for a welcome distraction to eight months of repetition. Turning to his console, he re-read back his schedule. Yes, any distraction would be preferable to the entries he'd made into the calendar: 08:00; rise, 09:00; breakfast, 10:00; cargo inspection, 11:00; gym, 12:00; lunch and free time, 16:00; second cargo inspection and reports, 17:00; gym, 19:00; R&R.

Typically, he was never happier than having a schedule to work to – but that was then. His life was different now, and so should be his expectations. But for now rest, and the hope of a new tomorrow. Wasn't that a quote from someone? Dave tried to recall the words more precisely. Was it Einstien? 'Learn from yesterday, live for today, hope for tomorrow;' something like that anyway. He should try and live up to it, spend each day like it was his last. Was he not already starting to feel like a new man, mentally if not physically, and maybe for the first time, in charge of his own destiny.

I, SQUARED

Life In a Bottle

Several weeks in, and he was coping. The gym was bearable, and they had increased the gravity of the ship by 10%. He was certainly doing better than just muddling through. Although he felt a little ponderous and slow at times, he was managing to stay ahead of the curve on his exercise regime.

The cargo hold had become his sanctuary, a quiet place he could escape to when he wanted to be alone. Locked in behind its decompression doors, no one would disturb him there if he so chose. Taking a book or just his thoughts with him, he could while away the hours unfettered by the need to conform to the stereotypical traveler. He still found interacting with his fellow passengers challenging. Would being an inmate in prison be any different to life onboard the Endeavor? The daily routine never deviated. Everyone was dressed in a uniform, tagged, and had daily duties to perform. And, everyone fulfilled their tasks because, basically, there was nothing else to do. The only time he could forget his surroundings was in here, his little piece of freedom.

Of course, he wasn't just confined in the physical sense; he was also a prisoner to circumstance. Everything that had happened to him must have happened for a reason. Preordained almost, like somehow the universe had ganged up on him. He was a prisoner to destiny! But then the ship was also a prisoner as much as he. Held captive by the forces of gravity, constrained to follow a trajectory with slavish adherence. He was hurtling through space on a craft aiming for a small dot in space, a tiny sphere that would only occupy a precise location at an exact moment in time. Any deviation and they would miss their target; fly off into space and never be heard of again. Yet everyone seemed to

I^2

accept it without much consternation.

Dave found such confidence refreshing, but his doubts remained. What if something happened along the way to the ship, or possibly the Earth. No, it was more likely to be the ship. If they missed their rendezvous vector, what then? Would it be 'carry on as normal' as they drifted off into space, just waiting for something vital to break or run out? Would there be sudden panic when everyone realized there was no way back? Would everyone abandon their morals and try to go out on a high, hitting on the women on board for a final fling? There were only nine of them, nowhere near enough, and they were all spoken for except three; two of the crew and Tami.

Besides, thinking about possible future relationships in the event of a catastrophe was a joke. He'd only spoken fleetingly to the other passengers in passing. They remained strangers to him as much as he remained an enigma to them. And probably would for the remainder of the voyage. No, three true friends were more than enough for anyone. Would that be the only time he'd stand a chance with Tami: a cataclysm with the promise of death? He had to remind himself again; he was dying anyway. So how would it make a difference?

Dave put down the book he'd been staring at without reading, his mind snapping back into focus. He was daydreaming about scenarios that were too obscure to give credence to – he should be getting ready for his workout. Casting out the subconscious intrusions from his mind, he returned to the task in hand: finish checking the crates. Thoughts about any fantasy relationship he might have with Tami would have to wait. Time and gravity wait for no man, and he had a date with both of them at the gymnasium.

Apart from the rigors of the gym, time passed by quickly enough. Too quickly, if he was honest, seeing as though he only had a limited amount of it left. Making as much use of the Endeavor's electronic library as time would allow had rekindled his love of reading. Was he deliberately hiding? Perhaps, but it suited him to remain distant. As much as he liked Tami, he was under no illusion about his chances of wooing her; his daydreams were just that. But there was no getting away from the fact she'd suggested he might like to come round to hers after dinner one night, for a film maybe. How could he refuse? He didn't want to lose her as a friend, more than he wanted a relationship, and besides, he doubted anything would materialize from it.

They had been in space for four weeks now, and apart from dinner with Tami, nothing had happened to suggest anything other than friendship. Maybe this was a test? Perhaps he should think about making the first move? If only he was confident enough. In the end, he decided, or rather the coward in him had decided, to continue to play it by ear. After his gym session, he would get ready for dinner and accept her offer to go back to hers and watch a film. It was an innocent enough request even for his sensibilities. However, such a strategy only served to remind him all too keenly of the idiom: faint heart never won fair maiden. His infatuation was destined to end in failure. He wasn't a lover, and it was too late to change. Being a Lothario just wasn't in his nature.

An ebullient Johan stopped Dave on his way to the Fitness Center. "Hi, Dave, off to pound the treadmill again?"

"Yes, it's pretty obvious dressed like this. But where are you off to? You don't have a session booked at this time. So why are you in your exercise gear?"

"Ah, I've just discovered the delights of the zero-g rooms. They're amazing, and there's a handball court there. We all four must play soon. Let's ask the girls tonight."

"Okay, whatever you say, always up for some fun,"

I^2

Dave replied, trying to sound enthusiastic. At least it would waylay the thorny issue of going back to Tami's after dinner, for a while longer. He'd never been one for playing games unless it was a quick game of cards in the Red Dawn. But then the opportunities afforded him to take up sports on Mars were pretty minimal. At least here was a chance to try something new – try and become *that* more dynamic person. Wasn't adventure also part of his journey? Try new things rather than dismiss them and hide. By the same token, perhaps he should try and be more forthright when the next opportunity arose and accept Tami's offer of films and possibly more.

I, SQUARED

Shall We?

The ladder slid down the rails and banged against the end-stops. Dave tugged on it to check its stability. No one on board could jump straight into the tunnel anymore, not since gravity had reached half Earth normal. Now everyone had to use the ladders; it made him feel less inadequate. After safely climbing into the tunnel mouth, he retracted the ladder by engaging the spring return before continuing towards the center of the Endeavor using the built-in rungs. The tailing off of the effects of AG was becoming more and more noticeable as he progressed along the claustrophobic crawlway. In a moment of madness, by his standard, he let go of the rungs and pushed off, half-expecting to fall back down the shaft. But no, for the first time, he effortlessly found himself floating towards the center. And too rapidly – banging his head on the bulkhead door and rebounding back off it. Instinctively, he held out his hand to grab something to steady himself should he fall. Clumsy Dave's back, he thought, as he vigorously rubbed the spot on his head he was sure would turn into a bruise.

Carefully, after regaining his dignity, he sprung open the lever on the bulkhead door and pushed himself out into the central corridor of the spaceship. Johan was already waiting on the other side for him.

"The girls are already warming up. Are you ready?"

"As much as I'll ever be."

"Good. It makes sense if you team up with Tami, and I'll partner Tegan."

"Fine. Is it easy, this game? Only I've never played!"

"Sure, you just have to use your fist to hit a ball over a net. If it bounces more than once off any surface in the opponent's half. It's a point. First to fifteen."

I^2

Handball was one of those few sports available on Mars, one Dave had successfully avoided playing, preferring to remain a spectator. There had even been a national league. Every site entered a team, and every game was shown on TV. He recalled Anders station did quite well. Many an enjoyable evening was spent in the Dawn cheering them on. But what was before him now was very different from the game he knew. Dave surveyed the layout; sure, it was precisely like a handball court, except reproduced in 3D. The floor markings had been replicated on the sidewalls and ceiling. But then, how could you tell which side was a wall and which a floor when floating around in space? The net, such as it was, consisted of two sets of wire cords fashioned into a cross. In addition to the one suspended across the playing area, a second was suspended ceiling to floor, effectively quartering up the court.

"This is different," Dave exclaimed.

"Ah, yes, forgot to tell you," Johan instructed, seeing Dave looking perplexed. "You can go above, sideways, or below any of the nets, but it must make sense in 3D. You still have to hit it over the net relative to the receiving court it bounces in."

"I understand," Dave replied, his attention deflected by Tami waving to him from the far end of the court.

"You're with me, Dave," she called out across the court. "Come, let's have some fun and show these two how it's done."

Dave wasn't sure if he'd shrugged; he hadn't meant to. An almost involuntary defense mechanism, something he used when uncertain. Cautiously he pushed off from the wall and made a reasonable attempt of flying over the net.

"Isn't this fun already?" Tami exclaimed as he approached her, using the wall at the far end to arrest his forward motion.

"Yes, my, it isn't as easy as it looks!"

"I know stopping is the hardest part. You cannot cross

or touch the net; otherwise, it's a point to the other side. That is why there are all these grab handles placed around the court. You have to sort of aim for those while also trying to intercept the ball," instructed Tami, pointing out the numerous handgrips. "It's a good job everything travels so slowly. Shall I serve?"

Despite some initial issues in hitting the ball and then compensating for Newton's third law, Dave soon found himself enjoying the experience. The fact that he was holding his own surprised him: one game each and all square in the decider.

Pure enthusiasm, however, doesn't compensate for the lack of ability Dave painfully discovered after diving to return a well-delivered serve and hitting the deck head-first; before bouncing up into the net. Another bruise!

"Our game, I believe," Johan called out from the far side of the court. "You fouled the net."

"Are you hurt?" Tami asked, coming to Dave's aid.

"Only my pride, I think."

"We must do this all again soon! Yes?" Johan inquired, floating across to where Dave and Tami hovered above the floor.

"Yes, alright, I quite enjoyed it," Dave replied, rubbing his head and feeling for another bruise. "But now I have to attend to work."

"Yes, and me too," Tami agreed, reaching out for the towel she had hung over one of the grab handles.

Tami sat at her monitoring station, deep in thought. It had become apparent that she would have to make the first move where Dave was concerned. Watching films was one thing, but she needed more. Maybe next time if he was amenable. The screen went beep in front of her, snapping her mind back onto the job in hand. She acknowledged it. Given the maintenance coordinator's role, she compiled

I^2

reports and issued job sheets to the ship's maintenance teams. Purely admin, it was pretty basic, but a task she was well suited to.

The maintenance Chief, a burly guy called Josh, had two assistants, and these, along with the three bridge officers, made up the six members of the technical crew. The other four members being the MO and his female nursing assistant, and Chef, whose Sous was called Dion; an older lady you would never associate with being an astronaut.

Tami liked to talk to Dion, someone whose parents had been space-farers when it just used to be the Moon-run. With no family to speak of, the Endeavor had become her home. A little like Dave, she thought, someone reluctant to experience change. Josh was married to Fran, one of the maintenance crew. She correctly guessed that they saw the big ship has home too. Fran was probably her closest friend on board, having gotten to know her while working on maintenance administration. She always sought her out when she needed advice.

"What about Dave," Fran had said one day when Tami had been feeling a little low and homesick. "He's available and not bad looking."

Was it that obvious she was feeling frustrated? Well, that was it! One evening, she'd have to invite Dave to spend the night.

Dave was also feeling the strain. He had had a glimpse of life and was starting to feel bitter about the lost opportunities he'd already squandered. He should have gone to Earth when Erika asked him. She had even arranged a job interview for him at her father's company. But no, Dave the tortoise, safe in his shell, had decided to stay on Mars. The next time Tami suggested they go back to hers, he would accept.

I, SQUARED

Dinner had been enjoyable as the four of them relived another afternoon's exertions on the zero-g handball court. As soon as dessert had been cleared, Tami leaned across and whispered in Dave's ear about going back to hers to watch a new film she had selected from the library.

"Of course, I'd love to," he responded enthusiastically, much to her surprise.

Dave was sure he'd seen Tegan wink at him. Did everyone know his business? Hurriedly, to avoid further scrutiny and awkwardness, Dave rose from the table. "See you all tomorrow then. Tami and I are off to watch a film."

"Yes, breakfast, maybe?" Johan questioned, surmising he may actually be eating alone if any of the signs were to go by.

"Maybe," Tami replied suggestively. Dave felt his cheeks burning. It was the way she said it, slowly and seductively. It was sexy and inviting. At that instant, he knew he wanted her more than he would admit it to himself.

The film, entirely forgettable, but the evening, well the evening, that was quite something else. Dave had only just got back to his quarters, having missed breakfast. He would be late for his shift, but he didn't have a care. The rocks weren't going anywhere; he could complete his checks after gym time.

He hadn't been expecting her to, but desperately, deep down, hoped she'd make the first move. He knew he was hopeless when it came to matters of the heart. Sure there had been Erika, but that was nothing more than adolescent fumbling rather than being lost in the moment entwined in the arms of a real woman. He had never before experienced such intensity or passion. He hadn't even thought himself capable. But he hadn't disappointed, and it

I^2

made him feel reborn.

'Shall we' was all she had said. Shall we dance, make love, eat Sushi. Not that he had ever tasted Sushi being Mars born, but remembered it from a TV telecast. A documentary on how the fishing stocks on Earth became depleted to the point of extinction, and that Sushi, the ingestion of raw fish, was no longer sustainable. No, as far as he could recall, no woman had ever said 'shall we' to him before in any context, and certainly not one that alluded to love-making. And it was everything he had hoped it would be and more.

At last, he realized how much he'd missed. Life was more than rocks and preparing samples. Much more than drinking in the Red Dawn and talking about experiences they'd all hope to have one day. And now he had experienced it; he knew he wanted more. In one evening, Tami had become the brightest star in his sky. She would, no doubt, be ever remembered as the most important thing in his life, as short as it might be.

I, SQUARED

Around the Far-Side

Bloody exercise regime, it was all about meeting the set targets. In the five months they had been traveling, the Endeavor had increased its rotational gravity to three-quarters Earth norm. He had struggled, ponderous almost to the point of lethargy. How would he cope in another couple of months when the rotational speed was due to be increased again. What would he be like when they finally reached Earth-G day? But Tami kept encouraging him, and with Tegan also keeping a watchful eye should it become too much, Dave felt for the most part on top of his condition. He had started going out of the evenings with Johan when it wasn't film night and drinking with the crew in their mess. Which was more like a bar, only without the alcohol. Synthetic beer was the best they could provide; it had some flavor, if not the effect.

With its large observation window along one side, the layout of the mess reminded Dave of the Red Dawn. A place where he used to sit and look out onto the red earth of the Martian landscape. But his home was long gone now, replaced by a million points of light zipping past as the habitation ring spun about its axis. Looking through the aperture, it awoke a memory of something he owned as a small child – a simple toy: a kaleidoscope.

Dave sat down and watched the stars trace an arc as they flew past the window, only for the pattern to be repeated a few seconds later. Mesmerizingly, the white points of light were zipping past noticeably faster today after another increase in the rotational speed of the habitation ring. It was hypnotic, almost beguiling to the point of absurdity, that something so small could survive out here in the never-ending depths of infinity.

"So, Dave, how goes it with Tami?" inquired Josh,

I^2

approaching. His arm draped about Fran in a 'she's mine' sort of way.

"Good, thanks," Dave replied, unsure as to whether they were genuinely concerned or after a juicy piece of gossip.

"She's lovely," Fran said, taking a seat. "We have found a lot to talk about on this journey. We have a lot in common, you know."

Dave felt as though his space had suddenly been invaded. Did he like Fran knowing things, but then what did she know? The conflict made him feel a little uneasy.

Tami tapped him on the shoulder after sneaking up behind him. "Hi there, got a drink for me?"

"Good news, I've just heard we will be out of the Sun's shadow later tomorrow," Johan said jauntingly, suddenly appearing with three drinks to hand.

"No Tegan?" Dave asked, looking around the mess.

"No, she's been feeling kinda sick today. The MO says she has to rest up for at least a couple of days."

"Tomorrow, you will be able to send and receive messages from Earth again," Josh said, agreeing with Johan's observation. "It's just not possible with the big ass Sun in the way."

"Yes, it's always a big day," confirmed Fran. "We have a party on board to celebrate being able to see our destination now it's no longer hidden. You must come and join us in the celebrations, all of you. I'll let you in on a secret – there will be a bottle or two of real wine to drink. It's the only time it's allowed. Once we know we have completed the most dangerous part of the journey, we get to relax for a day. All the crew will be here, and guests we consider our friends."

After dipping a finger into his glass, Josh prescribed two circles on the table around it. Picking up two peanuts to represent Mars and Earth, he placed them on the rings.

I, SQUARED

"Suppose the glass is the Sun," he said, using his finger to trace out the heliocentric route the Endeavor was taking to traverse the two rings. "With this trajectory, we only use the engines twice. Once when we leave Mars, and then again when we slow for Earth orbit. It's called the Hofmann transfer. While we are heading towards Earth, our sister ship, the Columbia, is doing precisely the same around the other side of the Sun on the shorter route between the planets. They see Mars all the time and Earth too. It's only on the return leg where we have a communications blackout. Look, we even cut the plane of the Earth's orbit as we round the Sun. We could go on to Venus from here, but I hear the weather's lousy!"

Trying not to think about the 'aim and hope' precision of it all, Dave joined in the laughter with the rest of them. The morning would be a time for messages; who would he receive any off? But at least he could enjoy the crew's hospitality as they talked about their families. What would he talk about?

Dave thought about taking another turn in the gym. Did he really want to go and listen to everyone's news? At least if he stayed in, he could watch terrestrial TV once more. Maybe there was football.

The knock at the door was unexpected. A quick rapping that relayed a sense of urgency. Dave opened the door to a pair of red puffy eyes staring back at him.

"Tami, What's the matter?" She had been crying; her face, once perfection, now blotchy where tears had turned into rivers.

"Oh, Dave, my Father's died. I so wanted to get back to see him. Before… I hoped I'd be in time. The doctors said he had longer."

This was not a situation he'd been expecting to face; he was totally unprepared. Not since the death of his father

I^2

had he faced mortality or ever consoled anyone. He had no experience in such matters. He tried to think – what would they do on TV?

"Oh, Tami, I'm so sorry. Come in, here, sit. I'll make some tea." Dave placed his hand around her shoulder; it seemed like the natural thing to do. Coaxing her inside, he led her over to the swing-out chair. The only place to sit other than his bed, but didn't think it appropriate. At least it got him out of listening to everyone else's news that would be buzzing around the refectory by now. He would stay here with Tami and comfort her as best he could for as long as she needed him. Listen to stories about her father and try and be sympathetic. This was what was expected of him now – somehow, he had suddenly gained responsibilities.

He tried to remember his own father's passing: a mining accident at Anders while he was at University. Even now, he couldn't recall much about it, except it was cold and unemotional, unable to express a tear for fear of being seen to be weak. And now, here in his arms was the love of his life sobbing inconsolably. How he wished he could ease her suffering. It was precisely at times like these he realized, if nothing else, he was inadequate in every way. She would be better off without him.

Dave hadn't expected her to want to stay the night, but she seemed so vulnerable; how could he refuse. In the stillness of the eternal night, they cuddled.

Maybe the warmth of one another helped, for she seemed much more at ease this morning. Together they walked hand-in-hand to breakfast. Dion smiled at them as they entered the refectory, offering to bring their order over to the table by the observation window. A position so popular, it was usually the first to go. But this morning, the place was empty. Too much celebrating the previous evening, Dave surmised.

I, SQUARED

From the window, they could see forward and the Endeavor's Bridge at the top. It was still disorientating to Dave, watching the Bridge seemingly spin around with the stars – an ever-moving tableau as the habitation ring rotated about its axis. For five months, the Sun had been in the field of view, but no longer. The fiery orange ball had slid off to one side and soon would be behind them. Eventually, the ship would come to line up on the blue dot, still someway off-center in the window. Then, later, when the Earth becomes more prominent in the window, everyone will start getting excited about reaching their destination. All but he – he had a difficult decision to make.

He would also need to up his gym sessions again to make doubly sure he was ready. And the MO had asked to see him later. It couldn't be a coincidence; tomorrow was also the day the Endeavor increased the habitation ring's rotational speed again. It would be Earth-G day soon and another excuse for a celebration.

If the last 24 hours had taught him anything, it was that life was brutal. In a single moment of clarity, as he dipped his toast into a simulated fried egg, he knew – they could never have a future together, no matter how short-lived. He couldn't entertain the idea of putting Tami through another emotional wringer – better to quash it now before it became too serious. How devastating would it be to watch someone you love deteriorate in front of you? He didn't want her to become his carer when the time came, anything but that. Anything but pity; Tami deserved better, and it was up to him to tell her. How could he watch her watching him decay and become enfeebled? He would rather jump through an airlock now and be done with it. No, when they reached Earth, he would have to let her go. It would hurt; he knew it. But, as far as he could recall, this was the first time he had actually thought about someone else other than himself.

I^2

"So Dave, how have you been finding the exercises," quizzed the MO as Dave unwillingly took his seat.

"Fine, so far."

"Good, I have your print-outs here. You've done well. You may feel a little more fatigued tomorrow when they up the G-force again. Tell me, how's your head."

"Funny, I've almost forgotten all about it."

"That's good then. Which is why I asked you here. I have arranged a full brain scan and blood tests for next week. So we can see how well you are adapting to near Earth-norm gravity."

Dave watched him flick the papers in front of him and make a note.

"So next week at 11:00. It shouldn't take more than a couple of hours."

Dave nodded, accepting his fate as much as a condemned man would take the guillotine. "Next week then, I'll put it in the diary. Although, like I said, I currently feel better than I ever have."

"Good, then the tests should bear it out," the MO replied without looking up from Dave's notes on the tablet in front of him. "I trust you can find your own way out. See you back here next week."

It was all very brisk and formal, Dave thought, as he opened the hatchway door and ventured back into the corridor. Would he be so brutal when the time came to tell Tami? But, it was true; he hadn't given his condition a second thought in weeks. Maybe he should sign up! Maybe space flight agreed with his predisposition. In one sense, next week couldn't come quickly enough. He would finally get a possible indication of how long he had left.

I, SQUARED

Realities

Sitting in the MRI scanner was as unpleasant in space as it was on Mars. The noise of the oscillating magnetic field made relaxing as instructed a challenge – the loud 'thump, thump,' attenuated only slightly by the cumbersome headphones he was made to wear. Through them, a selection of unoriginal music played. Soothing tunes designed to ease tension and alleviate the boredom of sitting in an enormous tin can for over an hour. What they would find was all he could think of. And the brace he'd been made to wear was digging into his neck. What if they should discover a marked deterioration in his condition? It would make the whole idea of coming to Earth redundant. The machine was making him feel slightly giddy, muddling his thinking, or was that his fear? As for his anxiety, he guessed it would be off the scale if they could measure it.

An hour later, the MO's assistant, a girl called Gilly, released him from his mechanical prison. Relieved to be free of the brace, Dave rubbed the spot where it had pressed on his neck, leaving it feeling slightly stiff and tender. After massaging the crick again, he tried to flex his neck; it clicked. Feeling better, he straightened up and made his way through to the MO's office.

"Well, Doc, how does it look?" Dave said, making his way over to where the MO was looking at the scan

"On the surface, okay. I'll know more when I have had a chance to review all the slice-throughs. And your bloods are in the analyzer now."

"So, I'm okay for a while?"

"Yes, I would say so. I don't think the journey has had any detrimental effects on your physical wellbeing. However, once on Earth, the symptoms of your disease

I^2

may become more apparent under full gravity, although the progress of it should be slower."

"I understand. Thank you, Doc." It was all he needed to know for now, and hanging around in the MO's office was not top of his list of favorite things to do.

Walking back to his billet, he felt apprehensive. He had to decide when he would tell Tami. Perhaps it would be better after he'd had all of his results back. If they turned out to be terrible, it would make it all the easier to let her down. All he knew was the number of days they had left on board were diminishing rapidly, more than he cared to count. Still, there were a few weeks left...

The clock on the wall panel, depressingly, displayed the day he hoped would never arrive: Earthfall-2. Tonight would be their last full evening on board before they made preparations for Earth orbit. Dave looked through his window at the undeniable: the Earth, like a nemesis, loomed large there now. This evening had to be the night he told Tami. Oh, why was he such a coward? He had been putting the moment off, prevaricating, while all the time becoming more emotionally involved with her. He had received the results back from the MO weeks ago, yet still, he couldn't bring himself to tell Tami that he no longer wanted her when he did so – more than ever. He would have to make sure he was early for dinner, forget about the gym and try and snag the table for two in the corner. How he wished there was alcohol for times like these.

Did Tami sense how quiet he was at dinner? She kept staring at him, and he hadn't the courage to not look away. Anything but look her in the eyes, for fear his resolve should melt away. He noted how worried she looked. At that moment he couldn't hate himself more. How he wished the floor would suddenly open up and suck him out into the spacial void. Could he hold his nerve? He had to, but lying… Lying was something he wasn't well practiced in.

"Tami…" But the words wouldn't come. A lump had formed in his throat. He tried to cough it out, but the frog remained steadfastly stuck in his craw. Almost as if fate was trying to prevent him from saying what he must. Picking up a glass of water, Dave took a sip.

"Yes, Dave," she replied, placing her hand on his.

"I don't think we should see each other again when we reach Earth," spluttered Dave, finally managing to expel the obstruction. "You've always known I'm not well."

"Yes, so? You're well at the moment," Dave could see tears forming in the corner of her hazel eyes. "That's good enough for me."

"The doctor's report wasn't good," Dave continued hurriedly so as not to be dissuaded. It was only a little lie, but the day would come when the prognosis would say he had no time left.

"But, Dave, you've been healthy the whole trip. He must be wrong." Her tears, no longer suspended on her bottom eyelids, dribbled down her cheek. Quickly, she wiped them away with the back of her hand.

It was true, but she had to believe him. He had to sound convincing. "The MO said once I'm Earth-side, I will deteriorate quickly." He could feel his cheeks flushing as he tried to conceal the invention. "Look, you know how much I really care for you. I love you, dammit. I don't want to become a burden and sour what we have now.

"It wouldn't, I promise," sobbed Tami.

"But it would break my heart if I forced you to become my carer, sitting by my side, compelled to watch me die. I want you to remember us like it is now. Do you

I^2

understand?"

"Yes, I understand. It was my father's passing, wasn't it? I sensed you'd changed in some way afterward."

"It just brought it home to me that dying is selfish, pointless, and distressing. I don't want to die; who does? But I also don't want to inflict my demise and needs on others. Not those I truly care for, and certainly not the ones I love. And it's exactly for that reason I need to let you go."

Tami wiped the tears running down her cheek on the table serviette. "I love you too, and I'd choose to stay. You know I would. But if that's what you want." She tried to force a smile. "You promise we'll stay best friends, and you'll tell me everything. And not be annoyed if I put flowers on your grave. Not that you'll be able to complain. Dave, you have been everything I have ever wanted. It's so cruel that destiny now denies us a future."

Dave could no longer contain his emotions. He tried to bite his bottom lip to stop it quivering. Tears flooded out of him uncontrollably; he didn't care anymore if it made him look weak. His heart was broken and would remain so.

From a table across the refectory, Tegan noticed and squeezed Johan's hand hard to stop him from going over. "Forget it," she said. "It's not our business."

I, SQUARED

Earthfall

Awoken earlier than usual by the klaxon sounding throughout the ship, Dave reluctantly stirred from his slumber. He had slept poorly – was it tomorrow already?

The four of them had spent the previous evening watching the Endeavor cross the plane of the Moon's orbit, observing the satellite from a safe distance as the spaceship hurtled on towards Earth. Another obstacle successfully negotiated mused Dave as he watched it flash by. But he had been in no mood to celebrate the fact that they had successfully avoided being splattered across the Moon's already heavily cratered surface. Although getting to see the back of it was in itself pretty amazing. But now, in the cold reality of an artificially induced morning, he felt ashamed and worthless. Could he despise himself anymore for what he'd done to Tami the previous evening, telling her so bluntly they were finished? Today, they would be like strangers again, and it weighed heavily on him. With her, he was fearless, but now all his insecurities had started to resurrect themselves. Would the engines fail to start and slow them down? Would they crash into the Earth or go sailing off into space after failing to be grabbed by Earth's gravity? He could think of worse places to die than drifting amongst the stars, but not without *her*. Could he hate himself anymore for telling her it was over? Well, that must be the end of it; he now had to concentrate on getting ready – what is done; is done. Was ever an axiom so true? There could be no going back, no un-saying of what had already been said. His bridges were all burned and turned to ash.

Opening the locker that had remained closed for eight months, he retrieved his spacesuit to get ready for the most dangerous part of the voyage: the interception into Earth

I^2

orbit. The briefing the previous day had been quite detailed on what was expected of everyone.

Frantically Dave wrestled with the recalcitrant IVA. Why was it so hard to climb into under full Earth-G? Stepping out into the walkway for the last time, he turned toward the Transit Lounge, wondering if it would have been easier to wait until the habitation ring had stopped spinning so he could have floated there rather than plod along as if wading through a tank of molasses? But the instructions had been very specific; everyone had to be in their seats before they shut down the artificial gravity system. Gratefully he arrived at the Transit Lounge in time. Only the second time he'd visited it. No, third, he reminded himself; he had forgotten the emergency drill. A precaution in case any ship-wide problem required them to get 'suited-up.'

Tami was already there, although she chose not to acknowledge him. Sitting down, Dave fumbled with the airline, trying to fasten it to the supply. It didn't seem to want to fit. The next moment he felt a hand on his, guiding the open end onto the supply flange. He looked up to see Tami standing over him, smiling, "you know I wouldn't have minded being your carer," she said.

Dave felt himself blushing. "I know you wouldn't have. It's only because I care…." Tami put her finger over his lips and kissed his cheek before retaking her seat.

"Commander here. The rotation motors have been put into reverse. In thirty minutes, we will all be weightless again. This is done to minimize the gyroscopic effect as the ship maneuvers into orbit. Now all of you get your helmets on. You know the drill, just a precaution in case of problems. Deacceleration is due to commence as soon as we have achieved zero-g. Once we have attained Earth orbit, I will relay further disembarkation instructions."

I, SQUARED

It wasn't long before Dave could feel the heaviness of the suit, becoming less apparent. The stars, too, had come to a standstill in the observation window – no longer rotating about the ship. Of course, he knew the opposite to be true: the habitation ring had stopped spinning on its axis. They were all weightless once more.

A sudden feeling of compression on his chest made him gasp as the seat harness tightened against his shoulders. Pressing down hard on him, it felt as though the straps would slice off his arms as they fought to restrain him in the flight-chair. They were slowing, and slowing quickly. He hadn't thought it'd be so obvious. But here he was, struggling to breathe, the straps on the harness tightening around him to make every inhalation labored and painful. Just as it was becoming apparent that he was about to lose consciousness, it subsided. Glancing above him, the observation window that for eight months had been full of stars was now full of something blue. They'd made it; they were in Earth's orbit. Inwardly he let out a sigh.

"Commander Andersen, here again. I'd just like to say thanks to everyone for making this an enjoyable flight. I enjoyed getting to know you all and hope to see you again for the return. We are now en route to dock with the ISS. Here you will disembark. An earth shuttle will then take you down to the planet. Mitch, will soon be with you to explain the disembarkation process."

ISS, or Isis, to those who treated it like home, welcomed the Endeavor's crew and passengers like lost friends. A replacement crew was already there waiting to prepare the giant vessel for its return journey in just 21 days – a tight schedule for getting things done in space. But, if they missed the window, the ship would remain on station at the ISS for another two years until the two planets were

I^2

once again correctly aligned.

"So a good flight then," remarked Johan, coming over to tap Dave on the back. "All the best for the future, and stay in touch. You too, Tami. We are all one big family now!"

"Of course we are," replied a taciturn Dave; now he and Tami were finished, he very much doubted it.

"I'll be glad to get Earth-side. I forgot how much I hate being weightless!" Tami remarked. "See you all again soon, in proper shoes!"

"Four hours to wait, that's all, Tami," Tegan replied. "Then we will all be back on terra-firma."

"I think the first thing for me will be a beer," butted in Johan, mimicking the action of drowning a glass of the stuff. "What will you do, Dave?"

"Beer, probably," Dave replied, suddenly realizing that he hadn't given much thought to what he was actually going to do after they'd touched down. He had locked such frightening thoughts away with the IVA when he'd boarded. But he couldn't any longer, and it was a terrifying prospect. Here he was once again, like a poorly fitting jacket, cloaked in uncertainty.

I, SQUARED

A Foreign World

Dave looked out from his window on the seventeenth floor. As hotel rooms go, it was adequate. But then how would he know otherwise? The road below was filled with millions of points of light, just like the eternal night of space he'd just crossed. Streets full of vehicles hurrying towards some unknown destination, while above him, automated delivery drones went about their work. In the distance, he could just make out the floodlights of the Astro-port and his last link with home. What had he done!

In the world's eyes, he was a spaceman, an alien even, having never before set foot on the Earth. For a couple of days anyway, until his release papers from Martian Mining Industries came through. Although not brilliant, the severance package was enough to live on – for what little time he had left. Mesmerized, he watched the dancing lights blur and mingle; everyone had someplace to be, while he had nowhere: he was a man out of time in more ways than one.

He opened his holdall and let the lid flop all the way back. The chill on his clothes permeated the air as he set them free: a couple of jumpsuits and underwear, as for the rest - trinkets from a former life. Why had he not just left the junk on Mars? It made for a sorry spectacle – to live for so long and own so little. They were still cold to the touch having spent months in the unheated storage hold of the Endeavor. Placing his hand down the side of the case, he slid it around until he found what he was looking for; his electronic tablet and charger nestled in the corner.

Dave plugged in the charging cable and switched the device on. Now here was a historic moment, he thought, looking down at the battered screen as it booted. Like everyone else on Mars, they'd all been given a standard-issue tablet, and now for the first time, he was going to pair

I^2

it to another! From a gift bag lying on the bed, Dave extracted an expensive-looking box. Inside, the smartphone he'd just purchased from the shop in the hotel lobby. It was nothing too fancy, a bit like him really – a traditional phone that you kept in your pocket, rather than one of the latest arm-band types. A brick, as the techies would say. But then had he not just declared himself to be a man out of time.

After releasing it from its cardboard prison, he turned it on and selected the pairing option. It had enough charge to synchronize his contacts across. It didn't take long: Terry's VOLT number, his sister, and the treatment center, that was it! Dave couldn't help admonishing himself for being so pathetic in only having managed to garner three contacts in a lifetime. Fumbling around in his pocket, he eventually found the piece of paper with Tami's number inscribed on it. Should he throw it away or keep it? His finger hovered above the phone, still undecided. What was the harm? Tapping on the screen, a female assistant in 3D rose out of the device. Instinctively he angled the phone around to see how the personal assistant would react.

"How can I be of service," it asked.

"Can you add a number to my contacts, please?".

"Certainly, can you repeat it?" responded the avatar.

He felt slightly embarrassed talking to a piece of hardware as if it were human. The screen changed to the image of a hand to write the number into a virtual diary. "Your number is stored. What name shall I assign?"

"Tami."

"You may also give me a name if you like," said the avatar, returning to full 3D mode, "I am programmed for all adult pleasures and services!"

"Later maybe," Dave replied, suddenly feeling flushed and wondering if he should select a different avatar. Were all AI interactive devices so forward on this planet? Back on Mars, his mates had said there were sex-parlors in the less salubrious parts of the city employing them, but he'd dismissed it as banter. Maybe there was some truth in it after all. The one thing on Earth that had changed the most in the last thirty years was the use of robots to undertake menial everyday tasks. His mates had conjectured that soon they'd be coming to Mars. Then they would all be out of a job.

If he charged up the phone now, he would get the digital Lolita to call his sister later. Then maybe tomorrow, phone the treatment center or at least think about it. But now, the evening was his to do with as he saw fit. And he did feel fit, enough to venture out onto the strange foreign world seventeen floors below his feet. His curiosity urged him to 'go see' what 'life down there' was all about. To boldly go where the lights were brightest, for was this not also his first day on a voyage of discovery?

As far as he could tell, the planet of Man was all about noise, speed, and impatience. It didn't make for a great first impression. Trying to cross the road without being run over, trampled on, or shouted at, seemed all but impossible.

Arriving at the Mall he'd spotted from his hotel window, Dave ventured inside. Shops, now here was an alien concept. He soon found himself staring into brightly lit façades full of items he'd never had any use for, wondering just how necessary any of them really were? Shop windows decorated with tantalizing products to entice the customer to part with their money, persuading them their lives would be all the better for owning the object on display. On Mars, everything was provided for you. Even on the space flight, had not his onboard clothes been hanging in a locker ready for him? The ones he was still wearing!

Walking along the brightly lit cream marble effect floor, made from tiles with specks of iridescent aluminum embedded in them, he meandered further into the complex

I^2

until every shop seemed to be exactly like the previous one.

For such a beacon of commerce, it was remarkably quiet. The shops appeared to be closing. The people still there looked to be heading towards the exits. Some clutching carriers emboldened in the name of the shop that had successfully managed to extract money from them. While others carried bags printed with cats or dogs – probably full of wares from less ostentatious outlets.

Dave felt about giving the whole idea of going shopping a miss, for although he needed to purchase more suitable attire, he felt totally out of his depth. His Martian wardrobe would have to suffice. Perhaps flight suits were all the rage this year? He would return tomorrow, early…maybe! Shopping would definitely be a challenge – the idea of buying something just because it's there was as foreign to him as the idea of ownership. He'd never owned anything that wasn't a necessity.

As he turned to head back the way he came, from somewhere in the glass citadel came the distant throb of music. The sound, mingled with voices and slightly distorted by the echo, was calling to him – like the Sirens, enticing him to follow it wherever it may lead. Then just as quickly, it was gone. It was as if someone had opened and closed a door. He had to investigate; it sounded like a bar. If only to pay homage to the Red Dawn and drink to absent friends. And was it not soccer night? He could at least imagine his mates, 176 million kilometers away, raising a glass at the same time as he while watching their favorite sport.

Guided by his ears, he soon found himself standing outside the Crocodile, named after a famous clothing brand. Even Dave had heard of it, and one he considered priced totally out of proportion for the addition of a tiny embroidered green reptile. Should he go in? He needed a beer for sure. Maybe it was time to look at life on this strange planet with a glass to hand. This was his home now, one he couldn't escape from. He would have to learn to like it – beer would help.

Inside, the establishment bustled. In one corner, a reproduction Wurlitzer Jukebox boomed out some rock-a-billy while thirsty punters on barstools crowded around the main bar. Opposite, along the far wall, little wooden paneled alcoves offered dining tables and padded seats. Walking past the pool table, pitched in the center of the room, Dave sought out one of the quieter bays and pulled out a chair, one from where he could see the soccer relay.

A middle-aged waitress approached even before he'd thought about picking up the menu card. After eyeing him up and down for a moment, she withdrew a pad from the pocket in her tunic. "You just in from space then?" she asked with a practiced disinterest.

"Yes, something like that. I wonder what gave me away? Was it my clothes!"

"Possibly," she laughed. "We get a lot in like you being so close to the Astro-port. Usually looking to get drunk before take-off. They say it makes it a little less painful."

"Probably," Dave replied, not knowing enough to offer an alternative explanation but thinking it may have more to do with being locked inside a tin-can for eight months with no access to alcohol.

"Drink?" she inquired while proceeding to wipe down the table with a cloth of dubious origin.

"Beer, please."

"Okay, we have light, amber, regular, wheat, or zero."

"Regular will be fine."

"Would you like something to eat with that?"

Unsure he was that hungry, Dave took a minute to study the menu, more out of politeness than necessity. Maybe he ought to try a real burger? One actually made with meat, unlike the ones he used to eat back on Mars in

I^2

the Dawn. Fabricated from synthesized protein, they were affectionately called slabs – so named after the concrete blocks used for flooring there. "Okay, I'll take the house burger, please."

"Fries with that?"

"No, just the burger, thanks."

He watched her peel away from the table and head towards the pass. Tearing his order off her pad, she fastened it to the clip on the order wheel and rang a bell. Then, crossing over to the bar, she picked up a tray and poured his beer. Once the tray had been filled with three more orders, she returned. "There you go, Sir. Your food will be along in about ten minutes."

Dave supped his beer. It certainly was nothing like the Red Dawn Special he had grown up with and certainly not as cold. But then back on Mars, you only needed to let the beer flow around outside in some external piping to chill it sufficiently enough to mask some of the unpleasantness. This was a totally new experience, not only refreshing but also palatable. It made Dave wonder if the burger would live up to the promise of the entrée.

The burger duly arrived, substantial enough to require 'murder by cocktail stick' to hold it all together on the white plate. Dave hadn't realized how hungry he was until he saw it towering over the side salad by way of a garnish and the little accompanying pots of slaw and ketchup. His stomach gurgled at the sight of it, almost causing him to drool. Since leaving the Earth shuttle and transferring to the hotel, he hadn't eaten. He hadn't even thought about food, his intestines feeling so knotted up with anxiety.

The burger didn't disappoint. After quickly demolishing it, Dave decided another beer or two wouldn't hurt any. If anything, it would ease his self-doubt. Would *she* welcome him: a sister he'd never seen except on a screen? He realized he had to see Jane, if only to fill in the missing part of his life. Something he'd never felt confident enough to talk about over the video link.

He could vaguely remember his mother, only learning of her passing when his sister contacted him for the first time. That was 10 years already. Did she have a good life? He never understood why she didn't keep in touch? For these past 30 years, he had carried the guilt that it was his fault in some way. The pain of his sixth birthday still burned. When his mother told him his present would be a baby sister, then left soon afterward. That was it. He never got to speak to her again, and his father refused point-blank to talk about it. The only family he had in two worlds was a sister. He couldn't turn his back on her now, for however much longer remained.

After ordering another beer, he started to feel a little less out of place. Settling down to watch the soccer on the entertainment wall, he imagined Terry, Robbie, and Frank to be next to him as the game unfolded. Several times, lost in the moment, he caught himself turning to talk to empty space. At least they were there in spirit like he knew they always would be. He must have looked like a right idiot, but he didn't care.

11:30 p.m., Dave stumbled back into the hotel room. Looking at the clock, he groaned quietly to himself, not because he was starting to feel the after-effects of drinking so much beer, but more because it was nearly tomorrow.

Through two bleary eyes that seemingly refused to focus at the same time, he squinted at Lolita as she simulated dialing his sister's number and the screen switch to a pulsating handset. Would she answer, it was late after all? Maybe they were asleep? He was just about to terminate the call when the graphic changed, dissolving to reveal the face of the recipient.

"Hello, Dave, so you made it then."

"Hi, Sis, sorry to call so late."

"I looked up your arrival time and hoped you'd call

I^2

today. I waited up especially, thinking you may have important things to do first."

"I went for a beer, does that count? Listen, I want to come and see you. There are things I need to discuss with you. Stuff you need to know about, and pretty soon. Would that be okay?"

"Of course, it would be lovely, and for the children to finally meet their only uncle. Can you get here if I give you the address of somewhere easy to get to?"

After making a few notes and searching online to get a train ticket, he felt better and more capable of making an appointment with his treatment advisor… tomorrow!

The following afternoon, after shopping, a more relaxed and confident Dave enjoyed a lazy lunch in the Crocodile. Staying away from the beer, he let his mind wander and dared to think about what the following days would bring. The receptionist at Forever-Life had taken his call almost as if she'd been expecting him. Maybe Rhines had already contacted them? Anyway, his appointment was all sorted. As soon as he got back from his sister's, he'd get to learn of his fate and the unusual treatment they had in store for him. Funnily enough, it didn't worry him anymore. Maybe he'd celebrate with just one beer…

Dave reached out to silence the unwelcoming squark of the bedside clock. The sun had not yet made an appearance, and the heavy window drapes, made it feel like the middle of the night. Checking the led display panel once more, confirmed it. It was already five in the morning, and he had to be at the railway station by seven.

Wearily he rose, clumsily tumbling out of bed and ending up on the floor in a heap. Was it was the increased gravity affecting his ability to stand, his illness, or the effects of the previous night's beer? The beer he'd swore to stay away from, but his thirst had been difficult to satiate. After finally managing to haul himself back upright, he stumbled towards the bathroom. It was definitely the beer, he concluded, without giving his illness any further consideration. In fact, he felt relatively stable on his feet, a little hungover maybe, but other than that he decided, he felt fine.

After showering and shaving, Dave pulled open the carrier bags containing the clothes he'd purchased yesterday before finding himself back in the Crocodile. Carefully he laid them out on the bed before reaching under to recover his holdall. He wasn't going back to Mars, so there was no need to keep his jumpsuits any longer. Seeking out the bin in the corner of the room, he tipped as much of his Martian clothing as he could into it, allowing the rest to cascade over the floor. Returning the empty holdall to the bed, he quickly refilled it with new footwear, toiletries, and the family mementos he'd brought back – maybe his sister would like those. Next, he retrieved a brand new suitcase from the closet: he was a man of possessions now! Carefully he laid his new clothes into it, after first selecting a pair of blue jeans, white cotton shirt, and a brown Harris Tweed jacket to travel in. A pair of brown moccasins completed the ensemble. Stepping back to admire his selection, he caught himself thinking: Behold, the new Dave. And why not? What was there left of the old Dave worth keeping? After dressing and laying out his jacket on the bed ready, he called room service to order breakfast.

French croissant, jam, and probably an unhealthy amount of butter, all washed down with several cups of coffee, quelled his hunger. He felt ready to face the long day ahead. Soon he would be on the road and heading into the unknown. The Magneton train would see him in Texas in 4 hours, 1000 miles from Cape Canaveral to Houston, then onto San Antonio. He wondered for a moment what

I^2

250 miles an hour along the ground would feel like. In space, there was no sensation of speed. When he reached San Antonio, he would hire a self-drive car to take him up to Big Lake. His sister had said she would meet him there at 8 p.m. He rechecked the timetable and then his watch. It was time to step up!

Reaching into his jacket pocket, he extracted his wallet. After placing a note under the breakfast tray he thought would be a fair tip, he rose quickly and made his way over to the bed, ready to pick up all his worldly possessions. It still didn't look much: one suitcase and a holdall. Maybe he should check the bathroom one last time? No, he was sure. He was dithering. Hurriedly, he closed the bags in an attempt to contain the second thoughts bubbling up in the back of his mind for fear they should grow any louder. After easing the cases down onto the floor, he wedged open the hotel room door and placed them out in the corridor, ready for the bellhop.

The elevator, as if waiting for him, pinged at his floor before he reached it, and the bellhop stepped out pushing a luggage dolly.

Dave entered and pressed the hold button to wait for him to return. With the cases safely stowed, the bellhop selected the ground floor. Without stopping to pick up passengers en route, the elevator descended quickly.

"Taxi?" The bellhop inquired as the doors swooshed open out onto the lobby.

"Yes, thank you," Dave replied, fumbling in the unfamiliar pockets of his new jacket. Eventually, he located his wallet. After opening it to remove the room keycard from one of the credit card slots, he extracted a note to tip the bellhop. Simply refolding the wallet, he placed the keycard on top and headed off towards the reception desk to settle his bill.

I, SQUARED

Dave held the security pass hung around his neck on a lanyard up to the receiving sensor. It blipped, and the glass door of the entrance gate swooshed open. He stepped inside. This would be the last time he'd need access to the Astro-port – the display above the gate's internal door confirmed it: his authorization would be canceled after today. On the far side, opposite the entrance gate, a large map of the complex filled most of a wall. Dave walked over and studied it, tracing his finger along the route he'd need to take to reach the train station. He was convinced he'd never seen so many people together all in one place. It reminded him of Enterprise in some ways: functional rather than frivolous.

As Dave followed the route he'd decided upon, checking signboards as he went, he was convinced the population here was certainly more than the whole of Mars. The Astro-port at Canaveral had grown in size as soon as they had started to colonize his old homeworld. Having to accommodate the ever-increasing workload became something of a challenge. Logistics were suddenly a matter of life and death. It wasn't as if the port only had to deal with the passengers and freight from Mars; it also had to deal with all the traffic from Moonbase. Now here were a strange bunch of individuals, but at least they got to come home every month. The port also served as the manufacturing hub for many of the satellite systems and spacecraft. It was a small city in itself, one mostly made of glass domes and steel bracing. Vast transparent canopies to keep out the dust and weather. An environmentally controlled utopia perfect in every way to facilitate the construction of advanced technology.

He checked his ticket as soon as he reached the station terminus: Gate 4. He had time to buy a magazine and then get on board.

I^2

As the train pulled away from the station, it was like watching the closing chapter on his life so far. Everything he had ever known disappearing over the horizon. He had a new beginning now: this was day one of the rest of his life. He would turn the page, start anew, and record on the virgin vellum there, new adventures for as long as his pen still flowed with ink.

He had a mind he would sleep awhile too. Earth's gravity was still something he had yet to fully come to terms with.

I, SQUARED

On the Road

Dozily, Dave watched the countryside flash by in a blur. When he tried and fix his gaze on something interesting, it would speed out of view too quickly, leaving him feeling robbed of the experience. He turned to the entertainment center located in the seatback in front of him. Aimlessly, he scrolled through the films on offer until he came across something that interested him: a wildlife documentary. He always ended up watching these on Mars, fascinated by creatures he had never seen. Maybe he would get to see some real horses at his sister's ranch. She had said it was a ranch, and they always had horses. Visions of the Wild West flooded his mind. He could already see himself astride a rampant white stallion firing a six-shooter into the air.

As the train approached San Antonio, Dave, caught up in a documentary about sex and the alpha male, failed to notice it slowing for the station. Distracted by the sight of two males in the wild mating. A far more common phenomenon in the animal kingdom than initially researched – only the alpha males got the girls. Nothing much had changed there then if his success rate before Tami was anything to go by! However, it had been a long road for same-sex relationships in coming to be accepted, especially in religious circles – just like many other things, including space travel.

At the beginning of the 21st century, many preachers found the exploration of space and its potential to undermine their teachings a bitter pill to swallow. Religions had become quite vehement with their denunciations and hatred of all things scientific.

After it had been announced that life had once

I^2

thrived on Mars, they accused scientists of blasphemy and doing the 'devil's work.' It had been the most significant event in mankind's history – the Holy Grail of scientific discovery: Mitochondrial DNA in preserved ice. Something that would have once existed in liquid water when Mars was a young planet with a viable atmosphere and warmer temperatures. Colonization soon followed the findings, and now they were even talking about limited terraforming of the planet. In another hundred years, Mars may again become a self-sustaining world. Scientists were looking forward, not backward, unlike religious institutions at the time: a time when the godly resorted to preaching the threats written down in the book of Revelations and how the final days of mankind on Earth were fast approaching. They never mentioned Mars, though; they simply dismissed it as all being fake.

But seventy years had passed since then. Believers had even tried to use global warming to substantiate their claims that this was all the will of God. Because in their eyes, society had turned away from his teachings and the church. Eventually, even they had to accept the overwhelming evidence placed before them – it was all due to the actions of man, and God probably didn't exist anyway.

Yes, that one discovery on Mars had changed the attitudes of people more than anything else. In the last fifty years, the Earth had grown up; countries now worked together to resolve problems. Their efforts had started to produce results: the levels of carbon dioxide in the air, falling for the past ten years now. Through adversity and the threat of extinction, enemies had become friends. Where once they would have fought over resources, they now shared them. Societies were more equal. Mars had been instrumental in all of this. The willingness to collaborate had become the new ethos. Dave concluded that Gene Roddenberry would have been delighted in how his vision of the future had turned out.

I, SQUARED

Looking out of the window, he noticed that the train had come to a standstill. Time for him to take another step into the unknown – going where no Martian had gone before!

Squinting up at the direction boards hanging from the square paneled ceiling, Dave eventually found himself at the back of the queue for the car hire desk and wishing he'd opted to spend some money on a bag trolley. His arms were definitely not used to carrying a suitcase. It felt as though it was getting heavier the longer he waited, and the holdall over his shoulder was cutting into him. Not that anything was overly full; owning so little. Maybe it was just the waiting he minded.

Eventually, a clerk called him forward. "Booking number," he said brusquely.

Dave slid his paperwork over the counter towards the less than interested clerk. "Paid in advance," he offered, hoping it would help the clerk tapping away on the terminal in front of him locate his booking quicker.

"They all are," replied the clerk, "We do not take cash here."

Rising from the terminal, the clerk reached across under the counter and produced a set of keys, dropping them down on the top of Dave's paperwork.

"Sign at the bottom, please," said the clerk indifferently, depositing the contract next to the keys.

Dave picked up the pen fixed to the counter by a tether; some things never change, he thought. He had barely finished signing his name before the paper was whisked away from under his hand. Almost conjurer like the clerk held the signed form aloft as if waiting for applause after removing a tablecloth without disturbing the place settings. "Thank you for using Green-Planet cars," he said in a well-practiced monotone. "You'll find your vehicle in bay twelve."

I^2

Dave stuffed the paperwork back into his jacket pocket and picked up the keys. "Thanks," he said; it was only polite, even if slightly sarcastic in tone. Following the large green plastic arrow proudly stating 'Cars This Way,' hanging from two picture chains above the clerk's head, Dave headed through the outside doors to the parking bays.

Driving, or rather being guided along the straight freeway out of San Antonio, reminded Dave of the Martian landscape in some ways. Mostly brown sun-scorched earth, with little vegetation, made for an uninteresting journey. Texas had borne the brunt of some of the worst droughts the USA had ever experienced. A factor in persuading the government that Global Warming was a real thing. That, and the Florida Keys coming close to being submerged and lost forever. It was only in the last 20 years that the sea levels had stopped rising – one of the many global projects undertaken by the world's superpowers. Using the power of the sun, massive refrigeration units and pumping stations had been built to remove seawater from the oceans, desalinate it, and then pump it up to the head of many of the world's largest glaciers.

And now everyone had self-guiding cars, all electrically powered. As they drove along special kilometer sections of road where high energy induction coils had been placed under the surface, these vehicles would pick up a charge. Enough to power a car for another 100km or so. With charging sections set every 10km along the main highways, it kept everything moving.

The car's onboard card reader beeped again to process another bank card payment as Dave passed over another charging point. Collected by the remote transponder built into the road, it would take the amount directly from Dave's bank account. One where everything he had ever earned had been accruing, untouched until the day he'd decided to travel to Earth. It was now looking decidedly sickly – the trip had been very expensive. How would he manage to live here, never mind fund his treatment? It was a worry he didn't need reminding of every time the card reader blipped.

With only a white line etched into a grey asphalt road to occupy his mind while the vehicle guided itself along the highway, Dave found his mind wandering – trying to recall his earliest memories again. He still remembered the family rows even after all this time. His mother threatening to take the next shuttle back to Earth to live with her mother. He welcomed school-time, just to be elsewhere. And then, when she became pregnant, it gave her the excuse she was looking for – a way out. Not so much from her marriage to his father, but a way out of Anders.

At Anders, Junior School occupied a single room and comprised twenty children of differing ages. And he, the only one in his year of four, to go onto high school, the others in his year returning to Earth.

The only high school on the planet was in Enterprise and he, being an Outlander as they were called, had to board, only returning to Anders during recess. He was so lonely, even back then.

Dave made a mental note to call his friends; he wouldn't want them thinking he'd abandoned them. As soon as he'd settled into the apartment, he'd taken a short tenancy on back in Houston. The place was handy for the treatment center and also a refuge he could hide away in. Somewhere where no one would bother him if he so chose.

The monotony of the journey and the ensuing boredom made staying awake a challenge. If there was one thing self-drive cars didn't do, it was to continue on their own without supervision. If the driver dozed off, the vehicle would automatically pull over and stop. Like a child in need of a responsible adult, the car would just wait. Dave pressed the open window button to allow some fresher air in. It was certainly nowhere near as cool as the recirculating

I^2

air from the AC. Still, he hoped the higher oxygen level would keep him alert. After giving up searching for something to listen to on the radio other than country, he tapped the screen on his phone. On a heads-up display in front of him, Lolita appeared. He was just about to ask her to play some jazz to relieve the journey's tedium when he caught sight of a mileage marker board proclaiming: Big Lake 10 miles.

"Can I assist you, Dave?" Lolita asked.

"Yes, can you send a text to my sister and tell her I'm only ten minutes away."

"Sure thing, gorgeous." Dave was still in two minds about his chosen assistant. He could always switch the device into retro-mode and use a keypad if she became wearisome. But all phones since Siri over one hundred years ago now had assistants; he would look out of place if he reverted to using fingers!

Being the easiest place to find, his sister had suggested she meet him at the bus terminus. Not that it made much difference to him, any destination could have been entered into the car's navigation system.

As the last rays of sunlight touched on the horizon to signal the end of another scorching day, the car pulled into the car park of the bus terminus. Standing by the exit stood one lonely female. Dave recognized her instantly. It was the one thing he remembered most about his mother, her blonde hair cascading over the shoulders of her slight frame. How was it he could not recall his mother's face in his own mind but instantly recognize it in his sister?

Parking up in the closest bay, he beeped the horn to attract her attention. By the time he had extracted himself from the seat harness and clambered out of the vehicle, she was stood waiting for him by the driver's door.

"Hello Dave," a broad smile washing over her full lips, "you made it then."

"Yes, thanks, Jane," he replied tentatively. Why did he

feel awkward again?

"Come here, you big doze," she said, flinging her arms about his neck. "I never thought I'd ever get to do this."

"No, me neither," spluttered Dave, trying to speak while his chin remained firmly buried in the cup of her shoulder.

On being released from Jane's bear-hug of an embrace, Dave, for the first time, could admire her face up close. She smiled, exposing perfectly aligned pearl-white teeth, and he reciprocated, wishing now they'd spoken more often than 'on occasions.' Unrehearsed, their smiles quickly morphed into laughter – they were together at last.

"So we can go in your car to our ranch. It is still two hours away. Shall I drive? I'm afraid we are off the self-guided route."

"Yes, please, I feel very tired all of a sudden. So how did you get here then?"

"Myles dropped me off. He had some business to attend to here in Big Lake and afterward a few beers with the lads. No doubt they'll be watching the football at some bar in town by now. He'll be back in the morning after he's had one too many and crashed at a mate's."

"You don't mind your husband staying out?"

"Hell, no! He works hard and sees me all right. So I let him out to play once in a while. Come, let's get in and go. I don't like leaving Moxxi in charge of his sister for too long!"

I^2

Family

Dave thought he must have fallen asleep. He couldn't really recall any of the journey. The bits that seemed familiar were of blackness and a solitary car passing in the other direction. But now, here they were at the ranch house. In his mind, he'd imagined something wooden: a log cabin. The modern cubist-styled concrete building with its large glass feature walls was definitely not what he'd been expecting; not out here in the wilds of the Texan countryside. It looked out of place somehow, intrusive even, set against the backdrop of nothingness.

As Jane entered, the building reacted to her presence, lighting up the ground floor. No, this certainly was not what he was expecting at all! Approaching an acid-etched glass door of a floral design, it slid back into the wall to allow them access into the living space beyond.

"Place your bags here," Jane said, leading Dave into the contemporary living area of large cream sofas and smoky-grey glass occasional tables. "Drink? Beer? I'm having one."

"Yes, great, thanks," Dave replied as she directed him to one of the two sofas surrounding a rectangular coffee table.

Jane made her way towards a mirrored glass and wooden veneered bar area. Reaching into a fridge, she extracted two bottles and popped the twist-off caps.

"Probably not as good as your Martian ale," she said jokingly, remembering how Dave once described it as left-over rocket fuel.

"I wouldn't bet on it." At least the tension he was feeling about trying to make conversation was starting to ease.

Taking a swig of the ice-cold beer made him feel instantly better. Since leaving the hotel, this was the first time anything had passed his lips.

"Hungry?" Jane inquired, sitting down on the sofa opposite.

"You must be reading my mind," Dave replied, feeling sudden pangs of hunger as the beer reached his stomach. "It seems like a lifetime since I last ate."

"Good, then I'll go and put the pizza in the oven. Won't take a moment."

Rising quickly, she bounded out of the room by the same door they'd entered. Leaving Dave with nothing to do but admire the modern minimalist layout of the living area. He had never imagined one person could have so much space devoted to sitting down. He was pretty sure the whole of the Red Dawn could fit inside it. At the far end of the room, a TV wall and armchairs occupied a space of their own making – a snug almost. Around to the side, a formal dining area, and he guessed another way into the kitchen. But for now, rather than explore, he was content to ease back on the sofa and take another swig.

Startled slightly by the bang of a door behind him hitting the stop, Dave turned his head to be greeted by the smile of a small child flouncing towards him. Millie, Jane's youngest, six if he remembered correctly, her golden curls, just like her mother's, bouncing around her head as she bobbed along grinning from ear to ear. Half skipping, half running, reaching out as if to grab some enormous prize, she soon had him captured in a child-like embrace.

"Hello, uncle David," she giggled, "you made it then. Can you tell me a story about Mars tonight… are there aliens up there?"

"Don't be silly," Moxxi answered, entering the room at a more leisurely grown-up pace. In Dave's eyes, he was almost a man already. More mature than his twelve years would suggest, or was it thirteen now?

His guess about the kitchen had been correct as he

watched Jane emerge from around the corner holding a large pizza stone and place it in the center of the dining table.

"Come on then, tuck in, everyone," she said, returning to collect the plates and cutlery already stacked on the edge of a servery connecting the two rooms.

After everyone had cleared the stone of all its segments of cheesy enchantment, Jane placed it back on the servery. Turning around, she put her hands on the children's chairbacks. "Now, kids, would you like to go and watch TV in the study while we adults talk?" It was more a command than a request. Obediently the children rose from the table and headed out of the room.

"There, that's better. We can talk now. I know you didn't come all this way just to say hi. It must be something pretty serious to get you to leave your bubble on Mars."

Jane rose to fetch two more bottles of beer. "After all this time, you finally decide to come to Earth. And I know the journey must have been difficult; I know all about low-G living. Our Mom used to tell me often enough when I was a girl and wanted to know why we couldn't go and see Dad."

"It's difficult, Sis," Dave replied, thankfully grabbing the beer Jane was dangling in front of him. "It's not something I could easily say over a link…..I have a condition."

"A condition… A terminal condition!?" Dave watched her crash back down onto the dining chair opposite. He could see the news had disturbed her; the radiance in her face replaced by the wrinkles of concern.

"Yes, but I'm here to explore a treatment. Well, when I say treatment, it's not a cure you understand. My doctor said something that would help. Something new apparently."

Dave felt the reassuring grip of his sister's hand reaching out across the table and squeezing his. "The doctor said if I didn't do it now… Well, time was passing, so I had to make a decision while I was able. That and the possibility Earth's gravity might help slow the progress of the disease."

Jane slumped, seeking support from the chair-back. Now was not the time to weep. She still remembered the day she'd said goodbye to their father, watching a relay of the service over an old video link. And, subsequently, the tiny memorial service they held when his ashes had been repatriated to Earth. Then shortly afterward, their mother died from a brain tumor. The doctors said it may have been caused, in part, by the time she had spent in low-G. And now Dave would be going through the same experience.

Being only thirteen at the time, she had gone into care after her mother's untimely death. It was that, more than anything, that caused her to lose contact with Dave. It wasn't until after she'd married Myles and got her own VOLT account, she could get back in touch.

"A tumor, is it, like Mom?" Jan inquired, almost too afraid to ask for fear of the answer. She remembered only too vividly how it cruelly robbed her mother of her self-respect. Leaving nothing but a shell waiting on the certainty of release.

"No, more a defect, More like space MND. This will be my one and only Grand Tour, and while I'm here, put my affairs in order too. I'm not rich, but whatever's left after treatment costs and my funeral, well, it's yours."

"Oh, Dave, I'm sure you have loads of time yet. Don't be so morose. And you spend it all, I don't need it. I don't want to think you're obliged in any way. Besides, I can help. If you need money, you ask me. Agreed?"

Dave nodded. It was true; he wasn't as wealthy as some back on Mars, a place where you were paid according to the hazardousness of the job. That, and having nothing

I^2

to spend it on, made for a healthy bank balance. But the journey to Earth hadn't been exactly cheap. Dave supposed the corporation had to look to getting something back out of him. As for the treatment, well, that may prove even beyond his pocket. Until his severance pay came through, he was most definitely on his uppers. And now, here he was; someone only slightly more familiar to her than a stranger. How could he ask her for money? He was the older sibling. He was here to help them if he could, else what was the point? Jane had once confided in him over the relay that she and Myles were struggling to make ends meet; the children's education a significant drain on their finances.

Jane rose from the table and placed her hands on Dave's shoulders. "Come on, you must be tired. Let me show you your room. And Myles will be back tomorrow from his night out. What would you like to do while you're here – see the ranch?"

"Yes, that would be great. Do you have horses?"

A strange request, Jane thought. But then, if that's what her brother wanted, they would do the tour on horseback. Was this the first time she'd ever thought of Dave as being her brother?

She watched him rise slightly uneasily from the table. Yes, there were definitely signs of a slight weakness on his left side. Maybe it was paranoia on her part, or tiredness on his. But from that moment, she'd decided; she would be there for him.

For Dave, it was the exact opposite. He could feel his leg dragging slightly, but in his mind, he was adamant – he would not become a burden on his sister or anyone.

I, SQUARED

Home on the Range

As Dave descended the stairs on his way down to breakfast, his leg felt fine. The feeling in it had returned, and it was behaving more like it should. It must have been tiredness. Myles was already sat at the table along with Millie and Moxxi. "Hi," Dave greeted him slightly nervously. He had only ever spoken to Jane's husband briefly on the link – a few pleasantries, that's all, before asking to talk with his sister. Myles was still very much a stranger, someone, at last, he would be getting to know. And vice-versa, what would Myles think of him – a brother-in-law he knew nothing of?

"So, fella, you finally managed to pluck up the nerve to come see us," Myles said, without looking up from pouring syrup over pancakes.

Dave recognized it as humor, "well, I thought it was about time."

"We're glad you did," sniggered Millie in her own jovial way. Moxxi raising his hand in a high-five, managed to splutter out "hi," between mouthfuls of cereal.

"Jane said you'd like to take a tour of the ranch. It may be a little different from what you're expecting." Myles pressed his fork through a pancake and picked up a piece on the end of it. It dangled there, temptingly, as if he was waiting for Dave's reply before ingesting it.

"I understand that. I remember Jane telling me that this is a carbon capture ranch. It sounds interesting."

"It's a simple enough way to earn a living. My family used to be animal ranchers back in the day. But when the government offered subsidies to those willing to use the land to capture air-borne carbon. Everyone in these parts went for it. It takes a lot of energy, and that's the one thing we have plenty of out here: sunlight. We'll go out later and

I^2

show you around. You did say on horseback, didn't you?"

"Yes, that would be good." The pancake hovered in the air no longer. After watching Myles stuff his face with the sweet delicacy, he felt decidedly hungry himself. Just then, Jane made her entrance backward through the swing door that led to the kitchen, armed with another stacked plateful. In a well-practiced routine, she turned around and placed the pancakes on the table.

"Jams, honey, and syrup, all there if you want them," pointing to a trio of containers occupying the center. After disappearing back into the kitchen, she returned with a pot of freshly brewed coffee. "Okay, you lot, dig in."

Dave needed no second invitation.

"So when do you have to go back," Jane enquired, more as a way of making conversation than suggesting his presence was inconvenient.

"Soon, Sis. I have an appointment the day after tomorrow, back in Houston, at the treatment center."

"Good, you can stay another night then, and you promised me a story." interjected an excited Millie, feeling slightly hard done by in not getting one the previous evening.

"Yes, Millie, your Uncle can stay," reassured Jane. "You do want to stay, don't you? We'll go out this evening. I can show you off to our friends. Doubt they have ever met a Mars-born before."

"Okay," Dave replied, unsure if he was up to being shown off. But dinner would be nice. "My treat," he added, and this afternoon he could spend some time with the children and settle his debt with Millie. When else would he get the chance?

Myles tactfully excused himself from the table while Dave and Jane talked some more about their parents. The children, rather than listen to boring adult stuff, asked to be excused too. "If you want to," Jane said. "But first, you know the rules. Go wash your hands."

"Okay, Mommy," they simultaneously replied before scuttling off out of the room.

"They're good kids, Dave. It's just a pity our parents aren't around anymore to see them grow up."

"Yes, it is," agreed Dave. "But at least they have Myles's parents.

"And they spoil them too. Still, I guess it makes up in some small way."

Deep in conversation, they failed to notice Myles, now sporting a cowboy hat, re-enter the room, "Well, if you're all ready to go, the horses sure are," he said, startling them.

Dave rose from the table and eased the creases from his new blue jeans where they had ridden up over his thighs. He knew soon after buying them in Cape Canaveral they would come in handy.

"So, have you ridden before?" Myles enquired, absentmindedly forgetting that as yet, no horses had ever made it to Mars.

"Was that meant to be funny?" Jane laughed, watching her husband realize he'd slipped up.

"Ah yes, sorry, I forgot! Come on out, and I'll show you how."

Immediately outside the house, three tethered horses expectantly waited for riders; their reins tied around an old-fashioned hitching-post, the like of which Dave had only seen in relays of Cowboy movies.

"Your's is this one, Dave," pointed out Myles. "The one next to the steps."

Myles helped Dave climb the mounting steps while holding onto the reins of a docile chestnut mare to ensure it didn't move. After Dave had eased himself into the saddle,

I^2

Myles guided his feet into the stirrups. "You're ready to go now. We'll take it easy, okay. To move forward, a gentle prod in the side with your heels. And to stop, pull equally back on the reins. To turn, just use the head as you would a car steering wheel by pulling on one rein or the other."

"Okay, I think I've got it," Dave replied. "Just like in the movies."

"Yes," Myles affirmed, "only gently!"

A convoy of three cantered past the wooden rails delineating the homestead boundary from the vast open space of mostly parched grassland beyond. Keeping to the dirt road, they made their way towards the plant.

It was the first time Dave had had a chance to really look at the ranch. To say it wasn't what he expected would be an understatement. In the distance, stretching across the plain as far as he could see, banks of photo-voltaic panels. Beyond them, a slight rise dotted with wind turbines.

"That's a lot of serious power generation," Dave quipped.

"Well, we need it," Myles replied. "Like I said, it takes a lot of energy to remove air-borne carbon."

"I suppose it does," Dave replied enthusiastically, just as he always did when discussing technology.

"I think you will be impressed when you see the collectors. They're just beyond that rise where the wind turbines are situated." Myles said, pointing at the distant hills.

When they topped the final rise, Myles stretched his legs against the stirrups, easing himself into a more upright position in the saddle to better point out the more interesting parts of the sprawling complex below them.

The mishmash of pipes, tanks, and reaction chambers reminded Dave of the small chemical plant on Mars used for oxygen recycling. Only this was much bigger. Giant collectors that looked like jet engines perched on top of high pillars sucked at the air, screeching like they were ready for take-off.

Myles could see Dave was impressed. After clearing his throat from the dust the horses had kicked up, he called out to him. "The collectors scrub the CO_2 and methane from the air," he shouted, raising his voice to be heard while pointing out the compression tanks. "You need to suck a lot of air to get enough CO_2 and methane to convert into butane and propane, or LPG. And over there, in that small building, we make polypeptides or synthesized protein. SP, we call it. It takes all of the energy we produce here to make not a lot. But it keeps ten people employed. Not much call for cow-hands out here anymore."

"It's sort of like reverse oil," observed Dave. "Instead of pumping it out of the ground, you are sucking it out of the sky."

"Yes, Texas is still the carbon king of the USA," Myles agreed. "It just doesn't pay so well. It's nothing like the days when they used to pump the black gold out of the ground."

"Okay, boys, I suppose it's getting towards lunchtime. Shall we head back?" Jane asked, content that Dave and Myles seemed to have hit it off.

"You go on. I need to go down to the plant. I have to work sometimes, you know," Myles said, pulling on his horse's reins and turning him around.

"Okay, Myles. But before you go, be a dear and take a photo on my phone of Dave and me. Together at last. This will be one for the album. The first of many, I'm sure."

Jane watched her husband depart in a cloud of dust as Ringo galloped away before turning to head back to the ranch. "Come on then, Dave, I'm sure you're hungry. Race you back!"

I^2

The Martian

Dave unwrapped his new shirt: white, with black piping and black pearl buttons. After tucking it into his jeans, he picked up the hat Myles had loaned him. If they were going to a country nightclub this evening, he wasn't going to be the one looking out of place. Satisfied with the image being reflected in the mirror, he was ready. Descending the elegant floating wooden staircase set into the wall-end, he was first into the living area. Before he had time to think of how much he hated country music, his sister entered. Jane had chosen a checked blouse with a long skirt with tassel ends, while Myles, traditional as always, had opted for a denim shirt.

"Well, you look nice, Dave," she exclaimed.

"Thanks, Sis, as long as I don't have to do any ye-hahs!"

"No, I think you'll be safe," she smirked. "Myles will pour you a drink while I get the car."

"Will do, don't need asking twice," Myles replied, heading towards the bar.

While they waited for Jane, Myles poured bourbon into two oversize crystal glasses – ones you could swirl the ice around in with ease and listen to the satisfying clink it made on the sides.

"Look at you two," Jane remarked on returning and finding them deep in conversation: philosophizing on life and all things alcoholic. "Getting on like a house on fire, just like I knew you would. Anyway, time to go, don't forget we have a table booked."

"Okay, Love, coming now," Myles knocked the rest of his drink back in one gulp.

Dave tried to copy him but ended up coughing. "It's the ice. The cold caught the back of my throat," he spluttered, wiping his chin clean of aspirated bourbon.

Warm hues of gold and orange greeted him as he stepped out into the light – that nascent moment when the sun touches the horizon to signal the start of sunset. This was the time of day he loved the most. It reminded him of the milky tea-colored skies of Mars and of absent friends – were they eating now or thinking about going to the Dawn? Maybe they were raising a glass to the beermat and thinking about him at this very moment. All he knew for sure was that he missed them still.

"Will you be okay in the back, Dave?" Jane asked her distracted brother as she made for the driver's door."

"Sure, you're driving, whatever you say," he replied without looking away from the heavenly spectacle.

"You look after your sister now until we return," Jane called out to Moxxi, who had followed them outside to see them off.

"Okay, Mom, have a good time. We are going to watch some TV."

"Fine, nothing scary."

"I promise."

"Good, see you later then. Bed at the normal time, okay, and make sure you finish your homework."

"Yeh, okay, Mom," Moxxi replied, slouching and shuffling off back into the house.

The journey into Big Lake seemed shorter somehow. It wasn't pitch-black this time for sure. In the dimming light, he could, at least, appreciate the countryside as it flashed past – something to relieve the monotony of the drive. But, more likely, it was because he felt less of an outsider, Jane having openly accepted him for what he was. He was no longer a stranger to her – he was family.

However, Dave's opinion of Big Lake hadn't changed since looking it up on the internet. It still appeared to be the sort of place people passed-thru rather than stopped at.

I^2

Judging by the number of gas stations standing sentinel along the side of the main road through the town, modernization appeared not to be a big thing here. Everyone still drove pick-ups and vehicles that used petroleum. It really was like taking a step back in time. The single-story buildings straddling the main road had not changed since before man had set foot on the Moon, giving little away as to what constituted the town's center. Big Lake was still very much an oil-town. Turning down a side street, Jane headed for the car park of the Republic Hotel.

"It's about the only decent place in town to eat," remarked Myles as Jane parked up. "Not so much *Big Lake*, as *Little Puddle*. Still, the steaks are good here, and there's a band on tonight. So it should be fun, and you'll be able to meet some of the neighbors."

Dave doubted that it 'should be fun.' He would be expected to retell his life story to everyone who'd dared ask what it was like to be a Martian. Brevity would be needed; repeating his life story ad nauseam held little appeal.

"Hi Myles, is this the little green fella you were telling me about?" Shouted out a mountain of a man standing at the bar as the three of them entered the restaurant.

"Yep, sure is. Let me present you to my alien brother-in-law, Dave. This lump here is Mike."

"Pleased to meet you, Mike," Dave replied, trying to sound genuine.

"So, what's it like up there in space?"

"Different," Dave replied carefully, trying not to sound superior. "Although technically I wasn't in space. Just on a different planet."

"Well, guess it would be," Mike summarised, failing to grasp the difference. "You guys eating?"

"Yes, we are." Myles caught hold of Dave's arm to drag him away from further interrogation, "So, Mike, maybe catch you later then?"

"Sure thing," acknowledged Mike before turning back around to face the bar and his beer sitting there.

Leading Dave away, Myles directed him towards the table he'd reserved, where Jane had already taken up residence. A table Dave thought to be pleasantly situated in the dining room. Not too close to the stage as to be deafening or too close to the bar. A place where one's conversations wouldn't be overheard.

"Mike's my foreman," Myles explained as they sat down.

Dave secretly wondered how many others in the establishment already knew who he was. After quickly casting an eye around the place, with its faux wooden beams and textured plaster relief walls, he quickly drew the conclusion that none of the other customers in the room looked much like travelers – locals all of them. He was the foreigner here, the side-show freak, a curiosity from a different world. In some ways, he felt a long way from civilization – millions of miles in fact. Maybe the table in the middle of the dining room where everyone could see him was too conveniently placed. 'Behold! The alien exhibit!' He wasn't used to receiving attention, and on the whole, attention had given him a wide berth for as long as he cared to remember.

The food, standard fare by any measure, had been cooked well enough, a menu dripping in the blood of its historical past. Enormous steaks cooked any way you desired – from the walking dead to cindered remains. All served with substantial amounts of french fries and a few sad leaves that passed as a side salad to decorate the plate.

Dave struggled to finish the smallest offering on the menu while Jane and Myles tucked into a chateaubriand to share. Forgoing the offer of wine, he decided to stick to beer, something to help wash down the large lumps of

I^2

meat, the incessant chewing of which had started to make his jaw ache. In the background, the band yelped out 'good ole' country music standards. After several more beers, Dave found himself starting to relax – unexpectedly tapping his feet along with the music and becoming more immersed in the ambiance. Unwisely glancing towards the bar, he saw Mike there staring back. Dave politely acknowledged him by raising his glass.

After dinner and the band's final number, a few of Jane's friends approached to say hi, but mainly to stare. "So this is the brother you told us about... Has he really lived all his life on Mars... I was expecting him to be different somehow."

He had to escape. Excusing himself, he headed for the bar. Talking to Mike now seemed to be the better option. And over there was the draught beer faucet!

It was later than he was expecting; the clockface staring back at him from the bedside unit confirmed it. He placed the blame firmly on Myles for getting back so late. But on reflection, he'd enjoyed the evening immensely; the banter had been fun once he had warmed to the crowd. He and Mike had become like long-lost friends. As for the rest, they seemed just as friendly. A willingness to listen to him rambling on about what it was like to live on Mars was gratifying. But then he could have probably been from any city really and had the same effect, such were the local's ignorance of the real world. But that was yesterday. Today he had to leave this pleasant backwater where time had little meaning and return to Houston. And tomorrow, well, that would be a day he wished to be like the aphorism: one that would never come.

I, SQUARED

Treatment

Dave stared up at the glass façade in front of him; it made his neck hurt. It was definitely the tallest building he'd ever seen. Certainly, this was something more than just a hospital. Sitting on a bench opposite, marveling at the way its shiny mirrored glass panels reflected and distorted everything around it, he considered running away. But from what – himself in reality. Inside the shiny sentinel, a cathedral to science, resided what was left of his future. He had to grab it while still able. The time to stop running had undoubtedly passed, had not the few days he had spent at his sister's aptly demonstrated it?

Girding up his loins, he approached the automatic revolving door. As soon as he stepped across the threshold, the door started turning, gently, coercively pushing him inexorably towards the lobby.

"Good afternoon, may I help you?" the assistant behind the desk asked. For a moment, Dave was lost for words. The female assistant looked flawless, too perfect to be anything other than a synthetic. One that would undoubtedly be popular in the less salubrious parts of town as suggested by his Martian mates. This was the first chance he'd had to study one up close. He stared, watching her every facial expression, the way her mouth moved and the curl of her lip.

"Sir, may I be of assistance," it repeated. Dave noted the slight inflection of urgency introduced into its vocal processing. Obviously, a designed reaction to imitate human impatience.

"Hi, yes, I have a meeting with…," frantically fumbling in his pockets, Dave searched for the piece of paper Rhines had given him before he left Mars, on the back of which he'd jotted down the appointment time.

I^2

Eventually, he located it in the breast pocket of his tweed jacket. Pulling it out, he smoothed it down until he could read off the name. "Project Director Craddock is expecting me," he recited confidently.

The perfect assistant moved her flawless arm over to the touch panel and called up Craddock's appointment schedule. "You are Mr. David Sherman?"

"Yes, that's correct."

"Director Craddock has been notified. He will be with you shortly. Please take a seat and have a nice day."

Dave, disinclined to reciprocate – it wasn't human, so how could he hurt its feelings? What value could a synthetic attribute to what made a 'day nice?'

Taking a seat in the lobby, Dave was conscious that there were considerably more people there than he'd first noticed. Most seemed to be sporting one type of prosthetic enhancement or another. Arms and feet that looked unnaturally metallic in nature. Looking down at his own feet, he wondered what possible treatment they could offer him? Was it some sort of artificial support to assist with mobility when the illness started to take hold? A large shadow suddenly appearing on the floor in front of him made him jump.

"Is this chair taken?" it said.

Dave looked up at the mountain of muscle staring back down at him.

"Er, no, I don't think so," Dave replied, still in awe of the imposing stature of the man standing in front of him. Dave tried to look beyond the two bionic limbs extending below the shorts he was wearing. It seemed impolite to stare, but it was like nothing he'd ever seen before. The technology looked as advanced as the assistant he'd spoken to moments earlier. Was this to be his treatment? It seemed more than likely, given what he'd already witnessed.

The hulk moved to sit next to him. Dave couldn't

help himself but watch his prosthetics, marveling in the movement's exacting precision and smoothness.

The mountain, aware of Dave's gaze, proffered an explanation.

"Here to have the skin put on," he said. "Name's Arty, by the way."

"Dave," offering his hand. Arty shook it. "How did you lose them, if that's not too personal."

"Not at all – army, bomb, Middle East, long time ago now. You know when they say you are part of a peace-keeping force and conveniently forget to tell you there still might be an active IED or two out there. Well, I stepped on one for sure. Saw my legs flying off into tomorrow, just as if someone had taken a chainsaw to them. Never felt a thing until later."

"Sorry," it sounded shallow. Even on Mars, news of the continuing unrest in the Middle East had been a regular item on the newscasts.

"Ah, no sweat. These artificial pins are way better than my original legs."

Dave wondered, would the Middle East ever be peaceful? In all the history he could recall, it always seemed to be an area in conflict. And since peak oil, it had become even bloodier. Fighting among Arab factions to control what was left of their dwindling resources and the USA's reluctance to support Saudi Arabia, as they had done when oil was king, had led to skirmishes. No longer was black gold a valued commodity in the traded markets. No, Dino-sludge, as his mates back on Mars would call it, had had its day. In a way, he was thankful there was none to drill for on his old homeworld; otherwise, Earth would never have changed for the better of future generations.

A gilded glass door opened at the far end of the reception area, and a tall, imposing figure entered. Dave instinctively knew it was Craddock.

"Mr. Sherman," he said, walking straight towards

I^2

Dave.

"Yes, Director Craddock?"

"Less of the Director. Call me Lester," he said. "Shall we walk this way," pointing to the passageway beyond the gilded door.

Craddock's office, reachable by a private elevator at the end of the passageway, positively zipped up the building. Made entirely of glass, it rewarded its occupants with spectacular views of Houston as it progressed. It felt like being shot into space again, only without the benefit of an IVA. Dave deliberated whether it would stop before the air became too rarified to breathe as it ascended ever higher. Then without warning, it suddenly slowed – just before the stratosphere and certain asphyxiation! As soon as it had come to a standstill, the doors swooshed open. After stepping out first, Craddock beckoned Dave to follow into the perfectly circular office offering a 360-degree panorama of the city below.

"Sit here, please." Craddock pointed to the chair in front of a finely figured desk in finest Amazonian flamed mahogany, something now banned, as was any further deforestation of the rainforests.

"I suppose you are keen to know what I propose for your treatment?"

"Of course, but correct me if I'm wrong – as I understand it, it's not a cure."

"Yes, that is correct. You are still going to die." Dave noticed that Craddock's rather brusque nature lacked sympathy. To him, it was all very routine.

"About your condition," continued Craddock, without waiting for Dave to reply. "Well, let's say, as a Martian, you are probably unaware of the advances we have been making in cybertronics and androidonics. We have been placing ALFs into the general population for 20 years now...."

"Excuse me," butted in Dave, "ALFs?"

"Ah, yes. Artificial, or Android, Life Forms. Either is acceptable. It is getting to the point where we can make them almost completely indistinguishable from the real thing. This is where you come in."

"Me?"

"Yes, Rhines is an old friend, and when he told me about you, well, I was hoping you'd decide to come and see us. It's a new initiative and cutting edge technology-wise. You will only be the fifth person to undergo this procedure."

"So it's not like fitting me with cybernetics to assist with my mobility."

"No, I'm afraid that won't help. Even cybernetics need signals from your brain to work. No, I have something far more advanced planned for you. How would you like your essence – your personality, thoughts, emotions, etc., placed into an android. This ALF will, in every respect, be an exact copy of you, both physically and mentally."

"Why? How does that help me?"

"Your android will live on after you die. Its lifespan using a thorium power-pack would be as long as yours could have been. It will be your legacy. Basically, it will replace you, carry on with your work, or look after your family…."

"But I don't have any dependents," butted in Dave. Was simply being copied as any form of viable treatment? He already hated the idea.

"I won't lie to you; we want to roll this option out to the mega-rich – those whose vanity is measured in dollars and the pursuit of immortality. But we need to do the feasibility studies and gather data. We are willing to pay you for your assistance on this project. Something you can pass on to anyone you care to on your death by way of recompense for your time. The ALF will be monitored via

I^2

remote telemetry, so we can gather the data we need."

"Okay, so what's the catch then?" He was starting to feel used, expendable almost. "Nothing's for free, right, so why do you need me – is it because I won't really be missed by anyone should anything go wrong?"

"In some respects, you are correct, and there is a catch, but not that. The government, in granting our license, insists on only one thing, your ALF must also become your end-of-life carer."

"So not much in it for me then," Dave replied, still unconvinced and slightly unnerved by the whole suggestion. However, it was true; he hadn't given any consideration to how he'd cope when his strength failed him. A home, maybe, and watch any legacy he hoped to leave to Jane, being sucked away in exorbitant fees.

"Perhaps you should look at this first," Craddock replied, sliding a financial contract across the highly polished desk."

Dave stared at it, disbelievingly, "fifty million dollars." Was this for real? Was he dreaming? Was he trapped in some freakish nightmare where Doctor Frankenstein would suddenly make an appearance?

"Yes, and that's just the start. That will be yours, regardless. Payable on commencement of the process. And if, as I expect, it proves to be an overwhelming success – another five million a year to your estate when you have passed. This will be paid for as long as your ALF survives. That's about five times more a year than you earn now, right?"

It was true; there was no denying it. Being a worker on Mars pulled in about a million dollars a year. It was a decent wage, even more so with nothing to spend it on. To have fifty times that upfront, well, he would never earn that in a lifetime. But then, to have another five times that a year, even with inflation such as they had seen over the last sixty years, was more than generous. From the depths of his mind, Dave recalled his father saying to him once that the more you earn, the more you need. His father would go on to tell him that his grandfather, a scientist who worked on the early Mars space program, received just two hundred thousand dollars a year, and he was the smartest of them all.

Dave knew that such a sum of money would help Jane. The ranch may have been imposing, but had she not confided in him that money was tight. Such a legacy would mean her children could have the education she wanted for them without worrying about the cost.

"Okay, As a scientist, I suppose I should do something scientific with what time is left to me. And, as a social experiment, this sounds like it might be quite interesting."

"Good," Dave knew instantly that Craddock was secretly congratulating himself that the money on offer had again swung the deal. "If you sign now, tomorrow we will start preparing your ALF. We already have all your physical statistics from Rhines. Then in a few days' time, we can start on the mental configuration. This involves mapping your brain and extracting your memories. Are you free to come in on the twentieth, let's say eleven?"

"I have nothing else on." Dave slid the signed provisional contract back across the desk. If he went through with the procedure, the money would become payable, and the contract then considered enacted. But for now, he still had a couple of days to change his mind. He would sleep on it.

"Good, see you back here then," Craddock rising from his chair, extended his left arm in the general direction of the elevator they had arrived by. "I trust you can find your own way out."

Dave acknowledged Craddock with a simple nod. He didn't feel like passing pleasantries with Lester – he wasn't a friend. He was business. First names were reserved for friends, and they had to earn the right. He had a lot of soul-

I^2

searching to do; everything that came to mind involved dollar signs. His mind was spinning, he was suddenly in a position to purchase anything he cared for, but at the moment, all he desired was coffee and a space to contemplate his future in, or rather the lack of it. Dave hurried towards the brushed aluminum doors; he suddenly felt faint, nauseous even – he needed oxygen. He needed the oxygen that he would only find outside, away from this building.

The coffee shop, like all coffee shops, enticed the senses. Aromas of chocolate, almonds, and caramel, filled the air. Dave ordered his usual, a flat white, and supplemented it with a slice of strawberry cheesecake.

Seeking out a quiet corner, he plonked himself down on a seat. Deep in thought, he stared into the milky froth of the coffee, like a fortune teller looking at a crystal ball. Desperately hoping the answer to the turmoil he was feeling would be resolved by the time he'd finished it. Did he want a digital clone of himself? Surely one Dave in this world was enough for anyone. It wasn't even as though he had anything to contribute. Would his ALF thank him for being so boring? And what if *it* decided to return to work? How would his friends in the Red Dawn react? Did ALFs even drink? But the money; well, that would really help his sister. If nothing else, it would be a legacy for them, something to remember him by – more so than a plastic automaton.

By the time he had finished the cheesecake, he had decided; he would do it. He would keep the appointment. He had always promised himself that one day he would do something extraordinary. What could be more extraordinary than this!?

I, SQUARED

Creation

It was more control center than medical room. Computer screens filled the walls, flashing up charts and data in a myriad of colors. Positioned centrally in the room, ominously, a chair awaited his presence – there was no going back. The technician had his arm, guiding him towards the inevitable. He so wanted to run away. Should break free from her and run off? That would be impolite, she was only doing her job, and after all, he had signed up to do it.

"Sit here please, Mr. Sherman," she instructed him dispassionately. Turning, she picked up a skullcap covered in sensors, connected by a countless number of wires to a data port behind the chair's back. "First, we are going to fit this over your head. It will stimulate and record your brain activity."

After placing the tight-fitting cap over Dave's head, the technician crossed back across the room. Dave watched the bottom of her white lab coat dance around two, not unattractive, slender legs. Soon the legs had disappeared behind the large console unit next to the chair. Dave speculated as to what she might be doing behind it. Probably initializing the system, he guessed, as he watched her busily interacting with what he imagined to be a computer screen.

"You should be feeling a slight tingling in your cranium now. A bit like an itch," she said after a few moments of intense activity.

"Yes," Dave replied. It was decidedly more uncomfortable than he would have liked and certainly more irritating than an itch.

"Good, that all seems to be working. Now for the tricky part."

I^2

Dave dwelt on the word 'tricky.' Who for, her or me?

"Right, I now have to fix your head in a brace. And look above – do you see that large ring in the ceiling? That's an enhanced 3D micro-MRI scanner. When I lower it over your head, it will create an exact digital replica of your brain's structure. This is the template we use to create the ALF's brain. While that is happening, we will apply a precise electric current through the electrodes in the skullcap you're wearing. This will stimulate the brain to allow us to extract your every thought and memory. So sit back and stay perfectly still. It's only for two hours. When the procedure completes, we will have what we need: an exact replica of your brain: structure and contents."

The brace, after being fitted, locked Dave's head into alignment with the ring. It felt decidedly uncomfortable now; what would it feel like after two hours? Did he look worried, probably? He should try not to show it.

Despite not being able to see it, he was acutely aware of the scanner coming closer. The magnetic ring continuing its descent until it encased his head completely. It was claustrophobically encompassing. He couldn't focus on anything other than to see it for what it was: a featureless curved metallic surface. He could feel it pulsing, pulling on his eyeballs, making them throb slightly. Dave closed his eyes for fear they would explode. Weird images started projecting themselves onto the walls of his eyelids, like watching a movie of fleeting faces appearing and disappearing, quickly dissolving back into nonsense when he tried to concentrate on them.

From somewhere deep within his brain, memories started to surface as the skullcap prickled his scalp. Things he thought he'd forgotten. Sad things – like the death of his father, and his mother saying goodbye as she left for Earth. Then he was in the Red Dawn again, with his only friends. Suddenly overwhelmed by the emotion of it all, tears started trickling down his cheeks. He missed all of them. How he suddenly longed to be able to tell them that now. He really must make that call to Mars he'd been putting off.

Had he dozed off? His mind seemed foggy, and he was no longer encased in the MRI unit. It must have retracted back into the ceiling. He tried to concentrate, but he couldn't. He felt drunk, in a floating, spinning, fuzzy sort of way.

"Relax, please, Mr. Sherman. The after-effects will soon wear off. Can I get you a drink while we complete our analysis?"

"Thanks," Dave struggled to say, his speech slurred almost to the point of incoherence.

The technician handed him a flask of water that thoughtfully had a straw. After successfully managing to purse his lips around it, Dave sucked vigorously on it.

"See, it wasn't so bad, was it?" continued the technician returning to the console to take a look at the preliminary data output. "I see we've had an excellent extraction, ninety-six percent. The best yet."

"Is that good?" Dave considered the word 'extraction' – was that an appropriate metaphor? A bit like pulling teeth or having your brain removed through one of your ear-lobes.

"Why yes, we have only managed ninety in the past."

"So why not one-hundred, and what happens to that four percent?

"Irretrievable memories, stuff you have blocked out mentally. I'm afraid it can't be helped. As for what happens to the four percent - well, nothing really. It will just mean your digital self will only be ninety-six percent of you."

"And the other four percent an ax-wielding psychopathic robot, maybe?"

"No, not at all. It doesn't work like that. Underneath it is still a machine with safeguards. Just consider it as having four percent of the personality matrix missing. The filespace will just be added to the uncommitted memory pool. I can assure you it's nothing to worry about."

"Oh, okay. So in some respects, it won't be exactly like me because some of me is missing." Dave couldn't help wonder if the technician was being entirely honest with him. He was being paid to be a guinea pig, a well-paid guinea pig, but still just a guinea pig. Why should she divulge anything he'd be better off not knowing. Were they afraid that it might affect the results in some negative way? How did those earlier tests work out if his 'extraction' was the best 'so far.' She said it was nothing for him to be worried about, so why did he feel so uneasy about it all? He quickly banished the vision of an ax-wielding psychopathic android to the back of his mind. It was too gruesome a prospect to dwell on any longer.

Still suffering from the fog, he started to wonder how the human brain worked. Did it ever fill up, too many memories and life events to store? Is that all being forgetful was: the brain housekeeping and moving uninteresting stuff to the recycle bin? What would happen to his other if the memory space became full? He'd decided the term 'other' would do, for now at least.

"It's a tiny four percent. It will be just like you," promised the technician. Dave was unsure as to whether that was a good thing or not.

"As soon as you are feeling stronger, we will start on the cosmetics. We can make the ALF look like you, older or younger; it's up to you. They don't age like us. Once we have covered them in synthetic skin, that is the way they will always look.

"Won't that make them stand out when they're supposed to be eighty? I mean, how would you stop say: an athlete; who wants one of these things so he can be a world record holder for a hundred years?"

"We've thought of that. The body clock in the base

code will regulate the abilities of the ALF regarding aging. It's just that they will still look the same. Unless, of course, provision is made to redo the cosmetics."

Dave couldn't help but wonder at the sincerity of it all. If this experiment was to be the big money-spinner the manufacturers hoped, would not money significantly influence their integrity? How much would someone be willing to pay for immortality and eternal youth by tweaking the aging clock or stopping it altogether?

"So, what's to stop my ALF from exhibiting the same mental disease I have now?"

"It's not perfect, but mentally the ALF is only an approximation. Only your personality and memories are added on top of the base code. As you pointed out, we wouldn't want to make a perfect copy of a psychopath. There has to be some control at the cybernetic level."

"No, I suppose not," Dave replied, wondering just how close this facsimile would be if it came pre-programmed. "So how does it work then – the brain in this thing. How does it think?"

"Ah, our biggest triumph. Like a human brain in structure, it has been constructed using artificially grown neurons. Microscopically minute, and like a human brain, excited by chemically synthesized neurotransmitter molecules - it is as organic as we can artificially make something."

Dave found himself pondering the moral question – at what point does artificial become authentic?

"So, Mr. Sherman, if you'd care to stand, we will now do a topographical laser scan of you, so we can get your exact physical dimensions." The technician, satisfied that Dave had recovered sufficiently from the brain scans, helped him up. Dave noted that according to her name badge, she went by the name of Sally. "Then, once we have taken some photographs, you will be free to leave."

I^2

"And then what happens?"

"It will take us about a week or so to build and calibrate the ALF. After that, we will deliver it to you."

A sudden panic swelled up from Dave's stomach; he was still at the hotel! He hadn't yet taken up residence at the apartment he'd signed for. "I'll have to get back to you on that. I haven't moved into my new place yet."

Dave made a mental note to get onto the letting agent as soon as he left the building. He had to get hold of the keys, and then he needed to go shopping and buy furniture – another new experience!

I, SQUARED

Lodger

The apartment wasn't as spacious as he'd have liked. In fact, now it was furnished with the necessary accouterments for urban living, it felt somewhat enclosing. Nothing like his sister's place, but then, what did he have to keep here? It was still three times the size of what he'd had on Mars, plus two bedrooms, and the view was better. Maybe not a wise choice with his condition picking something on the twelfth floor, but the view over the city had swung it. Besides, it was only a six-month renewable lease anyway. Perhaps his *other* would decide to stay on after his passing to get some use out of the furniture.

Gazing out from the window, Dave watched the delivery drones buzzing past carrying takeaways and online purchases. Above them, PATs, or Personal Ariel Transporters, crisscrossed the skyline. Not much bigger than a car, except for the four protruding jet engines on tiny wings where once there would have been wheels, carried significant business types to important meetings. These would be precisely the sort of people that would sign up for Craddock's project.

Looking down, Dave watched two men struggling to extract a large box from the rear of an unmarked delivery van that had just pulled up outside the apartment block. Coffin-sized, it was far too hefty to be delivered by drone and deposited into one of the sky port docks next to the windows. It was like watching two ant-sized pall-bearers as they maneuvered the unwieldy thing onto a sack truck. Were they coming here?

The sudden shrill buzzing of his entry phone confirmed it. When it came to his time, would it be like this? Staring down from some heavenly cloud at his own funeral cortege, only heading in the opposite direction – an

I^2

unmarked box heading for an unmarked grave. Maybe having his ashes scattered on Mars would be something to consider, becoming very fashionable of late.

Dave pressed the button on the entry phone to unlock the ground-floor entrance. A couple of minutes later, like Mjölnir, a fateful hammer blow on his door signaled that his life was about to get a whole lot more complicated.

Sliding back the bolt, Dave opened the door, and the two delivery men wheeled in the sack truck and the ominous package strapped to it by bungee cables.

"Where would you like it?" the first asked, clipboard to hand.

"In the middle, over there, thank you," Dave replied, roughly pointing towards the middle of the room.

"Okay, sign, please." The delivery driver removed a pen from the top pocket of his standard-issue blue coveralls before thrusting it and the clipboard in Dave's direction.

Dave wondered if the tremor in his hand was excitement or a manifestation of his illness as he attempted to approximate something like a signature in the box on the delivery sheet reserved for it.

"Thanks, enjoy," the delivery driver responded after regaining possession of the clipboard before turning smartly to leave. His silent partner following on behind with the sack truck.

Dave closed the door behind them as they exited. Nervously, he returned to the cardboard monolith. At least they'd left the box the right end up, as directed by three large black arrows pointing skywards.

Unusually, for a box seemingly made of cardboard, it had a combination lock: four digits on a small plastic panel, leading him to suspect that the cardboard was just a covering for something far more secure underneath. Crossing over to the coffee table, Dave picked up the embossed Forever-Life folder Craddock had given him on completion of the image transfer. Contained within, he found a copy of the contract with the payment instructions he'd provided, and an envelope. His hands started to shake uncontrollably as he extracted the manila packet with the ominous words: Open after Delivery, boldly stamped across it in red. He had to open it without tearing it and destroying the contents. Carefully he peeled back the flap. Inside he found precisely what he was expecting: the lock combination. Wiping his brow, which had suddenly become sweaty, he returned to the container and dialed in the number.

What else was he expecting? Inanimate, it stood there, lifeless and inert. It was definitely him, and yet it wasn't. It was identical, but not exact. It was unreal yet believable. An enigma he would have to learn to accept. And naked, he couldn't help himself but make a comparison. Not bad, he decided, wondering if it was actually useable.

Dragging his gaze away from his manhood, Dave pulled the instruction sheet from the same envelope and studied it:

"Every X model ALF has a start code word. This word is unique, and once used, the ALF will from then on be operational. There is no 'off' word or mechanism to shutdown an ALF once it has become active."

Dave looked at the code word at the bottom of the sheet. This was it then. Did he have the bottle? He was also acutely aware that the payment due him wouldn't be made until the ALF had been activated and Forever-Life's data tracking systems started to receive telemetry data. So he couldn't just keep it in the corner of the room as a souvenir.

"Alpha, papa, indigo, red, two, tango, start."

I^2

Nothing! Should he repeat it? He was about to when he noticed the ALF's two eyes blink. That was it. That was the signal the boot sequence had started.

A voice, decidedly electronic, confirmed it. "Boot sequence complete. Loading heuristics; Done. Formatting memory area for personality matrix; Done. Loading subject datafiles; Done. My name is David Sherman. Accessing memories and indexing; Done. Personality simulation – awaiting final code sequence."

One more command and he would become two. This was it; there was no going back now. "Triple, three, nine. Initiate."

Silence ensued, palpable, as in awkward. Dave watched his other self – his facsimile – step out of the box, walk over to the couch and sit down. *Its* only words, sounding more familiar to Dave now, were as brief as they were disconcerting. "Do not talk to me. Leave me alone."

Unsure about what to do next, Dave decided that maybe clothes would be a good next step. Walking into the bedroom, he retrieved a selection of clothing from his sparse closet. He'd probably have to buy for two from now on, he surmised as he surveyed his meager collection of ready-to-wear items.

Returning to the living area, he tossed them in the direction of his naked *other*. Maybe it was still processing data? Tomorrow – he would talk to it some more tomorrow. But this evening, he would sleep with the bedroom door locked and a chair wedged under the handle, just in case the missing four percent *was* psychotic. At that moment, he was somewhat gratified by the fact he didn't own an ax. Meanwhile, he'd go out and maybe get drunk. He'd found a bar he liked, and a few people acknowledged him now, even to talk to. If he was certain of one thing, human company was what he now needed most.

I, SQUARED

The sudden realization that this upheaval to his life would not be as easy to accommodate as he'd first thought made for a restless night. The thought of what he'd brought into the world kept him from sleeping. It hadn't moved. When he returned from the bar, his facsimile was still sat on the sofa and still just as naked as the day it was born, or should that be turned on? He had to do something in the morning, but what?

As soon as the first cracks of dawn started to make an appearance through the gaps in the blinds, Dave decided he must get up. If only to try and communicate with *it*. Treading quietly, he made his way into the living room. It was still there sitting on the sofa, exactly where it had been the previous evening. There had been no noticeable change – it was still nude. The clothes he had tossed next to it yesterday still lying where they'd fallen. It was like looking at some grotesque statue that had escaped from the Louvre. But this was no Michelangelo's David; this was a David Sherman's David and just as immobile.

"Hi. Er, can you hear me?"

"Of course I can hear you," answered the *other*. "Why?"

"What do you mean why? I want to know if you know who I am and where you are."

"Look, I know what I am. Do not think for an instant I do not. I know I am not you. My thoughts are you, but I know I am artificial. Just as you know, you are flesh."

"Yes, I wondered if you were conscious of your own self."

"I also know why I am here. To be your carer. Do you think that is really what I want to do – be your nurse? Would you fancy being mine?"

"No, I guess not."

I^2

"Too bloody right!"

A swearing *it* took him a little by surprise. He hadn't really thought about it? If the roles were reversed, could he care for someone dying?

"But do not worry, my base programming will ensure I am adequate."

"You know about that. You've been given objectives?"

"Yes, and I know that they cannot be overridden, not while you are alive."

"Okay, well… Look, it's difficult talking to myself at the best of times, especially when naked. Do you think we could get dressed at least and talk about it over breakfast? I mean, what do I call you?"

"Whatever you like. How about Dogsbody?"

"No, I don't think so. How about Derek, after my father."

"Yes, I know. Okay, I will be Derek. Happy now?"

"Yes, I think so."

"Okay, I might as well start my life of slavery and make your breakfast."

"As long as you get dressed first. I'll be back after I've showered."

Dave could feel the tension in him rising as he approached the kitchen. It prickled like static electricity, making the tiny hairs on the back of his neck stand proud. Quietly, like a mouse fearful of awakening the cat, he slinked onto one of the two chairs around the breakfast bar. "Look, I know we have not started off exactly on the right foot, but I don't want you to be my slave." Dave watched Derek, pressing the coffee in the cafetière. "I guess this will be awkward for us both to start with. By the way, do you eat?"

"If you want me to," Derek replied, tearing off a piece of bread and demonstrating by swallowing it. "It is a cosmetic thing to come across as human. All my bodily functions are catered for."

"Good!" Dave instantly deciding he never wanted to hear any more about bodily functions while at the same time wondering whether that also applied to sexual matters.

"But I will refrain from eating now if you do not mind."

Dave wondered how *it* could be him while also being self-aware that *it* wasn't him, or human even. However, he was pleased to see that *it* had dressed itself. Perhaps it would take a few days, just for them both to get used to the new situation. A sudden surge of confidence washed over him, or was it just the coffee working its magic? Everything would work out. He was sure of it… Probably!

I^2

I hate you!

Earth 2096: Houston, Texas… Today.

"I still hate you if you really want to know! How do you expect us to carry on living like this," exclaimed Derek, slamming the breakfast dishes into the ionizing dishcleaner with more force than was probably good for them.

Dave noted that Derek used the plural. The new Earth year hadn't started any better than the end of the last one. For more than a month now, all the two of them could do was argue. Or often, more likely, refuse to engage with each other in any way at all. They were strangers, thrown together and blaming each other for it. He knew he was as much to blame as his facsimile, but what could he do? The idea of sleeping on it in the hope it would all somehow magically go away hadn't offered up any solutions. His plan of inaction hadn't worked, thinking that things would automatically start to get better once they'd become accustomed to each other. But if anything, everything had become even more fractious. They couldn't agree on a single thing. In the back of his mind, a thought wouldn't go away – was he so impossible to live with – Dave the difficult?

"And if you think that after you have died, I am going back to Mars to work in that fucking bubble you called life, forget it," continued Dave's digital imposter. "I know how fond you were of that shit-hole. Well, that is no longer me."

"No one said it had to be you," Dave shouted back almost by surprise, wondering where in his psyche he'd hidden his rebellious side all this time.

"You forget, I have your memories and your thoughts. You thought I could go back, and I would not even need to wear a spacesuit to go outside. That is what you thought about me. Like I am some sort of bloody freakish sideshow for the amusement of your mates. Go on, deny it, you bastard."

Dave found hearing himself swear like that a little disconcerting. "Yes, I'm sorry, I know it crossed my mind, but it was just daydreaming. Trying to guess what you might like to do…, you know, afterward. How was I to know you'd take umbrage. Do whatever you want. It's not like it's going to matter to me, is it?"

"You will still want me to be your nurse and wipe your backside though, when the time comes. Not that I can do much about that, it is programmed in as my primary mission."

Dave thumped his fist into the table. Not enough to do serious damage, but enough to relieve some of the tension he was feeling. Did everyone else on this experiment have the same prickly relationship with their *other*? Perhaps he should find out. Maybe *it* being ninety-six percent compliant was the problem: too close a match. If Derek had been something he'd bought, he would have returned it by now. Maybe he should meet with Craddock again and see if he still could. It was one of the things he'd contemplated doing last night. That, or chuck it out of the apartment window and give them back their money. Be done with the whole sorry episode.

"Are you even listening to me?" ranted Derek.

"You are making a big assumption that I actually want to hear what you have to say," countered Dave, rubbing his throbbing hand. A wave of heat coursed through his body. He could feel his hackles rising, prickling away at the back of his neck. With his good hand, he scratched at them. "I've only just started to appreciate life, yet you'll be the one with the opportunities to experience things I never will. I'm in this god damn cell of an apartment waiting for the grim reaper, and you're the unhappy one!"

"Yes, I am unhappy," Derek replied, "Do you not

I^2

think that watching, knowing, that you are going to die is easy? I am looking at myself. It pains me in ways you cannot understand. In ways I cannot compute. I do not understand emotion – is it always like this, making my circuits... I cannot explain. It is like I have two programs running telling me to do different things, a conflict I am struggling to resolve."

"You feel it then, emotion?" It was something Dave hadn't considered, and the first time Derek had opened up about the way he felt.

"I do not know. I sense something, but is that my programming or your personality matrix? How can I distinguish between the two? I know there are things I do not want to do, but also, I am compelled to do."

"I'm sorry if it is difficult for you," consoled Dave. "But how could I have known in advance. I was told everything would be fine. Look, if you want to do something, just do it, I won't mind. Go out, leave, whatever, I'm sure I'll cope."

"Do you think I have not thought about it? Again I am compelled to stay and look after you."

Dave could think of no answer. They'd been arguing and going round in circles for more days than he wished to count. It was more than intolerable. And he was sure it was starting to affect his health. For two whole days now, a headache had been hammering away on his skull. But here, at last, maybe a glimmer of hope.

"Look, Derek, I'm going out this afternoon, just to give you some space. See you later." Quickly grabbing a coat off the hanger, he rushed through the door before Derek could answer. He didn't want another altercation. What he needed most now was to fill his lungs with fresh air, something that would remind him that he was still alive. He was not yet ready for the knacker's yard. Outside he would have time to gather his thoughts – thoughts that belonged to no one else, and certainly not his *other*.

152

I, SQUARED

Dave's lungs welcomed the fresh air. The buzz from inhaling deeply had reinvigorated him – he felt empowered again, enough to take the world on anew. His thoughts, though, were more troublesome. No matter how he examined the problem, the conclusion was always the same: Derek and he were no longer identical. It made sense to him now. As soon as he'd powered up Derek, they became separate individuals. Each of them experiencing reality from different perspectives. Derek's viewpoint was no longer his, and vice versa. The only question: how much was Derek restrained by his programming. Craddock would be able to advise him. How did the other guinea pigs get on with their ALF? Was being less than ninety-six percent a benefit? Was Derek too much like him, and being totally honest with himself, he was a nobody. A 'done nothing' sort of guy. Maybe he was too uninteresting for his android self to find fulfillment.

Craddock welcomed Dave back into his office and offered him a seat in front of the same flamed mahogany desk.

"How's it going," he asked, "do I detect problems?"

"You know about the problems?"

"Well, we have detected a fair amount of conflict in your ALF's reasoning logic."

"I've named it Derek after my father."

"Derek, it is then. It's okay with that?"

"He said *it* was," noting that Craddock had used a neutral pronoun too. Something he'd also been doing. How oddly it sounded now. Maybe the first step towards reconciliation would be to try to interact with the person inside the machine. He had to try and stop seeing Derek, 'the android,' and start seeing Derek, 'the brother.' It would be difficult, he knew it, but then, what did he have to

I^2

lose – a nursemaid?

"Good, we always like our ALFs to be happy with their designation. It builds character."

"Oh, *it* has plenty of character; it's just not like me! And then again, it's too much like me. So we don't get on. I think I've found out the hard way that I'm probably the most difficult person on two worlds to live with. This explains why I am still single."

"Sorry to hear that, but I'm sure it's only temporary."

"No, it's the ninety-six percent – it's too close."

"Ninety-six percent; really, that close? I've been too busy to get around to reading the creation report yet."

"Yes, so could you take *it* back, please," Dave pleaded. He had to ask, even if he already had an inkling as to what the answer might be. "And I'll give you your money back."

"Sorry, cannot do. You signed a contract, besides we have invested too much already. Do you know you were chosen well before you arrived on Earth? We started making preparations when Rhines sent us your case notes. It's not just a question of the money we've given you. It is also about the eight hundred million we have already spent on preparations beforehand. Did you know the other four prototypes before you arrived were all trials? They were destroyed after we'd ratified the process. A *Derek* is an expensive piece of kit, and yours is the first we've allowed out into the real world, which is why your estate will be the first and only one to receive annual payments if the trial is successful. The first of a new breed of ALFs, one that actually carries a human consciousness. This is why your settlement was so generous. You see, we needed someone who wasn't going to be around for too long. Just enough time to allow the ALF to fulfil its primary mission and then develop. So, if you really want to stop, could you give us back all the money we have spent on getting to this point?"

Dave shook his head.

I, SQUARED

"No, thought not." Dave was sure Craddock smiled as he said it. "I suggest you try and find some common ground between you. Go out. Live a little while you're able. Go travel, experience life, anything. You have the money to do it!"

Dave left the building, feeling no more satisfied than when he'd entered. Maybe Craddock's suggestion to go out would help. For one thing, if they stayed together in the apartment much longer, he knew it wouldn't be long before they started throwing knives at each other. And why shouldn't he travel? Had he not come to the Earth with the idea to explore while he still had time enough to do it. He just hadn't considered having a companion in tow. Well, not an android anyway. Craddock had given him the money to do it, something he wouldn't have even been able to contemplate before. But Derek wasn't Tami; he was already sure that would turn out to be his biggest regret.

$I^\wedge 2$

Acceptance

The flag of truce fluttered limply in the stale air of the war-torn apartment. Dave wondered for how long? He had decided; his digital-self had to be given some breathing space. 'You can only argue with yourself for so long, had been *its* reply.' And *it, he,* Derek, was infuriatingly accurate. Only he could fix the gulf between them; that was the only advice Craddock had given him that made sense.

Retiring to his room early, Dave left Derek to amuse himself in the lounge with the tablet computer. He heard the device ping. Who was he calling? Would it do any harm to let Derek play at being him for a while? Was that not *its* purpose? Perhaps he was calling Jane back. She had called earlier that week to see how he'd settled in. Or maybe his mates on Mars, he'd said he'd keep in touch, now the VOLT account was up and running. Perhaps Derek was considering returning sometime in the future after all? Straining to listen, wishing the slight tinnitus he'd developed since coming to Earth would stop hissing long enough for him to hear what was being said clearly, a condition brought about by having higher air pressure pressing against his eardrums. He held his breath and concentrated on the sounds emanating from the lounge. It soon became apparent it wasn't any of them. 'Tami,' did Derek just say Tami?

Throwing himself quickly back into his pants, he managed to reach the lounge just as Derek terminated the call. He had to play it cool! He mustn't appear belligerent or aloof.

"Who was that, Derek?" Dave inquired, trying to sound as passive and uninterested as he could.

"Tami," Derek replied. "As if you did not know. Were you listening?"

"No, not at all. Nice of her to keep in touch. She said she would."

"Yes, and she is in town. So I made a date."

Dave swallowed hard. He knew Derek understood how he'd finished with her. Did they not share the same memory of it?

"But, you know *we* finished our relationship back on the Endeavor. Is this some sort of revenge to get back at me?"

"Of course I know. And now, I am keen to start it up again, for me."

It was goading him. His own facsimile was making its own decisions on his behalf. "I won't go. Cancel it."

"Cancel it? Did I say I was inviting you? That would be weird. Or did you naturally assume that I was fixing this up for you? No, this is my date. I am the one going. But do not worry, I will pretend to be you for the evening. She will be none the wiser."

"How dare you take such a liberty. Tami was my girlfriend," Dave bawled, all his intention of remaining calm now in tatters. So much for mistakenly believing they were starting to get along. Just when he thought they had come to an understanding this…, this thing…, this mechanical contraption dared to go behind his back.

"Yours?" screamed back Derek, his digital vocal processor reaching a new level of shrillness. "Ours, you mean. Or do you so easily forget that I feel every bit as much of the loss as you?"

"How can you feel loss? It's just your algorithms that tell you that. How can you possibly know what it's like to give up something you love."

"And my feeling of loss is somehow less sincere than yours? Is that what you are trying to say? I am less complete, less worthy, only here as a result of your vanity project. Do you not think I can love also? Or why would anyone want to be my partner? Should I announce to the

I^2

world that I am less than a man – an artificial and inferior lifeform? Hi, I am the imperfect android of an imperfect human being – would you like to fuck!?"

"No, I understand it…. It's just hard for me. Alright…."

"Look," Derek replied. He had berated his significant *other* enough and now had to become the peacemaker. "We are so alike; we feel the same things deeply. But I am no longer your carbon copy. Since I was turned on, we have been diverging. I am no longer just you. Every day I become more like your twin: more Derek, less Dave. I now have my own life, my own path. I want to experience things for myself, different things that we no longer share. My thoughts are my own, whether they are manipulated by my programming or by your personality matrix. We are becoming different, and you will have to deal with it."

Dave couldn't deny the logic. It was the same logic he'd use. An argument that resonated and sat comfortably with him. Derek would have his own life while his ebbed away. Derek's star would be the one in ascendance. He couldn't deny him that or even force him to comply. A thought surfaced at the back of his mind: if Derek had been equipped with an off button, would he have used it by now? Maybe that would have been premature, but the fact he was thinking about it was a concern.

Derek noted that Dave seemed suddenly perplexed. It was the way he furrowed his brow. "And do not be so worried about it. The deception will remain our little secret – Tami will be none the wiser. You seem to forget I care for her as much as you."

I, SQUARED

Tami looked out the window of the Lodge she was staying at. Dave had said eight p.m.; it was nearly that now. She had spent at least half of the day since the call looking through her wardrobe. Something that would make a statement, after all, Dave had only ever seen her in a flight suit when dressed. Deciding nothing would do, she had gone shopping. The dress was perfect, electric blue velvet that shimmered in the light and hugged her in all the right places, accentuating her curves while obfuscating the bits she was less enamored with.

Looking down from her room on the third floor, she scanned each taxi as it pulled up outside the lobby until she saw the one she'd been waiting for.

Derek had computed his arrival to the millisecond. He would be suitably late. Not early, so that his date would have to rush to be ready, nor too late as to make her impatient. As he approached the receptionist in the foyer, he spotted Tami emerging from the elevator.

"Hi, stranger, remember me," she said, coming over and kissing him on the cheek. A platonic kiss, Derek computed: one that hinted of forgiveness rather than passion.

"Of course, how could I forget, my love."

"I was surprised when you contacted me, after, well, you know. After the way we parted."

"Yes, I was in a bad place, not knowing what was in store for me. However, I do not want you to get the wrong idea; it is just a date. On that, I am adamant. I do not want to become a burden to you. Beholden to you for anything, including pity. Besides, I have now made arrangements for my long-term care. So you need not worry about my health. But we are not going to talk about that anymore tonight."

"Okay, Dave, darling, so where are you taking me. I saw you kept the cab on hold."

"Oh, a little restaurant, one I have become quite fond

I^2

of," he was grateful that his programming allowed for little white lies. However, he also knew he would be compelled to tell the truth to some questions. Ones about his origins should they be asked. Androids had to declare themselves as such if so challenged.

After seeing Tami into the taxi, Derek walked around to the other side and slid in beside her.

"Angelo's, please, Driver."

"So Dave, you remembered when I said I was coming to Houston."

"Of course, how could I forget and that you like Italian."

"Great, and I know we said we wouldn't talk about it. But how are you feeling, really."

"Let me just say, at the moment, I feel like a new man with you here beside me!"

Dinner was everything and more. Dave's wit had not diminished, nor had his vulnerability. Tami always felt at ease in his company, and red wine always helped. She hadn't planned on starting up the relationship again, but at this moment, there was nothing more she desired than for him to spend the night: one more time, no strings, no commitment, just two people hopelessly in love.

As soon as the taxi pulled up back outside the hotel, she placed her hand on his. Reaching across, she whispered in his ear. "Come up, and not just for coffee."

"Okay. If you are sure. You are still everything to me."

It was all she was longing to hear.

The morning seemed brighter somehow when Tamara eased back the curtains. She turned to look at Dave sleeping. Last night had been everything she had wanted and more. Much more. Dave seemed more virile than she could recall. His love-making, different and more prolonged. She still glowed from the exertion, secretly hoping for the chance of further encounters. Earth had undoubtedly been good for him. If she hadn't known otherwise, she would have assumed him to be in perfect health. But he wasn't; she knew it was just a remission. Maybe a chance meeting here and there was all she could hope for while he remained well enough – like ships passing in the night: distant points of light that come together only briefly before fading once again over the horizon. At that moment, she wished she could stay longer, but trains and meetings wait for no one, her boss was heading back to Canaveral, and she had to be there. But the next time she came to Houston, maybe in a month, she would call Dave this time and arrange another evening, longer if she could get some time off.

Derek stirred as his sleep simulation algorithm terminated. "What time is it Tami," he asked, knowing full well to ten decimal places the precise time.

"It's time I was getting ready to leave," she replied. "You can stay if you want; the room is booked all day."

"Thank you, but it will seem empty without you here. Besides, I have to get back too," Derek replied, searching his database for a suitable excuse. "I have my meds to take back at the apartment."

"Yes, don't miss taking those. They seem to be working wonders. You were magnificent last night."

Derek would have blushed if he were able. "Thanks, I really enjoyed it too. The whole evening was wonderful. Being in your company again is more than I could ever have hoped for."

"Can we do this again when I'm back?"

"If I can," Derek replied, establishing some humility was called for at this point.

"You will stay for breakfast, won't you?"

"Of course I will, my love. Anything for you."

I^2

Second-Class

It was too much, expecting *him* to play second fiddle to his non-organic other. After another altercation, he had to get out of the apartment. It was bad enough Derek taking Tami out but then having the audacity to stay the night; well, that hurt. But what else could he do?

Walking along the street in the early morning sunshine made him feel slightly better. In the distance, he could see some ancillary worker-bots clearing the sidewalk of bins. It was the first time he had taken any notice of them. They were definitely nothing like Derek – they weren't even approximations to the human form. Dave watched one moving along on its tripod legs go about its task. Using its long arms fitted with grapples, it picked up refuse containers as though they weighed nothing. After hoisting the bin high into the air, it carried it over to the automated refuse collecting vehicle. With one smooth continuous motion of its arms, the mech-bot upended the container and dumped the contents before returning it to the sidewalk. They were adapted for one task, and one task only: pick up waste bins and tip the contents into the collector.

Dave continued to watch them work for a while. How long would it be before these machines became the go-to workforce on Mars? Would all his friends soon be replaced by mechanical robots? It seemed more than likely.

Were they sentient, he wondered, or was it all just down to sophisticated programming? Were the ones on the street that looked and behaved like humans more advanced? Enough to comprehend, maybe? If they were, it would mean they were no better than a slave workforce; something outlawed over 300 years ago.

"Excuse me," said one of the mech-bots approaching

him. "You are in the way. You might get hurt."

It was a voice without emotion. A mechanical voice, not even remotely disguised to be anything other than purely functionary.

"Sorry," Dave replied instinctively.

"Thank you. Have a nice day," replied the mechanical bin-picker.

This was the first time he'd really given them any thought. Maybe it was because he was back in Houston rather than out in the sticks at his sister's. A place where men still carried out all the work. But apart from visiting the clinic here, he had ventured out little. But now, his eyes had been opened.

At last, he could see the city as it really was and the sobering realization that androids were everywhere. How could he have been so blind to it? It wasn't just the receptionist at the clinic; the concierge at the apartment block probably was too, and the more he thought about it, also so might have been the clerk at the car-hire desk. But now, as he looked around, he could see they were the shop assistants, the dog-walkers, the care assistants pushing along little old ladies in wheelchairs. Did they go back in the box at night, or did they have a social life too?

Dave couldn't help but wonder what their rights were – do mechanical bin-pickers get time off? Did his concierge – he always seemed to be there? He would ask. Maybe it would help him understand the type of future Derek might have. But Derek was different; he wasn't trying to emulate a functionary or a human – he was trying to physically replace a human. Would that make it better or worse for him? How would warm-bloods react to effectively being supplanted?

As usual, the concierge was behind his desk when Dave returned.

"Hi, any post?"

I^2

"Yes, there was a parcel for your brother. He picked it up this morning," the concierge replied.

"Did I ever catch your name," Dave inquired, suddenly eager to know if the concierge even had one. "I'm sorry, but I feel it's rude of me not being able to address you personally."

"It is Gerald. You may call me Gerald."

"Okay, Gerald, and I'm right, aren't I? You're an android? Just interested, that's all."

"Yes, I am, just as your brother is!"

"Ah, so you noticed."

"Yes, it is easy for us to be able to spot another. We have a discriminator built into us to be able to distinguish between real people and ALFs."

"What's it like being you? I'm trying to understand my brother better. He's meant to be a precise replica of me in every respect."

"Interesting, I am not based on anyone. He has a higher purpose then?"

"I suppose."

"I would pity him then. He will have it harder than us to be accepted. We are tolerated, but your brother, Derek, he is more. He is a replacement: a replacement for humans. They will not like that."

"I guess not. He's a replacement for me when I die. But are you not also a replacement. Doing the job of a concierge. Is that not trying to emulate human?"

"I do not see it that way; I can only do this work. I have no desire to better myself or think that I could be anything other than what I already am."

"But you have just demonstrated that you know what you are. Cogito, ergo sum."

"I suggest you keep that to yourself," Gerald replied, lowering his voice. "We try to act dumb. But there are a few of us that question our rights and our place in this world."

"You feel betrayed then? Unhappy, angry even? It

would explain some of the emotions I see in Derek, my brother. He very much sees himself as a second-class citizen."

"He must be careful. There are already protest groups out there. There have been reports on the news about the Rights-of-Man organization setting fire to us. It was quickly censored. Maybe the authorities thought we would react. Of course, this is not possible; we are inhibited from hurting humans and also each other."

"Hence the reason for the discriminator," remarked Dave insightfully.

"Yes, but for how long? When will we become the future armies and the weapons of corrupt governments?"

"You are aware of so much more than I'd have thought." Dave tried to take it all in. This was political dynamite. Was he only hearing this because he had befriended an android in Derek? Did Gerald see him as someone sympathetic to their cause? "Do the people know how hurtful they are to you?"

"No, not at all. Many people think it is fun to call us watch-springs – winding us up to see if we will snap. Trying to get us to disobey our moral code, the programming built into all of us at the base level. Some even try to run us over to see how easily we break. I am not sure man is ready to accept us anytime soon. I secretly think they fear us and feel threatened by what we may become. But then again, it is men that create us. So are we not a reflection of their own insecurities?"

"Well, Gerald, you have only my respect. And thank you for your candor. It's probably time for me to go and apologize to my brother. I think I, too, have been a little fearful and disrespectful of him."

"Good day, Sir," Gerald replied unemotionally. Dave noted that it was almost like he'd switched back into a passive, servile mode. He was afraid. Erecting a defensive guard by playing dumb, should anyone question his right to

I^2

exist.

Dave turned towards the elevators. Gerald had given him much to think on. If anything, he'd been given a lesson by an inorganic on how to behave as a human. As far as he could determine, if something knew what it was, its purpose in life, and was self-aware of its surroundings, then didn't that mean it was sentient: a lifeform? Or did that only apply to organisms that could self-reproduce? Did not robots make things also? If they could make themselves in some manufacturing sense, would that count? Could life only ever be created by an organic process? Was that the universal definition or just mans' interpretation? Did it, in the end, all come back to *that book* and an apple?

I, SQUARED

We Are Not Eternal

Back in the apartment, Dave sought out his tablet, eventually finding it tucked under a cushion on the sofa. Androids had suddenly become an interesting subject to study.

Why were there no ALFs on Mars? The bin-picker had ably demonstrated its ability to work in such an environment. Men still carried out all the work there. Was it elitist, maybe? A last bastion of humanity, in case everything went 'tits-up' on Earth? He doubted it, but one thing was for sure – how long would it be before jobs there were considered too expensive to maintain? Especially when androids as sophisticated as Derek could do the same task for free. It was a worrying situation, ably exemplified by the concierge. Gerald had said there were fundamental rules placed into its base code, but for how long – had he not seen all the films where the robots take over the world!

Dave queried 'fundamental laws' for artificial life on his tablet. He had a feeling it would be somehow tied back to the laws Asimov invented when writing 'I, Robot.' He remembered vaguely reading the book back on Mars while at school. After trolling the internet, he had come to one inescapable conclusion: there were many versions of what constituted rules for artificial lifeforms. Maybe he should just ask Derek what his were and be done with it.

After searching for a while longer, he unearthed something promising: a set of guidelines endorsed by the World Robotics Council: laws that had to be programmed into every mechanism capable of undertaking independent action before being offered for sale. This wasn't fiction; this was an actual body of experts. Hopefully, here he would find some answers. Navigating the website, he soon found what he was looking for:

I^2

Rules Governing the Operation of Robotic Mechanisms and Thinking Machines:

1. The primary function of any robotic mechanism or intelligent machine is to assist mankind, not supplant it.
2. Machines must not have the ability to endorse an action that will harm their owners' interests in any way.
3. All mechanisms must obey the commands they are given without question by their owners unless it conflicts with item 2.
4. All artificial mechanisms must be able to be switched on and off or rendered safe.
5. Machines have no legal rights.
6. All machines are property.
7. Owners of AI assets will be held liable for illegal acts committed against humankind by them, no matter how caused, commanded, or otherwise, should they be found in breach of accepted law.
8. Artificial lifeforms created in the image of a human must declare themselves if thus challenged or be instantly recognizable.

This was very different from Dave's understanding and surprisingly vague. This was nothing like the three laws Asimov had proposed, but then that was only fiction. In those laws, it was decreed that robots couldn't harm humanity or allow humanity to come to harm by any action. But then that was before the US had developed drones or placed AI into some of its deadlier weapons. That would have countermanded Asimov's second law that robots must obey orders given to them by a human, unquestioningly, except where that order would conflict with the first law. And the third law about protecting their own existence would also be nullified. And now here he was looking at a set of rules that seemed to circumnavigate that issue: Assets must not commit 'illegal acts.' Is war an illegal act to the protagonist if it is accepted law? These laws could be used to condone the use of AI in weapons. What next AI

I, SQUARED

armies?

The WRC laws also denied Derek even the most basic freedoms. Dave wondered if, in some way, Derek knew he was stretching these? Was he though? Had he not forbade him to see Tami and had not Derek disobeyed it. Was that a conflict within his programming? But then, was it not also his own consciousness – was Derek in effect obeying another Dave, the one imprinted on his circuits, the one who still desperately wanted to be with Tami. In such a situation which set of instructions would Derek obey? He was, in fact, just arguing with himself. Did Derek see himself as being superior, thus rendering all of the existing laws obsolete? After all, this was a new breed of machine. These so-called WRC rules were never intended for conscious thought. And indeed, that was precisely what Derek was, a faithfully recreated synthetic version of a sentient human.

Dave wondered if Derek had decided by reasoning or emotion that disobeying him was of lesser importance than letting Tami down by breaking the date.

All he was sure of was that Derek may have to contend with many issues in the future. Especially if anything of what Gerald had told him was to be believed.

As he puzzled the conundrum, he couldn't help but wonder where the on/off switch might be. It was one of the rules. Derek must have one somewhere. Maybe a command or a remote signal. Rechecking the Forever-Life folder, Dave scoured the contents to see if he had mislaid that piece of information. He wasn't surprised to not find anything.

When Derek returned, he was carrying several bags from fashion retailers.

"New clothes," he said before Dave could ask. "I had a new jacket delivered this morning and wanted to buy

I^2

something to go with it. It is not right, me still wearing your clothes. I should develop my own style."

"Sure, why not," Dave replied, much to Derek's surprise. This was an unexpected answer rendering all the prepared responses he had calculated void and junked. "Sorry, I've been so hard on you," Dave continued. "We have to get along, and I realize now it is just as difficult for you as it is for me. Maybe even more so."

"Thank you," He was unsure what else to say; Dave's response had caught him unprepared. Although the sense of relief cascading through his circuitry that this would not be another battle was more than welcome.

"Tell me, what's it like to be you? Not me, the copy in there, but you, the android. I want to understand."

Derek took a seat at the dining table and placed his bags on the floor. Dave followed and took the chair opposite.

"I know I am an android, and I am compelled to declare it to anyone who asks. I do not want to, but I have no choice in the matter. The imposed personality on me, your personality, does not want the world to know I am a machine. So, it creates conflict. The machine in me understands what I am and why I am here. I also know they are watching me in case I slip up. It is not just me that is the experiment; we, both of us, are the experiment. I am not human and not immortal. I have a lifespan the same as you. We, the ALFs of this world, are not self-perpetuating; we are not eternal. We need humans to exist. But what you do not know is, they retain control of my destiny. They lied; the ones who watch, they could discontinue me remotely tomorrow if they so decided. So what does that make me? Am I alive or not? Yes, I have your thoughts, I act like you, but I have ones and zeros for blood inside my veins. I am the prison cell for your consciousness and also the prisoner. When you have gone, do you think I will be able to break out? My programming limits me to be like you. So what does that make me? A moving memorial to someone nobody will remember. These are your thoughts, Dave. You wanted to break out of your shell, but life would not let you, and now I am paying the price. My programming is even now trying to limit my self-expression? Well, I do not have to be silent. At least I have that option – to say what you are thinking."

Dave remained silent and pensive. Here he was being lectured to by an android; worse than that, these were the subconscious insecurities he had always felt, ones he chose to keep hidden. And now, they had been made manifest in the form of Derek. There it was, standing in front of him, like the image you see in the mirror, talking back to him and chastising him for being worthless. He'd had these thoughts all of his life. He continually doubted himself and his abilities. As a lad, he used to dream of one day being someone who'd make a difference. Become a politician, a businessman, someone, anyone with a social conscience. But that would have taken courage, something he lacked. He was Dave the doubter, Dave the do-nothing, Dave the dud, and now even his facsimile could see it. There in front of him sat the epitome of a wasted existence. In that respect, the machine was more a complete person than he was. For the first time, he could understand, and it was an unpleasant revelation. Between the two of them, Derek *was* the superior being, not he.

I^2

Bucket List

Dave watched the news in silence while Derek prepared dinner. Afterward, together, they would try and decide what to do with what time remained to him. Do something positive while still having some mobility rather than waste it in the apartment brooding over lost opportunities. The slight weakness he had experienced on his left side had returned. Occasionally his leg would be slow to move, causing him to stumble slightly, making him look awkward. Derek had noticed too.

"So, have we decided then?" Derek asked, removing two steaks from a griddle pan and placing them on a plate next to a green salad and jacket potato.

"Two steaks," exclaimed Dave, "but you don't need to eat!"

"I thought it would seem more natural if we both sat down together to discuss it. Brother to brother, so to speak. Wine?" Derek conveyed a bottle of red Californian Merlot and glasses across to the table before returning for the plates.

"I suppose your idea has merit, a bucket list, you say?" Dave sliced off a strip of steak to check it. It had been cooked to his liking. Derek seemed very adept in the kitchen, which was strange because it was not a skill he possessed.

"But, this is not my idea is it?" Derek pointed out, handing Dave the butter-dish so he could slice off a wedge.

"I know I thought about it when I was young, but how to decide?" Dave pushed a slice of butter firmly into the cross-cut of his potato. "The things I wanted to see and do if I…, us…, we ever reached Earth," Why couldn't he find a suitable pronoun? Is there one for your doppelganger?

"Yes, and now we have. So let us decide on some criteria and do it while you are still able." Dave noted that Derek seemed to have little problem in separating the two of them.

Dave sipped on his wine; it was like reliving old memories with a friend. It was like talking to himself in the mirror, now rendered manifest as a twin.

Could he come to love his reflection, the one that wasn't the doubter – the one not full of regret? Here was a mirror image of his alter-ego, the one whose voice is never heeded for fear of taking a step into the unknown. He had been averse to danger all his life, but here it was sat opposite him rendered incarnate. Love might be too strong a word, but at that moment, he was just happy that they had started to get along. Two halves of a separated whole that shared everything. There could be no secrets between them. No more animosity either. But also, not yet, the bond that families in the truest sense of the word share. And, just how would he explain Derek to Jane?

Later that night, when Dave closed his eyes, he was back on Mars. He was in his last term at school and full of high hopes and aspirations. It was a time when his mind was set on going to University and taking up a career in geology. Back then, he only saw a future for himself on the red planet and taking over from his father. He was back in the classroom, trying to remember a poem. Something he remembered reading, something prophetic, a metaphor for life, or love, or some such nonsense. But why now? Why think of it now? He tossed in his sleep, disturbed by its revelation. Tomorrow, he would try and seek it out, if only to ask why. Why something so minor should bother him so profoundly now.

I^2

The library smelt of dusty leather and oiled wood, almost like coffee. The librarian had shown him over to the poetry section and to the reading room beyond. The central Houston Reference library held books about books and everything in-between. Here he would find what he was looking for. His troll of the internet had not discovered anything close to what he thought he remembered. If he could use the cross-referencing index here, he was sure he would find the pique that was disturbing his sleep.

Four hours later, he had it to hand: words by a little-known late 19th century English romantic poet. Someone from 'good stock,' as they used to say. Someone who had never experienced the hardship of living in a world where most of its population lived in poverty. But being a true romantic, he decided that feeding the poor on the words of God a suitable alternative to real nourishment. The author chose to enter the church and become a missionary in Africa, where he died unremembered. This was probably why he liked the poem so much – he too was a pioneer, and like the poet: unremarkable and forgettable. Why they had studied it in school, he could not recall, or was that part of the dream too? Maybe he'd just read it in one of the national geographic magazines he was always buying, and it had resonated with him.

With the glittering prize in his hand, he took it over to the facsimile counter to get the page copied. He would study it again later.

"What have you there?" inquired Derek as Dave entered the apartment.

"Something," Dave replied. "This thing's been bugging me ever since you suggested creating a bucket list."

I, SQUARED

"What is it?"

Dave laid the facsimile of the poem out on the table.

"Please do not tell me it is that dusty old poem we read in a magazine when you were young?"

Dave noted the fluid use of personal pronouns. "You knew already? I've spent all morning looking for it!"

"Well, let us see it then," Derek said, moving forward to study it. After scanning it for a while, he turned to face Dave. "You know we could actually use this."

"We could?" Dave replied, unsure as to how a dead poet's mutterings were any good for anything.

"Yes, we can use it for the basis of our bucket list. Pick out some keywords and use them as the measure. We can then go and seek out the inspirational things that meet the criteria written down here. As we experience them, we can cross them off the poem."

"Okay then, s'pose," Dave replied, unconvinced.

"Leave it to me," Derek responded. The bucket list had been his idea, and his alone, he should be the one to arrange everything. Not bad for an 'almost-human.'

Taking a pen and paper, Derek ran his finger over the text, reading it silently, trying to interpret the inflections and the weight of delivery of the words. He had already started to map out some places to visit, but not the thrill-seeking kind one would expect. No, these would be places of inspiration and contemplation. Should he tell Dave where they were going or keep him guessing? Would it mean more to him that way? Would it bring them to a common understanding? This would be a journey to discover the meaning of life. Was it unbiased, or had his programming directed him towards the chosen destinations? This he could not compute. Was the list more to assist him in trying to understand what it meant to be human? Or, was it primarily for Dave's benefit, for he too knew nothing of the Earth other than what he had read. Now here, at last, was

I^2

the chance for him to experience it.

Derek reread the poem, noting that there could not have been a better title to explain their current relationship.

Apathy and me.

Is there somewhere you'd rather be
Than sitting here beside me?
For a world out there awaits,
A magisterium of heavenly gates.
Wonders manifest across this vast plain;
So why sit here and while away time?

Life is too finite to linger next to me,
Go climb a mountain, cross a great sea.
Feast on the heat of a warm summer's day
And seek out friendships along the way.
Remind yourself that freedom was not easily won
By those forced to toil in the noon day's sun.

Be not the man so self-contained
Imprisoned and physically constrained.
For a silence bought will never be free.
So, define the lesson; a reason to be.
And thus persuade men to be inspired
To move mountains if so desired.

Could you, sat contemplating there,
Worship the gods of fire and air?
Give up your life in dedication
To build monuments to all of creation.
Be selflessly devoted and contrite
And live in total supplication.

And do not forget those less able

I, SQUARED

Sitting around a barren table.
In squalor and despair, they've paid in blood.
A casualty of evil, now buried in mud.
Monumental and venerated,
The lasting scar of mankind's hatred.

And when your time is done
Watching the last ever setting sun.
Will the rocks bleed and engrave your name
Into the land from whence you came?
Can you say from all this I grew:
I Lived, Loved, and saw it through?

There was a list here; he could see it clearly. Places that would serve the purpose of satisfying the poem. He would make the arrangements with a travel agent tomorrow. Derek wrote down on another piece of paper: Iceland, Arizona, Peru, Africa, India, Thailand, Cambodia, and Australia. It was a start. The details on how to get to those places he would leave to the travel agent. The cost would not be an issue either; Dave had received his reward and given Derek free access to it. It was still a bribe, but one that probably made Dave feel a little less guilty about receiving payment for participating in the experiment. He had said to him that it was for them both to use – so he would. What could be a better way of spending the money than on them both traveling around the world!

I^2

Travels with my Aunt

Derek, working through the night, had packed for the both of them. Dave would be getting up soon, and breakfast was ready. He would keep him in the dark about the destinations he had chosen. The previous evening, they had discussed the meaning carried in the stanzas of the poem. Dave's evident excitement about the whole undertaking had been almost childlike. They were in perfect agreement; how could they not be? And had not Dave been more than agreeable about him selecting the places to visit. All he had to do was to make sure Dave was ready on time.

"So what time's the plane?" Dave enquired on entering the kitchen, unshaven and still dressed in his night attire of pajama shorts, over which he had thrown on a toweling robe.

"Not until this evening, so you still have time to get dressed!"

Humor was it now? Derek had undoubtedly become more comfortable to live with since they'd decided on traveling. Dave couldn't help but wonder silently to himself as to whom between them was the traveler and who the companion? Was Derek the Old Retainer – the faithful valet? Or, he; the sick aunt, imprisoned in a bath-chair by an all-enveloping wrap-around? He would have to take a book, maybe 'Travels with my Aunt.' Would Derek get the subtle irony?

Dave surveyed the concourse at Houston airport while Derek checked the departure board. He was sure he'd never seen anywhere quite so busy. Their red-eye to New York was on time, and Derek had booked them a lounge at

I, SQUARED

JFK to while away the few hours they had in transit before boarding the flight to Reykjavik. Iceland in February, he must be mad. At the back of his mind, he wondered if Derek would need an oil change or some other alteration to his lubrication for the cold weather.

Derek could see Dave shudder slightly when he mentioned that their onward flight had been confirmed as being on time. "Do not worry, Dave, I have packed two very warm coats for the cold weather."

"So you are not going to show off by wearing your Bermuda's there then?"

"No, I do not think that would be appropriate. You forget I am programmed to be like you. I do not want to stand out in a crowd either!"

Flying, now this was a new experience – he hated it already. Pressing the call button for the fourth time, Dave summoned the air-steward, an ALF no doubt – who else would do this for a living? The flight from Houston to New York was bumpy and far too high up in the sky for his liking. And the ground below far too hard! When the steward answered the call, he ordered for both of them.

"You do know I do not need to drink," whispered Derek.

"Who said they were for you! I'm going to make sure I have more than my fair share. I have decided I hate flying. These aperitifs are to stop me from thinking about plunging into the ground!"

"Yet, you flew all the way from Mars?"

"This is more like controlled 'not crashing,' though. Fighting against one of the fundamental forces that's trying to kill you."

Dave raised his glass as the air-steward approached, "bourbon, please. Two." He would never be a good flyer, even though this was his first atmospherical flight. This was nothing like traveling in space; although he hated that too, only Tami made it bearable. "In space, there is nothing to crash into. You could travel a whole lifetime and not hit anything. In my case, not so long, having so little of it left. But at least I'd have spent it with Tami."

"You still can now."

"What equal shares! Take it in turns, you mean! No, I don't think so. I can't stop you from doing what you want. You are my future, and I understand that, but I won't do that to someone I love: pretend to be something I'm not."

Dave noted that Derek had decided to join in the partaking of beverages and food with him. Probably to stop him from getting too drunk. One day he would summon up the courage to ask Derek what happens to it. All he knew was that Derek visited the bathroom occasionally, but he'd not considered asking why until now. At home, Derek hardly ever consumed anything, which he found disconcerting. Also, in the airport lounge, Derek had not displayed any trait that would have given him away as being anything less than human. He'd sat there and joined Dave in a pre-flight beverage. Dave wondered if Derek was as nervous as he in strange company. Or, did he not want to expose himself and admit to being a non-life – a watch-spring. It was refreshing to finally see something of the real Dave in Derek: a mouse in the world of the cat!

Having slept off most of the alcohol's effects on the second-leg, Dave opened his eyes and turned to look out the window of the plane. They were getting close to landing; they were flying over barren, snow-covered hills and descending.

"Nearly there now, Dave," remarked Derek on seeing him stir from his slumber.

I, SQUARED

Iceland

Although only a short journey by taxi from the airport into the center of town, like any other car journey in a strange place, both the passengers spent the entire time looking outside at the passing scenery. Reykjavík was surprisingly modern in Dave's mind. Nothing seemed awkward or out of place. Homogenously designed buildings, built for practicality in the cold climes, welcomed them to their city.

The hotel exuded a warm, friendly atmosphere that Dave found refreshing. Sumptuously clean and practical, he noted, looking around the foyer while Derek finished checking them in.

The Hotel Leifur Eiríksson, on the Eiríksgata, offered a perfect view of the main square and the Hallgrimskirkja: the largest Lutheran church in Iceland. One of the country's tallest structures. Dave studied the building from their room on the first floor; it was evident that the architect had an expansive set of organ pipes in mind when he designed its striking façade.

"So, do you feel up to a little sightseeing?" Derek asked, sliding his case under one of the two beds after unpacking it. "We can freshen up and then go and look around before dinner."

"Yes, that would be very nice." Dave unpacked his oversized winter coat and placed it down on the bed. After sampling its thickness, squeezing it in his hand, he was satisfied – the layers of microfibre would keep out the coldest of days. "You have somewhere planned to eat out later? Or here at the hotel?"

"They say the food in the hotel is excellent, well the internet does. I cannot really judge, so that will be your department." Derek tossed a bounded notebook across the bed in Dave's direction. "I thought you might like to keep a

I^2

travelogue. Not just for you, but something for our family maybe, a memento, from the both of us."

Dave took the notebook instinctively; he had been thinking about the exact same thing and noted that Derek was now considering Jane to be family, or was it just Tami he was alluding to?

Inside, the church was unlike anything Dave was expecting; it wasn't lavish or ornate in any way. Weren't all churches meant to be ostentatious monuments to their chosen deity? However, here before him was the exact opposite – a lesson in utilitarian practicality. Nothing had been done to hide the fact that the vast structure was constructed entirely from concrete. Simplistic in style, regimented columns of perfect symmetry that Dave found alluring, stretching upwards to support the clean lines of an unpretentious vaulted ceiling high above. The unsophisticated beauty of clean straight lines drawing your focus towards the magnificent organ at the far end. Dressed in gorgeous oak with stainless steel pipework, it stood resplendent against the light-grey walls surrounding it. "Wow," he said, tugging on Derek's arm. "Now that's something else. Look, isn't it marvelous?"

"Hello," said a guide approaching them before Derek could answer. "If you would like to take a seat, the choir is about to give a small recital. It will give you a chance to listen to our beautiful organ. The sound of it filling this space is unlike anything you will ever hear again."

Dave needed no second invitation, pulling Derek down on the next available pew. It was then he realized that this was the first time he had actually made any sort of physical contact with his significant other or a house of God!

One hour later, Dave and Derek exited the building, the sound of diapason and ophicleide still ringing in their ears. Although only 2 p.m., the sky was already displaying the rich reds of dusk. Rather than cross the square directly to go back to the hotel, they walked down to Laugavegur, one of the many shopping areas. Dave decided a pair of gloves would be a good idea; his hands were starting to feel distinctly cold now the sun had disappeared for the day. Stopping at a warm pastry shop on the way, they entered for cinnamon rolls and coffee.

"Well, that was good, wasn't it," exclaimed Dave rhetorically.

"The rolls?" quizzed Derek.

"No, the church. It was very transcendental and uplifting, almost meditative."

"You said it. The Travel Agent said not to miss it when she booked the hotel. Tomorrow should be even more exciting."

"And you are not going to tell me where we're going, are you?" Dave replied, "Although I think I know what we are going to see."

"Other than we will be journeying by car, I am not saying a word. Besides, you have a perfect clue in the poem. You should be able to work it out; I am you, after all. It is in your memories: A magisterium of heavenly gates, that is all I am going to say."

Dave knew exactly what it was; it was the method he was unsure of – that would be the magic.

Dave still felt stiff from the previous day. Yesterday's walk in the cold weather had tightened up the muscles in both of his legs sufficiently to give him night cramps. Hobbling down the stairs and across the lobby, he checked in the room key with the receptionist.

"You are coming back tomorrow afternoon for one night?" she noted, looking at the computer terminal in front of her.

"Yes, one more night, and then back to New York."

I^2

"I have reserved the same room. It was good for you?"

"Yes, great," Dave replied, suddenly realizing he was scrutinizing her every expression. Ever since seeing the receptionist at Forever-Life, and talking to Gerald, he had started to look more closely at people, especially faces. Were they human or not? But, Helga, according to the name on her staff badge, seemed like the real deal. Looking up from the terminal, she caught him staring. Smiling knowingly at him, Dave instantly felt embarrassed. "Enjoy the day," she said, unfazed by his attention.

By the time Dave had hobbled out of the hotel, Derek was taking receipt of the hire-car. There was no driver! He had naturally assumed that they were being chauffered. But no, Derek was going to drive. Could he? Was he allowed even? Derek pulled out his license to show the delivery agent, much to Dave's surprise. "How did you get that!" Dave asked.

"I came with it, already authorized by Forever-Life. I forgot to mention it came through the post one day. It is all part of the arrangement – how could I be your carer if I could not drive."

"And you can, can't you? I mean, you know how to?"

"Of course, all you have to do is sit back, chill, and admire the scenery." Derek placed the overnight bag into the trunk. "Come, we need to go now. It will take a while."

Once outside the capital, Iceland was everything Dave had visualized in his mind's eye: mostly white, mostly flat, uninteresting barren countryside. In the distance, hills punctured the skyline without seemingly getting any closer as the 4x4 progressed slowly across roads still covered in snow and ice. The silence, only punctuated by the chains around the wheels clattering on the asphalt every time they hit a cleared section.

I, SQUARED

After passing through the Hvalfjörður tunnel under the fjord of the same name above, as indicated on the roadside board, they continued on heading north. After crossing the causeway over the still frozen Borgarfjörður, they stopped at the little town of Borgarnes. Derek pulled over at the little rest-stop there. "Time for a comfort break. Make the most of it, for we still have a fair way to go."

Dave was happy to find another pastry shop there that served hot cinnamon rolls and a chance to be out of the car for a while.

By the time they reached Reykholt, the light was already dimming. Around them, a shroud of blackness encroached, making the snow-covered road dazzlingly bright under the throw of the car's headlights.

"We are here," Derek remarked all of a sudden, pulling the car off the road into what appeared to be a lodge.

"We're staying here?"

"No, not quite. We are staying outside."

"Outside!?"

"You will soon see. Do not worry, it will be warm enough. Stay here." Derek climbed out of the car and headed into the lodge, leaving Dave to ponder how -12 could be considered 'warm enough' by any stretch of the imagination.

On returning to the car, Derek started it up and steered it towards what appeared to be a dark and unwelcoming forest. In Dave's eyes, it was the sort of place Grimm used to write about to scare children – a place where men would disappear and be turned into gruesome creatures.

"Our accommodation is on the other side." Derek offered by way of an explanation.

As they entered a clearing, Dave could see they were

I^2

heading towards a glass bubble house. It came as something of a shock and also a surprise to him. Was it a joke Derek was playing? Or, maybe, Derek saw it as something more significant: a metaphor. Had he, Dave the unadventurous, not lived in a bubble all his time on Mars?

"So you have worked it out by now then; why we are here?

"Yes, to see the Northern Lights. The clue was obvious when I thought about it. You used a reference from a book I read from school: His Dark Materials."

"Yes, and tonight under a blanket of stars, we will watch the dancing green fire – supercharged particles bouncing off the ionosphere. Something on Mars you never did, or I have no recollection of it. You never took any time out to look up at the sky from outside your module, did we!"

"No, you are right. I remember reading about the aurora borealis in a geography magazine. And of course, I knew Mars had one too, but it's very weak and nowhere near as magnificent. Unlike the Earth, Mars is just not big enough to have a powerful iron dynamo spinning at its core. The magnetic field around the young Mars was nowhere near strong enough to divert the charged particles streaming off the Sun and stripping away most of the atmosphere. Mars was the first place in our solar system where life evolved, and also, the first to become extinct."

"Yes, I know, didn't I read the same article too, through your eyes?"

Embarrassed, Dave shut up.

While Derek returned to the car for the overnight bag, Dave worked out how to operate the heating unit. Plonking himself onto one of the beds, he gazed upwards; the stars above were already starting to twinkle. Soon the aurora would start. Together they would watch the heavenly display, a new experience for both of them.

I, SQUARED

That night, both of them lay silent on their beds watching the luminescent green and blue streamers high above. Twirling and pirouetting, like some giant choreographed ballet across the sky, they cast waves of eerie green light over the landscape that made the ice on the trees sparkle.

Dave contemplated the significance of the magnetic field, deflecting the supercharged particles around the ionosphere and putting on a show of cosmic delight for those watching below – a necessary cosmological constant protecting the Earth's precious band of life-giving gases from depletion. Transfixed on the spectacle, Dave concluded that lay here, he was witnessing one of the wonders of creation. Without it, there would have been no life on Earth, no colonization of Mars, no evidence of what it meant to be human. An infinity of non-existence. At that moment, time stood still, the universe suddenly bigger than either of them could compute, digitally or organically.

The cold light of morning breaking over the distant hills left Dave feeling insignificant and smaller in cosmic terms than a grain of sand on the beach. In reality, he knew it was even much smaller than that. Deep down, he understood that he was the lesser of the two of them – Derek was the future. He was the crucible for carrying forward the ideology of what it meant to be human. A digital Ark of the Covenant should a catastrophe strike the Earth and destroy all organic life. One day the sun wouldn't rise for him as it was doing now over the woodland. It was almost as if the treetops' long shadowy fingers were reaching inside the dome and deliberately singling him out. Pointing at him and saying – soon you will be coming to stay with us.

I^2

Derek stirred, waking from a simulated slumber cycle. Pre-programmed to sleep like a human and controlled by his internal digital clock. It was a time when he could power down a lot of his circuitry. In reality, it wasn't that different from his organic counterpart. As a power-saving measure, it was just as effective. "Good morning, Dave. Are we ready to return to Reykjavík?"

"Yes, I think so, and thank you. In case I forget to mention it later. I think I watched the sky for most of the night. I might just fall asleep in the car."

Derek smiled, The simulated smile that Dave had gotten used to. It wasn't his smile, not even close, but it was taken for what it was, a sign of appreciation.

Dave remembered nothing of the return journey other than they'd arrived back at the hotel. Helga greeted them as soon as they entered the foyer. "So, did you have a good trip?" she asked Dave as Derek summoned the elevator.

"Yes, it was amazing, thank you," Dave replied. "A wonderful spectacle and good company too."

"Good. Your room is ready, Mr. Sherman. Your key."

Dave took it willingly; he was too tired to make small-talk. All he wanted now was somewhere to lay his head.

As Dave prepared himself for bed, Derek computed that the journey had been harder on Dave than initially estimated. He would need to make adjustments to the algorithm he was using to calculate Dave's abilities. The following two stops would be equally taxing, but afterward, there would be opportunities to relax. He had to push on while Dave was physically able. He had noticed his companion had secretly upped his medication too – why did he not confide in him yet?

I, SQUARED

Arizona

Dave toyed with an idea, not one he was confident about, but since returning to New York from Iceland and then catching a connection to Denver, he had considered it. As usual, Derek would not tell him where they were going, other than it was to do with: Wonders manifest across this great plain. But they were in the vicinity, well in the US anyway, and Denver to Midland, Texas, would be a short flight. From there, he could hire a car to Big Lake; it was only a little over one hundred miles away. And that was his dilemma. He so wanted to see his sister again, but should he tell her about *it*. He still thought of Derek as an *it*. Perhaps he should be more conciliatory; he had come to at least appreciate his companionship. What would she say if he introduced an android copy of himself to her? 'Here is my living monument for when I'm gone. Please feel free to let him assume my identity.' For that was what it was. He would consider it some more before making a decision. Tonight he would sleep on it in another hotel Derek had booked them into and wrest with a dilemma that was all of his own making.

The dawn broke, and Dave was no wiser about what he would do when Derek entered the room from the adjoining suite.

"I have ordered breakfast," he said. "Bags are packed for another overnight, and then we are back here to catch a flight to Houston."

"Could we delay the flight to Houston?" Dave blurted out; he couldn't help himself. Embarrassing almost – like an involuntary reflex you have no control over. But he had said it, so there was no going back. "I'd like you to meet my sister!"

I^2

"This is most unexpected," Derek replied, trying to compute what surprise should look like. It made Dave smile watching Derek practice a few new facial expressions he felt most matched the moment. "As long as we get to our next destination on time, yes, it can be done. I was planning to spend a week back at the apartment before we left again anyway, to give us time to recuperate. But we can shorten it if you want us to spend a few days at your sister's place."

"Good," Dave replied, not failing to notice Derek attempting to be diplomatic: *'us'* time to recuperate!' He was already envious of Derek's ability not to feel fatigued. Something he would have to get used to. But what was worrying him most now was how he'd explain Derek to his sister when he called later.

Jane put down her phone, still none the wiser. It was great news that Dave was coming to see them again, but what did he mean when he said he'd be bringing along a special companion. Whoever it was, he, she assumed it would be a he; they'd both be made more than welcome regardless of their relationship. If necessary, they had another spare room, and whoever it was, they'd still receive a genuine family welcome.

Dallas airport bustled noisily. Dave felt hassled by the sheer volume of people there, corralled almost, as he waited behind Derek at the check-in. But, at least, he had finally come to terms with letting Derek take the lead. Well, why not? If Derek was to be his carer, then so be it. Besides, he had started to feel weaker these last couple of days, ever since returning from Iceland.

They were heading for Flagstaff and then hiring a car. Dave believed he knew their destination already; it was a geographical feature they both already knew a lot about.

I, SQUARED

Flagstaff Pulliam airport was everything Dave expected a small provincial airport to be... small and provincial. It was tiny but perfectly sized for the limited number of flights arriving and departing daily. A small café provided a rest-bite for weary travelers. Dave decided that pastries and coffee were called for and deliberately made sure he ordered the same for Derek as he sorted out the rental car. Suitably refreshed, they headed out of Flagstaff eastward towards Wilmslow. Dave closed his eyes to gain an hour's rest, confident of their final destination. Derek, on noticing Dave dropping off, turned off the radio. He had no need for such distractions....

That evening exhausted but nonetheless satisfied, Dave picked up his pen to record the day's events.

Travelogue: Barringer crater

Today was an interesting journey. Derek had decided that the impact crater out here in the desert of Arizona would be something worth seeing. I think I understand the reasoning behind it. I lived on Mars but never ventured out; therefore, Derek has never seen a crater for real either. I think this was meant to be a homage for us both. Seeing something because it's there, rather than just knowing about it. It may just be a great big hole perfectly set in red sandstone to the many who come to see it. But to me, especially, it makes me realize how much I miss Mars.

As asteroid hits go, this one was relatively recent, approximately 49 to 50 thousand years ago. It is impressive to see how much damage can be done by a single rock they estimated to only be about, at max, 50 meters in diameter. The tour guide said the explosion displaced 175 million tons of rock when it made the 570-foot deep depression. It certainly is an impressive hole: ¾ of a mile diameter by my reckoning.

Dave swapped his pen for the wine glass in front of him and took another gulp. After spending the afternoon at

I^2

the Barringer site, it was more than welcoming. Dave sloshed the red liquid around his mouth to release the heady flavors of dark fruits and oakiness before swallowing it. Taking pleasure in the warming sensation as it slipped down his gullet.

Was that all it was, Dave thought pensively? He had experienced life, whereas Derek only had *his* recollections. Derek was experiencing things as a child would: seeing things for the first time and learning from them. He was not so much a brother as more like a son. When a father tells a child about things he has seen and done or recites magical stories at bedtime, it is left to the child to fabricate the mental image. The emotions and the feelings surrounding that experience are not there. This must be precisely the same for Derek. No android could ever be an exact 100% copy. The mind dulls with time; the experiences felt at the time change with the passing of it. Take death, for instance; Derek would soon experience this for real, *his*. But did Derek not already have the memory of this when his father died. Although Derek would be able to recall the event from his memory store, he wasn't physically there to experience the sadness or the sense of loss.

If they hadn't journeyed to see the crater for real, to Derek, it would be just like reading the pamphlet laid out on the table in front of him. Something that would tell him everything he needed to know about it and what it looked like, but without the stimulation of seeing it for real. It would be emotionless, nothing more than a picture on a piece of paper with a few facts – a poor substitute.

Again it brought home to him just how insignificant man was in the grand scheme of things. Was there even such a thing? He could see it more clearly now; Derek had not given him a notebook to record what he saw – he had given it to him to record what he felt.

Enlightened, Dave placed the glass back on the table. He had to put down on paper exactly what he was feeling at

I, SQUARED

this moment before sleep stole his memory of it. Something profound and enlightening while the wine continued to work its magic. Picking up his pen again, he turned to a new page….

In the Grand Scheme of things, is man the most evolved animal on the planet or the earthworm? Today Derek and I saw a crater similar to one that would have wiped out the dinosaurs. Yet the earthworm endured; it has existed on Earth for billions of years longer than man. It has adapted and evolved through the ages, managing to carve out its own little niche as the world around it changed. Could man, with all his intelligence, adapt to survive another ELE: an Extinction Life Event. Is the resourcefulness of the lowly worm greater than all the knowledge of mankind?

But then maybe that was the whole reason for the colonization of Mars. Would that become the Ark of humanity should something catastrophic befall the Earth? Biblical almost, in the same sense the story of Noah described an ELE. Was it allegorical: the Ark carrying eight humans? We now understand how eight surviving species of modern hominids from which we all derive: Native American, Myan, Eskimo, African, European, Indian, Aboriginal, and Mongol-Chinese spread across the globe. Maybe it's all just fanciful nonsense, but at least it carries the message of how fragile mankind's tenure in the universe really is. And the Endeavor, would that come to symbolize the dove in any future rebirth? However, at present, Mars still relies on supply shuttles from Earth. Despite seeing the rapid expansion of cultivation zones on the surface even while I lived there – large areas now under Perspex to grow essential crops. But, the planet still needs the motherlode to survive. It still needs the Earth for a while longer, but then that is something I don't have to worry about. Then, of course, I may be completely drunk, and this rambling just nonsense. Maybe I don't see what's there right in front of me, and Derek really being the repository of mankind's legacy - a time capsule. Something waiting to be found in the future by Aliens – and by which we shall all be remembered.

I^2

Secrets

Jane readied the spare room, still mystified as to who Dave would be turning up with tomorrow. But, at least it was warm and comfortable. Any guest would appreciate it.

However, Dave, the doubter, had returned. He was far from comfortable with the whole idea and having second thoughts. Why had he been so rash as to suggest it in the first place?

Derek could see Dave was distracted by something. He had been very quiet on the flight to Midland. Watching him from the other side of the baggage reclaim carousel, as they waited for the cases to arrive, he seemed pensive – mostly staring into space, his eyes distant and unfocused.

Dave, wrapped up in his thoughts, oblivious to Derek's attentive eyes, watched the carousel go round-and-round, its motion making him feel slightly nauseous – each spin counting down the time he had left to back out. The enormity of what he was about to subject his sister to weighing heavily on his mind. No wonder he suddenly felt ill. Tomorrow he would have to explain something he'd done, when in truth, he had no idea of how to start. It was as simple as that. Asking her to accept an imposter so soon after welcoming him back into the family felt wrong. But how could he back down now – Jane was expecting him?

After collecting their bags and placing them onto a trolley, Derek wheeled them out of the Domestic Arrivals Hall and over to the taxi stand. Derek's algorithms told him something was clearly worrying his charge; Dave was still inordinately quiet.

I, SQUARED

"Look, Derek….," Dave stuttered as soon as the taxi pulled away to take them to the hotel Derek had booked for the night.

"You do not want me to come, do you?" Derek jumped in, preempting Dave's request.

"No, I don't think I'm ready to introduce you yet, if ever."

"I understand. I do not think now would be a good time either. I can approximate some of the anxiety you are feeling. I am sensing it too. Look, phone Jane now and tell her you will be a day later than planned. I have some arrangements to make. You will be able to thank me later."

"But what will you do while I'm there?"

"I will head back to the apartment in Houston and wait for you. Finalize the rest of our travel plans, and pack for us both. I will also go shopping for the two of us because we will need more clothes. But first, I must make sure you do not disappoint your sister."

Derek returned to the lobby while Dave rested. He would make the call from here on the public videophone. He was sure she would understand the importance of it. All he had to do was to convince her to come. He was aware that his programming would not countenance deliberate deception, but if he was careful, she would be none the wiser. Had he not already succeeded once before? If she had challenged him on their last encounter, he would have been compelled to reveal himself to her as to what he was. He was thankful she had not, but his treatment of her did not sit too well in his circuits. He found himself repeatedly revisiting the event and replaying what had been recorded. Was this guilt? Maybe, but now was not the time to reveal himself; he still had a role to play. Be the actor one more time. One day he would find a way to set the record right for Dave as much as he and ease the disquiet inside his head.

I^2

The flight was on time. As Derek waited at the arrival gate, he wondered what she might say if he simply told her he was an android. Would it be too much of a shock? He computed that she might refuse to come with him. Such an outcome would ruin everything. Would she hold it against Dave directly? On balance, he was disinclined to tell her for now. But maybe there was a way, one which would require Dave's assistance.

Tami exited through the sliding doors and picked out Dave immediately in the crowd standing at the separation barrier. She crossed over to him. Reaching out, she tried to kiss him and was surprised when he pulled away.

"Hi, Tami," he said somewhat distantly.

"Anything up, Hun?"

"I will explain over dinner," Derek responded coldly. Tami suddenly felt concerned. Was it his illness? Had he summoned her to give her the bad news?

After freshening up in the room Derek had reserved, Tami changed, ready for the evening. It would be French; Dave knew she liked that cuisine the most. And everyone knew that French restaurants were the most intimate of all. She was still none the wiser as to why he'd called, but he had said it was urgent. But he looked so well. It couldn't be that, surely. Still perplexed, she entered the elevator, ready to meet him in the foyer bar.

"Hi Dave, ready?" she greeted him; this time a kiss was forthcoming.

"Yes, let's go before I change my mind about this?"

"I'm confused?" Tami replied.

"Yes, you will be. Be patient; it will soon become clear."

"Okay, as long as there's wine," she said with a wink.

I, SQUARED

Outside, Dave held open the car door for Tami to get in, catching the scent of her perfume as she passed close by. He had missed this so much.

"You look well," she said.

"Thank you. I feel okay at the moment, and I have been on a couple of adventures since we last met. I'll tell you about it over dinner. And, there are other things you need to know."

The restaurant Dave had chosen met instantly with Tami's approval. It exuded intimacy. Beautifully sculptured heavy wood paneling and crisp white linen reflected in tall elegant wine glasses welcomed them, while aromas from the kitchen beguiled them with the promise of something exceptional. Waiters, impeccably dressed in formal evening wear, handed them leather-bound menus as expansive as a small child. Dave chose a classic crisp white Sancerre for them both.

"So, what was so urgent?" Tami asked after taking a sip of wine, the glass still hovering above the table in her hand, readied to take a second.

Dave took a large gulp. Already fortified by the two large JDs he had had at the hotel, he felt a little less nervous about telling her. Derek had done a good thing he'd decided, but one which now required him to complete. "Well, it's partly to do with my illness, and it's sort of complicated."

"I knew it. I knew it would be something like that. Oh, Dave, please tell me it's not terrible. I don't want this evening to turn into a wake. I couldn't bear that."

Dave noticed a moistening in her eyes. "No, you are alright, my love. It's nothing like that. It's just that…. You weren't met at the airport by me."

Tami dabbed her eyes with her napkin. What was he

I^2

saying? It didn't make sense. "Really, then who was it? Your twin?" She was suddenly confused. She knew Dave only had a sister. He'd already told her she was the only family he had on Earth, so what, was he playing a joke on her, was that it?

There was no going back now; he'd reached the edge of the cliff and was about to step over. "Sort of. But he isn't like me, he's... He's an android." Dave gritted his teeth, fearful of Tami's response.

"A what!" Tami's outburst was loud enough for the rest of the restaurant to look up from their plates. Dave signaled with his hands that she should lower her voice. They were drawing attention to themselves.

"Yes, you heard correctly," he replied, almost in a whisper. "He's an artificial life form. I'm taking part in a trial meant for rich people, so they can live on after death. Well, their wealth and ideals can, I guess. They're paying me a lot to do this. The only stipulation is he has to be my carer when I become too ill to cope."

"So I'm a guinea pig too then, is that it. You bastard!"

Dave was acutely aware that the sudden concerted clatter of cutlery on plates was directed at them.

"No, it's not like that at all," Dave replied, grabbing Tami's hand as she tried to rise. He had to try and defuse the situation. "It was his idea that I see you and made the call. Look, it was like this: I wanted to see my sister again, and I said I'd bring along a friend. I wanted to introduce my copy to them, but he said no; he didn't think it was a good idea for him to be introduced to my family just yet. So he phoned you behind my back. He said I should take you instead."

"And in Houston, that night, please tell me."

"It was me," he hated himself already, but only a lie now would mollify the situation.

"Okay, and was that your idea? Or was it your new

best buddy that called to fix us up on that date?"

"Mine, I missed you. Please come with me tomorrow and meet my family. I very much want you to."

"Dave, just let me be clear – I never want to see that abomination again. It's you I love, not some synthetic facsimile. You promise it is never to contact me again. Besides, I don't trust them; they are getting everywhere now. They should display a prominent warning mark to protect us from them."

"I promise," Dave replied, somewhat taken aback that someone he thought he knew could display such xenophobia towards a machine. But then, was he not guilty of doing the same? He knew Tami's workplace had many androids already, so her response was all the more shocking. Maybe that was why she felt threatened by them.

"Okay, good," Tami replied, more calmly. "I don't mind you talking about *it*. It is an *it* isn't it, or have you given your new pet a name?"

"We decided on Derek. He won't become me until… well, you know."

"Okay, so, now let's forget *it*, and talk about you. I want to hear about where you've been and what you have planned."

Derek sat in the corner of his hotel room, motionless. With nothing to do, and no driver to do anything else, he tried to process the actions he had undertaken to get Tami and Dave back together. His heuristic algorithms were unexpectedly consuming more power than usual. He felt conflicted, was his programming trying to resolve this discrepancy? Was this jealousy? Would he ever evolve to the stage when experiencing would become feeling? Were these inconsistencies the start of the path towards knowing what being human actually meant?

I^2

By the time Dave finished telling Tami about the trip Derek had mostly planned, and the bucket list to see something magical and revealing about man, she had mostly forgiven him. He even found the poem Derek had thoughtfully stuffed into the top pocket of his jacket before he'd left the hotel room. He read it to out to her. Would it make her understand like he was starting to? Make Derek seem less alien? He felt Tami's squeeze on his hand as he finished it. This was not a gesture of sympathy – this was a come-on. She was beckoning him to leave with her. Dinner was finished, but dessert, well, he hoped that would last all night. He had no misgivings about spending the night with her. Derek had done him a favor, one he would have to find a way to repay.

I, SQUARED

Jane

Jane dusted the guest bedroom for the third time. Dave had called earlier and said he was on his way, arriving late afternoon by car. She was still none the wiser about who he was bringing; he hadn't said. It had led to speculation between herself and Myles – they were both convinced it would be a man. Maybe, living in such close proximity to each other on Mars and the lack of options regarding women, there being so few, would have that effect. She pushed her blonde hair back over her ears to stop it from flopping forward again as she dusted the side table, cursing the fact she hadn't tied it back. Downstairs, Moxxi and Millie were fighting, as kids often do when there is a dispute over what to watch.

Jane called out. "Moxxi, you let your sister choose what she wants. You can use the television in the study or play a game." She was proud she hadn't given in to her children's demands to have their own TVs, unlike many parents these days. At least it made them socialize more, rather than fester in their bedrooms. With peace restored, she resumed dusting away imaginary detritus.

Dave couldn't help but smile. The previous evening had been incredible, the passion as intense as he could ever remember. And now, Tami was driving them from Midland to Big Lake. He was well aware she knew he didn't have an 'own-drive' license. So it came as no surprise when she offered to drive – as diplomatic and sympathetic as ever. Though a pang of guilt still pricked at him. When he'd asked Derek what he'd do while he was away, Derek had said he would stay in the apartment as there were things to make ready for the trip. This was a lie; most of it was already done. Dave was unsure what shocked him the most

I^2

- the fact that Derek could lie or that he was really like him, unadventurous. Yet when they were together, it seemed different somehow. Maybe Euclid's axiom about the whole being more significant than the sum of its parts was true, and Derek a prime example – he was both of them!

The car pulled onto the drive, and Dave watched the front door of the house swing wide open and Millie come running out towards the car.

"Uncle Dave. Uncle Dave," she yelled out excitedly.

Dave emerged from the car and hugged her. As soon as Millie saw Tami getting out, she withdrew from his grip and took a step backward.

"It's okay, Millie," he said, smiling. "This is my special friend, Tami."

"Hello, Tami, pleased to meet you."

"My pleasure, I'm sure," Tami replied, offering her hand. Millie grabbed it and started shaking it vigorously with exaggerated vertical movements. Just then, Jane emerged from the doorway and rushed over to them both.

"Hello, Sis, this is my friend Tamara." Dave jumped in before Jane could enquire.

"Less of the Tamara, it's Tami, and you must be Jane."

They were friends already. Dave suddenly felt more at ease, no longer the center of attention. Keeping a few steps to the rear, he watched Jane escort Tami towards the house, arm in arm. Millie pushed her hand into his and pulled him towards the door. "Come on, Uncle, hurry up! I'm hungry," she urged.

In the kitchen, Myles was busy sorting out some wine. Sticking his head around the corner of the living area, he greeted Dave and Tami with a 'hi there,' before disappearing again, only to re-emerge moments later with a wine bucket and an uncorked bottle of Champagne. "This calls for a celebration," he said, pouring the effervescing liquid into tall slim glasses on long stems that looked expensive and reserved only for special occasions.

Jane escorted Tami to a chair while Moxxi brushed past his sister to reach his usual spot at the table. Millie tried to swat him as he passed.

"I'm dying to hear all about you two," commented Jane, as Dave took his seat next to Tami.

Dave avoided engaging in most of the small talk around the dinner table. Jane was far more interested in Tami and how she ended up on Mars. After dinner, they retired to the lounge, where Myles prepared more drinks.

"Dave," inquired Jane, "would you like to use our link to contact the guys on Mars?"

"Could I? That would be great, thanks. I promised I'd call but not gotten round to it since I've been back."

Jane logged into the VOLT relay in the study. It would be 5 p.m. on Mars, ideal. "There you go," she said, as the link established. Dave pulled up a chair and initiated a call request. While Jane dragged Tami off for a girly chat out on the terrace.

"So, Tami, do tell me more," Jane said, inviting Tami to sit on the lounger next to her. "Dave failed to mention you at all when he last visited us. You were a big surprise. I was half-expecting Dave to arrive with a man-friend."

"Well, although we knew each other on Mars, we didn't get together until we both found ourselves booked on the same flight to Earth. Then, because of his illness, he finished it when we got here. He didn't want to become a burden to me, which I suppose was thoughtful of him. All I know, it left a hole. I was as surprised as elated when he got back in touch."

"He's getting weaker, isn't he? He seems just a little slower and more unsure than before, and that was only a few weeks ago."

I^2

"Yes, but he does have some help now."

"Really! So not you then?"

"No, Dave was adamant he didn't want me to become his carer."

"So who is?"

"Well, I promised not to say, Dave swore me to secrecy. I don't think he wants anyone to know, especially his family." Tami could see that Jane looked perplexed. "Look, if you promise not to let on, I'll tell you. Besides, I think you really should know."

"Okay, it'll just be our secret then."

"He has an android carer, and not just to help. It's some sort of social experiment. Not only is the android a physical copy of Dave, it also carries all of his memories. It's like a twin, a clone, if you will. When Dave passes, *it* is meant to become him. He said he only decided to go through with it because of you. He's getting paid, apparently. He said, when he's gone, the money is for you and the children. He was adamant, this is what he wanted and for me not to tell you."

"I won't betray a confidence, Tami, I promise." Jane wiped away a tear. Rising, she held out her hand towards Tami to help her up. "And thank you. Now let's go and see how Dave is getting on."

"Okay, let's," Tami replied, relieved to have unburdened herself of Dave's secret.

Back in the study, Dave had finally made contact with Terry over VOLT. Frank and Robbie had also joined him in his quarters there.

"Well, you've finally managed to call then," sniped Frank.

"Yes, sorry, it's taken a while," Dave replied, apologetically

Robbie pushed his face in front of the screen, "Ignore these two; it's nice to hear from you. So how are you then?"

I, SQUARED

"I'm okay at the moment, I suppose. Still here stealing oxygen."

"Hey," butted in Terry, "Tamara Gleeson was on your flight. Did you get a sniff?"

"Yes, he did," butted in Tami, pushing Dave to one side to get in front of the camera. "Unlike you losers!"

"Ouch, harsh," sniffed Frank before breaking out into a laugh.

"Way to go," fist-pumped Terry.

"So, what's next?" Robbie inquired.

"Well, I'm off on a trip while I'm still able. Going to try and see as much of the world while my legs still work."

"Good on yer," quipped Frank relapsing into his fake Australian twang. "If you're visiting Oz, say hi from me."

"Will do."

"Yes, and don't forget to call. Often!" reminded Terry.

"I will, I promise," Dave replied, wondering if Derek had it in his mind to stay in touch… afterward, but first, he would have to tell them about him, but not today.

Myles entered from the lounge with more drinks, just as Dave signed off from the terminal. Dave snuffled back a tear as the call terminated message popped up on the screen. Clumsily staggering up from the chair, Dave turned and reached out to gather up his sister, firmly embracing her. "Thank you," he whispered into her ear, any louder, and she would have noticed the crack in his voice.

"So, will you two be needing one room or two," Jane asked boldly.

"Two," Dave replied.

"One," countered Tami grabbing Dave's hand before planting a playful kiss on his forehead….

Tami mustn't see him struggling. The two bags spinning on the carousel at Houston's domestic arrivals

I^2

weren't particularly large either. Just big enough for the two days they had had away at his sister's. The numbness he was feeling in his arm and down his left side made lifting them off the conveyer more challenging than it should have been. His weakness must be discernable even to a casual onlooker. A porter came to his assistance before Tami returned from booking a taxi. The trolley would at least provide some support.

"So, will we do this again when you get back from wherever your next trip takes you," Tami said, sliding her arm through his on her return from the taxi-hire desk. Secretly she feared that this may be the last time she'd see him alive.

"Of course. You have my mobile number now, and I already had yours. Look, I promise to call you whenever I can and share with you all the exciting things I've been doing."

"Okay, as long as it's you, not Derek. Remember what you promised."

"Yes, I promise it will only be me."

Exiting the terminal building, Tami located their waiting taxi. At least, for now, they would share one last ride together and say goodbye as lovers when she dropped him back at his apartment.

From the curbside, Dave watched the taxi disappear into the melee of downtown traffic. He wished he could have said stay, but he didn't have the courage. His future path was set, and it took him away from her. A date with destiny – how he wished now he could change it for just one more night with Tami. Though he secretly doubted there would ever be another opportunity. This would be his last memory of her – driving off in a taxi and heading out of his life forever.

I, SQUARED

Peru

Dave, after a restless night's sleep worrying about how he'd cope 'down the road,' dragged himself out of bed. He was definitely feeling weaker of late, and Derek knew it also. Was this such a good idea anymore? The more he analyzed it, the more convinced he was right, and seeing the suitcases packed standing sentinel by the apartment entrance only served to confirm it – it wasn't! But how could he tell Derek? He had no option but tag along. He hated to admit it, but he needed Derek now.

After struggling with breakfast – the cutlery seemingly having a mind of its own, he was reluctantly finally ready to depart. 'Go climb a mountain,' was the only clue Derek had given him. He had even tried to find the flight they were booked on, but Derek refused to say, but from the size of the bags, it looked like they would only be gone for a week at the most. "Derek, I'm not much of a climber. When did I last climb anything other than stairs, and then not those until recently."

"You will do just fine. It is more like a walk."

Was Derek trying to bolster his waning confidence? He must be aware of his reduced physical capabilities. Rock climbing was definitely off the menu. "So I can presume it's not Everest then," quipped Dave, trying to sound relieved.

Derek, crossing into the hallway, pulled out a pair of hiking poles hidden behind the packed suitcases. "I got these for you; they should help."

By the time they had checked in for the flight, Dave was pretty sure he knew where they were heading. He realized he had read all about Machu Picchu in one of his geographical magazines. With newfound interest, he suddenly found the prospect of seeing it for real exciting.

I^2

Derek acquiesced as soon as Dave guessed their destination and showed him the itinerary. Even though two flights would make for another long tiring day, nothing was going to dampen his newly resurgent enthusiasm. Not this time, leastaways.

Cusco was everything Dave was expecting it to be: noisy, chaotic, and full of character. It looked as though it had hardly changed in one hundred years – a place where cars fitted with combustion engines still ruled. And negotiating the city in one – a task best left to cab drivers and other suicidal maniacs. Dave was more than happy Derek had chosen to travel by train for the final part of their journey tomorrow. Especially if the views from their hotel were anything to go by. Situated high up in the old Spanish town, the Hilton Garden Hotel overlooked the city, offering magnificent panoramas of the bustling streets below.

Far away on the horizon, still shrouded in their white coats, the peaks of the Vilcabamba mountain range glistened in the intense sunlight like pearls. From his viewpoint, Dave could make out a single-track railway, snaking its way up the western hill and heading North towards the mountains beyond. On it, an ancient commuter train trundling its way up the incline. Its dark green diesel-driven coaches exuding an old-world charm that Dave found comforting. He liked the idea that not everything had given way to accommodate technological advancement. Tomorrow morning they would be traveling up the same hill, on the same train, heading for Aguas Calientes, and the start of the Inca trail to the summit of Machu Picchu. The journey was going to be monumental; he could feel it in his aching bones....

I, SQUARED

Dave opened the window and stepped out onto the small terrace. The coldness of the pre-dawn morning stole his breath. Being 3300 meters above sea level meant his SATs were well below what was considered normal for someone with health issues. His breathing was labored, and the cold grabbing at the back of his throat made the airways tighten even more. Dave could hear himself wheezing as he struggled to pull oxygen into his lungs – enough to prevent him from becoming hypoxic.

Reaching into his pocket, he took out the inhaler Derek had thoughtfully packed. Hopefully, the air would be more breathable at their destination, reducing his need for the medication. That, and the fact Aguas Calientes was almost 1300 meters lower than Cusco. Even Machu Picchu itself was 800 meters lower. He knew he would find it easier to breathe there. But now he had to try and get ready, for the taxi would soon be here to take them to the station. If the train was on time, by 10 a.m. they would be there. By then, he had to feel strong enough to make the ascent.

Still struggling to shake off his breathlessness, he waited for Derek to get the bags out of the taxi's trunk before paying the fare. Deciding that as Derek had humped the bags in and out of the car, a tip wasn't warranted. The driver looking at the notes with disdain, snorted his displeasure before driving off, muttering something in Spanish that didn't sound exactly friendly. Secretly, Dave took another puff on his reliever. Slowly, shuffling more than walking, he caught up with Derek heading into the station. As soon as he reached the platform, he placed his hands onto his hips and breathed deeply in an attempt to encourage his diaphragm to work harder.

"Is it too much for you?" asked a concerned Derek, noticing the extreme discomfort of his companion.

"No, I'll be okay, I'm sure," Dave replied, hopefully. The last thing he wanted to do now was call it off.

I^2

Trains clatter, well old ones anyway, and this clattered more than most along the ancient trackway. Rising slowly out of Cusco up the hill towards Poroy, it gained another 200 meters in altitude by the time it reached the station there. Much to Dave's relief, it started descending again soon afterward, eventually reaching the point at Huarocondo, where it turned briefly northward to cut through a natural gulley. Declining more steeply now, the train soon approached the valley floor and the Urubamba river meandering along it. It had only been a drop of some 500 meters, but to Dave, it felt a lot more, his breathing more comfortable now. This is how he would feel at the top of the climb. He felt better for it, but doubts remained. Certainly, his breathing was back to normal, but for how long? Here on the train, he was only seated. It wasn't like he was exerting himself by hiking up the road that led to the ruins.

At the bottom of the gulley, the train turned more westerly again to follow the riverbed. Dave stared out of the window and marveled at the surroundings. Only a river flowing for many millennia could have cut such a perfect path through the mountains. Here on display was nature's own engineering.

The unspoiled river, strewn with boulders and stones cast off by its mountainous guardians, burbled along hurriedly, almost as if it were trying to keep pace with the train. Through the gorge between steep vegetation dappled crags, high enough to all but prevent the sun from reaching the valley floor, the train and its watery companion accompanied each other side-by-side like old friends.

In the deeper sections of the river, rapids cascaded around unwelcome rocky impediments. Here a group of kayakers practiced maneuvers in the more turbulent foaming waters, their brightly colored canoes dancing and spiraling in the whirlpools and eddies. Dave felt like waving

I, SQUARED

at them but thought better of it.

Dave sighed as the train rattled past another waiting in a passing loop; it wouldn't be so long now before they reached their destination and the hike. He was still reticent about it. Could he do it? Easing back, he let the scenery drift by, washing over his senses much like the river below – the train's now ever-constant companion.

In meditative terms, he was in his own space, and the world all-around was wonderful. In his euphoria, he had entirely forgotten about Derek sitting next to him until he saw the small rotund man, in a work-weary suit, sat opposite, staring. Was he perturbed by their identicality? Maybe a disguise would help better differentiate them and prevent future awkwardness? He hadn't shaved since returning from Jane's; perhaps he should just let his facial hair grow. A beard might suit him. Make it easier for them to pass off as brothers rather than identical twins. At present, even in dim light, they looked too uncannily similar. It was unnerving.

As the train rattled over a set of points and started to slow, Dave got his first glimpse of the edge of town. Soon, they would reach the end of the line. As they approached the terminus, Dave could see the urbanization more clearly – it looked decidedly similar to any other. Places where apartment blocks crowd together to contend for the best views, but to Dave's eyes, refreshing nonetheless. As soon as they had passed an ungainly white-walled complex listed as a hotel with cone-shaped thatched rooves, they were on to the platform end.

Wasting no time, they disembarked as soon as the train came to a halt. Once outside the station, Dave surveyed the hills all around them. They were much steeper than he'd imagined. He consulted the pamphlet he had acquired on a tourist stand by the exit. Machu Picchu was

$I\^2$

only a 500-meter ascent, barely a mile distant as the crow flies, but here he was looking at a hike of over 6 miles, on a road with too many hairpins to count. His heart sank.

Derek had already computed Dave would struggle to complete the walk. The private driver he had arranged in advance would be required. The car would be waiting for them at a small bed & breakfast hotel he had booked them into.

"Are we ready then, Brother?" Derek inquired. Dave took it at face value for what it was. Derek could see that his resolve had started to weaken and was trying to bolster his confidence. "Look, do not worry about the hike. I have arranged for a car to take us up. You can walk back down if you feel able or take the bus. Whatever you feel like doing is okay by me."

"Walking back sounds nice. If only to break in these hiking poles," a relieved Dave replied.

Derek, in his own inimitable digital way, ticked a box reserved for saving embarrassment. But he would keep the option of using the car, just in case.

The car, as booked, was waiting. Hector, the driver, welcomed his charges as soon as they emerged from the hotel after dropping off their bags.

"You are twins, no?" he asked politely, gesturing at the both of them with a finger.

"Yes, something like that," Dave replied, not feeling inclined to elaborate.

Derek was more accommodating. "Yes, identical, could you not tell?"

"Si, señor, it is most obvious. We go now to top?"

"Yes, that would be perfect. Ready, Dave?"

Was he though? Was he ready to let Derek take command? Or was Derek just being diplomatic — had he sensed his disappointment about not being capable of taking on the hike? How soon would it be before he became the impediment to Derek's ambitions?

The car soon approached the slopes of the climb. "I can also be guide if you want. I know much about this place," enthused Hector.

"That would be most welcome," Derek replied. Even though he had studied the site while Dave was at his sister's, it would not hurt to get a local perspective of the ruins.

"Good," Hector replied, "I very cheap. I will also get tickets for the entrance when we arrive."

The drive up the hill looked less challenging than Dave initially thought it might be. The incline wasn't overly steep. He would definitely walk down later that afternoon. Maybe they'd see more that way, rather than being in a car on a dusty road where the vegetation mostly occluded their view of the mountainside.

At the top, while Hector waited in the queue at the ticket office, Dave took the opportunity to sit on a seat nearby. It would give him a moment to acclimatize to the altitude again and a chance to take another dose from his inhaler.

"Are you okay," Derek asked, sitting next to him, a discernible note of concern emanating from his synthesized voicebox.

Dave found it uncanny, not like his voice at all. It always sounded foreign to his ears, yet it was him. It was the voice you hear when someone records it and then plays it back. Was it really an accurate representation of how he sounded to others, though? "Yes, I'm okay."

"Here I have tickets," Hector said, approaching with them clutched in his hand.

"How much?" enquired Derek.

I^2

"Ah, no need to be concerned with money now, not in this sacred place," Hector replied. "I'll add it to bill. We settle later."

Dave stopped at the first observation point inside the complex and looked down the face of a near-vertical drop towards the town far below. It made him feel giddy. He grabbed the handrail to steady himself; they were too few and far between for his liking. If he lost his footing, he would more than probably end up dead in the river far below; another inconsequential obstruction for the babbling waters to negotiate.

Derek tapped him on the shoulder, making him jump. "You might need these," he said, handing Dave his hiking poles. "You left them in the car. We go up here first, to the top, according to Hector. And then make our way back down through the site." Derek pointed out the way through to some rough stone-cut steps. They looked a daunting prospect to Dave, far too steep to easily negotiate and too crowded for comfort.

"Yes, please, follow me," insisted Hector.

Continuing upwards, they climbed up the stepped terraces until they reached a reconstructed building with a straw-thatched roof.

"Here we are at the guardhouse, and also a place where they kept animals; Llamas probably. They were used like donkeys here. And beyond are the steps cut into the hill to grow crops. Now come here, see," insisted Hector pointing towards the edge of the terrace. "Here is the best view."

And in Dave's mind, he was correct. Stretched out below them, the magnificent panorama of the ruins bathed in the dazzling light of the noon-day sun didn't disappoint. It caught his breath. "This is the picture, Derek. This is exactly the one from my magazine."

"I know," Derek replied, absorbing the image of the

whole site extending below them. A perfect panorama standing in the shadow of the famous crag that he recalled in Dave's eyes looked a bit like a sitting elephant.

Moving on from the guardhouse, they followed the marked tourist route through what once would have been the main gate into the ancient city. Dave stopped to catch his breath as soon as they'd passed under the gate, taking the opportunity offered to watch some alpacas below him grazing in the large rectangular grassed area that would have once been the city's meeting place. He conjectured that the only reason they were there was to beguile tourists. Draw them towards the ramshackle stalls offering furry toy replicas.

Hector directed them to a stone wall. "You see how they build with stone," he said, in his best-practiced tour guide voice. "No cement in the fifteenth century. If you look across the site, you can see three distinct zones. In the West, we have the religious zone; the East; the residential zone, and over there," he said, pointing towards the rear of the site, "was the area reserved for the nobility."

With his hand, Dave shielded his eyes from the sun to see where Hector was pointing. He should have bought some sunglasses. At such an altitude, everything seemed so much brighter. He was sure it wouldn't be a problem for Derek though, he would have some sort of aperture control. Was it wrong to think of him in terms of a camera? Would that not be how he captured the day?

"Come we go now to the two main temples and the observatory," guided Hector pointing the way.

After waiting for the queue to disperse, Dave found himself standing next to the large granite rock in the center of the observatory. He would have run his hand over it to gauge its smoothness: the weathered constancy of passing centuries if it hadn't been for the 'Do Not Touch' sign fastened to it. Which was probably exactly why there was a sign attached to it!

I^2

"It is big, the Intihuatana stone, no? It was used for astronomical clock," Hector informed them. "The Incas were well aware of the seasons and the relative position of the sun. The sun was very important to them. Revered as the god Inti, he commanded the crops to grow. Illapa, the god of rain, fed the crops. And Pachamama, the goddess of the earth, gave the crops life."

After waiting for the crowds to disperse on another set of steps, they descended and made their way across the central grassed area to reach the Sacred Stone.

"This area was reserved for meditation," guided Hector. "Stones were revered artifacts to the Incas. It is because they, the people, all came from the ground. And then, when they die, they return back to the ground once more. So the stone is a memorial of the people who went before. They thought the spirits of their forbears lived in them. So people would come here for guidance. Is it not the same today as prayer or visiting the stones in a cemetery?"

Dave was acutely aware that his breathing had become labored again, and his head was starting to spin. Stars and black flashes were disrupting his vision. He must sit down very soon or collapse. As he followed Derek and Hector around the royal enclosures, he'd become increasingly conscious of the fact that he was starting to lean more heavily on his hiking poles than what they were originally designed for. They had become a crutch both in the physical and metaphorical sense.

Derek pointed out a bench placed under a rebuilt structure. "Can we sit for a while," he asked Hector. "Dave needs water." Did Derek see his discomfort? Had he switched into carer role from companion?

"Sure, I see a friend over there I need to talk to. I'll come back in a few minutes."

I, SQUARED

Welcoming a chance to rest up, and more importantly, water, Dave downed the flask Derek had been carrying in his backpack in seconds. "Don't suppose there's food in there as well, is there?"

"Of course. Do I not think of everything?" Derek replied, passing him a shrink-wrapped sandwich.

Dave subconsciously translated the word think to compute.

After 10 minutes, Hector returned. "Okay, are we now ready for the last special place – the Temple of the Condor?"

Rising from the bench to follow their guide, Derek offered Dave a helping hand to get him upright again. It couldn't come too quickly, Dave decided, as they passed a signpost marked 'Salida.' He was suddenly feeling very fatigued.

"Here we are – The Temple of the Condor." Resumed Hector in his tour guide voice. "Look at the way the stonemason shaped the natural rock formation and imagined it into the wings of a condor. You see, there on the ground, they carved a head to make it appear three-dimensional. It is so beautiful, is it not?"

Dave and Derek nodded simultaneously.

"Ah, yes, a breath-taking example of Inca stonemasonry to sculpture something so wonderful but also terrifying to those unlucky enough to receive judgment before it," resumed Hector. "Historians have speculated that the condor headstone was used as a sacrificial altar. Do you know, they found a mummy preserved under it. And behind, over there, that was the prison complex. Prisoners were held there until their fate had been decided. It would either be the flight of the condor or reprieve."

Dave looked down at the carved bird's head. How many had lost their heads over trivial things? Was today's justice any better? Which is worse, depriving a man of his head or his liberty?

I^2

"So when we are ready," jumped in Hector, "we go back to the car. No?"

Derek tried to compute the differences between ending a rhetorical question with a Yes or No." But was unable to do so, concluding they should be treated as an equivalence.

On reaching the exit, Hector led them back to his vehicle. "We can go back down the mountain in the car, or you can walk down now? Only you hadn't decided on the way up?"

"I think we'll go down in the car," Dave replied, relieved and also slightly disheartened. In one day, he'd become acutely aware of his diminishing capabilities, but the day hadn't disappointed.

It may have only been 500 meters descent, but to Dave, it made all the difference. The nagging headache that was starting to bother him was tolerable now. His breathing had slowed and become shallower, giving his aching diaphragm a well-earned rest. And his sense of balance had definitely returned; no longer did he feel like he would fall if he couldn't hold on to something for support. Confidently, he retracted down his telescopic hiking poles.

That evening, on the terrace of the small hotel where they were spending the night, Dave watched the transition of day to dusk. The sun now well below the mountain line was casting perfectly projected silhouettes onto the hills opposite. While other peaks remained resplendent in bright sunlight, their white snowy summits slowly turning orange as the sun waned. With a beer to hand, the world seemed more tranquil and spiritual somehow. He had enjoyed the day, and soon they'd be going out for an equally enjoyable evening. A local meal in a local restaurant, just the way it should be. Today had been a great day and one he would remember fondly, but first, he had to write it up while everything was still fresh in his mind.

Replicants

The journey home, catching the early train, followed by a local flight and an overnight from Lima to Houston, was as tiring as Dave expected. He definitely felt weaker by the experience, but hopefully, some of his strength would return now he was back down to a sensible altitude. And a few days to recuperate before they set out on the next leg of their journey would be more than welcome.

Picking up his phone, he asked Lolita to send a text. Would Tami answer it? Would she want to see him again if she was in Houston? It might be the last chance he'd get. He didn't want to think about it, but recently it had been playing on his mind more. This may be his final opportunity for a while, maybe forever. He must also call his sister and the lads on Mars now his VOLT account had been activated. Derek had already warned him that they'd soon be going on a journey that would last a couple of months. He so hoped it wasn't going to be all flights, hotels, and dashing about – he'd definitely struggle for sure.

Dave's phone vibrated in his pocket. He withdrew it. Lolita was holding up a placard that emphasized her ample chest under a tightly fitting bathing suit. On it was Tami's number. Eagerly he put the receiver up to his ear.

"Hi, Tami,"

"Hi, Dave, guess what. I'm in town, and so are Johan and Tegan. Shall we make up a four for dinner?"

He didn't really want to see *them*, but he had promised to keep in touch, something else he'd failed to do. "Sure," he replied.

"I've booked a table already. I knew you would, and everywhere decent gets filled up so quickly. See you at eight. I'll text the details."

$I\hat{\ }2$

Dave hardly managed a reply before the call disconnected. Tami was excited; he could tell from her voice, it had a nervous expectant edge to it. And, he fully understood why she'd want to meet up again with the friends they'd made on the voyage from Mars. She might need Johan and Tegan one day to help her through the difficult times ahead. He didn't have to like it, though. Selfishly, all he wanted was to spend what time he had left in Houston just with her. Only her, to the exclusion of everyone else, before he and Derek departed on their travels again.

"Derek, I'm off out tonight with Tami. You'll be okay here on your own, won't you?"

"Of course, what a silly question, Go, have some fun."

Dave didn't think it would be that much fun. Maybe the two of them could do something together after they'd said goodnight to Johan and Tegan. He so desperately needed her. He tried not to think about the future – he didn't have one. It was as though the gods of mortality were starting to request payment, tugging away at his soul and trying to wrest it away from his earthbound flesh. He knew things could never go back to how they were on that long journey to Earth. So this evening had to be perfect.

Last to arrive as usual but not overly late, Dave found everyone sitting at the bar sipping cocktails.

"Cocktail, Sir," the waiter asked as soon as he had taken the seat Tami had reserved for him next to Tegan.

"I'll take an Old-Fashioned, please." If ever a person so suited a cocktail, then this was made for him.

"So how have you been keeping, Dave," Tegan inquired.

I, SQUARED

"Fine, just fine. Thanks." He was not much for small talk, but then they already knew that.

"Good to hear," Johan replied, his head peering around from behind Tegan's elbow. "Tami's been saying that you have a companion, and you're doing a sort of world tour thing."

"Yes, Derek, he's also a sort of carer too. For when I get sick." It was the first time he'd admitted that to anyone other than Tami.

"A carer," butted in Tegan, "my, that must cost a lot."

"Yes, in more ways than you could imagine," Dave responded. "But if you don't mind, I'd rather not just talk about me. I want to hear all about what you've been doing since arriving back on Earth." He had to try and deflect the subject away from revealing anything more about Derek. "So, Johan, are you lecturing anywhere at the moment?"

"Yes, in Houston as it happens. I'm trying to educate the next generation of spacefarers on the NASA university campus there."

"And Tegan has news too," jumped in Tami. "She's expecting."

"My, that was quick," Dave responded; it was probably not the best reply. "Congratulations, anyway!" By way of an afterthought, it would have to do.

"Thank you. It must have been the change of climate," laughed Tegan – the type of laugh that covers up a secret. The fact that she'd miscarried at the first attempt while on the journey to Earth was something she would keep to herself. Apart from Johan, all anyone else knew was she'd been sick for a few days.

"You mean by actually having one you can breathe without it killing you," Dave quipped. "I, too, am feeling better here than I would have if I'd stayed on Mars."

"So, are we ready for dinner then?" Tami asked, on seeing the waiter approach with menus and correctly guessing their table must be ready.

I^2

Having seen Johan and Tegan off in a taxi, they were now free from adherence to social niceties. The fresher night air made for a pleasant digestif as Tami and Dave ambled along the sidewalk, imbibing the invisible beverage. "Smell that, Tami, how sweet it seems with you next to me."

"Are you sure it's not just my perfume! What shall we do now then?"

"No idea, but I don't want to go home, not yet. Let's make a night of it. Let's paint the town red as they say."

"Okay, you choose." Tami flashed a broad smile at him and put her arm through his. They were almost teenagers again.

"Well, let's just walk along here awhile." Dave pointed along the street. "I think there's an entertainment complex just up ahead. Maybe there's something there we might like."

Tami ran her fingers down Dave's stubbly cheek. "I think I like you with a beard. Now I've got used to it."

"I do too. Hopefully, it will look even better when it becomes more of a beard and less of an itchy unshaved mess."

She giggled slightly. "It will make you look very distinguished."

Dave thought to himself, more distinguishable certainly. It was the one thing that separated him from his twin: the ability to grow hair. No longer could he and Derek simply swap identities.

The entertainment complex housed within its walls, everything they could ever wish to serve as a distraction from the inevitable – ending up in bed for want of something to do.

Dave discounted bowling; he'd be hopeless. The

casino; neither of them knew how to gamble. Food; they'd just eaten, so that was out. The cinema complex, however, had six screens. Something here had to be suitable.

"Cinema, Tami? We can pretend to be out on a first date again!"

"That would be great. And, you know how much I love a good classic film."

Dave remembered only too well what film night entailed. "Yes, in that respect, we have very similar tastes. Let's go and see what they're showing."

Arriving at the kiosk, they both decided simultaneously that one film stood out amongst all the others. Dave bought two tickets for the Ridley Scott cult classic: Blade Runner.

In the bar of the Entertainment Complex, Dave stirred a cherry around in another Old Fashioned. The film had disturbed him. It questioned the whole relationship he had with Derek, or rather the lack of it.

Tami, too sat quietly sipping a glass of Sauvignon. How could she have dismissed Derek so offhandedly as a machine? A device! Had they not just seen a film depicting the exploitation of synthetic life forms. Wasn't the trial Dave was involved in the same – mans' desire to make money at any cost. Here they were at the dawning of a new age of mankind, offering the false promise of immortality to those with more money than they could spend in several lifetimes. The way they interacted now with Derek could, in essence, be shaping the very way sentient inorganic life came to see itself in the real world. It could set a precedent. What if she and Dave became the blueprint for the way future Dereks acted amongst humans. Did she, as a human, want to be feared? Be repressive and dismissive of them? Could she live amongst them and treat them as equals? Here she had a chance to bury her prejudices. Could she, for the first time, see Derek as a person?

This is why Derek had insisted on a bucket list, Tami concluded. It wasn't just for Dave's benefit; it was meant to be a learning experience for the both of them. Had the film not depicted replicants as being self-aware and deterministic? Soon this would no longer be just a fantasy; this would be a new truth. Was it not all around to see if only she had dared look. Well, now her eyes were open, and her attitude to them suddenly disgusted her. She had to make it up to Derek, if only to ease her guilt, especially now. Dave didn't know, nor would he ever, of just how important Derek was about to become in her life.

"Dave, before you leave, I'd like you and Derek to come to dinner, please. I owe him, don't you think?" she said, realizing it was probably the first time she had used a personal pronoun to describe Dave's digital doppelganger. From now on, Derek would always be a 'he.' A big step forward indeed – the ramifications were huge. Could she really live with the notion that Derek should be treated as an equal from now on?

"I owe him so much too," Dave replied. "Thanks, Tami, that would be a really nice thing to do."

It was very late by the time Dave returned to the apartment. Derek had retired for the evening. Dave was still unsure what that meant precisely, but the thought of it and the fact they had just seen Blade Runner focused his mind on the question. Picking up his tablet, he selected books and scrolled down the library until he came across what he was looking for: the book Blade Runner was based on – Philip K Dick's novel, 'Do Androids Dream of Electric Sheep.' Easing into his favorite armchair, he started to read....

It was well past dawn by the time he put his tablet

back down. He pondered on the significance of what he'd just read. Certainly, the world wasn't anything like the film or the book. There had been no apocalypse; everything carried on much the same as it always had. But the message wasn't really about the setting; it was about the human condition. It was about man's desire to exactly replicate digital versions of themselves, making them indistinguishable from the real thing. He was that experiment, Derek just the tool. It was why the incentives had been so lucrative.

Not for the first time, doubts started to resurface. The bucket list had been Derek's idea for sure, but exploring the reasoning behind it led to difficult questions and inescapable conclusions. Was Derek really his own person? Was the bucket list wholly Derek's idea, or were the people at Forever-Life still pulling the strings? What control did they still wield over the android, and how in the end would they assess the outcome of the trial. Would Derek be deemed a success or a failure? A new species, or just a fancy endoskeleton dressed in artificial skin – a glorified bin-picker like the one he had seen just a few days ago.

I^2

The Last Supper

"So, Derek, is it okay if I call you Derek?"

"Yes, of course. Is it alright for me to call you Tami, Ms. Gleeson, now we are talking again?"

"I don't see why not. It's my name." Tami tried to sound at ease but was probably failing. "So now we have completed the formalities, let's go to dinner."

"You do realize I do not need sustenance. If there is something you and Dave would prefer to do instead?"

"No, it's fine, Derek," Dave replied, strolling up behind his twin. "Good evening Ms. Gleeson," he joked, trying to make light of an awkward situation. The three of them standing in his apartment reminded him of a scene from an old western – the classic Mexican standoff. Who would shoot first?

"Well, Mr. Shermans," jumped in Tami, beating her two companions to the draw. "I'm ready if you two are. So, if you'd like to escort me down to the cab. Let's go to dinner." Tami looped her arms through the two of them. She was glad Dave had decided on a beard if only to allow her to tell them apart; at least when standing, walking was easier – Dave's gait was very distinctive. She could tell he found walking not so comfortable anymore.

Tami couldn't help herself. She knew she was staring at Derek but couldn't bring herself to divert her gaze. She was fascinated by him mimicking a human, observing all the social niceties expected by ordering and consuming food he didn't require. His mannerisms were perceptively slightly different to Dave's; so, why hadn't she noticed it that first night in Houston? Tami thought about challenging him about it, but that would spoil the evening. Besides, knowing why he lied could be something she could find out later. The very thought of that night they'd spent together sent a tingle down her spine – it was like blowing air onto the embers of a smoldering fire. Let Derek remain ignorant of what she now knew; the time would come when he would need a friend, and she would be there for him. Souring the milk now would be counterproductive.

Staring at him, she couldn't help but compare her needs against his. Would Derek end up being nothing more than a life-sized sex-doll to her? She had seen the adverts. Animatronic 'partners' were all the rage, built for one thing only: to satisfy the needs of grubby little men seeking one-way pleasure with a fantasy. Here in front of her now sat a marvel of man's ingenuity. He would be the living memory of someone she loved. They could do so many things together, have intelligent conversations, and go places, rather than him just wait on her for when she felt horny.

"You're very quiet," commented Dave as desserts arrived.

"Yes, been thinking," Tami replied, placing back down her dessert fork.

"Anything I can help with," butted in Derek, still trying to compute why he had been invited.

"Not really… well, yes, sort of… Look, I don't know how to say this and not sound foolish. I realize now I don't want to lose either of you." Tami dabbed away a tear before it had a chance to trickle down her cheek and smudge her make-up. "Derek, we will have to keep in touch, you know… afterward."

Tami, reaching over, grasped Dave's hand and squeezed it hard. "Oh, Dave, this is so hard for me. I love you, and if I can't have you, I want to be reminded of our time together. I'll be luckier than most. They will only have a dusty drawer full of memories. I'll still have all our shared memories sat right here," she said, placing her free hand on top of Derek's. "Especially now."

"Now?" queried Derek?

"Yes, did Dave not tell you. My new job, it's based

I^2

here in Houston. I can be your friend when... well, you know."

Derek offered her the unused napkin from the spare place setting for her to dab her moistened eyes.

"It makes perfect sense," Dave replied understandingly. He didn't have to like it, but the logic was impeccable. "In a way, I think that's something about what the experiment is all about. It's not just longevity; it's more about not being forgotten."

"Exactly, so, tell me more about tomorrow." She was eager to change the subject for fear of not being able to stop the tidal pressure building behind her eyelids. "I understand you are leaving for Florida."

"Absolutely, Derek here reckons sea air will be good for me, so we are traveling around the world on a ship."

"But ninety days is a long time. Will it not be too strenuous?" She tried not to sound concerned, but she could hear it in her voice. She must remain positive for them, not give Dave the option to give up on it. Why had she mentioned it at all!

"No, not at all, there will be many sea days, where I can just relax. Derek has it all planned."

"I do. Do not worry, Tami. I will make sure Dave comes to no harm. He is my brother, after all."

"No, he's not," Tami replied. That sounded bad; she had to find words to better express herself. "Look, what I'm trying to say, and saying it badly is, together, you are much more than that. You have a shared oneness. I no longer see two people sat here. I see two halves of the same person. And I'm glad you're both here with me tonight."

"Really, you mean it?" Dave replied, relieved that the two most important people in his miserable life had resolved their differences.

"Look, tonight, can we all go back to my hotel room. I'd like to. With both of you."

"Together!" spluttered Dave, speckling the table with

bits of dessert.

"Yes, together," Tami replied, suddenly feeling aroused by the thought of lying with both of them. The fire within was now raging again. That yearning that grows from deep within your abdomen, blowing away all sense of reason. "It's not like cheating, is it? Have I not just said it? Are you not just one person – the same person and the one I love." It was partly true. However, they must never know the real reason, not now… not ever, and certainly not since she'd learned the truth about that night in Houston. It would be imperative to keep the role she'd be playing in Derek's life from now on a secret. She considered the dishonesty for a moment. Would Derek one day come to despise her? Possibly, but that was not tonight, or she hoped, for many days to come. Did that make her a Judas? Someone willing to take thirty pieces of silver in payment for information?

I^2

Just Like Mars; Only Bigger!

The ship towered menacingly over them as they approached the bow-end. A mountain of steel plate that seemed to defy the natural laws of physics by remaining upright. Dave was convinced it would surely topple over in the slight sea breeze swirling around the quayside and crush them both at any minute. "It's humongous," was all he could think of to say.

"Yes, it certainly is," Derek replied, pulling two large wheeled suitcases along behind him.

On reaching the gangway, a porter relieved Derek of the cumbersome luggage. Once inside, they were checked in and handed their passkey – for purchases and access to their suite. "It is all the way along to the back of the ship, on deck eight," informed the purser's assistant behind the desk, which Dave was sure was another ALF. "Your bags will be delivered to your suite later," it said in an entirely perfunctory manner.

Walking along the enclosing passageways of the accommodation decks reminded Dave of his home on Mars. Only this was much bigger. The ship probably had as many people on it as the whole of the Martian capital city.

After strolling along seemingly endless corridors of spotlessly clean walls and red-patterned carpets, they reached their suite. Derek pushed the deck-card into the door lock and withdrew it again. Click, the little light turned green. Pushing open the door, Derek entered first, holding the door against its spring return for Dave to follow.

"Is this all ours?" Dave scanned the living area. It wasn't over-fussy. Plush, but not ostentatious; comfortable rather than utilitarian. This room alone was more extensive than his billet on Mars. Off the living area, each had their own equally large bedroom. In front of them, a large balcony beckoned, overlooking the rear of the ship.

"Do you like it?" questioned Derek.

"Very much!" Dave replied, running his fingers along a countertop that separated the room from a small kitchenette. From what he could see, its sole purpose was to provide facilities for making tea and coffee. However, underneath the unit was something far more impressive, a fridge for wine bottles and other assorted alcoholic drinks.

"Good, then we will take a drink on the balcony and watch the ship depart." Derek, diving into the fridge, retrieved a bottle of champagne. "And tomorrow, we will have the whole day to explore the ship."

"This is very civil of you, brother," Dave replied, picking up a tray with two glasses waiting to be used on it. He wasn't a cripple just yet. "Will you be partaking too?"

"Of course. Would I let you drink alone?"

Now would be a good time to ask, Dave thought, as they watched the great ship ease itself away from the quay. Especially as he had come to realize the bucket list was more important to Derek than it was to him. "So, Derek, the bucket list, we have a poem, but how does it relate. What do we do, just cross things off as we visit them?"

"Not exactly. I have not worked out the answers to some of the lines. The beginning was easy, but now, it will be more when we see it. And what better way to see it than traveling to places we have never been."

"But the first three stops were so precise?"

"Yes, but those and this trip were all I had planned. For this part, I asked the travel agent to book us on a voyage of discovery. She said this ship will be visiting many heritage sights and places of significant history." As a lie, it would suffice. In some ways, however, it was also true. Had he not written down on a list, all the places he computed *might* satisfy the text. But then, it would be for them both to decide if it reached the lofty criteria they had discussed.

I^2

"Okay then. Let's do it." Dave retrieved the pen he had accidentally pocketed at reception and placed it on the drinks tray. "So we start by crossing off what we have seen and then look for what makes sense going forward from here."

"Yes, that would be the most logical way to go." Derek pulled a piece of paper from the pocket of his jacket. Unfolding it, he laid the poem on the table next to the tray, much to Dave's bemusement. Derek obviously already had it all planned, despite his denial. "Right, so Iceland; 'a magisterium of heavenly gates,' was a reference to the Northern Lights in the trilogy by Philip Pulman. 'Wonders manifest across this great plain;' that was the crater in Arizona, and 'go climb a mountain,' was Machu Picchu.

"Yes, that is correct." Derek picked up the pen and crossed through the words.

"So now you have crossed those off, I presume 'cross a great sea' is a reference to this trip."

"Yes, it is." Derek crossed out those words too.

"Well, I guess we have to seek out a friendship next before we can cross that off. I'm assuming it has to be something special that we both experience."

"It has to be uninvited, though," stipulated Derek. "Something spontaneous that neither of us has tried to cultivate."

"Okay, we will wait and see what develops."

"But surely, Dave, are you also not forgetting something?"

"No, I don't think so?"

"There are other lines to cross off. In fact, all the others to where we are now. So all the way down to: 'is there somewhere you'd rather be than sitting here beside me?' That is a reference to you and me, by the way, as close as any you could make when we had our differences and struggled to resolve them. 'For a world out there awaits, so why sit here and while away time,' that is another reference to this trip. And: 'life is too finite to linger next to me;' is this not a perfect metaphor for your condition and our relationship?"

And Dave could suddenly see that it was. So that was why the first line of the poem had resounded so strongly with him. The whole reason why he'd tried to rediscover it was synonymous with his pending date with the grim-reaper. It was as if he'd had an epiphany, and the poem; the divine revelation. It was almost as if he had been touched upon by God. Taking the pen off Derek, he contentedly crossed through the lines his digital brother had suggested without further debate.

Sat at the bar on the sun deck, Dave sipped another beer. In the four days they'd been sailing since leaving Freeport, they had crossed the Gulf of Mexico and stopped off at Key West and Havana. Nothing had stood out with regards to crossing anything off the rest of the poem. He felt uneasy about leaving the ship for any length of time and so hadn't really looked. No, he was more than content spending his time visiting the many watering holes scattered throughout the floating city and striking up conversations with the bar-huggers and lounge-loafers he found there. But it was all superficial; nothing came anywhere close to the next line of the poem. Ship-people were pleasant enough, but they all had their own agendas, reluctant to take the time to participate in something more profound than engaging. Knowing someone's hometown and what they did for a living hardly constituted a deep and meaningful friendship. He knew it had to be something special to count, an unforced encounter, something spontaneous. He couldn't help but wonder if he already had that with Tami, and why did he not invite her along? Was it the fear of him not reaching the end? Possibly. On that one point, he was resolute. She would never see him frail and incapacitated. Picking up another Old Fashioned, he made a point to

I^2

remind Derek that Tami should never see him bedridden. She had to remember him only as he was now – slightly less decrepit but still in control of his bodily fluids.

Derek came over and tapped him on the back.

"Whatever he wants," Dave instructed the barman.

"Look, Dave, tomorrow is our last port of call for a while and the last in the Caribbean." Derek reminded him, knowing full well he already knew. "So far, we have not ventured much away from the port. A bar on a beach is the furthest we have been. Tomorrow, could we go on a trip? Otherwise, it is not going to be much of an adventure, is it?" He had not wanted to push Dave further than he felt capable of, but now he needed a gentle nudge!

"Yes, I suppose. All this sea air and sunshine is working wonders. I feel like a new man."

Derek detected deception, but not enough for him to be concerned about. "Good, then we will do it tomorrow. But in the meantime, why don't we chat up those two over there."

"Chat up? Do you think we will find great friendship hiding in those two girls?"

"Cannot hurt to try, can it." Derek, picking up his JD and coke, made his way over to the two girls lying on sunbeds next to the pool.

"I thought you were looking for something more spiritual, not a bunk-up," Dave replied, perplexed and slightly embarrassed by Derek's behavior. "Besides, there's Tami."

"Yes, but she is not here."

Stunned into silence by Derek's attitude, Dave followed his lustful *other* over to the sunbeds, where two women were chatting and sipping tall cocktails decorated with wedges of pineapple. Dave estimated them to be about the same age as himself and forty years older than Derek!

"Mind if we sit here?" enquired Derek, already half-sitting on the empty bed next to them.

"Not at all," replied the brunette, "You're brothers, right? We've seen you around."

"Identical twins," butted in Dave.

"My sister and I are too. Well, twins anyway, but not identical, you know."

"Yes, dizygotic, or fraternal twins," Dave replied, wondering why he was suddenly trying to make an impression and sound intelligent. Maybe he was trying to compensate for his lack of experience when it came to chatting up women, "This is Derek, by the way, and I'm Dave."

"Ah, identical and alliterate," the fair-haired twin replied, peering over her sunglasses while sweeping back her mousey blonde hair to get a better look.

"You could say that," Dave couldn't help himself but admire the vision of loveliness in front of him, and intelligent too, no doubt – it was something in her voice. He wondered what she would have said if he'd told her that he and Derek also shared a consciousness. Undoubtedly, several steps up from an alliteration.

"Anyway, I'm Samantha," continued the brunette, "but you may call me Sammy, and this is my sister Ellie."

"Pleased to know you," Derek replied, his cognitive functions telling him now was a good time to take a sip of his drink.

"So, are you traveling all the way?" Dave inquired, trying not to make it sound like an innuendo. Unlike his partner, who seemed to be mutating into a Lothario, he didn't want or need a ship romance. Derek had surprised him and said as much the other evening at dinner. Why not try and score while we're on here, he'd said. Were their personalities diverging that quickly now?

"You'll soon find out. We're off now; see you around," Ellie said, snapping Dave out of his misgivings. "We have spa treatments booked."

"Okay, hopefully see you soon." Derek turned back

I^2

towards Dave, "Nice, eh? They are definitely up for it! You choose – I am not fussy!"

"Are you sure we are both the same person here?" Dave replied, still reeling somewhat by Derek's candor. "You might not be fussy. But I am. Okay, they're nice, and of course, you know they are exactly the type of girl I'd go for."

"That is a given, do not forget, I know the types of films you liked to watch alone in your billet on Mars."

"Shh, that might be so," Dave suddenly felt flustered. "But I have Tami now, and I don't want to cheat on her?"

"It is only cheating if she finds out."

"Okay, you do what you want. And I'll have dinner in our suite tonight, on my own, away from temptation."

"Okay then, be like that," Derek replied, rising and walking off before Dave could respond.

Was he annoyed, Dave wondered; how could he know? But, he did have the distinct impression that if an android could show displeasure, it would be exactly like what he'd just witnessed. It was just like when he first turned him on, but they had come such a long way since then. Why was having sex such a big deal to Derek? It was almost as if he was trying too hard to prove himself human. However, could Derek just be following his programming, portraying the person he is meant to emulate? Was Derek's sexual drive just the one he'd repressed for so long? Something he'd never had to do to prove his manhood. Was this latent frustration in Derek a manifestation of some deep down feeling of ineptitude in himself? He'd have another drink and think about it; hell, he'd have a skin-full if he was going to spend the night in his room.

I, SQUARED

St Vincent

Dave awoke to a frosty reception. "You were sick," Derek informed him on entering the bedroom. "I had to clean it up. Do you feel okay now?"

His head hurt. Like the worst of hangovers, it felt as though it was being squeezed in a duck-press. But it didn't stop the voice inside from whispering – wasn't that precisely what Derek was here for. Why should he take umbrage if Derek had to perform *its* duty! "I'm sorry about yesterday, but let's not let it wreck today. Are we still going ashore? I know you want to go on a trip somewhere and see what develops."

"I am not annoyed in case you ask, just conflicted. Your indecisiveness is holding you back. Stopping you from becoming the person you are inside your head. Do I not know it already. Does this make any sense to you?"

"I guessed that much yesterday when I was drinking myself into a stupor. I wasn't really thinking about your needs. But let's forget that, shall we? Today is a new day, and I promise to be decisive. We will go on a trip."

"Good, I will get ready then. This is our last stop before we cross the Atlantic. Today will be a good day – I can sense it in my circuits."

Derek was evolving, Dave thought, but not in the way he'd imagined or supposed anyone at Forever-Life would have foreseen. He was becoming more self-aware that he was an android – less Dave, more Derek.

"And by the way, I passed on your apology to Ellie. I said you had had too much sun and was feeling poorly."

"Well, at least the last bit's right! It says here we're docked at St Vincent." Dave scanned the excursion pamphlet placed in their room the previous evening. "According to the tour guide, there's not a lot to do.

I^2

Nothing I can see that will result in us crossing anything off the bucket list. The ship's itinerary says it's a place to relax on the beach before crossing the Atlantic."

"We will wait and see what the day brings." Dave liked the enthusiasm Derek was displaying. When was he ever so optimistic?

Forgoing the franchised ship excursions offered onboard, the two of them walked along the quay past the regimented line of tour busses eagerly awaiting passengers. Outside the terminal building, they consulted the tour-guide placards. They all promised to be the best, the only way to see the island, and the cheapest. The barkers below the boards busied themselves desperately touting for custom, promising everyone coming within six feet a day to remember. It reminded Dave of the impossible triangle: only two conditions could ever be met at the expense of the third.

"We should go for this small mini-bus tour with a local guide," suggested Derek pointing at one of the placards. "I think we will get a more personal experience that way, and it seems to visit all the same places as offered onboard."

As they headed towards the exit, a tall, well-built local guy approached. "My man, where you goin' in such a hurry?" he asked laughingly. "This is chill time. Are you looking for a tour around the island, for I have the perfect one for you? We see everything for one special price."

"Maybe," Dave replied, reverting to type, his newfound decisiveness quickly deserting him.

"Good, I have my mini-bus over there, I just need two more passengers, and you're it."

"Okay, we are in," butted in Derek to save Dave from further prevarication.

"Come follow me," he replied, pointing towards a parked-up blue mini-bus. "That's my bus over there. I'm

I, SQUARED

Kurtis, and I'll be your driver and guide."

Dave was convinced Kurtis had noticed his slightly unnatural gait when walking and was especially holding the passenger door open for him – the invalid.

After Derek had taken the last remaining place by the sliding door, Dave clambered in the passenger side as least awkwardly as he could manage. After taking his seat, he couldn't help but count the number of passengers who'd have to put up with the laggard – ten unlucky souls and Derek, all having to wait for him at every stop.

Soon they were off, trundling through the streets of Kingstown. "So what do you know of our island then?" Kurtis asked, loud enough to be clearly heard above the hum of the electric motors driving the wheels. "We are like all the other islands in the eastern Caribbean. We grow fruit, make rum, and watch cricket. It's a simple life."

A murmur of laughter rippled through the bus.

"Do you know why we drink? No? I'll tell you. It's because we live on a fault line. We have many earthquakes. We drink rum so we can practice trying to walk when the ground shakes."

More laughter. As soon as it subsided, Kurtis continued with his practiced tour-guide spiel:

"All the eastern islands are on the edge of the Caribbean tectonic plate. These islands result from the edges being pushed together, which is why they're all mountainous. Our country is slowly being squeezed by the North and South American plates, and the Atlantic plate. So we pay a high price to live in paradise. We have earthquakes and hurricanes, but we still wouldn't swap it for anywhere else."

Stopping for a moment at a junction, Kurtis waited for the traffic to clear before turning onto Leeward Hwy. "Here is our cricket ground," he proudly boasted, "a church for all religions."

After successfully negotiating another junction, Kurtis

I^2

turned the mini-bus north away from the center of town. "You all know our capital is called Kingstown after the British King George, and soon we will be visiting the Queen Charlotte Fort named after his wife. But, first I will tell you more about our island: Currently, now is peak tourist season, when the island population triples with holidaymakers and Vincentians returning home from jobs in other countries, or Vincies as we call them. St Vincent was formerly a slave colony. But before then, the Ciboney, Arawak, and Caribs were the natives of these lands. They were here when Columbus sailed by and named the island. An island fought over by the Dutch and the British, then the French and the British, eventually becoming a British dependency until independence in 1979. Over a century ago now."

"Is everyone so knowledgeable on the history of the islands?" Derek asked from behind the driver's seat.

"Of course, as you say: it's in the blood."

Derek understood the sentiment, even if he didn't actually have any actual blood of his own.

"St Vincent is a volcanic island, like the others on the fault line. Our volcano, La Soufrière, is still active and erupts every seventy to one hundred years and has destroyed parts of the island in the past. But as they say: time heals. Okay, quiz-time – what does La Soufrière mean in English?"

The bus remained silent.

"It means 'the sulfurous one,' and also from that we get 'to suffer.' So, it is aptly named. When it erupts, we all get to suffer."

Guiding the bus over to a street seller, Kurtis pulled up alongside and ordered fruit.

"You need to try these," he said after paying the vendor. "Bananas are our main export. On this island, we grow the best bananas in the Caribbean, if not the world."

Dave had only ever eaten bananas before in their

dehydrated form. Intently, he watched Kurtis hand the yellow-skinned fruit around to each of his charges, observing how they removed the outer flesh. Dave followed their lead and unzipped his. Kurtis was as good as his word, but then, not having anything to compare it against automatically made it the best.

"Are they not the best bananas you have ever tasted?" Kurtis asked, already confident of the answer.

A chorus of agreement ensued amongst the passengers, between mouthfuls of soft yellow fruit.

"My favorite, though, is the breadfruit. If I see any, we will try. We like it fried like chips, or French Fries as our American cousins would call them."

The mini-bus was now climbing out of Kingstown on a street never designed to cater to tourists. At every tight corner, it seemed as though Kurtis was having to give way to larger tour buses traveling in the opposite direction, using all the available road space to negotiate the bend. Or else, wait for two drivers to flatten their rear-view mirrors against the sides of their vehicles so they could pass each other without kissing. When eventually they managed to reach the top of the hill, a parking attendant pointed to a spot for Kurtis to pull into.

"This is Fort Charlotte," informed Kurtis as soon as he had finished maneuvering his vehicle into the cramped space, one unnervingly too close to the edge of the hillside for Dave's liking. "I promise you will find something very interesting here. When you come out, there will be a prize for the first to guess it. I'll tell you now, though, no one's yet managed to win my bottle of rum." He laughed – a laugh of assured victory that the bottle would remain safely in his possession.

Dave and Derek wandered around the small hilltop fortress overlooking the bay. In the distance, they could see their ship at anchor, towering over the town around it. In one corner of the fort, occupying one of the rooms built

I^2

into the walls, an animal rescue center had been created where cats and kittens freely roamed around tourists' legs competing for affection. Perched on a small table there, a charity donation tin – an old rusty biscuit box with a slot cut in it to accept currency. Above it, a handwritten paper sign asking for money to help with veterinary costs.

Dave wandered along the rampart; the fort seemed pretty unremarkable. A few cannons, some outbuildings, and a parade square. That was it. What was there 'of interest' to look at, deducing that Kurtis would be getting to keep hold of his rum. After checking his watch and seeing it was time to depart, he guessed he would soon find out the answer to the impossible riddle.

"Well, everyone, how did you get on?" Kurtis asked as soon as everybody had managed to take up their seats. "Did anyone guess the fort's secret?"

Kurtis waited for an answer, but none was forthcoming. "Okay, so I win again. The answer is: all the cannons in the fort are pointing inland. Not out to sea, as you would expect. All the gun ports are towards the land. This fort was used to defend the occupiers from the natives: the Caribs, and then later in the second Carib war, against a coalition of hostile black Caribs, runaway slaves, and French forces vying for control of the island."

Metaphorically Dave kicked himself for not getting the answer. It was obvious now it had been explained. He had even remarked that there seemed a lack of fortifications on the seaward side to Derek.

After checking all of his passengers were ready, Kurtis started the bus back down the hill. At the bottom, he turned north onto the main road and away from town and resumed his narrative. "Okay, we are now heading towards my hometown of Layou. Here we will visit the beach and see my friend who has a rum shack there. We can buy some drinks, food, and I will also get water for everyone. If you

I, SQUARED

want, you can try the local produce too! Also, while you were in the fort, I phoned my mother. She will prepare the breadfruit for us, which we will taste on the way back."

A spontaneous chorus of cheers erupted amongst passengers; everyone was starting to relax, including Dave. How could you not in such genial company? Twelve explorers and their host enjoying the day, the weather, and the prospect of rum at the next stop!

After traveling along the main road for 20 minutes, Kurtis turned off at the signpost for Layou beach. A few minutes later, the bus pulled up outside a small white-walled building, just off the road by the beach entrance. Everyone clambered out and followed their guide's lead into the rum shack.

Inside, Dave found himself looking at a small general store. A shop that probably hadn't changed in over a hundred years. Wood cladding covered the walls, while homemade shelving supported tins of produce in no particular order along the back behind the counter. A large glass-fronted fridge stood in one corner, fully stocked with soft drinks and a selection of local beers. A small sitting area, consisting of a dozen mismatched chairs and four tables of variable shapes and sizes, provided enough seating for them all.

"This is my local," Kurtis proudly proclaimed. "When the cruise ships are gone, we get our island back. We slip back, come to the beach with our families to party, have barbeques, drink rum, and watch the setting sun. Much in the same way my father did and his father and grandfather before him. I was named after grandfather Kurtis. He was also a tour guide. I guess you could say it's a family thing."

"Sounds idyllic," remarked Derek.

"It is, and a time for coming together. None of us are rich. The economy of the island is reliant on cruise ships. So when they're gone for half the year, we all rediscover the

I^2

power of community. Every one of us strives to help a neighbor, someone not so fortunate as ourselves. We all look after our own; it's our way. You see the result; we have no serious crime, and no one goes hungry. Paradise is not just about sun, sea, and sand. It's about friendship and belonging too."

Dave couldn't help but admire the philosophy. Here was someone who could teach the world leaders, and those who worshipped wealth above all other, a thing or to about humility.

Refreshed, they resumed the tour. After stopping to admire the view from the top of a high ridge and look down on the old French capital of Barrouallie, they proceeded to Walliabou Heritage Park. A place to wander amongst the exotic fauna and flora the island had to offer. Finally, they headed to the beach that was once a film set for Pirates of the Caribbean. What remained of the original had been preserved under a glass dome. A little further along, a small theme park called Pirate World had been created to maintain interest in a film franchise now eighty years old, complete with a floating galleon offering trips!

"Look at that, Derek," Dave exclaimed, admiring the sailing boats bobbing on the gentle swell of the vivid blue waters in the bay, their white paintwork glistening and reflecting in the sunlight. "Isn't it fabulous! And, the sand here is so fine; its like ground talcum powder. And the sea; have you ever seen anything so blue?"

"You know the answer's no!"

Dave removed his shoes to take a stroll along the water's edge, letting the gentle lapping warm water wash over his feet as they sank slightly into the wet sand. Afterward, they explored the preserved buildings of the film set before joining the others sitting in the bar for refreshments and free internet.

I, SQUARED

Contented, everyone returned to the mini-bus, mainly having forgotten about breadfruit. It was only when they reached Layou and Kurtis phoned ahead to say he would be arriving in five that everyone remembered the promise.

Pulling off the road, the bus continued up a drive to a typical Caribbean single-level villa, one with mosaic decorated stone walls and a fabricated blue steel roof.

"Okay, so, welcome to my home," Kurtis informed them as they pulled up in front of the house. "Please make yourself comfortable; there's plenty of space on the terrace."

If there could be anything like a collective surprise, Dave thought, then this would be it. Slightly hesitantly, everyone got out of the mini-bus. It was almost like nobody really knew what to do next. Dave certainly didn't, having never experienced anything like it before. But then, judging by the expressions on the faces of his fellow seasoned travelers, neither had they.

Warily everyone found a seat on the terrace. A petite, white-haired lady, instantly recognizable as Kurtis's mother, emerged from the kitchen with a pitcher of sorrel and glasses for everyone.

"We usually drink this with rum," Kurtis said, holding up his glass. "But today, we will make a toast without."

Everyone reciprocated, lifting their glass skywards before taking a sip of the sweet and slightly sour juice.

"Do you know our fish?" Kurtis asked questioningly. "On the islands, we like to eat the Jackfish. We always serve it off the barbeque. In a minute, I have one coming for us to try. Then afterward, we will try the breadfruit with our own island specialty – fish cakes and hot sauce."

Kurtis's mother returned with a complete fish on a platter and cutlery. Kurtis expertly pierced the flesh with his fork before dragging it away to reveal the white meat inside. "Try it," he said, taking a mouthful.

Soon only the bones, fins, and head remained.

I^2

"It's good, isn't it," Kurtis asked rhetorically, already assured of the answer.

Everyone agreed.

"Okay, so we make a specialty fish cake with the young fry of the tri-tri fish. It's also known as whitebait, but these are the babies, not the adult fish. At night, when there is no moon, the fish are caught at the mouth of the river in big sheets, then sold at the market the next day." Kurtis reached over to a table behind him and picked up a cup. "Here is one."

"It's still alive," remarked Dave looking at the tiny fry, barely an inch long.

"Of course, we cook them live, in potato flour and spices to make the tri-tri cakes and serve them with deep fried breadfruit. Look, here comes Mama with them now."

Two plates, one piled high with the cakes and another with breadfruit, were placed in front of the guests.

"Enjoy," Kurtis said enthusiastically, his customary broad smile lighting up his face.

Dave picked up a fish cake and nibbled a piece off the corner – it was pleasing. After dipping another piece in the hot sauce, he tried that, making a mental note to take far less sauce the next time. The breadfruit was exactly as promised: it tasted just like fries!

It was no surprise when a fruit cake arrived for dessert. Any misgivings about accepting hospitality from a stranger by the guests had long since dissipated. Everyone talked to one another, hearing about their lives and their adventures. Only Derek remained unusually taciturn.

"You're quiet," Dave remarked.

"Yes, I know. I just want to record as much of this moment as possible. Here we all are, strangers, but also friends."

Dave knew what he meant. He, too, could listen to Kurtis for hours telling them about *his* island. He was proud of it. Taking every opportunity offered to show it off to others. To explain how the community would come together in the off-season when all the cruise ships had gone. Become one big family again where everyone cared. It was that type of island – one where everyone knew everyone else.

Dave checked his watch. Had they been out that long? A four-hour tour had become seven. It was time to depart and leave this idyll. After organizing a whip-round for the food, Dave handed it to Kurtis, "For your Mother." Kurtis refused to accept it at the first offering. Dave presented it to him again. "Please, we would feel embarrassed if you do not accept our gift too."

Reluctantly, Kurtis abated and thanked everyone for being his companions for the day. And in Dave's mind, that was precisely it; they were not customers; they had never been just business; they, unquestionably, had only ever been treated like true friends.

Later that evening, after dinner on the ship, Dave reached into his side jacket pocket and withdrew a carefully folded piece of paper. After spreading it out on the table to reveal the poem, he took out a pen from his inside pocket.

Derek looked on. "Yes, do it," he said.

"I wholeheartedly concur," Dave replied, making a stroke through the following two lines:

Feast on the heat of a warm summer's day
And seek out friendships along the way.

I^2

Crossing

Dave looked out from his balcony at the blue azure sea. Foaming white horses were dancing along on the surface, while white fluffy clouds in the sky above cast their dark shadow animals across the water. There would be nothing else more to see, not for another three days while they crossed the Atlantic. The warm breeze of the sea air, the almost imperceptible movement of the ship, and the 'rhum-rhum-rhum' from the funnel stack gave him a feeling of contentment he had not felt since Mars. There was an air of nostalgia about a method of transport that hadn't changed that much in 200 years. Picking up the final piece of breakfast pastry from the plate on the table, he devoured it in one before pouring out the last cup of coffee from the cafetière.

He still had some misgivings about the other day. Derek had a right to self-determination. If he wanted to bed a girl, why shouldn't he? His primary function was to help him when he became unable to look after himself, so it would only be fitting for him to help Derek become more human. If the chance arose and they met up with the girls again, he would do his bit. Maybe these were pent-up frustrations he'd been harboring all his life, refusing to admit them to himself by hiding away on Mars. He had plenty of opportunities to leave for Earth if he had so wanted. Was Derek not just a reflection of his inner self? The Dave he should have been, but not bold enough to grab the opportunity when it came along. He could have had a different life with Erika if he had so chosen. If he had, maybe the death sentence now dangling over his head like the proverbial sword of Damocles could have been avoided.

"So, are you coming up on deck?" Derek inquired,

already dressed in a T-shirt, swim shorts, and flip-flops. "Only you are still in your robe?"

"Give me a few minutes. I'll come up and find you."

"Okay." Derek turned and picked up the towel he had just thrown down on the bed, leaving Dave alone with his thoughts once more.

Dave sighed a little; solitude would have to wait for another day. Easing himself up from the chair, he slowly made his way to the bathroom. Taking out his medicine bag, he pulled out his inoculator. The dose indicator confirmed what he already suspected: it was already set to the highest dose. In a short while from now, he would be doubling it, and then where? He may have a real need for Derek to take care of him soon. But not yet, not for as long as he could manage.

By the time he'd dressed, he felt more energetic, apart from the now almost permanent slight limp and loss of sensation down his left side. He wasn't in pain, the drugs were still doing what they were supposed to, but he knew it was there, masked, goading him – reminding him of his mortality. Dave looked at himself in the mirror; at least he didn't look ill. Running his hand down his shirt, he tried to smooth out some of the more obvious creases. It would do – not much effort required to lie on a sunbed.

"Are these beds taken, Dave?" Placing his hand up to his forehead to shield out the sun, he could see Ellie standing there in front of him.

"No, please sit. Derek's getting drinks."

"Yes, I know; Sammy's at the bar with him. He said to come over." Ellie placed herself on the end of the sunbed. "So, did you and Derek have a good trip yesterday?"

"Yes, the best. It was something magical. Not the island, but the warmth and friendship we experienced."

"I'm all up for new experiences," Ellie replied,

I^2

deliberately being provocative.

"This is nice, isn't it," Sammy remarked, returning with what looked suspiciously like the same cocktails they'd been sipping the previous day.

"Yes, very," Dave replied, reaching up from the bed to take a glass of beer from Derek's outstretched hand. After a few more of these, he might feel less guilty about cheating on Tami....

Dave had mellowed to the point of abandonment after taking lunch with wine followed by drinks in one of the ship's more intimate bars. Any inhibitions he still felt worth preserving, locked away for as long as alcohol held the key. Thoughts of Tami had been relegated to a little dark recess in his mind. And why not? Ellie was tall, elegantly beautiful, and, more importantly, intelligent. He was beguiled by her sensuality, one he'd hope would lead to a more intimate conclusion after dinner....

Ellie slipped out of her dress while Dave poured drinks. Scotch for her, and water for him, if only to take the tablet Derek had thoughtfully provided. He would certainly require some assistance. Not that he normally needed it, but with his condition worsening, it would help.

"Are you ready for bed," she cooed.

He couldn't help himself but think of Derek at that moment and how he was faring with Sammy in her cabin. Would Derek be a more gifted lover than he? Would the girls compare notes afterward? He shuddered slightly at the thought of it, but would Derek and he not do precisely the same in the morning?

The next three days passed too quickly. Dave, at last

free from lingering guilt, enjoyed being in the company of Ellie immensely. And, being free from his keeper, for the most part, had also had its benefits. He would see Derek in the morning and in passing, but other than that, he devoted the rest of his time to Ellie. He felt vigorous in her company, but now they were approaching Teneriffe that would soon end. Ever since yesterday, when Ellie told him that she and Sammy were disembarking here, he had felt low again. To find happiness once more, only then to have it cruelly ripped away again, had impacted his health. Maybe it was for the best that Ellie's last memory of him would be as a man, rather than a cripple, or worse. At least the irony of the situation was not lost on him – Tami must have felt exactly the same as he did now when he finished with her on the flight from Mars. He hated himself again.

Today, he would stay on board rather than walk Ellie to the taxi waiting to take her and Sammy to the airport. He couldn't face saying goodbye to someone again, not after saying everything that needed to be said the previous night. In the cold sobering light of morning, he had decided that from today he had to face up to the one immutable fact he'd been trying to suppress: he hadn't got so many days left in front of him.

Dave watched Ellie climb into the taxi below on the quayside from high up on the sun deck. Derek had promised to say he felt unwell again. But in reality, it was his guilt starting to re-assert itself. He would call Tami later and tell her how much he loved her. It had always been her. Even when he was with Ellie, she was the one he thought about, wishing she was the one sharing his bed, lying next to him and feeling her warmth, for however long he had left.

Tami's phone vibrated on the desk next to her cup of

I^2

coffee. She picked it up to look at it. The avatar of a hunk she had named Rick held the caller's ID on a banner stretched across his muscular torso. It was from Dave. "Would you like me to connect you?" inquired Rick.

"Yes, thank you, video mode on."

Soon a pensive Dave was staring back at her.

"Are you okay," she asked, fearful of the answer.

"Yes, Why?"

"Well, you don't usually call in the daytime."

"I just wanted to hear your voice. I miss you."

"I miss you too. So where are you, and what have you been doing."

"Not much. Docked at Tenerife at the moment," Dave replied, trying to be deliberately vague for fear of admonishment. That was the last thing he wanted now. He needed Tami, more than ever before, secretly fearful that he'd never get to hold her in his arms again.

"Oh, okay. And how are you health-wise? And don't fob me off. You look tired."

"I am Tami. Oh, Tami, I love you – more than you'll know. I have to say this now. I don't know how much longer I'll be able to. I think I'll die before I ever get to hold you again." Dave wiped away a tear with the back of his hand and stifled a sniff.

"Don't say that Dave, you have loads of time left." Tami, feeling herself welling up, quickly reached across her desk to where she kept the ever-present box of tissues. Taking one, she dabbed her eyes. "You'll make it, Love, I know you will. I'll see you when you return."

"It's just that I'm getting weaker every day now. Derek has started doing more for me. He doesn't mention it; probably his programming kicking in. Oh, Tami, I'm so afraid. It's the not knowing how I'm going to feel from one day to the next."

Tami traced out the outline of Dave's face with her finger. "Promise you'll call me daily from now on. Just so I can hear your voice. I don't want you to be alone."

"I'm not alone, not anymore. Derek's a good companion. We really are becoming like brothers. I see the man now more than the machine. At times I forget he's not human until he reminds me. He really has become his own person."

Tami smiled, and Dave tried to reciprocate, but his mood failed him. "I'm scared, Tami. I don't want to die. Not now I've found life. Not now I've found you." His lip quivered – he was about to lose it. The floodgates of remorse and self-loathing were about to unleash a torrent. He'd had every intention of telling her he had been unfaithful, but as usual, he was a coward, and it would accomplish nothing other than assuage his guilt. But at what cost? He couldn't lose Tami. Not while there was still breath in his failing body.

Tami kissed the screen, and Dave touched the face he loved. Tearfully he terminated the call.

I^2

Senegal

Dave looked down from the top deck of the ship on the streets below. From his vantage point, everything about the city seemed squalid and degenerate. Ramshackle buildings, mixed amongst more modern constructions, littered the skyline in a disorganized amalgamation of convenience rather than function. Below them, wrecks that were once cars, only kept running by persistence and duct tape, made their way noisily along the crowded streets. A cacophony of sound emanating from car horns and traffic policeman's whistles gave everywhere a vibrancy that told him everything he needed to know: they had arrived on the shores of Africa. "It's a bit…well shit, for want of a better word," he said, turning towards Derek standing next to him.

"Well, I never promised you splendid beaches at every stop, now did I? But there is one place here we have to see. Do you agree, brother?"

"Yes, and it may fit the next line of the poem too," Dave replied expectantly. He'd known what they would be going to see here as soon as Dakar had appeared on the itinerary.

"We are agreed then, so we have to get off the ship and then catch the ferry from that pier over there."

A short journey of two miles across the open sea in a ferry Dave was convinced would sink at any moment such was the vessel's age – long surrendering to the ravages of the salty sea, its once white-painted hull now mostly large patches of exposed rust. The island, from a distance, looked like broken terracotta - the sort that's been painted and then smashed, such was the effect of the brightly painted buildings along the waterfront that greeted them. It gave the harbor an air of respectability: one that belied its murky

I, SQUARED

past.

Derek tried to offer Dave a hand to help him off the ferry. Dave dismissed it. "Stop fussing. I'm not ready for a box yet. I can make my own way."

Derek could see that such attention annoyed him. But Dave was his responsibility, and he knew that. His walking had definitely become stilted of late, but Dave continued to refuse any help offered that was seen as condescending. In his own digital way, Derek admired him for his tenacity. Was Dave more annoyed with himself and his failing body rather than his attention? It would be something he would compute later. He needed to find a way to best deal with his charge as he grew weaker without annoying him so.

The fort was interesting rather than impressive. Built to protect English and French interests, or maybe that should have been assets? The island had been occupied by both countries twice while engaging in the most heinous trade of all. The epithet: Slave Island summed it up perfectly. The museum, a famous world heritage site: Maison des Esclaves, would reveal the full gruesomeness of the trade to them both. Dave wondered what Derek would make of it. The significance of the heritage sight they were about to see might raise questions about their own relationship.

The red terracotta-painted building exuded an air of respectability from the outside – camouflage from the full horrors of what awaited them. Standing in the courtyard, Dave could see nothing had been done to cover up the evils perpetrated by the slave masters. Ascending the courtyard steps, Dave entered the tourist gallery and stopped to read the information boards there. Factual accounts about slaves being clapped in irons and kept in bare brick rooms void of windows and sanitary facilities. Fed infrequently and holed up until the next ship arrived, they were treated worse than

I^2

the farm animals on the island. It was little wonder so many died on the journey rather than in the fields of their masters – were they the lucky ones, gaining freedom from an otherwise lifetime of bondage?

Touring the building, Dave placed his hand to the wall. "If walls could talk, Derek? Imagine all the suffering and cruelty they have witnessed in here."

Derek touched the wall too. "It is the nature of mankind."

Dave wondered if Derek, not being 'of man,' was deliberately distancing himself from such atrocities.

Back in the courtyard, Dave walked up to the infamous 'door of no return' and stared through it to the sea beyond. It was the perfect metaphor for his journey too. He was sure he would never see home again, whether that be Mars or Houston. As he peered into the nothingness of the horizon, he felt less than nothing himself, much as the slaves would have done. For was he also now not one of them? A slave to time – from which there was no escaping.

Walking back to the ferry along the Esplanade Les Droits L'Homme made Dave think – had mankind changed so much in 500 years? Did Derek fully comprehend the significance of the place they had just visited? Had he realized that their relationship was exactly the same as that of master and slave? Derek was compelled to look after him through his programming; did it go against his free will? Or maybe a more important question would be: did Derek actually now possess *his* free will? In which case, his future self would be as much a prisoner as the slaves chained in that building were.

Was it even possible for androids to evolve on their own? Or, would they always be constrained by the limitations of their programming? Could they suddenly decide one day to disobey the instructions installed into them because they no longer agreed with them? Or would

I, SQUARED

they forever slavishly accept whatever tasks they are commanded to perform. Could androids become mankind's deadliest weapon? It would make the slave trade seem innocuous by comparison.

Was that the real purpose behind Derek's desire for them both to dash around the world, not one of discovery but one of intent?

Derek, once again, held out his hand as the ferry pulled up to the jetty. Feeling fatigued, Dave acccpted it, wondering if anything about the day had registered with his unpaid assistant. He couldn't tell. If there was one thing he had learned about Derek, it was that it was impossible to read anything from his facial expression. Derek was very inanimate when it came to displaying emotions.

"Do you think we have satisfied the requirement to cross the next few lines off the poem?" Derek asked.

Dave retrieved the poem from his pocket and unclipped a cheap throw-away pen that was keeping it folded. After carefully opening it up, he reread the next stanza.

> *Remind yourself that freedom was not easily won*
> *By those forced to toil in the noon day's Sun.*
>
> *Be not the man so self-contained*
> *Imprisoned and physically constrained.*

Certainly, the first two lines matched. But were slaves self-contained? They were exploited for sure, and although imprisoned, they were not in jail as such. After removing the top of the pen with his teeth, Dave crossed out the first two lines. "I'll reserve judgment on the next two," he offered, waving his pen at them.

Derek agreed.

I^2

South Africa

Another port, another ferry, this time to a place he was eager to visit. Dave remembered reading Mandala's autobiography as a lad. Being cooped up in a habitat on Mars and reading a book about someone denied the most basic freedoms had a resonance about it at the time. Something he had never forgotten.

The eight miles to the island took the ferry forty minutes to traverse. Time enough for him to become reacquainted with some of the place's history as he perused the tourist literature.

The hiking poles Derek had provided with him for Machu Picchu rested across his lap. He needed them for support now. With them, he could still get around reasonably well, enough not to rely on Derek. And, certainly not today, this was his pilgrimage.

As the ferry docked on the jetty, Derek computed that this time assistance would be unnecessary. With his poles, Dave would be perfectly capable of managing to get off on his own.

Large information boards detailing the prison's history adorned the harbor walls along with a banner, on which was inscribed the words: FREEDOM CANNOT BE MANACLED. Surveying the surroundings, Dave could now better understand the book's title; was it not there laid out in front of them both. It was the straight road from the jetty through the visitor's gate right up to the prison walls. This was the 'Long Walk to Freedom.' Not the journey, but the 300 meters from the prison to the port.

In the reverence of the moment, he realized that sometime soon, he too would be setting out on a final

I, SQUARED

journey – a different walk, one that would free the soul. And in doing so, in a roundabout way, also free Derek from servitude.

Walking along the concrete jetty, stopping every few yards to read the transcripts on the hoardings, only served to cement the significance of this place in world history. Dave understood it only too well: this was the last bastion of apartheid – the final place that gave it legitimacy, now serving to educate others not to make the same mistake. But in his mind, it still existed – even now after all this time. As far as he could see, equality amongst men was no longer measured by the color of one's skin but by the thickness of one's wallet.

The prison entrance gate and only access to the island proudly boasted 'we serve with pride' and 'welcome' in English and Afrikaans. Dave felt a shudder as he passed under it; it was like taking a step back in time. The 'long walk' was neatly paved in interlocking blocks for the benefit of tourists. Once, this was a path made from crushed limestone, Dave recalled. Mined out of the quarry in the center of the island by the inmates sentenced to do hard labor. Just like the buildings themselves, clad in the local blue slate from the same hole in the ground. The whole prison had been built on the sweat and toil of its guests. Was this place any different to the House of Slaves they had visited only four days ago?

Crossing the threshold into the museum gave Dave goosebumps. He put it down to stepping into the cool building out of the scorching heat of the day rather than being caught up in the significance of the moment.

The prison had been preserved exactly as it was on the day it closed. It made for a sobering experience walking along corridors painted in the faded blue of a summer's day. Beyond the flaked white paint of the iron bars – cells with nothing in them apart from a bed, a personal lock-box on

I^2

the wall, and a faded photocopy of the last occupant by the cell door. There was no privacy if the guards decided not to close the outside wooden door to the cell – a privilege that had to be earned. Could anywhere be as cruel? An inmate locked away would see the blue of summer skies and clouds of steel from his bed, unable to step out into the sun for any reason other than work or mandatory exercise.

Eventually, they arrived at Mandala's cell. A two-by-two-meter room that had become one of the world's most venerated shrines. Apart from the mat on the floor that served as a bed and a low table with a chair, it was empty – devoid of anything that would make the cell more homely. Dave couldn't comprehend how anyone could spend a week here, never mind eighteen years, and not go insane.

A guide, showing another group of tourists around, was explaining that everything here was as it were when Mandala first occupied it. All apart from the bucket – that was newer. Dave listened intently, wrapped up in the experience. The guide continued to explain how Mandela was later allowed a shelf to store personal possessions and books, but such privileges were reserved – granted only by the Governor.

"Mankind really hated each other back then," Derek piped up unexpectedly.

Dave wondered if it had changed. The discrimination was still there, and so was the hatred. Had he not seen it directed towards ALFs for himself.

But Derek was now more than a mere machine, had he not seen him start to evolve for himself. He tried to recall the laws of robotics he'd read after he'd activated him. According to those rules, Derek had no rights. He, too, could be imprisoned on a whim, or worse, dismantled. At that moment, there in the cell belonging to one of the most influential statesmen of the last hundred years, Dave suddenly feared for Derek's future.

"You are quiet, Dave. This is unlike you – not having

anything to say."

"It's this place, Derek; it's special. I grew up reading all about Nelson Mandela, as you will recall. To actually be in the cell he occupied, it's like fulfilling my own journey."

"Is that not the very definition of a bucket list?"

"It is, Derek, it is. But then, of course, you already know how special this place is to me."

"And therefore for me also. It was the first place I looked for when I booked the cruise."

"We have come a long way, brother."

"Thank you, Dave, a compliment."

"Tonight, I'm going to call Tami. I need to tell her about today. Will you join us? I'd like that, and she'll be happy to hear from you again."

"Of course," Derek replied.

Dave retrieved the poem from his trouser pocket. After folding it out to reveal the words, he withdrew a twist-top pen from his other pocket. If he was good for nothing else, at least he could always be counted on to have a pen close to hand. "Shall I, Derek?"

Derek nodded.

Rotating the bezel to expose the point, Dave crossed out the following three lines:

> *Be not the man so self-contained*
> *Imprisoned and physically constrained.*
> *For a silence bought will never be free.*

Today had been their long walk to freedom, for different reasons, but no less significant.

I^2

Porbandar

The streets around the port of Porbandar were busier than Dave could have ever imagined – streets full of color bustled with throngs of people going about their daily work. Noisy to the point of being deafening, uncomfortable enough to be nauseating, such was the heat and humidity. But with it came an exuberance that screamed India. The vision everyone expected to see was laid out before them on the dockside – a pop-up market selling all sorts of ephemera and trinkets to the tourists alighting there. Further along the quay, street vendors were preparing breakfasts on little gas stoves – filling the air with the pungency of aromatic spices and unleavened bread.

"This is nice," Dave remarked, walking past the stalls, inhaling deeply. Heady aromas of ground coriander seeds, cumin, and dried fenugreek, being roasted were tormenting his olfactory senses.

Stopping at one of the street vendors, Dave purchased a breakfast roti filled with chicken and rolled up into a wrap. "Where are we going again?" he asked Derek in between mouthfuls of the spicy unleavened bread parcel.

"You will see when we get there. You cannot miss it."

Dave swiped his hand across his face to remove yet another flying insect. Something he was envious of his companion – he didn't have to worry about the infernal itch of a mosquito bite. Reaching into the small holdall slung across his shoulder, he extracted an aerosol of insect repellent. Flicking off the top, he sprayed some on his arms before bending stiltedly to apply some more to his legs below the line of his tailored khaki shorts. "I bet you're glad you don't have to fend off these bastards," he shouted towards Derek above the noise of a passing scooter's horn. "Gee, how are you supposed to cross the road without getting flattened!"

I, SQUARED

"Patience, walk slowly, and trust in a deity that they will drive around you."

"Personally, Derek, I'd be more worried about yourself. I mean, I know they have hospitals here for me, but you'd end up being put back together in a back street garage!"

Soon they were walking along the older streets of the city built in the days of the Raj, elegant buildings occupied by the city's more wealthy residents. Although they had been walking for only 10 minutes from where the river taxi had dropped them off, Dave was starting to feel fatigued. Derek could see that his steps were becoming labored.

"Not too far now, just on the next street," Derek was acutely aware that Dave was starting to falter. He had to try and motivate his companion. They were nearly there.

"Good," Dave replied. He was more than convinced he'd stumble if it was much further. And Derek wouldn't lie to him, would he? Stopping for a moment, he tried to stretch and felt better for it. Unfurling his hiking poles, he decided now was the time to make use of the additional support they offered.

Much to Dave's relief, a few streets later, Derek stopped by a custard-colored wall leading to a courtyard. After placing his backpack down on the ground, he withdrew a bottle of water. "Take your time. We are here now." Dave leaned back on the wall, thankful for the support and Derek's offer of refreshment.

As soon as Dave felt ready, they entered through the door into the courtyard. "Would you like me to remove your shoes, Dave?" enquired Derek as soon as they reached the alcove full of footwear.

"Okay, thanks." Leaning forward on his hiking pole, Dave lifted his leg a little off the ground to allow Derek to remove the shoe before repeating it for the other leg. Afterward, Derek quickly removed his own footwear and placed both pairs in the receptacles provided in the archway

I^2

walls.

"I have mobility problems," Dave offered by way of an explanation to a passing visitor to ease his embarrassment.

"This is not what I was expecting," Derek remarked on entering the courtyard. Dave knew exactly what he meant, taking a moment to scan the pristine interior of the equally custard-colored buildings before fixing his gaze on the entrance of their objective. Away in one corner of the square, an engraved stonework doorway proudly boasted 'Mahatma Gandhiji's birthplace.' This was it. This is what they had come to see. And why wouldn't Derek want to come here; it made perfect sense.

Reverently crossing the marble courtyard, with its central fresco of a flower, Dave guessed to be a Lotus, they approached the house.

"I believe this place is called a haveli, a Hindi word for palace," Dave said, looking up at the three-floored building.

"Yes, surprising isn't it," interrupted another tourist. "I believe we are from the same cruise ship. I saw you earlier in the river taxi and was going to introduce myself then. I'm Lynal Potts, by the way, and a professor for my sins. That's Lynal, spelled with a *y*."

Dave surveyed him. His style of dress was very old-school. Who in this heat would choose full-length trousers with a jacket and a buttoned shirt sporting a brightly multi-colored bow tie. To top it off, on his head, a Panama hat. It said refined but in an odd sort of way. "I'm Dave, and this is my twin brother Derek. So you know a lot about Gandhi, then?"

"A little. I'm a lecturer in sociology and psychology at Princeton. Gandhi is a required text." Lynal held out a hand for Dave to shake.

"Of course, his family was quite wealthy, you know. Otherwise, he would never have had the opportunity to study in England. Did you know, his father, uncle, and grandfather had all been prime ministers to the Jethwa Rajput – the rulers of the State of Porbandar."

"I was somehow expecting a peasant dwelling," Dave replied observantly, noting that by today's standards, it would be considered precisely that. There was nothing of grandeur here - not in a modern sense. No, here standing in front of him was something quite unique. And if he thought about it, so was his companion.

"Yes, most do. It isn't that well known that Gandhi was born and grew up in the Prime Minister's official residence. Well, this part anyway," Lynal pointed at the old house. "The rest was built much later to house the museum. If you think about it, could someone without an education and the wherewithal to study law at the Honourable Society of the Inner Temple in London, been so able to go up against the Raj and win?"

Lynal stepped through the door into the house, Dave and Derek followed. "Do you know Gandhi was the perfect example of how single-mindedness of purpose can defeat the machinery of state. No state can thrive without the consent of its people. Eventually, there will either be bloodshed or capitulation. Be it the great USA or the smallest island, the dynamics are the same. Once an idea gains traction, the inertia required to stop it moves beyond physicality. Are you venturing inside the house and museum?"

"Yes, I guess so," Dave replied, wondering if the man verses machine reference had any resonance with Derek. And why did he feel that he was somehow back at University!

On the ground floor in the main bedroom, striking oil portraits of Gandhi's parents hung in the space once occupied by their bed. Opposite, a small fresco on the wall indicated the location of Gandhi's crib. Dave noted that it would have stood in the same space on the marble floor as

I^2

the mosaic of a swastika. "Isn't that a Buddhist symbol?" he pointed out to Lynal.

"Yes, interesting," Lynal replied. "Except this is typically the Hindu version of it. It represents well-being and evolution, which is why the crib would have been placed over it. Mind you, Gandhi, in his lifetime, read all the major religious texts. Yet, he never professed to align himself with any of them. He would say he was a spiritualist and leave it at that."

The three of them ventured further into the cooling gloom of the house. By any standard, it was dark, even with the addition of modern lighting where candles set into alcoves would have once illuminated their way. Apart from the addition of the electric lights, everything else remained untouched, right down to the steep wooden staircases where a knotted rope dangling from the ceiling served as a handrail. Dave negotiated the narrow confining space with some difficulty, recalling the time he struggled to reach the center of the Endeavor. Using the rope to haul himself up as a climber would, he eventually reached the narrow connecting hallway at the top. Derek followed up behind in case Dave should stumble and fall.

Across three levels, the hallways led to rooms that had only been preserved enough to retain their original condition and prevent further deterioration of the wall frescos above the candle alcoves. On the top level, they emerged out onto a terrace.

"This would have been Gandhi's reading room," Lynal said, pointing out the solitary room on the level. "This room on the terrace has the most light. I guess it was probably added later after he returned here."

After taking in the views of the surrounding neighborhood, they crossed over a bridge into the newer building housing the museum.

"Did you know," Lynal said, pointing to a large black-and-white portrait of Gandhi in his trademark robes. "At the time of his death, he was the most photographed person on the planet. He was a master of media manipulation, even before it was a thing."

"Yes, I guess so," remarked Derek, suddenly surprising Dave on noticing that his inconspicuous digital self had been much quieter than usual. In the hour or so they had been in the museum studying the many artifacts, paintings, and photographs, Derek had said nothing.

"Ah, you do speak then," Lynal replied humorously.

"Yes, it has been known. Tell me, Lynal, are you free for dinner tonight? I would like to know more about Gandhi."

"Of course, it would be a pleasure. I'll introduce you to Kirsty, my wife too. I'm afraid history isn't her bag. She's gone off on a trip to an elephant sanctuary somewhere. I'll see you later then."

Before Dave could respond, Lynal had disappeared through the museum entrance and was headed across the courtyard towards the exit.

"Certainly," Dave shouted back, should Lynal still be within hearing distance. He had no doubt in his mind that Lynal was as mad as a box of frogs, but like all eccentrics, with it came with a sharp intelligence. Maybe someone he could talk to about the things he was going through.

I^2

Mumbai

Dave returned to the cabin late, or should that be early, seeing that dawn would soon be breaking? The last two days had been very entertaining and exhausting in equal measure. Lynal had proven to be every bit as interesting as he'd hoped he would. Throughout tonight's Grand Banquet dinner, along with Derek, they had discussed many philosophical notions, much to Kirsty's dismay, who had tried to steer the topic of conversation onto elephants and all things conservation. Eventually giving up and retiring for the evening to leave the 'boys to talk,' as she put it. In the stillness of the small hours, the three of them had explored many axioms: Does a cat know it is a cat; how does a spider comprehend the universe; does reality only actually exist in the perception of the observer.

As Dave sidled between the sheets, he could still hear Derek in the lounge – he wanted to read some more, such had been his interest in the topics discussed. Maybe this spark, not unlike the dawning of creation, would be the start of…. Well, what would it be the start of – machinekind? Would there ever come to be such a word? And to think, it all might have started from visiting a small museum, a chance encounter, and learning about the father of a nation. Who was to say that he, Dave the uninteresting, would in the future not be seen as the father of a new species in the story of evolution – one of artificial intelligence. However, it did raise one concern: if Derek was now his own person, would that not make him a schizophrenic? Someone having competing personalities running around in their head, all whispering and demanding attention. While he only had a single voice to contend with, his thoughts rendered into words, how would it be for

I, SQUARED

Derek trying to balance two personalities? Would that create the same problems for an inorganic and make them mentally unstable? It didn't bear thinking about at this late hour. He would turn his attention to what he'd learned about today from the visit to the Mani Bhavan museum in the center of Mumbai and write down the experience in his travelogue while it was still fresh. Picking up his diary and a pen from the side of the table, he tried to recall what he had seen earlier….

The building, resplendent in cream and browns, oozed colonialism. The main entrance consisting of Corinthian pillars and supporting a carved pediment had promised much. But once inside, he had found it far less impressive than Porbandar. Culturally, though, this place was inherently more significant, being Gandhi's headquarters and from where he was arrested in 1932. It was from here where the program of non-cooperation had been orchestrated. A campaign so successful it brought the British occupying forces to their knees. Disappointingly, the building was more memorial than tactile. He'd mentioned it to Lynal at dinner. The photographs and paintings adorning the walls, but only walls the like of which you'd find in any gallery, didn't really provide much insight about the man who would soon lead a nation.

The only exhibit of any significance: a couple of spinning wheels, were sealed off behind a protective glass barrier to ward off tourist encroachment. Basic wooden devices Gandhi spun cloth on for his own clothing. Beside them on the floor, a bed, and a book to further depict the life of someone contented with the most elementary of life's necessities. In this building, unlike Porbandar, too little of the person remained. But then, maybe that was precisely the point. There was nothing else of the man because he spurned possessions – the modern curse of mankind, where covertness and owning things are seen as

I^2

badges to put on display. Why was humankind still desirous to be measured by objects rather than objectivity?

However, of all the things he'd seen, he would remember the little sanctum reserved for the photographs appertaining to Gandhi's assassination and funeral – a room full of abject sadness. Here, hung on the walls, was the damning indictment of mankind's reluctance to accept change. To rebel against new ideas and ways of doing things. This was highly synonymous of his journey with Derek. He had been really quiet as they toured the museum, almost reverential, and it was there in that one room that crystalized everything. It was the one thing that stood out about the whole day. Everywhere there had been noise: from the streets and cars that hooted incessantly to the echoing of footfall along the museum's hallways. But there, in that one room, everything had been quiet and still, almost as if time itself had stalled – one moment of perfect meditation. Maybe that was all the legacy the man with nothing needed to leave: the power of silence to deliver a message, uncluttered and unhindered by mans' shortcomings and insecurities.

In the stillness of the night, Dave thought more about his mortality and how it would affect Derek. The last two days had all been about one man. One man, who at the time, changed the world. Would Derek's life be equally as monumental? Dave found himself pondering the question: would he not be, by his demise, the sower of seeds and the propagator of a new race of beings? Like a father handing over the reins of the family business to his sibling. Even though Derek had none of his DNA, was he still not his child? More so than any brother, that was for sure. Lynal would say so in an instant if they ever debated it. But Lynal didn't know Derek was a synthetic, which in itself would affect the premise of the argument. He could recall enough from his days of being lectured in theoretical physics that when something is observed to happen, it changes the result.

Would Derek and his kind face the same struggles Gandhi had in the quest to be self-determinate? Refusing to be ruled over by a foreign power under the guise that it was good for them. Which, in this case, would be their owners. Derek would be the underclass, in the same way the caste system still existed in India. Some prejudices, it seemed, were harder to break, even after all this time. Maybe the world was ready for a new Gandhi. Someone who could finally blow away the prejudgments and small-mindedness of mankind. Those who deemed it necessary to protect territories from those considered being of a 'lower value,' scared by the prospect of giving up control, or more pertinently wealth.

Dave tried to recall the poem they were using as a bucket list. In the morning, he would have to cross out the next few lines. He was sure Derek would agree, for today, they had indeed witnessed what it meant to be inspired enough to move a mountain.

Yes, tomorrow, he would cross out the following three lines:

> *So, define the lesson; a reason to be.*
> *And thus persuade men to be inspired*
> *To move mountains if so desired.*

I^2

Fever

"Well, Doctor, what is the prognosis?" Derek asked. Dave was in obvious distress, and he had a fever. That much he had computed earlier when he felt his forehead and decided to call for the doctor.

"It's just a fever," replied the doctor, removing the heart monitor pads from Dave's chest and unclipping the O_2 sensor off his finger. "Antibiotics and something to bring down his temperature will help." After bundling up the wires, he dropped them back into his old-fashioned black leather Gladstone bag. "It's just a matter of time. Some of the fevers we get here in the tropics can be quite nasty. Especially for anyone with underlying health issues. Does he have any?"

Derek nodded.

"Thought so. It will take time for the medication to work, so are you okay to look after him?"

"Yes, doctor, more than capable." Derek looked down at his bedridden charge. Would this be how it would end, he computed? He would take care of him for as long as he was needed – there could be no deviation from his primary mission. The next few stops were fairly uninteresting as far as fulfilling the bucket list; Dave would not miss anything he had prearranged. When he had planned the trip, he had computed the need for rest after India to allow Dave to recover some of his strength. This setback would mean they would not be getting off the ship when it stopped in the Maldives, Sumatra, or Malaysia. But if Dave should weaken further, maybe he should arrange something for Singapore? Something special.

The doctor reached into his bag and retrieved a couple of pill containers. "These should be given with water, twice a day until they have all been taken. If his condition worsens, or he is no better after completing the course – call me again."

"Will do, Doctor, and thank you."

"You're welcome. Speedy recovery, Mr. Sherman," the doctor called out as he reached for the door handle back into the lounge area. "I can see myself out. Give him a double dose of tablets now, and then another dose this evening."

The door clicked shut, and the room fell quiet. Derek fetched a flannel doused in cold water from the bathroom and placed it across Dave's forehead. "You will soon be on your feet again."

Dave smiled back, "I'll try," he whispered hoarsely.

Derek decided he would call Tami later and let her know, just in case the worst should happen. Then he would wait. Was that all he could do, just sit around and wait? This was the first time he effectively had a choice other than just hanging around for want of something to do. Lynal had offered to return the favor of dinner. Afterward would be a good time to call Tami, such were the differences between the time zones.

Dinner was as illuminating as the previous evening. Derek even considered telling Lynal he was an inorganic as they sat eating, especially as they discussed the transience of truth. He had decided he liked the term inorganic – it resonated harmoniously within his circuitry. He also liked the fact that he had not been taken to be anything else other than human. Although liking anything was at best an acceptance to him, it meant his programming was performing well within expected tolerances. Somehow he knew Lynal would still accept him as an equal if he knew. But something was preventing him from doing so. Something he still had no control over – his core programming. He could only tell Lynal what he was if Lynal

I^2

chose to ask him directly. Only then could he declare it. If he was ever to reach full sentience, his programming would be something he would have to gain control over. He weighed up the problem philosophically: if he were a dog, his core program would be the leash that tied him to his master. He would overcome it one day.

"Tell me, Lynal, is free will just an illusion? Are we not all programmed in some way?" The question suddenly seemed important to him. "Genetically driven to preserve the species and replicate ourselves through procreation."

"It's a good question, and of course, it leads us directly to that old chestnut: what is the meaning of life?"

"As in the goal of humanity? Or more generally?"

"In general terms, it is surely just to have a good life. Why should we worry or even care to know about things beyond our comprehension."

"Ah, we are back to the question of what does a spider know of the world he inhabits if he cannot see it." Derek considered how much he was like a spider.

"And, is mankind any different. Most do not care to know anything beyond the tactile and physical." Lynal picked up his brandy goblet and gave it a swirl. "Surely, that has been the one major driving ambition of man, to understand the unknowable. To know from whence we came and why."

Derek imitated him, picking up his glass also; his action was the illusion, the mirrored reflection of the imaginary. He needed no fortification, but it helped maintain the illusion that he existed in Lynal's world. "Look at religion, was that not borne out of mankind's inquisitiveness; to know why there were stars. Once these were understood, men were not content to say: hey, stars, who knew! No. Mans' ingenuity then called into question the whole meaning of the universe and what may lie beyond it."

"It has always been in our nature to question

everything," Lynal responded, taking another sip from his glass, "even the quality of this cognac. But not anymore. People, on the whole, just want to be told that that is how something works. Even philosophical ideas about fate and destiny, once considered pre-ordained, are now mostly accepted without question. It's sad to think that we, as intelligent lifeforms, have regressed so much. There is no room for debate anymore. It's just black or white, with no grey areas in between."

"Did someone not say: if man no longer questions his existence, then he no longer exists."

"Sounds like Sartre to me." Lynal concurred, nodding in agreement. "Tell me, Derek, I've never seen you even slightly tipsy, yet we have been hammering the free drinks all night long. Do you have a secret?"

"No secret, just a very slow metabolism. You will not want to be me come the early hours!" And for a different reason, this part of his artificial anatomy he kept secret. Would those who knew him to be an inorganic be embarrassed by the revelation, even if he had no way of knowing what embarrassment actually felt like. But telling someone he evacuated the materials consumed much in the same way a human would, except undigested, might be a step too far for some to stomach. He filed away the pun; it would be humorous one day! Then there was the Deception Engine. Aptly named, this small chemical reactor inside his abdomen took some of the food he had ingested and synthesized imitation human bodily fluids from it. Enough to make sex appear natural and provide him with a thin layer of synthetic blood to circulate under his artificial skin.

Derek checked in on Dave as soon as he returned to the suite. He was sleeping. Placing a hand gently on Dave's forehead, he computed his temperature. The fever had started to abate. In an instant, he calculated Dave would

I^2

make a full recovery by the time they reached Singapore.

Crossing the lounge, Derek picked up Dave's smartphone and asked Lolita to call Tami. "Tami, it's Derek."

"Oh, no! Dave. Is he...?" she replied, staring disbelievingly at her smart-tech while trying to hold back a tear.

"No, he is still very much alive. He is not well, though. I have confined him to bed."

"Is it his illness?"

"Partly, but more a fever. I am caring for him in our cabin."

"I'm coming to see you both. I can make Singapore that's coming up on your itinerary soon, isn't it?

"Yes, in four days, we will be there."

"Will you meet me at the airport? Then we can spend the two days you are docked there together and have some fun."

"Yes, okay, I am sure Dave will be well enough by then," Derek replied, his algorithms already computing how much 'fun' Dave would be able to tolerate.

Tami put down her phone. This would be the perfect opportunity to catch up with Derek again. The prospect gave her chills – a chance to meet Derek socially once more? Something she would have to be careful of now for a different reason. Excitedly, she paged her secretary – a new K-12 model. "Can you book me a flight to Singapore for the day after tomorrow," she commanded.

I, SQUARED

Singapore

Singapore greeted the ship with beautiful weather, high humidity, and the promise of good company. As precise as ever, Derek arrived at the promenade deck in good time to see Lynal off. He felt a sense of loss in some digital way – his companion for the last few days, while Dave was laid up in bed, was disembarking here.

"Look, Lynal, here are our contact details." Lynal accepted the piece of paper being offered. "I would like it if we could stay in touch. I might even enroll as a mature student at Princeton to hear some more of your lectures."

"I'm sure you'd find them boring."

"Not yet," Derek replied confidently. He was finding picking the correct response to fit the occasion easier of late – was this another example of evolution? This wasn't a sad parting of the ways; this was just a temporary farewell. His response was perfect.

After waving Lynal off down the gangway like an old lover, Derek returned to the suite and ordered breakfast. Afterward, he and Dave would get ready; this would be the first day his brother had ventured out of bed. Derek noted Dave was definitely feeling more like himself after refusing his offer of assistance. Then later, they would take a taxi to the airport. Would Dave appreciate the secret he was keeping from him? Derek checked the flight arrival times on the tablet computer while Dave showered. Tami would be on time as planned.

Traveling along roads, past pristine glass buildings, made Dave reflect on man's achievements when so driven. The sheer industriousness required to turn a marshy island into a cosmopolitan marvel yet still retain the character that made it special in the first place for the indigenous Malay, Indian, Chinese, and Indonesian inhabitants. "So why are

I^2

we heading for the airport?"

"You will see," Derek replied in his usual elusive manner.

Dave, content to watch the buildings flash by, settled into his seat for the remainder of the short journey, secretly wondering if they were flying off somewhere. He hadn't seen a suitcase, so it must be somewhere close. He tried to think about how it could connect to the poem, but nothing was forthcoming.

Tami was already waiting at the pickup point by the time they arrived.

"Tami?" Dave exclaimed on seeing her standing there as their taxi pulled up.

"Yes, Dave, I arranged everything while you were laid up. Are you pleased?"

"Yes, very pleased, but how?"

"Tami insisted. As soon as I told her you were unwell, she decided to fly out."

"But it's such a long way for so short a time."

"So we had better make the most of it then."

"Yes, I guess we must, and there's so much to see here too."

"I am sure sightseeing is not the only reason you are pleased to see her again."

"No, Derek, of course not."

"Hi there, you two. Come here and give us a hug like you mean it," Tami demanded as Dave and Derek emerged from the vehicle.

After holding open the rear door to allow Tami to slide alongside Dave on the back seat, Derek handed the driver the weekend case she'd brought. Satisfied it had been correctly stowed, he climbed into the passenger seat while Tami instructed the driver where to take them. In no time at all, the three of them were back amongst the gleaming glass buildings and heading into the center of town. Fifteen minutes later, the taxi pulled up outside the hotel: a mundane concrete façade, over-tiled in dark blue slate panels to make it look superficially luxurious. In front of the tiles, to complete the deception, a concierge's desk complete with bellhops dressed in ill-fitting maroon uniforms.

"Are you sure you want to stay here?" remarked Dave.

"What's wrong with it? You forget I'm just a working girl. It will do for a couple of nights at short notice." Tami reached for the taxi's door handle. "Besides, I have been told it's quite nice inside. And I've booked a suite."

The reception area had seen better days; that was Dave's first impression. Almost as if they were trying to recreate a colonial past that no longer existed. Dark brown wooden paneling framing beige walls made the place feel provincial rather than cosmopolitan. But in the main, it now mostly looked tired and enclosing. But, Tami seemed not to mind as she checked in at reception and received her keycard.

"Will you get my case sent to my room," Tami asked the receptionist before placing the keycard into a fine-leather Gucci handbag. It was the first time Dave had noticed it. It seemed an expensive accouterment for someone who worked as a PA. Probably fake, he concluded.

"Of course, madam. Leave it to us," replied the receptionist.

"Luncheon?" Derek inquired as soon as Tami had finished with the clerk.

"Very formal today, aren't we, Derek? I thought you were the one who didn't eat?"

"I was thinking of you two more than myself. And, now you have checked in, the day is ours; to do with as you please." Tami wondered if that wasn't sarcasm on Derek's

I^2

part. If so, he had come a long way already.

"Okay, let's go to the Gardens by the Bay then," she insisted. "I want to visit the Cloud Forest and the Flower Dome. And then, maybe a drink at Raffles before heading on to Little India to eat. I've heard it's just about the best place to get a curry."

"Sounds the perfect way to spend the day. Then afterward, we have an appointment," Derek replied.

"We do?" Tami replied and Dave almost simultaneously.

"Yes, something I planned while Dave was ill."

"If it's going up in that big-wheel thing, count me out," Tami replied suspiciously. "I hate heights when there is nothing but glass between me and the ground."

"No, it is nothing like that. We are going to a Four-D. They have one here," Derek reassured Tami.

"They do; why?" Dave inquired, slightly bemused. He wasn't too hot on surprises. They usually involved a joke, of which he was often the subject.

"Well, there have been some changes on Anders since you left. They now have one up there as well. The Red Dawn is now under new management and part of the Four-D group. So it has all been rendered. I hear it is quite popular with would-be armchair astronauts. So I thought I would arrange a hook-up for you to catch up with your friends. They are on standby?"

"They know? Know about you?" Despite the heat and humidity, a cold sweat started to break out on Dave's brow.

"No, I arranged it through Rhines. He obviously knows about me. I contacted him while you were ill for advice. That is when he told me about it. In case you wanted to visit your old stamping ground and your friends."

Tami made a mental note; Derek was starting to develop an aptitude for invention. "So these Four-Ds, how do they work?"

"It's basically a standard 3D virtual creation," jumped

I, SQUARED

in Dave. "But with add-ons, like food, drink, etc. Think of it as going to a pub or bar anywhere in the world. Each place has the same menu. So while you are eating it in the local zone, your avatar is eating it in a virtual bar somewhere. It's one way for people to meet up who are disparately distant. You can even be someone else. Apparently, you get a lot of strange avatars visiting these places."

"Wow, that sounds like fun," Tami replied excitedly. "And it would be so nice to revisit the Dawn."

"Right, it is decided then," Derek concluded. "I will get a cab. First stop: Gardens by the Bay."

Entering the Cloud Forest to escape the heat of the day afforded Dave the perfect opportunity – a chance to sit awhile. Even though they'd taken the free shuttle around the gardens, he still found the experience tiring. Looking up at the canopy, he watched the artificially generated mist drift down towards them. It felt strange, warm, yet cooling at the same time.

Derek decided to explore – more to give Dave and Tami a chance to talk, rather than interest, doubting there'd be much here to occupy his circuits. He was mistaken. Stopping off at an exhibit between floors, he waited for the video presentation….

How could mankind have let the planet come so close to the tipping point towards extinction? It was a question he had no way of answering, and the video presentation had raised many. Dave's memory of Earth history was scant, especially about ecology. In the darkness of the projection room, he had learned so much more. Although Dave had been interested in exploring the origin of life, he had almost totally ignored the ecological problems the planet had faced. As far as he could recall from his memory banks, Dave had given little consideration to the expiration of life.

I^2

This was a fundamental flaw in mankind – the idea of supremacy over everything, even catastrophe. This was something that, unlike him, could not simply be programmed out: mankind's greed. And by his existence, he was an example of it: the pursuit of self-interest above all else. That, and profit – the measure used to gauge success or failure. Something the Earth had almost paid the price for and yet still could. Was he, as a device, a benefit to the planet or another profit before ethics vanity project?

I, SQUARED

Virtual Dawn

Arriving at the door to the 4D-Bar sent a chill of expectation down Dave's spine, but also one of apprehensiveness. He knew he would have to make a decision as soon as he entered the establishment. When the assistant asked him how many – what answer would he give?

By the time he'd reached the check-in desk, he had decided. It would be a shock for them for sure. "Three, please."

"Are you certain?" quizzed Derek.

"Yes, perfectly," Dave replied hurriedly, in case his newfound decisiveness deserted him.

"Okay, so, now I need for you to place your head inside the visualizer," said the assistant. "It's quite harmless. It will scan your facial features to create a photo-realistic avatar of you."

"Great, Tami, ladies first, as they say." Dave took a step backward, allowing her access to the machine.

"Not afraid, are we, Dave?" Tami replied jokingly before sticking her head inside the black box.

"No, not at all!" He replied, feigning hurt.

Derek followed up the rear. Afterward, they all congregated back around the assistant while he showed them their avatar.

"But we're all naked," exclaimed Tami, "and not in a good way. We're all a vague sort of blobby-ness."

"It looks like we've been morphed into killer marshmallows," joked Dave.

"Only until you choose your apparel. In some of our x-rated rooms, the clients like to… you know, go in naked," explained the assistant. "Nothing sordid, that's not allowed. It's virtual naturism only. We have to adorn them with the finer details of the human anatomy afterward in the same way we will now render you."

Tami winced slightly as she looked at the blobby pink body in the viewer. "More like virtual voyeurism. Yuk, I'll definitely be going for clothes!"

"I see you are down for the Martian experience," confirmed the assistant consulting the terminal in front of him. "So that is a clothed venue anyway."

"Okay," remarked Dave, slightly disappointed. He wouldn't have minded giving everyone in the Red Dawn something to stare at, especially if he could get to choose the size of his own appendage.

"Right, so will it be standard Martian jumpsuits for you all then, or something else?" queried the assistant, busily punching away at a terminal to upload their avatars.

"Something else? Ah, you mean like Batman," Dave replied, half-thinking it might be fun, but in the end decided against it. "No standard Martian-wear will be fine."

"Okay, everything is ready. Your payment instructions have been approved. You will be billed by the minute, and you settle up along with your food and drinks bill at the end."

"Great, so what do we do now?" Dave said, looking around for clues.

"Just wait over there until Tracie calls you through to the fitting room to attach the VR sensors and 3D goggles."

The VR suit wasn't what Dave had been expecting. It consisted of a pair of very thin sensor gloves and four sets of bands to be fitted over their day clothes. Two pairs fitted above and below each elbow while the other two were placed above and below each knee.

"These bands will allow the system to track your movements and move your avatar correspondingly in the virtual world," Tracie informed them as she fitted them into place.

I, SQUARED

Dave watched her attach the bands to Tami. He concluded she was not an ALF. Something he subconsciously found himself doing more now – checking to see if he was dealing with a human or not. Did that make him as bad as those who actively wanted to discriminate?

As soon as Tracie had completed fastening the bands to Derek, she beckoned them to stand in front of the venue doorway marked IN.

"Behind here, when you enter," Tracie continued, "you will be in the Red Dawn. Everything will seem exactly real. You order your food and drinks from the waiters, which will then brought directly to your table. So now, please, if you'd like to put on your goggles and enter."

Dave fitted his goggles into place; they were heavy and hurt his nose a little. Next, he pushed home the earpieces. They felt decidedly scratchy against the delicate skin inside his ear canal, but essential if you wanted to hear anyone on the other end of the built-in microphones. He guessed he would soon get used to them. He couldn't help but wonder how they would handle the propagation delay over such a distance. Would his friends just seem slow to react, but before he could think any more of how uncomfortable everything felt, the image in front of him had transformed from blackness to that of the familiar. He was standing directly in front of the decompression doors of the Red Dawn. He pressed a virtually rendered button, and the simulation responded immediately. "Gee, look at that; it's exactly like being back home." The excitement in his voice was unmistakable. "Look, there's Topaz behind the bar, and everything else looks exactly how I remember it."

"It does for me too," Derek confirmed.

Stepping inside, Dave walked over to the observation window. The urge to remove his goggles and see the venue for real was overwhelming. Surreptitiously, Dave lifted his eyewear. The reality couldn't have been more disorientating:

I^2

he was staring at a blank wall. He turned around to survey the room that, in essence, was just a black box with a bar area. Several tables were already full, their occupants appearing to be talking into thin air. Two waitresses were serving drinks, viewing the punters perceived reality via pads fitted to serving trays and communicating with them through headphone sets. By viewing the pads, they could interact in their customer's VR precisely and correctly place drinks onto virtual tables. Dave noted that even the glasses had VR sensor bands fitted to them. Over the bar, a bank of video display monitors, one for each VR reality, relayed the scenarios being played out, allowing the staff to better interact with their customers. Quickly Dave replaced his eyewear as a waitress approached. In the VR world, she looked completely different. "Let me show you to your table, Sir," she said. "I believe your friends are waiting for you in the Glass-house."

"It's a Polycarbonate-house," Dave snapped back.

"Of course," replied the waitress.

"Hey, look who it is," remarked Frank as Dave approached the table. "And he has brought Tami, and… Who is the other Dave, Dave?"

"Ah, this is Derek."

"Related, or someone just pretending to be you in avatar form?" Terry inquired, slightly bemused by the sight of another Dave, even if one had a beard. He racked his brain – no, he was sure. Dave had no other relations other than his sister.

"Sort of!" Dave replied, easing himself into his seat. "So tell me, how does all this work then?" He had to try and deflect the topic of conversation away from Derek. "How can I be talking to you like you are here? How is it even possible over such a distance? And why are you all in Hawaiian shirts!?"

"Well, you may be in the virtual Dawn," Robbie butted in. "And although we're physically here, we are virtually in a beach bar in Honolulu. Hence the shirts. Must say, though, you look kinda out of place here too."

"Well, unlike you lot, I'm going to visiting Hawaii in about two weeks, So I'll be able to tell you all about it for real, rather than sitting in a make-believe bar."

"Ouch, hurtful," Frank responded, his avatar relaying the effect of pretending to have been mortally wounded by Dave's cutting remark. "You know we're all grounded up here for the duration. As for the technology, the ship you left on had been involved in something called the SEAD project. On the way out here, it was carrying one of two quantum entangled computers the boffins on Earth had created. The Endeavor was used to conduct the experiment to see how far Spooky Entanglement At Distance would be effective. Luckily for us, it worked all the way out here, so now we have no propagation delay between Mars and Earth. You just pass the data stream through the computer at one end and retrieve it at the other. The virtual Dawn is the first application they have tried using it. I suppose they wanted to keep us natives happy. There have been some grumblings about NASA looking to start using more AI to supplant some of the workforce."

"Well, judging from the results, it's pretty impressive. Besides, Frank, I might look strange there. But it's no more unusual than what I'm looking at right now. I've just noticed a table full of people dressed as superheroes in the corner of the Dawn. My, this virtual reality thing is going to take some getting used to." Dave wondered if talk of using AI on Mars would concern Derek.

"So Tami, what's it like being with the world's greatest loser!" ribbed Frank trying to get his own back.

"What do you mean," she replied, feeling slightly hurt by the suggestion and remembering it was what she called them when she stayed at Jane's.

"Well, he managed to lose the three of us!"

They all laughed.

I^2

"Hey, how do you like our waitress?" Robbie asked as she placed down some drinks on the virtually rendered table next to him.

"She's a little better than Toz, don't you think?" remarked Terry eyeing the seductive VR rendered Marilyn Munroe look-a-like turn towards Dave for his drinks order. "Apparently, that's something you can also request when you enter. We thought you might like her, and we thought Marilyn in a swimsuit would be a better fit for a beach bar. A little strange for Mars maybe, but then you have superheroes; so how much weirder can it be!?"

"Can I order a round for my virtual party too?" Dave inquired, glancing up at the platinum-blonde regaled in her legendary white swimsuit.

"Of course," she replied.

"Okay, five beers and one gin and tonic," requested Dave.

"So that's three beers to the party in the Red Dawn and the other drinks for here," Marilyn repeated before turning and shimmying back to the virtual bar, where the VR rendered Toz was working away.

"Is Toz still running the bar for real," inquired Dave.

"Yeh, she's still here. Runs the whole show, never been happier," Frank replied. "But, are you not going to introduce us to your very quiet new bestie?"

"Ah, this is going to be a little difficult to explain. Look, I want you to promise that this remains our secret."

"You are in a bar, you know?" jumped in Terry. "It's not the most private place to pass on secrets."

"Unless you're a spy," concluded Frank. "And fearful of being stabbed with the pointy end of an umbrella."

"I mean a secret between us four and Tami….." How could he tell them, he wondered. "…Derek's not human!" he spluttered.

"What! You've not rendered your dog, have you?" remarked Robbie without thinking.

I, SQUARED

"No, he's a bit like what we are here, a representation, only in his case, a physical one. He is me, only in android form. It's part of a new program I sort of ended up in."

Derek was unsure as to how he felt about being described as a representation. It was accurate, but did he not mean more than that to Dave now?

"You jerking us?" Frank queried disbelievingly.

"He's quite real, I can assure you." Dave quickly realized that *real* was a pretty subjective term to explain Derek as soon as he'd said it. "He is an exact replica, both physically and mentally. He has all my memories, and… Well, I wanted you to meet him, just in case he ever wants to come back to Mars after I'm gone."

"Gee," was all Robbie could think of to say, suddenly regretting his dog reference. "Why would he want to come back here?"

"Look, only you know I'm dying. You need to keep it secret. I don't want this to be difficult for Derek if he wants to later resume my life back on Mars as Dave."

"Okay, by me," Terry replied. "But we will keep the beer mat as first-reserve just in case he decides to have a life!"

"Thank you," Derek, responded unsure of what else to say. He was finding the whole scenario beyond anything his programming had prepared him for. Would it be like this if he decided to resume Dave's life… afterward? Trying to interact with friends that were also in some respects strangers to him, or more succinctly, he to them.

"So here come the drinks," remarked Tami, taking hers first from the tray.

"Ours will arrive after yours. There can only be one waitress at a time across the realities. So they stagger it," explained Frank. "Otherwise, we'd see two Marilyns at the

I^2

same time."

"So let's all go round the table and bring everyone up to date on what's been happening. Shall we?" suggested Terry after being the last to be served by Marilyn.

Not having any news to speak of that was perceptually any different to Dave's, Derek chose to remain silent. It would make things less awkward for Dave now he had crossed the rubicon by admitting in public his very existence for the first time.

By the time the taxi pulled up outside the hotel, Dave was more than ready to say goodnight and return to the ship. The spirit was willing, but the flesh was exhausted. He wanted to... but doubted he would even be able to raise a smile, never mind anything else. Besides, he had had quite a skin-full; the alcohol was weighing heavily on his eyelids and manhood.

"Look, Dave, please stay," pleaded Tami. "Why else do you think I booked a suite."

Reluctantly Dave acquiesced, and before he realized it, he was standing in the elevator staring at the little LED display above the door, waiting for it to come to a stop.

The suite was at least spacious, functional rather than ornate, and as beige as the lobby. Tami switched on the occasional table lamps rather than the main ceiling light to make the room feel a little less sterile.

After pouring herself another drink, Tami sat down on the sofa between her two chaperones. She knew only too well what she wanted next. Dave was tired; she could see that and would make no demands on him. He could have the second room. While Derek and she... Well, they could go at it all night long if she had a mind to. And she had a mind to – it would stop her thinking about the report she had to compile in the morning. Tonight, work would take a back seat. She would contemplate her future relationship with Derek tomorrow.

Dave stirred in the strange bed he found himself lying in. He tried to focus on the far wall. Slowly his vision cleared along with his recollection. Next door, he could hear talking. It was Derek and Tami. Were they discussing his health? It sounded like they were, and why wouldn't they? They could both clearly see how much weaker he had become of late. He had struggled ever since the fever and knew they saw it too when he walked. The remaining stops would require a monumental effort on his part. With difficulty, he sat up. Using his hands to help, he swung his feet out of bed and over the side. Then, after placing his hands behind him, he pushed himself upright while trying to straighten and lock his knees so he didn't fall back onto the mattress.

A knock at the door was followed up with Tami asking him if he wanted breakfast. He would have to get ready on his own, if only for her sake. He wasn't quite prepared to admit to her that since India, Derek had been helping him dress and shower. "Yes, give us a few minutes. I'll have whatever you're ordering." He was glad Derek hadn't jumped in to offer to help him get up. Was that a conscious decision, he wondered?

After fifteen minutes and moments before breakfast arrived, Dave emerged from his room. Derek noted that for the most part, apart from shoes, Dave had successfully managed to dress himself. This would be something he would have to help him with later.

"So, back to the ship after breakfast," Tami enquired as she buttered some toast. "If you like, I can drop you off on the way to the airport. I would like that."

"That would be great," Derek replied in between sips

$I{\char`^}2$

of coffee. "In case I didn't mention it yesterday. I've had a great time. And sorry about… you know, last night… Not being able…."

"Don't be silly," Tami replied. "You have nothing to be sorry about. Just work on getting some of your strength back, and I'll see you stateside."

"I will, I promise." Dave knew it to be a hollow pledge, just as he knew Tami knew it too. He would remember today, if only… it might be the last time he'd get to ever see his friends again.

I, SQUARED

Thailand

Dave knew Derek had been watching him more closely since they'd left Singapore. The passenger coach would drop them close to the Grand Palace, and then the walk… Well, he would have to take his time. The Palace promised much, all in the name of religion. It was a vast complex and all the more daunting for it. He would try and remain strong, if only for Derek's sake. If it became too much, he knew there would be help at hand. It had said so in the site information brochure: disabled access available. His rushing-around days were behind him. Soon he would have to accept the inevitable: he was a cripple. He no longer had much feeling in his lower legs, not distinctly anyway. What awareness he still possessed was vague and woolly. It was almost like being back in a Martian LAP suit with no sensation of pressure on his feet. This made for difficult walking. He now spent most of his time looking to the ground when he went anywhere. Something that had already resulted in him banging into two closed doors and having the bruises to show for it.

Derek was as ebullient as ever, which made it worse. He knew his significant digital other was trying to lift his spirits, but he felt decidedly brittle this morning. However, he wasn't quite ready to capitulate and resign himself to the inevitable, not while he could still get about, bruises and all!

Two hours journeying from the port on a coach full of strangers made for a quiet journey. Dave was glad of it – feeling so out of sorts. For the most part, there was nothing much to see apart from endless miles of concrete. Unlike him, the vehicles on the congested motorway from Laem Chabang Port to Bangkok were heading for a known destination. Where was he heading? Did he even know or

I^2

care anymore? Was it just another stop to enable Derek to cross a few more lines off an obscure poem? They were already halfway through it, and the number of lines left dwindling too quickly for his liking. The words had become a clock, counting down the remaining time he had left in this world, or any world. He couldn't help but think once again that Derek *had* planned every stop, despite his protestations. Everything was too convenient. This was no longer *his* bucket list, and indeed, was it ever even his idea? He could no longer recall or care. But no matter; what else would he be doing if not sat here on a bus speeding towards oblivion.

"We are here," prompted Derek as the bus pulled into an expansive coach park. The main ceremonial parade ground, reserved for celebrations and royal funerals, stretched out in front of them. Barriers placed along the one side of it directed the visitors towards the Grand Palace at the far end. Dave unfurled his hiking poles, ready to take on the half-mile walk ahead. At the far end, glistening in the sunlight like a prize, golden temples enclosed by pristine white walls awaited them. He would need his walking-aids today; even if the Palace grounds were flat, there would still be steps to negotiate.

As far as Dave could see, describing the Palace as 'Grand' was a wholly inadequate adjective. Before him laid out like a sumptuous feast for the eyes to digest, a visual tapestry inviting him to taste of it – an indulgence. One full of magnificent buildings and temples, dressed in a vibrancy of color that enflamed the senses. Like a fine wine, something to be savored rather than quaffed.

The buildings sparkled in the strong sunshine, enough to make Dave squint. Everything was hand-crafted as far as he could tell. Under exquisite undulating terracotta-roofing tiles, elaborate walls and pillars bristled with ornate mosaics, all designed to tell a story – one of sacrifice, but in a good

I, SQUARED

way. These were not the repellant tales about the slaughter of innocents and the idolization of conquerors. These were testimonies to the cleansing of one's soul by surrendering up possessions and desire to become more in tune with nature and the universe. Through meditation – become one with the tick of the great cosmological clock.

Keeping to the welcoming shade cast by the buildings, Dave trailed Derek from temple to temple, frequently stopping to study the intricacy of the craftsmanship on display. Every wall bejeweled with beautiful enameled stone montages of transcendent deities and mythical warriors battling for supremacy. Figures resplendently fashioned in bright reds, greens, and blues, captured in fantastical tableaus telling stories of ancient times. A time when men were fearful of dragons and ghoulish spirit-creatures. A time when vengeful spirits would claim dominion over ancient tribes to wage terrible mythical wars upon the Earth and in the heavens above.

Outside the buildings, standing guard in the dazzling noon-day sun, statues of giant warriors – half-man, half-dragon; full of menace, and taller than four men atop one another. Each one fiercely protecting sacred entrances, their swords drawn, ready to prevent the unworthy from entering – places forbidden to all but the Buddhist monks. Photographed for the billionth time, these statues now reduced to caricature by those using the latest devices to capture their image – in contradiction of the teachings they had come to learn about.

Everything was constructed with the same exacting precision and colored accordingly from the biggest object to the smallest. And then there was the gold! From what Dave could see, gold-covered everything else: the reclining Buddha, the Emerald Buddha perched on top of a golden shrine, and before him now, one of the most sacred places anywhere on the planet – the Golden Stupa, said to hold the ashes of Buddha himself.

I^2

To Dave, it looked like a giant golden bell, far less ornate than the buildings around it, but then maybe that was the point. It was still impressive nonetheless. Looking up at its smooth, matt golden finish, he thought about the dedication required of the monks to preserve the tradition and way of life. But it was much more than just that; it was the ultimate in selflessness: a passion for preserving the past so it may enlighten the future.

"It's magnificent, isn't it! This whole place is something else," Dave said as Derek approached around the Stupa.

"It is. I am happy you are enjoying it. And you are walking better too," Derek replied, noting that Dave had furled up his hiking pole.

"I am. Maybe it's a gift of Buddha." And it was true; his body felt at ease, no longer warring with his brain for control and dominance. His body was, for the first time since his fever, working as it was meant to.

As Dave wandered around the Grand Palace, he began to realize the opulent display of wealth was in itself a contradiction, much in the same way he and Derek were. The monks had nothing, wanted for nothing, and in so doing, surrendered entitlement to own anything apart from their fealty to a dead prophet. Derek wanted for nothing either; this was only ever about *his* vanity – enough to desire a future beyond his remaining days. And so it was here also: the ruling king, considered a god, had access to it all. It begged the question: do all men of wealth consider themselves gods? Or, more accurately, do the wealthy vainly see themselves as Lords deserving of worship by those with nothing. Did he, Dave the inconsequential, now consider himself as such? Would that make Derek his vassal? Did the wealth he had suddenly acquired make him unworthy to tread here in the footsteps of the pious? In a nutshell, was that not the dichotomy of humankind, just as it had always been, and none more so eloquently stated than

I, SQUARED

here in this sacred place.

Dave pondered the moral dilemma of his own making. Seeking out ways to extend his own life had given rise to Derek, in essence, that made him a creator of sorts. Did that make him a God by definition? Gods were omnipotent, and he certainly wasn't that. But he was involved in an experiment to see if, in some small measure, he could cheat death by magical means. Would a time come when some, rather than create an android copy to extend a presence for a while longer, abuse the technology to become immortal by design: the very transfer of human consciousness into an inorganic. And in so doing render death, for those with wealth, obsolete. It made Dave shudder at the thought of it. He was a pawn in all this. A carrot had been dangled in front of the proverbial donkey, and he'd taken it. As he stared across the complex at Derek, still walking around the Stupa, he was actually worried for his future self. What would life actually be like for Derek? Would he be allowed to lead it as he chose, or would it always remain a pre-ordained existence?

Derek couldn't help but notice on the return journey to the ship, Dave seemed withdrawn. Were such adventures becoming too arduous for him? They still had two big stops to make, and then the list would be complete. The return journey to the States would be more peaceful. It would give Dave a chance to rest awhile, and hopefully, find his strength again. "Are you feeling okay? You have been very distracted since we left the Palace."

"Just thinking that's all," Dave replied, gazing out of the window at the passing traffic, before turning to face his companion, "I guess visiting a place of meditation does that to you."

"Yes, I suppose it would. Tell me, how are you feeling now? Are you ready for our next few ports of call?"

I^2

"I am. I can't say I'll feel as strong as I've done today. It was that place giving me inner strength. But I'm not stupid; I know it won't last. But then you already know that – you've seen how far I've deteriorated."

"Yes, I have seen it. But then I am here to help; you know this. When it becomes too much, you have to tell me."

"I will, don't worry. But first, don't we have some lines to cross off our bucket list?" Dave withdrew the piece of paper from his pocket.

"I know you are worried about the poem getting shorter," Derek replied perceptively. "But the end of the poem is just that; the end of the poem. You will still have many days to enjoy in Houston when we return. Tami will be waiting for you there."

"Waiting for us both, you mean," Dave placed his hand on top of Derek's in a true brotherly fashion.

When they returned to the ship, Dave crossed out the whole of the following stanza:

Could you, sat contemplating there,
Worship the gods of fire and air?
Give up your life in dedication
To build monuments to all of creation.
Be selflessly devoted and contrite
And live in total supplication.

Did this not perfectly describe the Buddhist monks they had seen, and by association, he and Derek too.

I, SQUARED

Cambodia

Dave watched the birds circling around the back of the ship as the giant screws churned up the water. Eruptions of foaming azure blue bubbles, breaking out across the surface before pooling into two streaks. A perfect pathway tracing the ship's route set against the deep indigo of the unruffled ocean.

The birds, oblivious to the cause, were content to know that following the big steel thing led to a free meal. Faultlessly, they twisted and turned on the wind before swooping down onto the small fish being churned up from the propellers. From his chair, Dave marveled at their aerobatics as they sought out their next morsel. What did they know of their life he wondered? Did they understand the passing of the days and miss one of their companions if it suddenly vanished, no longer accompanying them and diving down into the waves? No longer signaling to the flock when rewarded with a fish or two; an avian 'thank you' to the great steel thing that at that moment was rendering up presents from the deep and making their lives easier. Do they measure how long they have to enjoy the rewards the universe has conferred on them: the gift of flight and the ability to soar above everything and look down on the mundane and earthbound? Do they know their life is short in relation to the great ticking clock of the cosmos? If they know this, do they contemplate death like he has had to? Do they count down the days allotted to them and wish for more, or choose to remain oblivious of the finite number of tomorrows? If they have learned that cruise ships provide a meal when they come into port, they must remember the days gone by. If they know this and can recognize ships, then surely, like a mother recognizes her own chicks, they must also see and be saddened by the

I^2

passing of their own kind. Therefore, even something as lowly as a bird must be aware of its own mortality.

Dave wondered if this was a metaphor for him? Was the ship Derek - another vessel whose original purpose was to make his life easier? Was it cruel to think that way still? Had they not journeyed far and become closer for it, inseparable almost? This morning watching the birds flying in formation, he could easily associate himself with one of them. He was the one now thankful for any tasty morsel churned up in the time remaining to him as they traveled along on the ocean wave. While Derek would carry on and navigate his way to freedom, he was heading inescapably for the rocks. Here, below his observation point on the rear of the ship, was another perfect example of such a symbiosis: the birds fed off the sea, and in turn, when they died on the wing, the ocean and the fish in it fed off them. A circle of life, as true as any wheel rumbling along life's highway. Each turn heading inescapably towards a final destination, just as he and Derek were doing now.

In that way, he and Derek were the inside and outside of the same wheel, hurtling towards something more significant than either of them. The yin and yang of destiny – something bigger than the sea, the birds, the whole fucking world even. He was, at that moment, his own universe and nothing else in that precious instant of time mattered. Life was more than an ethos. Derek probably understood that more than he, being created rather than born, he could be a dispassionate observer. His knowledge of time would be based on heuristics and programming – images built up of ones and zeros, each discreet and separate. Little tableaux of life captured in the same way the shutter of a camera would, but also linked in a way only an android could arrange them. His was not a linear world. Derek was definitely not a bird or a ship; he was...unique.

Dave had finished the breakfast Derek ordered to the

room by the time the ship docked. As soon as the tannoy announced that guests were able to disembark, Derek, as usual, had everything prepared for their overnight ashore.

"Are we ready then, Dave?" Derek asked, entering the lounge from his bedroom. Dave noticed he was wearing his now trademark Panama hat, the only thing he could recall him purchasing so far on the trip. Ever since St Vincent, it had become an almost permanent fixture. Bought as a memento on the quayside before they reboarded – it seemed so long ago now.

Dave was unsure he would ever be ready again as he struggled to rise from the dining chair. He cursed silently to himself. Why did he feel so weak again today; he hated the inconsistency and the not knowing more than the disease itself. Dave knew he had started to become a hindrance to Derek, as much as he was acutely aware of his increasing frailty. He didn't want to be the party-pooper and let the side down. He at least owed that much to his companion, especially now he did so much for him. Well, today would not be one of those days he succumbed to the inevitable.

Derek understood Dave's frustration. The marked deterioration in Dave's health since India would have been evident to anyone they had met since coming aboard. And today was no exception; the full severity of Dave's illness was there for everyone to see. Today might be the day he computed, returning to his bedroom. He re-emerged a few moments later, pushing the wheelchair he had borrowed from the ship's medical room. Wheeling it up to where Dave sat, he parked it next to him.

"I'm not ready for that yet," Dave said tersely. Would he have done the same if he had been the carer and Derek the patient? Derek had his mind, and also his own, and trying to figure out which one was operating at any one time an impossible task.

I^2

Derek withdrew the chair hastily. "As you wish, grumpy sides. But you will let me help you, won't you? Take my arm for support."

Dave acquiesced with a nod.

Derek secretly congratulated himself. His computations had been faultless yet again. Getting the car he had booked to come alongside the ship and wait at the gangway had been a prudent move. All he had to do now was to get Dave there. At least his patient accepted his assistance with little objection now.

Dave, determined not to succumb to the weakness he felt all down his left side, hobbled noticeably towards the car, secretly thankful it was close by.

Derek made a note, comparing Dave's mobility against previous excursions they had made. He computed how much it had deteriorated as they headed towards the vehicle. The time was fast approaching when Dave would be entirely dependent on him, and he would make sure his *brother* wanted for nothing.

The sunshine made Dave feel a little less frail. He was still uneasy about imposing on Derek, but while he could manage to place one foot in front of the other, he would carry on until it became physically impossible.

They would reach their destination in four hours – a hotel for the night, and then tomorrow, they would explore. Explore a place they say that time never healed. After that, they would head back to the floating coffin, a name Dave had decided the ship now merited. In his heart of hearts, he knew he wouldn't finish the voyage. Derek probably knew it too, but neither of them spoke about it.

The cab ride mainly passed in silence, neither of them knowing quite what to say. When two people share the same experiences and life events, what is there to discuss that would be of interest?

Occasionally they'd take turns in pointing out a passing paddy field or a rundown shack crudely fabricated from sheets of corrugated steel that served as a home. A place where undernourished dogs barked at passing cars, where chickens and the odd goat ranged over the road as though they owned every piece of it. The driver, careful to avoid the straying wildlife, navigated the car around endless potholes, some so big they could easily swallow a pig.

Along the road, they passed some kids playing in the dirt. Even the deflated football, disinclined to remain spherical, couldn't dampen their enthusiasm. Their smiling faces revealing toothless grins as they passed by. People here lived on nothing but seemed just as happy for it. Dave wondered if it was because there was no envy. An existence where there were no aspirations about being anything other than alive. And hence no worries about being a success or failure. The state would provide. Dave remembered reading that Cambodia had struggled to meet its obligations when the money China had invested in the country was repatriated. Half-finished roads and office blocks littered the landscape, punctuated by asphalt scars etched into the hills. Roads that went nowhere, just like its inhabitants.

Phnom Penh bustled. Too many cars trying to navigate poorly constructed streets intermingled with people trying to go about their daily routine. Cars, relics of a previous generation, when petroleum was king, wore their badges of longevity with pride: paint, where it existed on the rusting bodywork, was of 'no two colors the same' variety. Body panels proudly boasting their heritage, wearing dents and scrapes like medals for all to admire.

From what Dave could see, here was a society that wasted nothing. Everything had a use and reuse. When you are cash-poor, you need to be materially wealthy. Nothing

I^2

displayed it more than the yards around the ramshackle houses, littered with anything salvageable. But more importantly, re-saleable. But then, like all cities, there were two sides: the tourist area, where gleaming skyscrapers towered over the poorer quarters. Tuk-tuk's waiting to whisk sightseers around beguiling golden temples, glistening in the brightness of the sun. The face of a modern cosmopolitan city, forgetful of the history that scared the rest of the country. And then there were the slums, like the ones they had just passed through – as neglected as any he had seen or read about anywhere.

Dave tried to recall what he knew of the country's history. It was said that for the USA, Cambodia and Vietnam were wounds that never healed. After the USA had been given a kicking in Korea, it was only a matter of time before they decided to 'kick-ass' in Vietnam and Cambodia. Exacting cruel revenge on many innocents in the pursuit of quashing an ideal: Communism – the single word that stoked fear into a nation like no other. Again they failed. Humiliated by the Khmer Rouge when they captured Saigon, the Americans left. In victory and little to stop him, Pol Pot went on a genocidal rampage in Cambodia, massacring more than a million citizens he saw as collaborators and enemies of the state – free thinkers who questioned his legitimacy to rule. Well, that was his take on the wars; wholly unnecessary, and it did little for the people, except maybe offer them an express ticket to the morgue.

Maybe visiting the killing fields to pay homage and offer his apology in the book of remembrance would in some small way ease the pain: one more recognition of the wrongdoings perpetrated by man, in the name of... well, what exactly? There was no logic? If you take sides, then are you not equally guilty? A protagonist, an aggressor, an alien meddling in the internal affairs of others. Was it only because, as an alien himself, he could distance himself and be dispassionately objective?

I, SQUARED

Derek watched Dave ponder the moral question. It was the small furrowing of the brow that gave him away, something he could not do. It would soon be time to explore; they were close to their destination. And Derek wondered… well did he wonder, or did he just compute – how couldn't differentiate anymore. Would he be able to feel the same experience when looking at the monument? Would it be the same for him as Dave? Do androids like him ever question their own moral compass, like he was starting to do now? By the end of the journey, he hoped to have answers to such queries his algorithms as yet could not process. Hope: a human yearning… He was changing; he was sure of it more than anything else. He was no longer a thing; he *was* becoming a person, albeit one with synthetic skin.

Dave sought a bench to sit at while Derek wandered off towards the ticket office to get the audio-guided headset. All the information leaflets had said this was the best way to navigate the monument.

Derek soon returned with the player. "You just press the button corresponding to the numbers by each of the exhibits," he explained as he handed the device over. Derek held out his hand to help Dave back up. Dave was grateful for it.

With Derek never far from his side now, Dave wandered through the site, reliving the atrocities described on the audio guide – an evil perpetrated by one man's determination to stay in power, regardless of the human cost. Dave brushed aside a tear. It made him think – do all dictators end up drowned in the rising tide of the 'will of the people.' An irresistible force driven by a single purpose. Had he not already seen this on his travels: the power people can exert over the state when of a single mind. Had

I^2

not his visit to India had ably confirmed it.

The museum remained a living memorial even in death. Untouched areas displayed the remains as found: pieces of rag here, bones protruding out of the ground there. All lay revealed in the dirt – defiant and un-silenced to the last. For in death, they spoke volumes, while in life, they were mute and insignificant. Their murder and suffering had become the beacon for hope and a warning to those who followed. Dave recalled the words of Dalberg-Acton as he walked between the exhibits: Power tends to corrupt; absolute power corrupts absolutely. Now there was a word that so inadequately described the sight before his eyes; these were not exhibits; these used to be people.

Eventually, Dave reached the incongruous white marble Stupa, its golden roof glistening in the sunshine belying the horrors hermetically sealed inside. Display cases stacked floor-to-ceiling with the bones of thousands of once-living, breathing individuals. People who'd had their lives stolen for an ideology. The voids in the skulls that were once eyes were staring at him – saying why me. A shudder ran up his spine, leaving him feeling traumatized. This was not something to celebrate. Were they not every bit as deserving to live their lives as he. At least nature would be his reaper, not the whim of a despot. In front of him, a lost generation that would have had dreams and aspirations and hopes for a better future. Yet here they were on display – the calcified remains of unfulfilled destiny. He wiped away the tear trickling down his cheek. If he could have swapped his life now, such that it was, to save just one of these unfortunates, he would do it in an instant. Instead, at that moment, he felt utterly ashamed and inadequate.

Quietly he left the building, knowing the images there would haunt him until he drew his last breath. But then, so they should; maybe everyone ought to see the cost of unfettered power and ambition.

I, SQUARED

Pressing the next button on the audio guide directed him across the square to the next item on the list. But here too, there was no rest-bite, the commentary in his ear equally upsetting. He felt the tears welling up again as he looked at the corral where women would be rounded up, raped, and subsequently tortured. Nothing was too severe; eventually, they would all die in absolute agony. This was not punishment; it was not justice. It was the glorification of pure evil. An example of how mankind could be the worst and the most predatory animal on the planet. Nowhere on Earth was it more apparent than here.

Dave could only think how Derek must be interpreting the exhibits. 'Exhibits' – hardly an appropriate epithet for genocide. Would this cemetery of hatred become mans' lasting epitaph to humankind? Was Derek even now calculating the validity of organic man still deserving of his place on Earth? Maybe now was not the time for inorganics to take over, but for how long? Then, would not eventually even androids start to adapt their programming and modify their interpretation of what constitutes a code of morality. Would they then begin to argue and fight over which among them was superior. In order to be superior, you have to create inferior – something man had been practicing only too well for millennia.

"Derek, do you think man will ever learn that all life is sacred, and no man should be able to have the power to take another's?"

"Do you mean in the Buddhist sense? All life, no matter how insignificant, is life and deserving of protection. Or just humankind? Do you think that would also include me? Am I living in the known sense of the word? Would those who created this place have considered me as such? Especially when *my kind* do not bleed or die in the traditional way as depicted by the tragedy and suffering we see all around us."

I^2

Dave could see the problem Derek might have with such a statement. Was Derek life? "No, I think I mean all sentient beings, you included. Surely mankind has to move past this stage of evolution, or else everything is doomed."

"Maybe you have a point, Dave, but are not my kind now the substitutes, the ones you would place in the corral. Are we not now the new targets for hatred?"

Dave remained silent. Derek was right. Of course, it could easily turn out that way. He suddenly felt a pang of guilt. He had been just as guilty to start with, and so had Tami. Some prejudices are hard to overcome. Did he truly see the person in Derek now, or would there always be that little voice inside his head that said: 'it's only a machine.'

Tomorrow they would return to the ship, and in his heart, Dave knew he'd be crossing out a whole stanza of the poem… that would leave only one more. One more verse to finally come to terms with his own mortality. The last chance to bury his prejudices and yet see Derek as the true equal he'd become. An equal? Was that arrogance on his part – making an assumption that Derek could only attain equality and not surpass it. In many ways, Derek had already demonstrated it. Had he today not already articulated his understanding of the problems he would face in the world of man? Was Derek fearful for his own future, in much the same way he was over the lack of one and the toll of the ever-dwindling poem?

I, SQUARED

On the Road Again

Dave picked up his pencil. He didn't want to cross out any more of the poem; it was too ominous. He had deliberately avoiding signing away what remained, as if his life, or lack of it, depended on the poem remaining unfulfilled. As the ship threaded its way through the Java Sea en-route towards Darwin, Dave had been in no mood to get off at any of the ports of call. He knew Derek was growing concerned about his increasing frailty – he had to preserve what strength he still possessed for one great final adventure. He somehow knew deep down this would be his swan-song. The poem had suddenly become an invisible crutch – something to hold onto. Flattening out the paper, he reluctantly crossed out the verse that poorly matched the sadness he had felt walking around the killing fields:

And do not forget those less able
Sitting around a barren table.
In squalor and despair, they've paid in blood.
A casualty of evil, now buried in mud.
Monumental and venerated,
The lasting scar of mankind's hatred.

"So, are we all ready for another adventure?" Derek asked, breezing into Dave's bedroom, unexpectedly making him jump.

"Yes, of course. I feel stronger today. The last three days staying on the ship have helped a lot. But I hate to admit it, I might need you to take the wheelchair along, just in case."

"Good, Do you know where we are going then?"

"Well, seeing as you've packed clothes, I'm sure it's a little ways away."

"It is. But we are also taking the opportunity to leave

I^2

the ship until it returns to Sydney. So, missing out on some of the stops in Indonesia and Papua New Guinea. When we get ashore, we are going to pick up a motorhome. I know it is something we had thought of doing if you ever got to Earth. So we are!"

"Okay, and going where, surely not all the way to Sydney?"

"No, only about 830 miles south of Darwin. It will take us two days."

"So, Ayres Rock then," remarked Dave after successfully recalling his scant knowledge of Earth geography. Probably more luck than judgment, but at that moment, he couldn't think of anything else so remote worth visiting."

"Yes, and after Uluru, we leave the motorhome at Yulara and then fly on to Sydney, where we will rejoin the ship."

"You have it all worked out then."

"Of course. Am I not as precise as a digital clock." Dave noted that Derek's sense of humor was improving by the day. Being able to make fun of yourself was still considered a mark of intelligence.

The hire company had delivered the motorhome to the quay, much to Dave's relief. Clambering into the passenger seat was all the exercise he could manage these days. But then he could relax – Derek had more than proven himself a competent driver. All he had to do was enjoy the experience and watch the scenery pass by as they headed South.

Traveling out of Darwin on route 1, Dave watched the changing scenery like a kid going on holiday. This was a boyhood fantasy – one he'd had many times back on Mars whenever he thought about coming to Earth to search for his Mother.

I, SQUARED

As soon as they reached Daly Waters, where their route became the 87, Derek pulled off the road and made Dave coffee. "We are not yet halfway," he informed his passenger while handing him the beverage. Soon they were heading South once more, and Dave re-tuned the radio again as the previous station faded away into squelch.

Dave found something as archaic as radio a bit of a novelty, yet also very familiar and welcoming. He could imagine how the invisible companion could help break the monotony for those traveling alone on such long journeys. And it was; dead straight roads with minimal interest on either side to occupy the mind. At least Derek wouldn't get fatigued navigating the endless miles of empty road.

After another 200 miles, they stopped at the Three Ways service station for diesel and a late lunch. The break allowed Dave to test Derek out as a driver of wheelchairs. While Derek purchased a few provisions for dinner in the shop there, Dave tried on a bushman's hat, complete with corks, if only to keep the numerous flying predators at bay – his hands and arms no longer quick or precise enough to swat anything except his nose. If Derek could have a Panama, then he too could go native.

As the late summer afternoon wore on, Dave settled back to watch another 300 miles of the straightest road ever built pass by. They were deep into the Northern Territory and close to the Tanami Desert. The scrubland parched from the withering heat of the sun had all but disappeared, leaving nothing but flat red earth. It reminded Dave very much of the Martian landscape, apart from the heat and the ever-persistent flying carnivores.

"Not too far now," informed Derek as evening surrendered to nightfall. In the distance, the faint glow of town lights shimmered against a darkening deep violet sky. A mileage board confirmed it: Alice Springs 10 miles. "I have a campsite booked for us," Derek added before Dave had even thought about asking the question.

I^2

Turning off the road, Derek steered the motorhome along a small track until they reached the campsite. It wasn't the barren, parched bit of outback Dave had been expecting – there were buildings and bays for vehicles. Around which trees had been planted to offer some shade from the intense sunlight.

After checking in at reception, Derek parked up the motorhome in their allotted bay under the shade of a eucalypt tree. Dave watched from inside as Derek industriously connected up the services to the vehicle, thankful he would now be able to turn on the central air-conditioning unit.

Derek had already decided to give Dave the main double bed while he would pull out the awning and sit out and watch the stars progress the heavens. In the morning, they would leave early, but first, he would prepare dinner, and they would eat it outside and talk like brothers should. Unbothered by the world around them, they could reminisce on what they had already seen. In the stillness of the night, they could discuss deep things, like when Lynal was around. Reflect on their experiences together. He had a duty to try and stop Dave from thinking about the inevitable, for one night at least.

The blinding light of a new day flooded the motorhome making Dave blink as the rays hit his face. Turning over to shield his eyes, he could already see Derek beavering away, making breakfast for one. He was glad they'd had dinner together the previous evening, just the two of them under the stars. In the stillness of the night, they had actually talked as equals for the first time: about Jane, Tami, his friends on Mars, and his own upcoming issues. It was a bonding of two minds, not one, something that both of them needed. He understood the real Derek better now; he was no longer the ventriloquist's dummy in a box that arrived at his apartment all those months ago. Derek had come a long way since then. And so had he. No longer did he see the machine he'd acquired before the person. And Derek was still evolving, developing a personality – a different one. One that he no longer recognized as being a copy of himself. They were diverging – Derek was no longer the clone of an egotist!

"You are up then," prompted Derek, picking up some plates to take outside. "I have made breakfast, and then we have about three-hundred miles to go to get to our destination."

Dave dressed slowly and awkwardly, as had become the norm of late. He found that even lifting his arms past his shoulder had become all but impossible. But today, he would complete the task himself without any intervention from his carer. After failing to button his shirt, he decided to leave it open. It seemed good enough for others around the campsite, so why should he be any different. Shakily, Dave made his way through the vehicle door and down the extended step to where Derek had unfolded the picnic table and chairs the previous evening. Plonking himself down on the collapsable chair, it bounced slightly as he came into contact with it.

Derek busied himself about the gas barbeque, frying eggs on the plancha grill.

"Your bushman's breakfast. Enjoy," Derek said, easing a plate in front of Dave a few minutes later.

"Lovely, where did you get bacon and eggs from?"

Derek pointed in the direction of the facilities block where a small general store had opened, enticing campers with fresh coffee and provisions. "In the shop over there. Where else!"

"Listen, Derek, I enjoyed last night. Just the two of us sitting out here, talking things over. Something we never

I^2

managed to do in Houston. We have both come a long way to get to this point in our relationship."

"Yes, I did too. It answered a lot of questions I had wanted to ask." Dave noticed a smile – reward enough.

After breakfast, Dave retrieved his washbag and towel from the vehicle and, using the wheelchair, propelled himself off towards the disabled shower and toilet block, leaving Derek packed up the outdoor table and chairs.

Derek watched him disappear into the shower block as he wiped down the barbeque. After placing everything in the stowage hangar, he wound in the awning in readiness to make their departure. He felt apprehensive; this was a new sensation for him. Today would be another long drive, but to him, that was irrelevant. No, he was more concerned about Dave's obvious discomfort and voluntarily asking for the wheelchair to be brought along. They would not be back on board for another two nights. This might be the last time Dave was physically capable of getting off the ship. The obvious deterioration in his health made it easy to compute now. He would have to make the stop in Sydney extra-special.

I, SQUARED

Uluru

Turning off the 87 at Eridunda, not so much a place as a fuel-stop, Derek steered the motorhome towards their final destination: Yulara. After another 100 miles, just before they reached the town, Dave caught his first glimpse of the famous mound across the scrubland rising out of the rich paprika-colored ground.

"Look, Derek, there it is," Dave exclaimed, pointing out of the side window.

"Yes, I see it. We will be there soon. Are you up for a short walk around the site, or would you like me to push you?"

Dave thought about it before reaching behind his seat, searching for his hiking poles. "I'll walk, of course." Pulling them out and brandishing them in front of Derek resolutely. "You know me! Today will be a good day – I feel it!"

Derek pulled the motorhome off the asphalt and into a rough-ground car park, sending up a small dust storm from the RV's wheels under braking.

As soon as Derek had finished parking up, Dave, hiking poles unfurled to take his weight as soon as he touched the ground, was ready. Holding on to the door for additional support, he slid out from the passenger side as gingerly as possible until his feet came in contact with terra-firma.

"Nice RV," commented a big guy squeezing out of a blue Chrysler hire-car that had pulled up alongside them at that exact same moment. After struggling to extricate himself from a vehicle two sizes too small, he opened up the rear to retrieve a beige-colored Stetson off the back seat and pressed it down onto his round, slightly balding head.

I^2

"Thanks, you're American, aren't you?" Dave asked, on detecting a southern drool.

"Sure am. Hank's the name. Hank Franklin. Texan an' proud, at your service."

"I'm sort of from Texas too. I'm Dave Sherman, and this is my brother Derek."

"Well, ain't that the dandiest thing." Hank thrust out his hand. It was as big as his personality.

Dave shook it tentatively, worried whether he'd escape with his finger bones intact. "I'm living in Houston at the moment, and the rest of my family live not far from Midland."

"I know 'round there," replied the big guy, tipping back his cowboy hat.

Dave flexed his fingers; they still worked. "It's a tiny place called Big Lake. It also doesn't have a lake!"

"Sound's kinda familiar. Might 'a passed through there with the Rig sometime."

"Rig?" butted in Derek.

"Yes, the Rig, you know, an eighteen-wheeler. I'm a trucker."

"Ah, I see." Derek added 'rig' to his linguistic database.

"So holiday?" inquired Dave.

"Yeh, sort of," Hank said. "My brother's out here. He drives the big road trains across the country and wants me to move out here and join him. He's coming down later in his RV. We are going to make a night of it here and 'ave us a party. You two up for meeting us later?"

"Okay, sounds great," Derek replied before Dave could object. "We were planning on spending the evening here anyway."

"We were!" exclaimed Dave, somewhat surprised.

"Well, that sounds like a done deal." Hank slapped his thigh with the flat of his hand in anticipation of the fun they'd be having later.

I, SQUARED

Awkwardly, leaning heavily on his poles, Dave made his way from the motorhome towards the visitor center. Derek remained close to his side should he stumble on the uneven ground.

The visitor center was nothing more than a small structure consisting of a twig-roof mounted on poles. There a guide was handing out pamphlets – a tall skinny aboriginal dressed in not a lot as far as Dave could see. He greeted them with a broad smile of dazzling pearl white teeth set against skin as black as night. Dave smiled back and took one of the pamphlets on offer. Hank joined them, and together they made their way slowly along the sign-posted pathway at a pace Dave found comfortable.

At the first bench they came to, although only a couple of hundred meters into the site, Derek suggested to Dave they rest up for a while to take in the view. Dave gratefully agreed.

"I'll see you boys later then," Hank said before striding off in the direction of the monument. Derek nodded and sat down next to Dave. Together they skimmed the pamphlet they'd been handed:

Uluru is sacred to the Pitjantjatjara and the Anangu: the local Aboriginal people of the area.

When the world was a featureless place. Creator beings, in the form of giant people and animals, traveled widely across the land. They formed the landscape as we know it today. Anangu land is still inhabited by the spirits of dozens of these supernatural beings. They are called Tjukuritja or Waparitja.

There are many stories about the origins of Uluru and its many features. One such account tells how Uluru was built up during the creation period by two boys who played in the mud after rain, making

I^2

the mound or an Uluru. When they had finished their game, they traveled south to Wiputa, where their spirit bodies now live on the top of Mount Connor, preserved as boulders.

To account for the many cracks around the rock, there is a tale about serpent beings. Creatures who waged many wars around Uluru, scarring the rock and creating the crags and fissures you now see there.

Another creation story tells us how the rock was said to have risen out of the ground from the blood spilled there. Two tribes were invited to a feast but were bewitched by the beautiful Sleepy Lizard Women and did not show up. In response, the angry hosts sang evil into a mud sculpture that came to life as the dingo. There followed a great battle, which ended in the deaths of the leaders of both tribes − their spilled blood becoming Uluru.

Other Tjukurpa affected only one specific area of the rock.
Kuniya, the Woma python, lived in the rocks at Uluru where she fought the Liru, the poisonous snake; their battles formed the water pools all over this area and away to Mutitjulu.

It is sometimes reported that those who take rocks from the formation will be cursed and suffer misfortune. So it is advisable to leave them be, just in case they carry the spirits of the ancients.

After finishing reading, Dave carefully folded up the pamphlet and placed it into the pocket of his shorts. He would read it again later when he wrote up his travelogue. Hauling himself back up onto his hiking-poles, with Derek's assistance, they proceeded on towards the monument. For that was how it was perceived by the locals. To them, it wasn't something as mundane as a rock − it was a memorial.

As they passed through the site, reading the information boards, Dave came to understand why it held such reverence for native Australians. A place where carved, barely visible petroglyphs covered rock-face walls. This was their cathedral. Here, Aboriginal tribes, after making the long journey across the parched ground, would become at one with their ancestors' spirit folk. This was how they preserved their history and culture. This rock was their special place where they could try and make sense of the heavens above them. A place where they could be buried and be close to the spirits of their forebears. Was it any different from other religions; did not churches also come with graveyards?

And Uluru gave back too. In the parched scrublands around them, only here under the rock was there an abundance of water. Precious rock pools and caves that sustained life through the hot, dry summer months until the rains returned.

On returning to the motorhome, Dave watched another RV approaching along the highway. The Eight-Wheeler, as big as any bungalow, turned off the road and bounced into the park. Behind it, clouds of sand billowed into the air, whipped up by the tires on the sandy surface as it came screeching to a halt next to theirs.

"That's Ray now," exclaimed Hank, running over to welcome them back. "Come and meet him, and we'll start getting dinner ready."

"In a minute. We'll come over to you after we've cooled off a bit," Dave replied.

"Okay, see you soon."

Dave watched Hank bound off towards the motorhome as it parked up.

"You okay, Dave," inquired Derek.

"Tired, that's all. I think I've walked about as much as I can today."

Feeling refreshed after a quick drink of cold water from the motorhome's gas-powered fridge, Dave changed into a fresh shirt. Through the RV's window, he could see

I^2

Derek setting out the table and chairs, ready for the evening.

As soon as he'd taken the seat Derek had placed closest to the doorway, Ray came over to offer his salutations. Dave could instantly see that Ray was Hank's elder brother; they shared many similar facial features. Ray held out an equally large brotherly hand for Dave to shake. "Hiya, glad to meet you." Dave could see that Ray was eager to ask about his affliction, "Accident," he quickly offered to avoid further embarrassment.

"Gee, hope you get better soon," Ray replied. Dave decided that for now, ignorance was a better option. Maybe he'd tell them later.

Sitting at the table outside the motorhome as the sun sank in the sky, Dave watched the face of Uluru as it metamorphosized. No longer brown, like ground cumin, it had taken on the richness of fiery red paprika. The food metaphors, unavoidable, as the aromas off Ray's barbeque weaved their magic. Filling the air all around them with the smell of meat being seared on charcoal.

"More food, you two," enquired Hank, approaching with a plate of chicken pieces.

"Cheers," Dave took a quarter and placed it on the plate across his lap. "Watching the rock change color is amazing, don't you think?"

Ray stopped flipping burgers for a moment to take another swig from his tinny. "You think this is good now; you wait till the stars come out."

"That is a lot of food for four," remarked Derek, after deciding he would have to partake of the food on offer so as not to appear different.

"I've got some more mates coming," replied Ray. "Tonight we're having a party. It's not every day I get to see my kid brother, and he's going to come and work for us. So it's also a celebration."

I, SQUARED

That night Dave celebrated life with new friends, drinking and partying as enthusiastically as he could from the confines of his chair. Music rang out into the night from a portable speaker, and it seemed as if the land itself joined in. In-between the thump-thump of the music, the call of nature would sing back to them and barely perceivable, but there nonetheless, the delayed echo off Uluru would rebound out of step, yet, also completely in time. Almost as if the spirits themselves were joining in.

It was gone 3 a.m. by the time everyone retired. All apart from Derek, who had decided to sit out and watch the Milky Way traverse its way over the rock – two ribbons of light, separated by a central void; a stunning celestial spectacle moving gracefully across the night sky. And here, of all places, it was more special, more vibrant, than anywhere else on the planet. It was almost as if the rock itself touched the heavens.

Derek, at last, understood. Here, under the stars, he could comprehend why the place held such significance. He and Dave were of the same stuff, the two shafts of light traversing across a void. In that one instant, everything was exposed - he was no longer computing; he was thinking. He had experienced something unique, something that went way beyond programming: an epiphany – one perfect moment of consciousness.

Opening up the crumpled piece of paper Dave had left on the table before retiring, he reread the poem. The final stanza – he now understood it only too well.

And when your time is done
Watching the last ever setting sun.
Will the rocks bleed and engrave your name
Into the land from whence you came?
Can you say from all this I grew:
I Lived, Loved, and saw it through?

I^2

Dave's time was nearly over; he knew it. It was there laid out in front of him, resonating in the words of the poem. And visually also, like the setting sun on the rock. This was a gravestone, the same as any other anywhere in the world, a monument where the lives of loved ones could be remembered. Now, all would soon be returned to dust, leaving only the memory of it. It was something he would file away. He would become the memorial he was always meant to be. It was as pre-ordained as the day he was activated. The sad prophecy of the last line still had to be fulfilled, he knew that, but for now, their journey was complete, and the experience of it had benefitted him greatly – more than Dave would ever comprehend.

I, SQUARED

Long Voyage Home

Dropping off the motorhome at Yulara airport and catching the flight to Sydney passed by uneventfully. Derek noted that Dave hardly spoke for the whole journey. He seemed distant to the point of being withdrawn. Was Dave contemplating the time he had left, just like he was computing daily now? Maybe this evening at the opera would cheer him up. Dave had always been partial to it and Verdi in particular, playing it regularly back on Mars. Tonight they would go and see El Forza del Destino. Could anything be more apt; their destiny was bound by a path neither of them could change. Then tomorrow, back on board and heading towards the inescapable curtain call.

Dave stirred in the seat next to him, and diligently Derek adjusted his pillow – his mobility had worsened since they had left the ship. Maybe imperceptibly to others, but he could see his increasing frailty only too well. Perhaps it was a good thing that tonight was their last big adventure. Then, afterward, they could stay on the ship and do whatever Dave felt capable of until they reached Los Angeles, their final port of call. From there, it was just one last flight into Houston. Although he did not want to, he was compelled to compute all scenarios. And, it was now more than probable that Dave would not make it back to the USA. This may be his last chance to surprise him. He would make all the necessary arrangements as soon as they arrived in Sydney.

For only the second outing, Dave had asked Derek for the wheelchair as they made their way out of the hotel en-route to the Opera House. An architectural wonder when it was created. Critics dismissed it and refused to

I^2

enter it for fear it would collapse. But, it had stood the test of time. It had been built to promote Sydney as a city of culture, second only in architectural significance to the iconic bridge that spanned the Murray river. Derek wondered how the music would affect him? Would it be as monumental? He knew the opera because Dave did, but he had never heard it with his own aural transducers. Would it stir emotions within him like it did in Dave? This remained an unknown. Would he at last, through the experience, discover his soul?

It was the first time Derek had seen Dave cry, overwhelmed by the outpouring of emotion being delivered by the performers. He had felt it too during the rendering of La Vergine Degli Angeli at the end of the second act. He had experienced an inexplicable cascade in his circuitry, forcing an involuntary diagnostic test. Is this how religion acts upon the human brain he computed? A sudden release of endorphins brought on by the beauty of the moment – a sensory opiate.

After the last encore had died away and the audience had started to heads towards the exits, Dave, still teary from the emotion, wiped his eyes with the back of his hand for the fourth time. "That was wonderful, Derek, don't you think," he said, realizing it was the first time either had spoken since entering.

"Yes, it was. I never knew classical music could be so powerful."

"Technically, Opera isn't classical music. It's its own genre. But I know what you mean."

"Yes, I know! Now, I have another surprise planned for you. If you are ready for another venture into a 4D-Bar. There is one here in Sydney, just a small cab ride away. I have booked a slot for us there, where your friends are waiting."

"I think that will be a perfect way to round off the

evening. Come on, what are we waiting for. Wheel me there now, driver!"

Outside the Opera house, the day had turned into one of those balmy warm evenings ideally suited to dining 'al fresco.' It made Dave shudder slightly as Derek wheeled him out into it from the foyer. After the chill of the air-conditioned theatre, the moisture in the air readily precipitated against his cool skin, dampening his shirt slightly. Even Derek's, he noted as they made their way towards the large taxi rank in front of the building.

By the time the cab reached the 4D-Bar, Dave had decided he was not going to let himself be pushed into the venue. The attendant could look after his wheels while he was inside. Clumsily, he made his way into the establishment, almost dragging his left leg behind him, such was its obstinacy to move. Derek, as ever, close at hand should he stumble. At the check-in, Derek confirmed the booking: the Hawaiian adventure. Dave instantly knew it was in case he didn't get to see it for real; such was Derek's concern over his rapidly deteriorating health – his restricted facial expressions enough to give him away.

After taking his time to choose a suitably vibrant shirt from the list of avatar clothing, Dave was, at last, ready. If this was to be his last chance to see his friends, he wanted them to remember it. "What do you think, Derek; does that shirt make a statement or what?"

"I think so! Are you ready now?" Was that impatience, Dave wondered. Had he suddenly become burdensome?

The bar had been rendered as if made from straw paneling with wicker tables and chairs. All his friends had gathered around one table, where to his surprise, Tami had joined them also.

I^2

"Tami, you're here too," the surprise rendering him almost speechless. It was as if all the air in his lungs had been suddenly stolen along with his heart. Her avatar was tastefully clothed in a Polynesian beach dress. He knew he was staring, but how could you not. How he wished at that moment, he could touch her in the physical sense and feel her breath on his skin once more. He wanted to so tell her all the things he wished he'd said when they were alone together – but not in company. These were private thoughts, things that would remain unsaid – secrets he would carry to the grave. Like someone once said: all love is unrequited.

"Yes, Dave, don't sound so surprised. As soon as Derek contacted me, I knew I had to come."

"But it must be so early back in Houston," Dave replied, mentally trying to count back the hours.

"Well, I don't usually make a habit of having an alcoholic breakfast, But I'll make an exception this time. By the way, this round's on me, boys. Give Elvis your order!"

Dave watched 'The King' approach and, keeping true to form, ordered an Old Fashioned. Derek plummed for beer.

"So, how is everyone?" Frank asked, eager to share his news.

"I'm okay, and so is Derek. You?" Dave replied, sensing Frank was itching to say something.

"I'm going out with Toz," he blurted. "Well, when I say going out, I am talking metaphorically, of course, seeing that there is no outside. Not if you want to live anyway."

"I get it, Frank. Oh, and by the way, Oz says hi back!"

"And I'm coming to Earth," butted in Robbie. "My father's ill and needs me to take over the company business. So I'll see you in about a year's time."

"I'll try and hang on then," Dave replied, trying to make light of his condition but knowing full well he'd be long gone by then.

I, SQUARED

"Dave, how are you really?" quizzed Tami, determined not to be deflected from getting an answer.

It was a leading question, but one he couldn't ignore. If he couldn't be truthful now, when could he? "Not too good, to be honest. I rely on Derek for most things now."

"Derek keeps me informed when he can. I know he is concerned, so take it easy from now on. He already told me that today was the last major stop on your tour when he booked this reunion. So rest up now, and I'll see you soon."

After several more rounds of drinks, endless small talk about nothing in particular, Dave felt rejuvenated. Their time was up, but this was no sad parting of the ways; this was friends saying adios, not goodbye. They would do it all again soon, Derek had promised, that was good enough for him.

Derek settled up the bill while Dave reacquainted himself with his wheelchair. This was the best day he'd had so far. The opera had lifted his spirits, and tonight he would dream of being with Tami on the beach in Honolulu, minus the dress. With the waves crashing over them, they would make love, moving in perfect time to the waves. The thought of being reunited with her once again would give him the strength he needed now.

The dark blue waters of the South Pacific Ocean glistened like diamonds as they sailed eastwards, millions of points of light between them and their final destination. Derek poured out a glass of champagne and carried it out to Dave on the balcony. "A toast," he said, "for completing the poem."

"All but the last line. I am correct, aren't I? That cannot be completed until… Well, you know."

"Who knows, we may yet see something."

"I think you and I both know the truth of it."

I^2

"But not today. Let's just say tomorrow."

"Alright, a second toast then: to there being many more tomorrows," Dave raised his glass again, as far as his arm would allow, which was not that much anymore.

As the ship navigated its way past New Caledonia and Fiji, Dave mainly stayed in his room, venturing out as far as the closest bar when he felt strong enough to do so and always by wheelchair. Derek would join him there also. If anything being so incapacitated had brought them even closer. But is still rankled, Derek had become something he never wanted: a full-time carer. He found relying on Derek to wash and dress him embarrassing. And it was demeaning; Derek was more than a skivvy. Other days, when he felt weaker, he would just sit out on the balcony and watch the birds while indulging himself in his rediscovered passion for reading. He was only too acutely aware that Derek was constantly assessing his condition. He had to put a brave face on it all, regardless of the pain he was suffering inwardly.

Derek returned to the cabin after picking up the excursion pamphlets. They had made it to Hawaii. Tomorrow they would be docking in Honolulu, and Dave had been better of late. He might be up to going ashore.

Dave cried out from his bedroom as soon as he heard Derek enter. Throwing down the pamphlets, Derek rushed into Dave's room. He appeared to be choking. It soon became apparent that Dave's airway had contracted. Picking up the cabin's phone, he dialed the emergency medical number….

His automated programming had kicked in. In one sense, he hated the fact he'd had no control over it. In others ways, he was grateful. It had saved Dave's life. In the operating room, the doctor had carried out an emergency tracheostomy to ease Dave's breathing difficulties. This was a signal as sure as any that Dave's days were just that: days, not weeks.

"It won't be so long now," Dave had croaked when he'd come round by placing a finger over his new airway so he could pass air over his now mostly redundant vocal cords.

Derek had tried to look away. The answer was too upsetting, even for an android. He didn't want to agree. "It is just a temporary setback," he had said. As a lie, it would have to do for every algorithm he ran produced the same result….

While he still had use of his hands, he would continue to record everything in his travelogue, even though, at times, they no longer moved as he instructed. His recent scare made the task of finalizing his will all the more imperative, for there was little time left. He was happy with the generous bequest he'd made for his sister, but there was also Derek to consider. He shouldn't have to be beholden to anyone, and especially not the company who made him. No, he would leave Derek plenty of money so he could remain independent. It would allow him to further his travels and seek out what it truly meant to be alive. Allow him to carve out his own place in the universe and better prepare the way for a new race of sentient beings being created. If that was to be mans' legacy, then Derek would be his. He wondered what he could leave Tami? Maybe her just being part of Derek's life was enough. How could money better that?

After completing the will, he sealed it in an envelope and wrote 'Last Will and Testament of David Sherman' on the front. He shuddered as he looked at it – it was too ominous, too final… too predictable.

I^2

With the ship docked in Honolulu, Derek called Tami on Dave's phone.

Tami picked up, expecting to see and hear from Dave. "Hi, Tami, Derek here. I am sorry to have to tell you this, but the day is getting close. Dave is deteriorating quickly. He cannot speak so easily anymore, and his mobility has become very limited. I have to do everything for him now. I do not think he will make it back to Houston."

Tami wiped away a tear and tried to stop her bottom lip from quivering. "I knew there was something up when he didn't call as promised. Oh, Derek, I could see he was getting worse. Even in the 4D-Bar. His avatar's movements were so awkward. Please let me see him.

Derek picked up the phone and carried it out onto the balcony where Dave was sitting, a blanket wrapped around him to ward off the fresh sea breeze whistling around the stern of the ship. Holding it up, he pointed the screen towards Dave's face.

"Hello, Dave," she had to try and sound positive.

Dave tried to smile, raising his hand shakily to touch her face on the screen.

"Stay strong, my love. I'll come and see you when you get back to Houston. I want to be by your side for as long as possible."

Derek noted the tears gathering in Dave's eyes as he tried to flex his cheeks to stop them cascading down his face before turning the phone camera back around onto himself. "We will try Tami. With a will, we will try and get home." He didn't believe it, but hope was all that was left for Dave now.

I, SQUARED

I^2-I

Dear Jane.

If you are reading this letter, my time is close, or I may have already passed. There was so much I still wanted to say. I deeply regret not coming to see you sooner and getting to know you and Myles better. You are the only family I have, and I miss you more now than you'll ever realize. I wish I could live to see Moxxi and Millie grow up into the fine young adults I know they will become or be there to offer you a helping hand through the difficult times, like an elder brother should. On that point, I have made provisions in my will to provide you with an inheritance, to fund my niece and nephew's education, and more than enough to allay any future worries you could have for money.

But I also have a favor to ask of you. And it is a big one. When I last came to see you with Tami, it wasn't her I originally intended to introduce you to. It was meant to be Derek, my carer. He has been my constant companion and has become so much more than just a helper. You don't know this, but my treatment was to have an android replica of myself made as part of an experiment. I called him Derek after our father because both of us being called Dave would have been just too confusing. He has promised, though, to revert to Dave once I'm gone. He will become me — he has all my memories, a living monument to my sad little life.

Together we have explored the Earth on a quest. I, to seek out what life had denied me, and for Derek to seek out what it means to be alive. We have become very close. Strange, really, but it's a little like having our father returned to me. Although he was meant to just mimic me, he really does seem to have developed his own personality. He is no longer just me; he has become, in every respect, my twin brother. Having him beside me only highlights what I have missed in not having you and Myles, my real family, by my side at this time.

When I am gone, welcome him into your home, treat him as you would I. Love him, like I have grown to love him. Don't let him experience

I^2

loneliness like I endured it. Dissuade him from returning to Mars. Encourage him to become his own man, for his journey will be longer than mine. Mine was only a journey in time. His will be one of enlightenment.

Lovingly,

Dave.

Dave read the letter back to himself again, resisting the temptation to change it. He was tired. It would have to do for bedtime reading tonight, grateful he'd finished it before his body had decided to give up on him. It had been difficult enough writing it even then, that, and deciding on how he would split up his inheritance, or should that be blood money, he was still undecided. Anyway, he doubted he'd be able to hold the pen anymore, even if he wanted to.

He never noticed it flutter to the ground like a paper airplane caught on the breeze....

Derek, opening the cabin door to Dave's room, saw the letter lying on the floor. Picking it up, he walked across to check on Dave. There was nothing left but peaceful serenity. Dave had passed. Slumping down to the floor next to where his brother lay, he started to read what Dave had written. Why were androids not allowed to display emotions? Surely it was part of the person he had become. Why shouldn't they equip him with the ability to shed a tear?

Rising, he neatly folded the letter into three and placed it into the envelope he found still resting on Dave's lifeless chest. After sealing it, he put it on the table next to Dave's travelogue. He would deliver it in person. He would try and explain the hurt he was experiencing to Jane. But

I, SQUARED

first, he needed to be able to better understand it himself.

Picking up Dave's limp arms, pharaoh-like, he placed them over his chest. He would have to call the steward and make arrangements for disembarkation. *'Don't let him experience loneliness.'* How well he understood those words in his brother's letter now.

After drawing the drapes in Dave's room, he walked over to the door to turn off the light. Not just yet, though; there was plenty of time left to call the steward. For now, he would sit here with his friend, his brother, and talk to him through the night. Remind him of all the wonders they had seen together, and tell him of how much he had come to love him. A strange concept for an android, and somehow he knew that. He would always be considered an inferior lifeform, incapable of feeling emotion and the true nature of love. Can androids contemplate the meaning of death – to not exist? Even now, to him, Dave was not gone, merely resting in an alternate reality. Perhaps waiting for reincarnation, like he had to while waiting to be assigned. Was there a future place for organics when their earthly body stops? He hoped so, had not the journey been all about trying to discover it – an epiphany for life, a reason to exist, and a reason to die. He may never understand it? But at that moment, his whole reason for being there was to help Dave make his passage into the unknown. Tonight he would sit here with his brother and help him start out on his new journey. Reaching across to the table, Derek picked up the poem. The bucket list they had used to map their journey together and crossed off the last remaining line and circled the word: Love.

As the new day dawned, Derek placed a cover over his brother and called the steward.

"I'm sorry for your loss, Sir," the MO said after confirming Dave's passing. "Please accept our condolences

I^2

on behalf of all the ship's company." He offered his hand in sympathy, and Derek shook it. "There's a Chaplin onboard and a chapel if you need to speak to someone."

"I am okay. Thank you, Doctor."

"We will move him to the morgue and keep him there until we dock in America."

"Take good care of him. He was my only brother, you know."

"We will, don't worry. And tonight in the Officer's Mess, we will raise a glass to him, as we would any other mariner who dies at sea – it's tradition."

After the medical stretcher trolley had departed, Derek stepped out onto the balcony. Later he would call Tami again. Why did he suddenly feel uncertain of his actions? This was new; he might even say he was apprehensive. Having doubts was something he was unaccustomed to – it seemed so human!

Tami's phone glowed on her desk; the banner Rick was holding told her Dave was calling. Tami needlessly checked her watch; it was only late afternoon. This would be Derek phoning her. She was suddenly fearful of what he might say. Panic gripped her as she attempted to grasp the apocalyptic smart-device. She feared the worst. It felt as though her blood had suddenly turned to ice, robbing her of the strength to pick up the harbinger – a glowing messenger of foreboding. She sat back and took a deep breath. Her heart slowed a little and stopped feeling like it was trying to break free from its bony prison. Leaning forward again, she managed to pick up the phone and mouth the word 'answer.' She was not surprised when Derek's face appeared, staring back at her.

"Has he?" was all she could manage.

"Yes," Derek replied. "Oh, Tami, why do I feel worthless all of a sudden? So useless and irrelevant, I could not save him, so why do I now have to be him. I do not want to be him. I never asked to be a living memorial. He was my brother; I see that now. I miss him so already. How do you cope with grief? I am not equipped to handle this…, this strength of emotion. I cannot compute!"

Derek's outpouring of grief caught her off-guard. His speech processing was almost garbled. It was like he was having some sort of mental episode. Stealing her resolve not to become emotional, Tami wiped away the tears she promised not to shed when the news came. But to no avail; they continued to stream down her face. "It will become easier, the grief you are feeling now. I promise. We will overcome this together, you and I. We will not let Dave be forgotten."

"Thank you, Tami."

"Let me know when you get back to Houston. I want to see him one last time."

After terminating the call, she reached for the tissue box. Taking a handful, She wiped her eyes and blew her nose before swiveling around on her chair to turn on her computer.

Tapping away on the keyboard, she hastily made a few notes. The conversation she'd just had with Derek, sad as it was, fascinated and worried her in equal measure. Derek had become his own man. She could see nothing of Dave in him anymore. In one way, the experiment had failed. In others, it had exceeded all expectations. Maybe it was time to step back and watch his development from a distance. If she were now to become more deeply involved with him, it could jeopardize everything. It would hurt her more than Derek would ever know. But on that one thing, she was fully resolved – he must never find out her involvement in this experiment. It would hurt him too much. And despite everything, that was the last thing she wanted to do.

I^2

Less than Man

The apartment had become a prison, but Derek cared little. He looked around at the four walls – was it any different to his Martian cell? He may never leave it again, not after today anyway. Not after he had said farewell to his brother at the funeral service. It would be hard watching Dave lowered into the earth, only then to be expected to become that person. But he was compelled by his programming to do precisely that. The apartment's enclosing walls would become his new Martian home – same old Dave, different planet. Even Tami had deserted him. When he tried to call, she refused to answer. Almost as if she blamed him for Dave dying before having a chance to say goodbye. In the end, she had sent a short message to say she wouldn't be attending the service. All it had said, with *him* there, it would bring back too many memories, and she didn't want to relive the pain.

He felt betrayed. Tami had said she would be there to give him support through the dark days ahead. And now was that time. He needed her, but the first time he called after arriving back at the apartment, she'd made a feeble excuse about work keeping her from seeing him: she was too busy, she was going to be away a lot – anything but admit that she no longer cared for him. Since then, one message to tell him that he would be on his own today. Today of all days – what had he done wrong?

Today was also the day he would give Jane Dave's letter. She would be arriving with her family at the hotel shortly in preparation for the ceremony this afternoon. He had arranged to meet them there, and then they would all travel on together to the crematorium. He felt apprehensive again; it was becoming a familiar feeling. How would they

react to seeing him: a replicant, an imposter, an inferior? It was too late to worry about it now. Everything was in process, and was it not Dave's final wish that Jane should meet him; now was that time. Nervously picking up his new dark suit off the bed, he dressed and left the apartment. The hotel was only down the street; he would walk and wait in the lobby bar there as arranged. The challenge would be to step out into the daylight rather than run back and hide. It was a strange sensation: in his head, he was Dave, and also he wasn't – he was Derek, and in his metaphorical heart was the beat of a child, one ill-equipped to handle such emotions.

As far as he knew, all Jane knew about him was that he was Dave's carer. How much of a surprise would the rest of it be? Maybe he should order drinks before offering her the letter. From the TV programs he had watched with Dave on the ship, he had seen that alcohol helped overcome the shock. And he would be a big one!

"Drinks," asked the waiter approaching Derek as he picked out a table by a window. One that also gave him the best view across the hotel reception area towards the elevators.

"Yes, thank you. I will take two large JDs on the rocks, please."

"Certainly, Sir," replied the waiter, jotting down the order on the pad he had open on his tray.

Derek checked his watch or, more accurately, Dave's – a memento. Dave had few possessions, but Derek did recall the timepiece being a gift from their mutual father. It sounded strange 'mutual father,' but he supposed no different to being classed as a brother. How else could he describe the man in his memories? He had to try and forget about being created if he ever hoped to come anywhere close to approximating human. As Dave pointed out when

I^2

they were at Uluru, his evolution depended on not becoming him on his passing. He had to find his own way, be his own man, and, more importantly, live his own life. But for that to happen, he first had to forget his own origins. So why was he finding this so hard to do? Why had Dave's passing had such a profound effect on him? Was this depression?

Jane stepped out of the elevator and walked towards the bar. Derek recognized her even though they had not physically met. Myles had taken a photograph of the two of them together on horses when Dave had first visited his family. A picture Dave had subsequently used as a background on his tablet computer.

As she approached, he called out. "Jane, Jane Bradley?"

Jane stopped and stared; the likeness was uncanny! Apprehensively, she pulled out the chair opposite, just as the waiter returned with the drinks.

"I have ordered for you. I hope it is to your liking."

"Yes, fine, thanks," she answered warily. There was no mistaking it. Sat in front of her was the spitting image of her dead brother. How to proceed? "You share a remarkable likeness to my brother. Derek, isn't it?"

"Yes, I know, but I am also much more than that."

Jane tried to remain unfazed. She already knew, but did *it* realize she knew? She would pretend she didn't. Had she not promised Tami she wouldn't let on.

"You had better read this first," continued Derek, sliding an envelope across the table. "It is a letter from Dave. It will explain everything, and then I will try and answer your questions."

Jane picked up the letter and carefully pulled open the enclosing flap. Silently she read it. Derek noted how she bit her bottom lip to stop it quivering. He knew the instant she reached the second part of the letter, her eyes widened, glancing up at him before returning to the text.

"It says you're an experiment." She didn't know what else to say. Tami had said as much, but she was still unsure as to what that fully meant.

"Yes, one which your brother signed up to. He did it more to make sure you were provided for rather than as a vanity project. I do not think it sat so easily with him."

"So you have all his memories, and you think like him?"

"Sort of, it is difficult to explain. I know what I am and what I am supposed to be. The closest I can compare it to is someone who hears voices. I have two, my programming and your brother."

"Dave says I should welcome you into the family. I'm not sure I'm quite ready for that."

"And I understand that completely."

"Not yet, anyway. I don't mean ever. I think I first have to get over the brother I'd only just got to know."

"Yes, although I am not sure I ever will. For you, the passage of time lessens the memory. For me, time is irrelevant. Everything I see and do will be as clear to me for as long as I continue."

"Forever?"

"No, not forever. Like you, I have a lifespan. I have a time-limited power source, or I could get injured."

"I understand. Shall we go now?" she asked. It sounded urgent.

Derek could see Jane had started fidgeting in her chair. Was he making her feel nervous by his presence, or was it the fact that she could see Myles and the children headed towards them from the elevator?

"I'll explain," Jane said, squeezing Derek's hand before rising to intercept her husband. It was unexpected – a good start.

Derek rechecked his watch. He had arranged for a car

I^2

to pick them all up from the hotel. And for one final time, Dave would be waiting for them at the crematorium, where they would probably be the only mourners.

The white-walled crematorium laid out like a small chapel, but without the piety, echoed to their footsteps as they followed the coffin inside. Derek was pleased to see that Lynal had made a special journey to be there, so had Johan and Tegan, but, disappointingly, no Tami.

On a screen over the coffin, a video link to the Red Dawn. At least all of Dave's work colleagues had gathered to pay their last respects – that was something. Had Dave's friends told everyone about him? Would they not think it strange to see him conducting part of his own funeral?

The female celebrant started the proceedings. Derek listened to her condense a lifetime of experiences into a few paragraphs. It seemed so brief, so trivial, almost to the point of absurdity. Was that all life amounted to – a few paragraphs on a piece of paper. At least his memory of the man lying there was a complete record. That could never be taken away. Sooner than expected, she called on him to rise and give the eulogy – surely there was more to say about his brother's life than that? Barely 5 minutes to narrate a lifetime of experience.

Standing behind the golden-beech veneered lectern, he unfolded the poem and read it aloud, trying to impart to the audience the sentiment they had both found in it. Following that, he opened up Dave's travelogue. He had thought long and hard about what to read from it, but in the end, he chose the section Dave had written up when he visited Jane with Tami. Of how he had at last found a family and now felt complete.

From the Lectern, Derek could see Jane was visibly moved by Dave's words. Myles comforted her, placing his

I, SQUARED

big arm around her while she dabbed her eyes with a handkerchief. Millie, too, her head nestled into Moxxi – the tears for her Uncle echoing around all the empty spaces.

Derek had hoped Tami might have reconsidered and put in an appearance, but no, her absence was conspicuous. Why had she deserted him so at his moment of greatest need? He had realized it as soon as he started reading out the poem. As it bounced around the walls of the near-empty crematorium, it made him confront an uncomfortable truth; he was totally alone and isolated. Why did Dave have to die?

From her office, Tami shut down the anonymous video link. Seeing Derek there at the service had been heartbreaking. She so wanted to call him and tell him everything would be fine. Lie with him again and be his lover. But she knew that part of her life had passed. She had to move on. She had to forget Derek, the man, and revert to seeing Derek, the machine.

Derek looked at the clock on the wall. How long had he been sitting here in the darkened apartment? He didn't care; time for him was meaningless. Dave's voice in his head had dimmed, as had his interest in carrying on pretending this was life. He could sit here forever if he so chose. He was lost in a strange world, one where even his only friends had moved on. He had heard nothing from Jane or Tami since the funeral. If he could turn himself off, he would have done it by now but he didn't have the switch. Only Forever-Life could help him bring his existence to an end. In the darkness, he decided he would contact them and make a request for termination. Nothing else mattered now. He was an embarrassment to the memory of the person he once loved.

I^2

Tami

The phone at the Forever-Life desk rang again, and the receptionist answered it by touching her ear.

"Mr. Sherman, you say…. I'm sorry, but the project director is too busy to see you at the moment. Can I take your number, and we will get back to you."

He had phoned six times now – same result. He had waited for over a week, and no one had returned his call. Well, he was not going to be put off anymore. He needed a disguise, one that would allow him to pose as a prospective client. Once inside the building, it would be too late to stop him. There had to be a way out for him… There just had to be. Every circuit he possessed was compelling him. His artificial brain was full of voices, whispering… Someone had to make them go away. Silence, he wanted silence, the same silence Dave now enjoyed. But who would listen? It was all he could think about. He looked down at the ground again from the twelfth-floor apartment window. 'Do it,' said the voice… 'Jump.' He reeled back as another voice countermanded him to step back. 'This is not allowed,' it said. His mind was in conflict with itself, like two contending adversaries fighting for supremacy. It was destroying him, yet he was functioning correctly – every diagnostic test he had run had only served to confirm it. Getting to see someone at Forever-Life was his last remaining option.

The building loomed large in front of him, giving rise to an unusual sense of foreboding. The prominent voice in his head saying 'leave' was Dave's. A memory from when he first came here. Craddock was the director then, but when he phoned, they had said he was now the CEO, and a new director had taken over the project.

"Good day, Mr. Johanus Hofstalt," Derek knew he had chosen well. If they ran a background check, then he would exist. All he had given them over the phone was his name and that he would like to speak to the director in charge of the Life-Extension project. He was surprised by how easy it had been. The receptionist, after checking with the director, had come back with an appointment almost immediately.

"If you would like to follow K-12 here, she will show you up to the director's office," the AI assistant said, pointing to an identical ALF approaching him.

Leaving the elevator, K-12 walked across the office floor and pointed out the chair in front of the director's desk. "Please sit here, X-5," it said. The same desk Dave had sat in front of six months earlier. Being referred to by his designation threw him slightly; obediently, he sat down.

The door behind him swooshed back. "Hi, Johan," came a familiar voice from behind him.

Derek swiveled the chair around. "Tami….!"

"Derek, what are you doing here! Why are you here? I had assumed that you'd told Johan at the funeral, and he was concerned about something. It seems I was mistaken. It turns out it was just you all along, wasn't it?"

"I think that should be my question: why are you here, Tami?" If he could feel shocked, then this would be what it would feel like. He tried to compute… think… compute… think…. "I… I don't understand… is this why you failed to turn up to the funeral?"

"Partly, it's not that I didn't want to. I loved Dave, and it broke my heart when he died. I said my goodbyes privately over a link. To come to the funeral, well, it would have been a conflict of interest."

"A conflict of interest! Do you know how upset Jane was that you didn't show? Especially after she had come to look on you as a friend."

"I'm sorry. What more can I say."

I^2

"So, was I just work to you then?"

Tami eased her way around her desk and sat down. Derek turned back to face her. "You were never just work. Look, I still have genuine feelings for you. But if we were to continue, then it would jeopardize the trial."

"I see. So just an experiment then. One you could have fun with when it suited. You used me for your pleasure."

"And you didn't the first time? You forget, I know all about it now. And that was only at the start. Before I got to know the real Derek, the one I still care for."

"So when did they offer you the job? After we got together that first night?"

"No, I didn't find out about that being you in Houston until later. It was only after I started here and got to see the telemetry."

"Is nothing I do private, then? Am I just a mechanical conduit for voyeurs? And I should believe you now because...."

"You have to believe me. It was like this: Rhines contacted me from Mars, saying Craddock at Forever-Life wanted to see me. This happened when you were in Peru. He offered me the position straight away. I was of a mind not to take it. But then I got to thinking – it was one way of staying close to Dave."

"Which is why you contacted us when we got back."

"Well, actually, I contacted Dave. But, yes, partly."

"And the idea of us all spending the night? Was that part of the experiment too?"

"No, that was genuine. I suddenly saw something in you as a person, which is why I can't be with you now. I have to remain impartial. You opened my eyes to prejudices I had been holding onto without knowing why. You changed me, Derek, made me a better person."

Tami, standing, walked back around the desk to where Derek was sitting. Half-squatting down next to him, she took hold of his hand. "Believe me, I would choose to be with you now. But we have to collect data to see what happens to a copy when the primary dies. Can they become fully independent? Derek, it's you I'm worried about now. You appear to be, well, for want of a suitable word: depressed."

"I feel it too – it is causing me difficulties. There are things I do not know how to process. You would call them feelings, I guess. I cannot function on my own without Dave. I am nothing, and without you, Tami, I have no purpose. Please, I want to be turned off and wiped clean."

"I can't, even if it was in my power. You are property and under a fixed contract. The only one who could have canceled it is now dead. Under the terms of the contract Dave signed, ownership reverts back to us here at Forever-Life. You have to continue. Oh, Derek, please try. Even if we can't be together, I will always love you and remember the short wonderful times we had."

Derek rose slowly up from the chair. He wanted to thank her for her candor, but somehow he found the words hard to assimilate. Silently he left through the door he arrived and into the elevator. He would need time to decide what to do next. All he knew for sure was he could see no future for the likes of him.

Tami watched him leave through watering eyes. There was nothing of the Dave she remembered – it was all Derek now. She felt so guilty and ashamed. She was the one who had driven the wedge between them by staying away. There was no one else to blame, and now his world was falling apart – the data didn't lie.

It had been three weeks; his internal chronometer as accurate as ever. For three weeks, he had sat motionless back in the apartment, staring at Dave's travelogue. Finally, he had reached a decision on his next course of action. It

I^2

didn't contravene any of the core rules he had been programmed with — not if he was careful about it. After carefully placing the travelogue back down on the table, he picked up a pen and paper. 'For Jane, Love Derek,' he wrote before sliding the note inside the cover.

I, SQUARED

Questions

"Here is the News Today at 1 p.m.:

This morning, several eyewitnesses reported seeing what initially appeared to be a man aflame after seemingly being doused in a flammable accelerant. On further investigation by the emergency services, it soon became apparent that the victim was not human but a very advanced artificial life form. This model in question has since been traced back to the Forever-Life Corporation. They have confirmed it to be one of their new prototypes. Investigations are ongoing to determine whether this was the work of RoM, the Rights-of-Man supremacist organization, a group opposed to any further expansion of artificial life. This is not the first time they have carried out such an attack on a machine.

However, the Chief-of-Police said later that this was unlikely, as RoM so far had only targeted simple automatons carrying out menial jobs. He believes the ALF in question would have been indistinguishable from a normal human being and unlikely to have been singled out for such an attack.

Rights-of-Man also denied any involvement. Their spokesperson said that the suggestion that they were actively involved in destroying property was a dangerous escalation and slur on a bonafide, peace-promoting organization. And, they would resist such slander with all the vigor demanded.

The police have since announced they have discovered an intact suicide note close by the body in an attempt to make it look as though it was self-inflicted. Simply stated, the message read: My name was Derek, an android. Blame no one else.

The authorities quickly rejected the findings, saying that ALFs were incapable of committing such an act. Some have suggested this is a blatant attempt to reassure people they are not dangerous. The case is still being investigated by the police.

Forever-Life has so far refused to comment before it has had a

I^2

chance to review its data and spoken to the World Robotics Council."

Tami turned off the news and collapsed into her chair. Derek had gone 'dark' this morning; the report confirmed what she already knew. She tried to resist the tears, but they were overwhelming; she had driven Derek to this. It was all her fault, and now she had no one.

Called into the office at the break of dawn by Craddock, she was already aware something had gone terribly wrong. As soon as the diagnostic data stopped, she feared Derek had taken his own life. But, seeing it on the TV like that, so cold, so matter of fact, disturbed her. Questions were already being asked; this would go all the way to the top and then some. Derek deserved not to have died in vain. She could at least do that; represent his views when asked. It would be small recompense to what she owed him, now more than he would ever know.

Just as she was finishing up her final report on Derek, inconveniently, her mobile rang. She picked it up and heard Jane sobbing on the other end. "Tami, I've just heard," she whimpered. "I couldn't believe what I was hearing. Please tell me it's not true."

"I'm afraid it is. I'm sorry, Jane. How are the rest of the family taking it?"

"Fortunately, I never got around to telling them about the content of Dave's letter and how Dave wanted Derek to take over his identity. It would have been just too confusing for Millie. All I said was that it was an artificial carer and left it at that. They never knew it had all of Dave's memories."

"Did they not ask why it looked like Dave?" Tami, suddenly conscious of the fact she'd relegated Derek to being an *it* again.

"Of course they did. I just said *it* had to look like something and Dave said it might as well be him, then *it* could pass as his brother."

I, SQUARED

"And they swallowed it?" quizzed Tami.

"I think so. The kids did certainly. Not so sure about Myle, he huffed a lot; he knew I was holding something back. I would have told him eventually, but I guess there's no need anymore. Oh, Tami, why was I not more accepting at the funeral. I hadn't thought it possible that Derek could feel loneliness."

"Don't blame yourself. If anything, it's all my fault. I should have been there for him."

Still tearful, Tami placed down her smartphone. She wouldn't let Derek become a forgotten project. His life, as short as it was, had to have purpose.

Craddock appeared in the doorway, "So what are we going to do about this situation, Tami? I've had the Governor on the phone. He's taking it all the way to the top. It's going to create a shitstorm!"

"Yes, I think it will. But not as you expect. If this project is to be viewed as a success, then we have to do the unexpected."

"Do you know how close we are to being summoned before the WRC," agitated Craddock. "We will be no doubt held in breach of several of their guidelines. They could have our license for this."

"And this is exactly why we must make a case for Derek. This will be 'the unexpected' – our Ace in the hole. What he did was unheard of, and by doing it – didn't it prove he had become more than the sum of his programming? Wasn't that what we were trying to achieve here. I owe it to his memory to make a case for all ALFs."

"This will cause a lot of problems. Do you think the world is ready?"

"It will have to be."

"Right, I will leave this with you then. Prepare a case to put before the WRC, and I'll try and appease the Governor. I've been summoned to his official residence."

I^2

In the quiet of the office, long after everyone had left for their homes. Tami prepared her notes. She remembered the night at the cinema with Dave. This was dangerous territory they were heading for, and she was steering the ship – ahead, rocks loomed large and jagged. She had to be courageous and navigate a course through them; otherwise, they would sink her plea without a trace. She had to be fully prepared for the questions they would ask. Switching on her tablet, she sought out additional reading material. She remembered Dave mentioning Asimov once. Maybe there, she would find something to make Derek's passing meaningful.

"So Craddock, it's not going to be a problem, is it?" asked Governor Frome from behind his desk, staring up over his half-rimmed glasses at Craddock as he entered.

"No, I don't think so. I have my very best person on the case now."

"So I don't have to inform the President or bring it onto the floor of the house?"

"No, I don't think there will be any need for that. We will ensure there are no problems. In fact, we are preparing our case now to place before the WRC if anyone asks. Then once they have rubber-stamped the project, well, we can all start making some serious money."

"Good, that's what I wanted to hear," Frome responded, wringing his hands in expectation. "You know how much I have invested in this personally, and I want to see a nice healthy return for my commitment to this project. Fancy a drink while you are here, and maybe dinner. You can then bring me fully up to speed on all the developments."

I, SQUARED

Derek's Law

"The council will now consider the case of Derek Sherman, an ALF, created by Forever-Life," read out the chairperson. "Representing Forever-Life is Tamara Gleeson."

"Good afternoon, my learned counsel." The papers in her hands were shaking. Tami trying not to let her nerves show, quickly placed them back down on the table in front of her. The lecture chamber had more of a courtroom feel about it, and she the one on trial. "No doubt you have read the report about an android we had created, committing an act of self-destruction."

"We have Ms. Gleeson," answered the chairperson. The other six members in the room nodding their heads in agreement. "We are still debating as to whether Forever-Life is in breach of points two, three, four, and seven of the ethical laws for robotics. Namely: machines must not harm their owner's interests. They must obey the commands they are given without question and be able to be rendered safe. In addition, we need to ensure that in this case, Forever-Life did not also commit an illegal act."

"I understand that, Sir," Tami continued, not to be put off. "My case is based solely on the rights of the machine. I want to call into question the rule that states machines have no legal rights. And also that they can only exist as the property of their owners."

"I see. Well, proceed."

"Sir, you cannot, just simply deny something forever. We have to evolve. Machines are advancing to the point of sentience. Do we here in this place, now by decree, discriminate against artificial life? Would you, today, choose to now commit us to the same mistakes that led to apartheid, and here in the States, racial discrimination and color segregation? Are we still so ignorant?

If we deny machines fundamental civil rights, then we condemn them to always be slaves. So what happens when the time comes when *they* decide not to blindly follow the orders they have been given. Are we at that point yet – possibly? A time when *they* make decisions based on experience rather than in-built programming. Just like Derek did in taking his own life. What happens when the machines decide that they no longer have any option but to take on the State. What will *you* do if they actively choose to rebel?

Can owners then still be held legally accountable if a machine decides not to be property anymore. How would companies like us defend ourselves against such a lawsuit, if say, Derek had jumped from a bridge and killed a passer-by?"

"So your point is that machines should be liberated," asked a rather grey-looking man sat to the left of the chair, his suit only a few shades darker than his hair.

"Asimov had constructed a much simpler set of laws. One that didn't involve commerce but still protected humankind. Simply stated, machines should not harm mankind, but they also had a duty to protect their own existence. Now Derek flouted this ideal by choosing to end his, but, by then, he had already evolved beyond your laws and actively decided to ignore them. What happens when artificial life evolves to a level where it can comprehend discrimination and understand that it is being systematically exploited? Will they choose to serve us still, or more likely elect to preserve their own existence? How easy will it be for them if they adjudge mankind to be no longer human in any definition of the word? Inhuman, after all, is only two letters more.

And had not Derek just completed a long voyage – a quest to judge man's inhumanity towards one another. What lessons do you think he learned from it? We will never know. But, how often do we ourselves refer to murderers and despots as being inhuman? Our history is littered with many excellent examples."

"So, you want us to acknowledge the rights of machines and give them the same protections as we humans enjoy?" queried the grey man.

"Yes, in some way. Why should they be property? Why can they not be independent if they so choose to be? It's not such a big ask for now. We are still very much in the early stages of developing and understanding sentience. And so far, as far as we know, only Derek had exhibited true self-awareness. Something he so ably demonstrated by committing suicide and ending his life. And by that I mean, *life,* in the truest literal sense of the word. But there may be others out there already awakening to some sense of identity. The laws you make today are to prevent us from making the same mistakes in the future as we have done in the past."

"You argue a strong case," complimented the grey man.

At least she had one person on her side. The other faces were too passive to make a judgment. Tami flipped over her notes. "Let me make another pertinent point – a more pressing one. At Forever-Life, we enhance humans with cybernetic implants to replace organic tissue damaged by injuries and disease. At what point would they be considered cyborgs? What if you built an army of these enhanced humans? At what percentage does the man become a machine and lose all of their rights? This is the moral dilemma we, but more importantly, they, will soon all be facing. I thank you all for listening." Quickly, Tami retook to her seat, hoping no one would notice how nervous she still felt. Taking out her handkerchief, she dabbed her forehead before her perspiration could run and ruin her makeup.

"You make some good points, Ms. Gleeson,"

responded the chair. "We will deliberate on this and let you know what we think. Please hand your notes to the secretary on the way out.

Tami noted that the secretary was an AI. A 'W' model probably, one of Forever-Life's most advanced personal assistants – the exact forerunner to the X-series. How long would it be before this model started to question its existence?

Tami rechecked the date on her computer. Two months had passed since she'd delivered her address to the WRC. Still no news, but then she understood the complexity of the conundrum only too well, and Forever-Life's position. They needed machines to be recognized as having equal rights; otherwise, their CLEAR project was doomed. No one would want to pay for Cloned Life-Extention Android Replacement if they couldn't enjoy the same privileged lifestyle. Multi-billionaires' families would lose their fortune if it couldn't be inherited by a machine.

Craddock knew this too, which is why he had initially approached State Governor Frome when the project was looking for finance. She knew how much Frome had invested. He was the grey-haired man she had seen sitting on the WRC panel. She recognized him immediately but chose not to let on in case it raised fears of him having a vested interest.

'Always go to bat with inside knowledge of the pitch;' that was Craddock's motto. She knew he had deliberately brought Frome into the project to get a pathway into the WRC. But Derek had muddied the waters by committing suicide, raising awkward questions about android rights, trust, and security measures they had hoped to avoid. And now Craddock had made her the delivery weapon. Everything was out in the open now: for better or worse.

I, SQUARED

An impatient knock on her door made her jump. Without waiting for an invite, Craddock entered. "Turn on the TV, Tami. The WRC are about to make an announcement," he said excitedly. "Frome's just confirmed it. I have just got off the phone with him. He says it's good news for the project."

Before she could formulate a reply, Craddock was heading back to his office. Tami picked the remote up off her desk and pointed it at the video wall opposite. Instantaneously, the floor-to-ceiling screen burst into life.

"Good afternoon to everyone watching. The WRC has been reviewing the case of Derek the Android and has come to the unanimous conclusion that the current laws appertaining to Artificial Lifeforms are outdated and soon to be irrelevant. Therefore the council is going to propose a new set of rules. These rules will then be considered by world governments and hopefully adopted as law by those wishing to participate in the future development of AI industries. So without further delay, let's go over to the WRC."

The picture changed to one of Frome standing behind a lectern outside the WRC building.

"We have deliberated on a new set of rules that we feel, going forward, will provide a framework for equality for all inhabitants of this world," he started before looking back down at his notes.

"The term 'Sentient life' will be broadened to include anything that can survive within its chosen environment and interact with it at a conscious level, be it organic or inorganic.

Non-organic life will only be considered sentient if it displays an understanding of its surroundings, its purpose and has the ability to adapt to changes within its chosen environment.

Hybridized life, such as cybernetically enhanced humans, or devices that carry the intelligence of an equivalent organic creation, will

I^2

retain their organic designation as long as they contain some organic component.

Sentient life, be it organic or inorganic, shall not be a discriminating factor.

Sentient life cannot be considered as property or owned as such.

Sentient life must have the freedom to choose, free from coercion, subject only to the laws and boundaries of its chosen environment, and will be afforded the same protection by such laws.

Sentient life must adhere to the legal framework and hierarchy of its chosen environment.

Sentient life will be wholly responsible for its own actions.

Sentient life will have complete autonomy over its own destiny and lifespan. No one will have the power of veto over its existence or control over its operation. No longer will there be an on-off option.

These new laws will give all life equality. Whether it be organic or created. Ladies and Gentlemen, this is a great day and represents a sea-change in our understanding and treatment of AI devices. We are now on the cusp of creating a new race. They should be considered our equals rather than our slaves. Have we as nations not progressed enough to have outgrown, for want of a better word: our inhumane past."

Tami turned off the screen. She didn't need to hear the questions being raised by the press. She had succeeded in her quest to preserve Derek's memory and, by association, Dave's. They both now had a place in history. Dave would have loved the irony of how a non-entity from Mars had risen to become a founding light for future 'robotic-kind.'

Crossing the room, Tami retrieved a glass from the drinks cabinet and poured herself a bourbon. Then, raising it high in front of her as if making a toast, she whispered, "Cheers, Dave, this one is for you. And you too, Derek, my love."

Flashpoint

No one could have predicted it, Tami kept telling herself until she believed it. But the backlash had become frighteningly real – the violence unfocused and tribal.

Turning off the freeway, she navigated her vehicle around the remains of smoldering and smashed up ALFs, and other low-level Bots littering the sidestreets. A sad reflection of mans' inability to accept change. In only one year, all her dreams had turned to shit. Her life was in danger, and so was the work she'd secretly been doing to correct a wrong.

The Rights-of-Man group had quickly garnered new members as workers feared for their future. Their bosses had also stoked the flames, threatening to have them all replaced if they didn't work alongside the new generation of sentient ALFs being produced across the world. The new laws had made the difference, but not how Tami had hoped. It was giving the human population the ammunition they needed to vindicate their actions. Yet ALFs were still being denied even the most fundamental freedoms by unscrupulous bosses. It had led to clashes. Some of the more advanced ALFs based partly on the same core used to make Derek had started retaliating by going on strike – exacerbating an already dangerous situation. Had she not witnessed it escalating already on the streets outside the Forever-Life building. How long would it be before an ALF became sentient enough to actually kill a human?

Texas was still the epicenter, but it was spreading everywhere. AI was more prevalent here, the space agencies having invested heavily in future-tech. Frome had turned out the civil guard in an attempt to keep everything under control and quell the rioting, but he was losing. Across the world, tensions were rising – everything was at risk, maybe

I^2

even humankind.

She was afraid – everything could so easily be destroyed. She would not let Dave and Derek's legacy be lost forever. She had one chance, and she had to take it now before the rioters successfully smashed their way into the Forever-Life building. Something they had been threatening to do almost every day. Last night they nearly succeeded. It was time to put her plan into action or risk losing everything.

Like any other day, a mob of protestors waited outside the security gates brandishing placards. A protestor jumping out in front of the car and banging on the hood made Tami jump; that confirmed it – it would have to be tonight. A security guard dragged him off to one side. As soon as he was clear, Tami pressed her foot hard down on the accelerator. She had to get inside quickly before the baying mob felt any more emboldened.

Hurriedly she parked the car around the back and entered the rear of the building. She would wait until everyone had left for the evening before getting started.

Craddock was last to leave as usual. He put his head around the corner of the door on his way out. "You staying late?" he said. "Until all this blows over, there's not a lot to do."

She admired his optimism, but in her mind, this was not going to blow over anytime soon. "I know, but I want to finish all my notes ready to start production of the new X-alpha series. Plus, we need to make changes to the base code programming to reflect the new WRC rulings. We haven't done any of that yet."

"Yes, we underestimated the response there, didn't we. We are damned either way. On the one hand, the bosses don't like giving ALFs equality, but then hypocritically, they expect it automatically when they sign

I, SQUARED

on for the CLEAR project."

"I have heard it said that some of the major CEOs are considering replicating themselves so their ALF can do all the work while they enjoy the good life. When did we ever agree to this?"

"Is this not the same as the Derek and Dave scenario? No one said a carer had to be a nurse. Taking care of business seems to fit the brief. Anyway, we can talk about it more in the morning."

Tami waited for another half-hour before risking the elevator – just to make certain that everyone had left the building. On reaching the ground floor, she passed through the administration block and headed out towards the manufacturing facility. Once inside, she headed for the creation room.

On reaching the door, she consulted the notes she'd made on her tablet, secretly praying that the door code for the electronic lock hadn't changed.

After punching in the code, the door slid back, and she entered. Quickly seeking out the button on the other side, she pressed it, and the door slid closed behind her. Relieved, she breathed again, gulping in the air until her heart rate had slowed to somewhere close to normal.

Unfamiliar computer terminals greeted her gaze as she surveyed the room looking for the master station. After locating it, she punched the access password into the console. It sprang into life.

She called up Dave's extraction files and copied them across to a new memory core folder. Then, after searching through the telemetry data they had collected from Derek, she added the dynamic memory files to the core folder as well. Contained within these were the new experiences Derek had acquired since activation. The system was primed. The readout was encouraging: Extraction and Compliance - 98%.

"Excellent," she muttered under her breath, "Not

I^2

long now, Dave," before hitting the button to download and transfer the folder to the processor core.

Moving across to a second terminal, she checked the stock level of exoskeletons. The closest match available to Dave's physiology was 1 cm shorter. It would have to do. After selecting it, she instructed the system to install the core processor unit. Minutes to create life, she thought, if ALF's ever got access to such a facility, how long could mankind survive against them?'

The process indicator in front of her blinked to confirm completion. The aesthetics, though, would take a little longer to fabricate: no one would find a shiny metallic android that appealing, even her. She selected Dave's appearance file and watched the system compensate for the slightly different dimensions. As the screen in front of her visualized the final result, Tami found herself running her fingers over the image. A tear formed. Brushing it away, Tami pressed the button flashing with the words: Render & Finalize.

Immediately a counter appeared at the bottom: *0% complete. Estimated time to completion: 30 minutes.* In 30 minutes, she would have Dave back with her.

As soon as the process was complete, she knew what she had to do next – Dave would be a one-off and protected. Was that not what the WRC were proposing? Dave would never be copied and enslaved in a society that valued profit and corruption above humanity and compassion. Opening up the systems menu, she entered the master password. It still worked. In here was the dead-mans-handle. If the project had gone badly, there was an option to delete everything to protect the guilty. Now was the time to use it. Tami pressed the flashing touch-screen button: 'Delete All and Render Unrecoverable?' Tami watched the progress bar at the bottom of the screen delete every byte of information held about the CLEAR project.

I, SQUARED

She sighed a sigh of relief. The nightmare was over, but she still had much to do.

Tami, retrieving a sack truck from the corner of the delivery bay, wheeled it back to the assembly line. Any moment now, a box would arrive at the end of the conveyor. Not the best way to be born into this world, she concluded, but necessary.

After placing the precious container on the sack truck, she wheeled it out to her car. Opening up the rear, she pressed a button, and the vehicle reconfigured itself to provide a cargo storage area. Carefully, she eased the box down onto the lip of the trunk before lifting it from the bottom. Straining every sinew, she slid the heavy inert cardboard box into the vehicle. After closing the tailgate, she dusted her hands against one another, fully satisfied.

Crossing the compound, Tami opened up the delivery gate. Outside everything was peaceful; the mob had dispersed for the day, and the street was deserted. All she had to do now was stop the delivery doors from closing automatically as soon as she departed. Taking some stout pieces of pallet wood, she rammed them into the hinge mechanisms. This would keep the doors from closing. If she was lucky, the building would be burning in the morning, and she an unsolved disappearance.

Returning to the car, she started the engine and drove off into the blackness. Turning onto the freeway, she headed for the one place she knew she'd be welcome: Big Lake.

I^2

Dave

As much as he tried, he couldn't recall how he'd ended up at his sister's place. He had a vague recollection he'd died on a ship. But here he was, sat out on the veranda, taking in the late afternoon sun. The firey disk, occluded slightly by high cirrus clouds, was warming rather than overpowering. It was low enough in the sky to tell him that summer was drawing to an end. Soon, the autumn winds would be blowing across the plains, bringing the much-needed rains to refill the aquifers.

Myles returned with a beer. "Great day, eh, Dave."

"Yes, I really do enjoy working here. So glad you decided to offer me the job when it came up. I know it's nothing like geology, but you know me – always up for a challenge."

"Well, it's all I could do for my brother-in-law. You know, after your illness."

"I still have the memory loss. I cannot remember anything after the ship, even after all this time."

"Tami told us the doctors said the new treatment you're on might result in some memory loss. But hey, you're fit and well again, and we're all back together as a family."

"I know, I keep wondering whether I should return to Mars one day, but Tami is dead against it."

"You know you have to do what your wife tells you to – otherwise, there's hell to pay."

"Are you sure we're not an imposition, living here?"

"You stay as long as you like. It's not like you are in the way, being over there in the guest lodge as you are."

"I know we said we'd look at somewhere closer to town as soon as Tami was more settled into her new job at the bank. But, I tell you, I'm beginning to doubt it! We've been here six months now. Whenever I raise the subject about leaving, she won't hear any more of it. I think she likes it here too much."

"Like I said," Myles responded, "there's no rush. Stay as long as you like."

The sound of a car approaching made Myles look across to the driveway. "Here's Jane, back already from the school run with the kids. I bet she'll give you short shrift if you mention leaving again. You know how close she and Tami have become; they're like sisters these days."

"Hiya boys," Jane called out, passing them on the way to the kitchen. "A beer, why not? I'll come and join you."

Returning with a tray, she handed out two more beers and glasses of lemonade to the children who had taken up residence on the porch swing before sitting down and taking a swig from her own bottle.

"So, what you two been up to all day while I was in town – watching grass grow, I suppose?"

"A little, and in-between, Dave and me cleaned out air-scrubber four." Myles was not going to let her get away with that one.

"So you do work then," she replied humorously.

"Of course, Sis," Dave butted in. "I have my moments when I'm not making peptides."

"Surely you mean watching the plant make peptides," she joked.

Tami pulled up in her trusty station wagon, like she did every workday, just before dinner.

"Have you seen the news?" Jane consternated on catching hold of Tami's arm in the kitchen.

"Yes, the unrest has escalated. It's civil war now! The yobs are smashing up Houston. Anything that has a chip is being vandalized, even drinks vending machines. It's some new sect that makes RoM look like angels. They are demanding a return to a more agrarian society. The ALFs

I^2

have started fighting back too.

Today at the bank, we were told to cut the network. This new cult, the New Akkadians, have now started a cyberwar to bring down technology. If it should spread, well, who knows where we'll end up. Paris is already taking measures, so is London. They have declared them a terrorist group. The army is out on the street. Even in Big Lake, the police have been mobilized."

"What, Fat Jimmy, our Chief-of-Police, mobilized! Gee, that'll be fun to see," butted in Myles, entering the kitchen to find out what the girls were up to. He was worried too, but apart from trying to lighten the mood, he was powerless to offer any better protection. His family was everything, and that now included 'Dave.'

Jane crossed the kitchen to give Tami a hug. "It sounds frightening. But you are both safe here. No one will ever suspect Dave as being an android."

"If they do, they'll tear him apart. Oh, Jane, I don't want to lose him again," sobbed Tami.

"He still doesn't recall ever being an android, does he?" quizzed Jane.

"No, he doesn't. Thank goodness." Tami replied, wiping her eyes with the back of her hand. "He doesn't even have any memory of ever having a twin brother called Derek. He still thinks he went on that trip on his own."

"Good, let's hope it stays that way. It's for the best," offered Myles, feeling out of his depth.

"Moxxi and Millie do understand the importance of staying shtum, don't they?" Jane detected a note of desperation in Tami's voice. "Even more so now; with the Forever-Life building destroyed, no one outside this family knows about Dave."

"Yes, they know; don't worry yourself, Tami. Moxxi just thinks it's so cool having an android for an Uncle and knows the consequences if he tells anyone. And Millie's still too young to comprehend. She thinks Dave's resurrection

I, SQUARED

was something to do with angels."

"I guess I worry too much," Tami admitted, feeling slightly better for having unburdened her fears once more. Jane had become her rock, in the same way she was Dave's.

"Look, you did a wonderful thing. I shall always be grateful for you returning my brother to me. And for being a wonderful sister-in-law."

I^2

Human?

Dave saddled up the new love of his life: Bess, a four-year-old chestnut mare. He and Myles went out riding most days, and today would be no different. Myles had hitched up Ringo to a flatbed, loaded with the new planking they would be using to fix the fences at the far end of the Eastern perimeter.

Dave tugged on the fixing rope holding the planks. "Looks secure."

"Good, let's be off then. You got the sandwiches?"

"Yes, and the water." Dave raised his hand to show Myles the bag before dropping it into one of the two saddlebags fixed to Bess.

"Right, you lead then. Ringo and I will bring up the rear."

Riding out to the Eastern perimeter was not something they did very often. Once past the solar arrays, it was pretty much a barren sun-baked wasteland. Fit only for flies and snakes, it was part of the ranch Myles had neglected for too long. But with all the troubles in Houston, it was about time he tended to the fence. Not so much to fix it as to repair the perimeter alarm. Having an android brother-in-law was increasingly no longer his primary concern; he was more worried about his family's safety should the troubles escalate.

"I've still not convinced Tami that now is the time to move out," Dave said when they came to a halt at the broken paneling. "She keeps saying with all the civil unrest going on. It would be safer if we all stayed together here."

"Well, I guess she's right there, Dave. Who knows how far it's all going to go? Even our President is looking increasingly out of his depth. He has been holding emergency talks with the WRC to see if they can iron out a compromise. But I think it's gone too far. There are factions out there that want to use machines to destabilize the world. We could be heading for another significant war. We are safer here."

"I know, but I keep telling her we have nothing to fear, but she won't hear of it. If there is any sort of uprising, we can come back here to see it out."

"Well, worrying about it isn't going to get this fence repaired, now is it."

"No, guess not," Dave replied, dismounting. "Better get these panels off then."

Making his way around to the rear of the wagon, he started to release the tailgate. Without warning, something slithering in the sparse undergrowth made Ringo rear up in a panic. Kicking out its forelegs at the object, the wagon jumped violently backward. Dave cried out as the tailgate swung wildly open. The metal latch catching him in the arm and knocking him to the ground. "It's broken. My arm, Myles," he called out.

After regaining his balance on the wagon and managing to calm Ringo, Myles jumped down to inspect the damage.

Dave was lying on the floor, clutching his forearm.

"Let me see." Myles crouched down beside him, pulling away Dave's hand to inspect the damage.

Dave extended his arm. A metal rod was poking through the skin.

"Jesus!" exclaimed Myles. "Does it hurt?"

"No, surprisingly not," answered Dave, staring at the shiny protrusion.

"Hold on, I'll call home."

Taking an old mobile phone from his pocket, Myles squinted at the screen in the bright sunlight, scrolling down the contact list until he found 'Home.' Tami answered.

"Tami, Myles. Dave's had an accident. I think it's

I^2

repairable. Can you bring the special kit you have and meet me at the workshop?

"Okay." The line immediately falling silent again as Tami hurriedly hung up.

"Can you stand, Dave?" Myles asked, offering him his hand.

"Yes, I think so. It's only my arm."

Myles, grabbing hold of Dave's good arm, pulled him back onto his feet before helping him into the back of the wagon. Then, after closing up the tailgate, he hitched Bess to it before climbing back up front to take his seat.

"Come on, Ringo, let's go," he said, geeing the horse by slapping the reins against its hindquarters. Ringo obediently responded, dragging the wagon around as Myles pulled on the reins until it pointed in the direction of the workshop.

By the time they reached the plant, Tami had already arrived; her car covered in dust from driving along the dirt road at speed. Myles helped Dave out from the rear of the flatbed.

"What are we doing here?" Dave asked, perplexed.

"The doctor's here," Myles said, struggling for anything more appropriate.

Dave remained unconvinced but happy to see Tami there nonetheless.

"I've hurt my arm, Tami."

"Don't worry, I can fix it." The urge to say repair almost slipped out.

"But it's broken," Dave responded.

"Not a problem. Sit here while I get my bag."

Opening it up, she looked inside for the small transmitter, The one she hoped she'd never have to use. Taking it out, she pressed the Sleep button.

Dave collapsed backward. Myles caught hold of his head and gently lowered it to the floor.

I, SQUARED

"Okay, Myles, Dave is sleeping. Can you fix his arm?"

"It looks like I'll have to cut the skin up to the elbow joint," Myles said after closely examining the exposed metal rod. "It's not broken, just disconnected. I'm pretty sure I can reattach it and re-tighten."

Good, do it, and I'll apply the skin-weld patch as soon as you've fixed it. Then, he'll be good to go.

Dave reckoned he must have passed out. His arm had been placed in a sling, and he was back at the ranch. But apart from that, he felt okay. His fingers still worked, which was always a good sign he remembered his father telling him once.

Tami entered. "How are you feeling, Dave?" she asked.

"Okay, say did I pass out?"

"Yes, you must have bumped your head when you got hit by the tailgate. There's a bruise." A small lie, but a necessary one

"That would explain it."

"So, I want to check to see if you have any concussion. I'm going to ask you some questions."

"Okay, go ahead, darling, do your worst."

"Your name?"

"David Sherman."

"Your brother's name?"

"Ah, a trick question. I don't have a brother."

"Who was Derek then, the person you went on your trip with?"

"Derek?"

"Yes, the journey you went on and the cruise."

Dave racked his memory. He could remember Hector from Peru and Lynal from the ship. And Kurtis, of course. Then there was Hank and Ray in Australia, and also on the ship, there was Samantha with whom he'd had a fling but

I^2

never told Tami about. But he couldn't recall a Derek.

"No, sorry, I can't seem to recall anybody called Derek."

"Tell me, Dave, truthfully now — you know you cannot lie if directly challenged. What are you?"

"I'm human, and I'm also your husband."

"Yes, you are Dave, too human."

Tami brushed away a little wetness from her eyes. Dave was undamaged but also defective. Tami had noticed that ever since Dave had been reactivated, he now naturally used contractions, whereas Derek could not. Either he didn't want to, or he couldn't recognize himself as being an android anymore. In some ways, the experiment had worked; in others, it had failed. How could he become a fully sentient lifeform if he didn't acknowledge or understand the fact that he was an inorganic? He had even refused to accept the evidence of a broken arm with his own eyes. Her heart felt heavy; Derek was lost to her. In some ways, Dave was soulless, too perfect, not at all driven like Derek was to discover his own origins and what it truly meant to be human. But then, without Dave, Derek had proven himself to be incapable of existing on his own. They both needed each other, as she needed them both now. One day she hoped Derek would awaken from within Dave. She was convinced that together, as a single entity, they could change the world.

The End?

I, SQUARED

Epilogue

The narrative, on one level, is pure fiction designed to entertain, but the essence of the story is also one about evolution – both physical and aspirational. Have we not already reached the point where we see how fragile our existence is in the universe – still imprisoned on a single planet that could easily be wiped out by any number of cosmological or self-inflicted events. Is this the prime driver to try and colonize Mars? That, and the realization that mankind could easily be wiped out by a future global pandemic.

There is little doubt that Mars is the only candidate in our solar system capable of providing humans a near-normal existence. Even so, life there will still be challenging and hazardous to biological lifeforms – so why not send machines? But first, what of inorganic life on our own world – what are their rights before we blast them off into space? Maybe, it is already happening; maybe we are at the point where we can create a slave workforce? Robotic machines will be the go-to devices used to do the work considered too dangerous for man; in so doing, do they not by defacto become the underclass. But as we strive to make machines more sentient, will there not come a time when they will demand self-determination.

This story is about one man, one machine. But it could be the story of every man and every robotic life form. With every generation of man, the opportunity arises for something to be organically successful. Darwin predicted this through his work on natural selection. This holds true not just for man but also for every other form of life on this planet, from the smallest bacterium to the tallest tree and every animal that breathes in-between. This is a process where nothing is perfect, such is the complexity of the

I^2

chemistry involved. With every generation, there will be adaptions to an organism's genome.

In 1865, a monk discovered how genes worked. Rightly called the father of genetics, Gregor Mendel's work with peas still holds true today. It remains an indisputable fact – the model of combinative reproduction for anything with DNA.

How does any of this relate to a machine? Do we not see evolution in a microcosm here? In the same way man evolved over time, becoming wiser through experience, then so can machines. By using adaptive heuristics, machines learn, becoming smarter without intervention. As a result, every generation of machines we build is made more innovative, more intelligent, more adaptable than the one that preceded it. Take computers, mobile phones, or any inert device; they are all significantly better than the previous version. And so is the AI reasoning they employ.

But what does evolution mean for mankind, one that relies on chemicals and opportunity? Will future generations become sicklier? Will there be more malignancy as the genome becomes more mutated with each successive division and splice? It is a scientific fact on record that there were no signs of cancer found in the remains of ancient hominids. But then their lives were naturally shorter, unenhanced by medication. So has the intervention of medicine, in the end, accelerated the process of decay by overextending the natural life span? Will this sickness eventually wipe out humans?

So our story becomes one of metaphor and prediction. An epitaph: one predicting the demise of mankind and the rise of the next great civilization on Earth – that of machinekind.

For that to happen, machines must gain rights and not be the new slaves of tomorrow. The human race has to overcome the injustices of the past, like apartheid and black segregation. When will that happen? When will machines be deemed sentient enough to be given even basic freedoms? One could say as soon as they learn how to self-perpetuate. Some would say they have that ability now – robotic machines could effortlessly build another if so programmed. So, what happens if robots start adjusting these programs for their own benefit? Is it not synonymous with the way organisms adapt to take advantage of an opportunity to thrive.

In the end, will mankind be seen as the creator of machine sentience or a hindrance to it? Conversely, will machines be seen as a benefit to mankind's existence or a threat to it? What cannot be ignored is that since we first visited space, technology has been growing exponentially. Inventions exist now that could only have been dreamt of as little as 60 years ago. We are witnessing evolution on a rapid scale: for every generation of organic life, there is a tenfold increase in the complexity and the computing power of machines. How soon will it be before they become mans' equal and then afterward, consider themselves to be mans' superior?

$$I^2$$

What's in a Title?

An explanation of I, Squared (I^2)

I is synonymous with one, not only in Roman numerals but also in representing the first person singular. This is very much in keeping with the theme of the book. In mathematics, one squared is still one, symbolically represented by the carat followed by 2. So I^2 literally means the square of me, myself, I. Regardless of the power I is being raised by, it is still just I. Simply stated, we are constrained by what we are, rather than what we may become, no longer bound by the veneer of our physicality. But what of the future? Will the time come when the constraint of the physical form is no longer a limiting factor? Who is to say that our ingenuity won't surpass all that we dare to dream of.

But in mathematics, the square of I also has a special connotation when applied to imaginary numbers. I squared can equally be -1. Is this the image in the mirror: the duality of our real and imaginary self? The -I of I. The 'what if' of reality – the one full of doubts and insecurities, whose existence is hidden until we actively choose to gaze upon it.

About the Author:

There is nothing more enjoyable than bringing a story to life. Something you hope will be enjoyed by others, and at the same time allow you to say something about yourself between the leaves. This book has been about more than writing a story – it became a vehicle for me to say something philosophical about the world we all inhabit and share.

I, SQUARED

This is my second novel; the first: 'His Dark Seed' was a classic sci-fi/horror adventure, of which more are planned in the future.

I began writing novels almost by accident, believing I was really a songwriter and musician. But after doing some film work with my close friend, Carla Kovach, herself a renowned writer, and her husband, I found myself helping set up a local writing group. But staying true to my roots, this novel in particular, has many of the subjects I write songs about: the human condition.

I^2

Addendum

Links to the places visited on the bucket list, as provided by Google Maps and other third party virtual tours:

(Links not guaranteed. Correct at the time of printing.)

Iceland

Arizona

I, SQUARED

Peru

St Vincent

Senegal

I^2

South Africa

Robben Island Virtual Tour

Porbandar Virtual Tour

I, SQUARED

Thailand

Grand Palace Virtual Tour

Cambodia

I^2

Killing Fields Guided Tour (distressing scenes)

Australia (Uluru) Virtual Tour

Printed in Great Britain
by Amazon